Praise for Jill Shalvis

"Hot, sweet, fun, and romantic! Pure pleasure!" —Robyn Carr

"Jill Shalvis will make you laugh and fall in love."
—Rachel Gibson

"Fall in love with Jill Shalvis! She's my go-to read for humor and heart."
—Susan Mallery

"Romance . . . you can lose yourself in." —*USA Today*

"Irresistible mix of sassy wit, snappy dialogue, and surfeit of smoking hot sensuality." —Booklist

"She's a *New York Times* bestselling author, and there's a reason for her popularity: her writing is character-driven, accessible, and just the right kind of sultry." —Bustle

"Witty, fun, and the characters are fabulous." —Fresh Fiction

"Sexy, engaging, and fun." —Kirkus

"Engaging writing, characters that walk straight into your heart, touching, hilarious . . ." —*Library Journal*

"Heartwarming and sexy . . . an abundance of chemistry, smoldering romance, and hilarious antics." —*Publishers Weekly*

"Ms. Shalvis's characters leap off the page." —RT Bookclub

lost and found sisters

Also by Jill Shalvis

Heartbreaker Bay Novels

Sweet Little Lies

The Trouble with Mistletoe

Accidentally On Purpose

Lucky Harbor Novels

One in a Million

He's So Fine

It's in His Kiss

Once in a Lifetime

Always on My Mind

It Had to Be You

Forever and a Day

At Last

Lucky in Love

Head Over Heels

The Sweetest Thing

Simply Irresistible

Animal Magnetism Novels

Then Came You

Rumor Has It

Rescue My Heart

Animal Attraction

Animal Magnetism

lost and found sisters

JILL SHALVIS

WILLIAM MORROW

An Imprint of HarperCollins*Publishers*

This book is a work of fiction. References to real people, events, establishments, organizations, or locales are intended only to provide a sense of authenticity, and are used fictitiously. All other characters, and all incidents and dialogue, are drawn from the author's imagination and are not to be construed as real.

FIRST EDITION

Designed by Diahann Sturge

Library of Congress Cataloging-in-Publication Data has been applied for.

ISBN 978-0-06-244811-8
ISBN 978-0-06-267564-4 (library edition)

17 18 19 20 21 LSC 10 9 8 7 6 5 4 3 2

No author writes in a vacuum. It takes a village and all that. And this one is to my village: Alpha Man, Oldest, Middle, Youngest, Special Edition and The Boy(s). Thanks for understanding me and letting me do my thing, love you all.

lost and found sisters

Chapter 1

I walk around like everything is fine but deep down inside my shoe my sock is sliding off.

—from "The Mixed-Up Files of Tilly Adams's Journal"

Here was the thing: life sucked if you let it. So Quinn Weller usually worked really hard to not let it. Caffeine helped. For up to thirty-eight blissful minutes it could even trick her into thinking she was in a decent mood. She knew this because it took forty-eight minutes to get from her local coffee shop through L.A. rush-hour traffic to work, and those last ten minutes were never good.

That morning, she got into line for her fix and studied the menu on the wall, even though in the past two years she'd never strayed from her usual.

A woman got in line behind her. "Now *that's* a nice look on you," she said.

It was Carolyn, a woman Quinn had seen here at the coffee shop maybe three times. "What look?"

"The smile," Carolyn said. "I like it."

Quinn didn't know whether to be flattered or insulted, because she smiled all the time.

Didn't she?

Okay, so maybe not so much lately . . . "I'm looking forward to the caffeine rush."

"Nectar of the gods," Carolyn agreed.

Something about the pleasant woman reminded Quinn of an elementary-school teacher. Maybe it was the gray-streaked hair pulled up in a messy bun, the glasses perpetually slipping down her nose, the expression dialed into sweet but slightly harried.

"You're up, honey," Carolyn said and gestured to the front counter.

Trev, the carefully tousled barista, was an L.A. beach bum and aspiring actor forced to work to support his surfing habit. His hands worked at the speed of light while the rest of him seemed chilled and relaxed. "Hey, darlin', how's life today?"

"Good," Quinn said. She didn't want to brag, but she'd totally gotten out of bed today with only two hits of the snooze button. "How did your audition go?"

"Got the part." Troy beamed. "You're looking at the best fake Thai delivery guy who ever lived. It means my luck has changed, so say you'll finally go out with me."

Quinn smiled—see, she totally *did* smile!—and shook her head. "I'm not—"

Trev piped in along with her, in perfect sync, "—dating right now," and then shook his head.

"Well, I'm not," she said.

"It's not right, a hot chick like you. You're way too young to be in a rut. You know that, right?"

"I'm not in a rut." She was just . . . not feeling life right now, that's all. "And hey, I didn't tell you my order yet," she said when she realized he was already working on her coffee.

"Has it changed?" he asked. "Ever?"

No, but now she wanted to order something crazy just to throw him off, except she wanted her usual, dammit.

Okay, so maybe she *was* in a rut. But routine made life simpler and after the complications she'd been through, *simple* was the key to getting out of bed and putting one foot in front of the other every day.

That and the badly needed caffeine, of course.

"You should go out with him," Carolyn whispered behind her. She smiled kindly when Quinn craned her neck and looked at her. "You only live once, right?"

"Not true," Quinn said. "You live every day. You only die once."

Carolyn's smile slowly faded in understanding. "Then make it count, honey. Go hog wild."

Hog wild, huh? Quinn turned back to Trev.

"I'm all for the hog wild," he said hopefully.

Quinn went for it. "An extra shot and whip."

Trev blinked and then sighed. "Yeah, we really need to work on your idea of hog wild."

WHEN QUINN FINALLY got to Amuse-Bouche, the trendy, upscale restaurant where she worked, it was to find her fellow sous-chef Marcel already in the kitchen.

He glanced over at her and sniffed disdainfully. Then he went back to yelling at Skye, a good friend of Quinn's she'd brought on board a few months back.

Skye was chopping onions exactly as Quinn had taught her, but apparently Marcel didn't agree. His voice had risen to a pitch designed to split eardrums as he went on and on in a mix of English and German that no one understood but him.

"Leave her alone, Marcel," Quinn said.

He slid her a glacial stare. "Excuse me?"

"I'm the one who taught her how to chop. She's doing it correctly."

"Yes. If you work at a place flipping burgers and asking what size fry you want with your order," he said, dropping the fake German accent as he sometimes did when he lost his temper and forgot to keep it up.

So here was the thing. There were days where Quinn surprised herself with her abilities, and others where she put her keys in the fridge. But she was good at this job. And yes, she understood that at twenty-nine years old and quickly rounding the corner kicking and screaming into thirty, she was young and very lucky to have landed a sous-chef position in such a wildly popular place. But she'd worked her ass off to get here, going to a top-notch culinary school in San Francisco, spending several years burning and cutting her fingers to the bone. She knew what she was doing—and had the tuition debt to prove it.

Oddly, Marcel wasn't that much older than she was—late thirties, maybe. He'd come up the hard way, starting at the age of twelve washing dishes in his uncle's restaurant not all that far from here, but light years away in style and prestige. He was good. Actually he was excellent, but he was hard-core old school, and resented a woman being his equal.

Quinn did her best to let it all bead off her back, telling herself that she believed in karma. What went around came back around. But though she'd waited with pent-up breath, nothing had kicked Marcel in the ass yet.

"You," he said, pointing at her. "Go order our food for the

week. And don't forget the pork like last time. Also, your cheese supplier? She's shit, utter shit. Find another."

Quinn bit her tongue as Marcel turned away to browbeat a different kitchen aide who was dicing red peppers, swearing at the guy in German as if that made him more intimidating. Quinn thought it made him more of an idiot. He jerked the bowl away to prove his point and ended up with red pepper all over the front of his carefully starched white uniform shirt.

Ah, karma at last—fashionably late, but better than never.

"I'm sorry about that," she said to Skye.

"You've got nothing to apologize for," Skye said. "If it's got tires or testicles, it's gonna give you trouble."

Wasn't that the truth . . .

On Sunday, Quinn drove to her parents' place for brunch. A command performance, since she'd managed to skip out on the past two weekends in a row due to working overtime.

She hoped like hell it wasn't an ambush birthday party. Her birthday was still several weeks away, but her mom couldn't keep a secret to save her own life and had let the possibility of a party slip several times. Quinn didn't like birthdays.

Or surprises.

She parked in front of the two-story Tudor cottage that had been her childhood home and felt her heart constrict. She'd learned to ride a bike on this driveway, right alongside her sister, who'd been a far superior bike rider. So much so that Quinn had often ridden on Beth's handlebars instead of riding her own bike. They'd pilfered flowers from the flower gardens lining the walkway. Years later as teens, they'd sneaked out more than a few times from one of the second-story windows, climbing down the oak tree to go to parties that they'd been grounded from attending—only getting caught when Quinn slipped one year and broke her arm.

Beth hadn't spoken to her for weeks.

Once upon a time this house had been Quinn's everything. But now coming here made her feel hollow and empty. Cold. And deep down, she was afraid nothing would ever warm her again.

It'll get easier.

Time is your friend.

She'll stay in your heart.

Quinn had heard every possible well-meaning condolence over the past two years and every single one of them was a lie.

It hadn't gotten easier. Time wasn't her friend. And as much as she tried to hold on to every single memory she had of Beth, it was all fading. Even now she couldn't quite summon up the soft, musical sound of her sister's laugh and it killed her.

Shaking it off the best she could, she slid out of her car and forced a smile on her face. Sometimes you had to fake it to make it.

Actually, more than sometimes.

Late April in Southern California could mean hot or hotter, but today was actually a mild eighty degrees and her mom's flowers were in full, glorious bloom. Quinn ducked a wayward bee—she was allergic—and turned to watch a flashy BMW pull in next to her, relieved to not have to go inside alone.

Brock Holbrook slid out of his car looking camera ready and she couldn't help but both smile and roll her eyes. "Suck-up," she said, gesturing to his suit and tie.

Brock flashed a grin. "I just know where my bread's buttered, that's all."

He worked for her father's finance company and no one could deny that Brock knew how to work a room. He was good looking, charismatic, and when he looked at her appreciatively, her entire body hummed with anticipation. Or it used to.

But these days she didn't feel anticipation for anything. She sighed and Brock tilted his head at her, eyes softer now, understanding.

He knew. He'd been there when she'd found out about Beth's accident. But his understanding didn't help.

She wanted to *feel* again, dammit. The thrum of blood pounding through her veins in excitement. Happy butterflies in her belly . . .

The front door opened and Quinn glanced over. Both hers and Brock's parents stood in the doorway, the four of them smiling a greeting at their chickens coming home to the roost, where they'd be pecked at for every little detail of their lives.

Quinn loved her parents and they loved her, but brunch promised to be more invasive than a gyno exam on the 405 South at peak traffic hours.

Brock took Quinn's hand and reeled her in, smiling as he planted a kiss on her lips. It wasn't a hardship. He looked good and he knew it. He kissed good too, and he knew that as well.

It had been two years since they'd slept together, two years since she'd felt the zing of sexual awareness or desire, and she didn't feel it now either. Still, the kiss was nice, and normally she'd try to enjoy it—except he was only doing it for show. So she nipped at his bottom lip.

Hard.

Laughing, he pulled back. "Feisty," he murmured. "I like it."

"I'm not going to sleep with you."

"You should."

"Pray tell why."

"It's been so long . . ." He tugged playfully on a strand of her hair. "I'm worried you're depressed."

This was just uncomfortably close enough to the truth to have her defenses slam down. "I'm not depressed."

"Not you," he said. "Your vagina."

She snorted and yanked free. "Shut up."

"Just keep it in mind." He took her hand back and held it as he led the flight-risk chicken up the front path.

"I should've bitten you harder," she whispered, smiling at the parentals.

"Feeling vicious today, I take it?"

"*Annoyed*," she corrected.

"Ah. I guess turning old does that to a person."

He was nine months younger than she and for just about all their lives—they'd met in kindergarten when he'd socked a boy for pushing her—he'd been smug about their age difference. She nudged him with her hip and knocked him off balance. He merely hauled her along with him, wrapping both his arms around her so that by all appearances *he'd* just saved *her* from a fall. His face close to hers, he gave her a wink.

And suddenly it occurred to her that this wasn't about her at all, but him. His parents must be on him again about giving them grandbabies. And she got it, she did. The truth was, everyone expected them to marry. Brock had been her middle *and* high school boyfriend, and they'd gone off to college together. During their freshman year, they'd had a wildly dramatic and traumatic breakup involving his inability to be monogamous.

Oh, he'd loved her, she had no doubt of that. But he'd also loved anyone who batted their eyes and smiled at him.

It had taken a few years, but eventually they'd found their way back to each other. He'd grown up a lot and so had she. They were best friends—at times friends with benefits—and at others mortal enemies. But after Beth's death, their physical connection had fallen by the wayside . . . and that was all on her.

They'd eventually had the hard discussion about their different needs, and as a result, they'd gone from lovers to friends. She knew Brock would go back to lovers in an instant if she showed the slightest interest.

But she didn't feel interest, and was starting to be afraid she'd never feel it—or anything—ever again. "You're only making it worse for both of us," she said quietly as they moved toward the mother ship.

"If they think we're working on things, they'll leave me the hell alone."

She had to concede the point as they hit the porch and were enveloped into the fold.

"Still not used to it," her mom murmured to Quinn, clinging to Quinn for an extra minute. "It never feels right, you here without her . . ."

She didn't mean it hurtfully, Quinn knew that. Her mom wouldn't hurt a fly, but as always, a lump the size of Texas stuck in her throat. "I know, Mom."

"I miss her so much. You're so strong, Quinn, the way you've moved on."

Had she? Moved on? Or was she just treading water, staying in place, managing to keep her head above the surface? Burying her feelings deep had been the only way to survive the all-encompassing grief, which at the moment sat like a big fat elephant on her chest. For the most part, she kept it locked away in a dark corner of her heart. She'd even built a wall around it, brick by painstaking brick, to contain the emotions that had nearly taken her down.

But she reminded herself that she was lucky. She had a job she loved, parents who cared, and a best friend/fallback husband if it ever came to that. And yes, she was turning thirty soon, and a surprise party still lay in wait regardless of the fact that she didn't want it. But while she'd like to pretend none of that was happening, it wouldn't derail her. Compared to what she'd been through, nothing could.

A LITTLE OVER a week later, Quinn was in line for her usual before-work latte when she felt the weight of someone's gaze on her. Turning, she found a guy around her age with tousled black hair and black-rimmed glasses who looked a lot like a grown-up Harry Potter.

He was staring at her with an intensity that caused her to blink and then crane her neck to peek behind her. No one was there, which meant he was staring at her. She shifted away and did her best to ignore him, instead tuning in to the two women in front of her who were chatting.

"Orgasms after the age of fifty suck," one was saying. "No one tells you that, but they totally do."

Her friend agreed with an emphatic head bob. "I know. It's like sandpaper down there in Lady Town. Takes an entire tube of lube and a bottle of gin."

The first woman snorted. "Don't get me started. Alan will spend thirty minutes looking for a golf ball, but he can't give me ten minutes to find the G-spot."

Quinn must have made some sound, because they both turned to her with apologetic laughs. "Sorry," Dry Vagina said. "It's just one of the many, many things you've got to look forward to, along with hot flashes."

"Don't forget the murderous urges," the other woman said. "And we're talking premeditated too."

Yay. Sounded great.

"Excuse me," the man behind Quinn said, tapping her on the shoulder. Harry Potter, her stalker. "I need to speak to you."

"Sorry. I'm not interested."

"Wait, honey. There's no need to make a hasty decision," one of her new friends said. "What if he's suitably employed, with no baggage?"

"Impossible," Dry Vagina said. "That'd be like finding a unicorn."

"Are you a unicorn?" the first woman asked him.

Harry Potter looked at Quinn with more than a little desperation. "Can I please talk to you . . . alone?"

"Not alone," the first woman said. "That sounds like stranger danger. You can do your pickup-line magic right here, or better yet, do it online like the rest of the world."

The guy never took his gaze off Quinn. "You're Quinn Weller, right?"

Wait a minute. *How did he know her name?* "Okay," she said. "You're going to need to go first."

"I'm Cliff Porter," he said. "I'm an attorney and I really need a word with you. Privately."

She stared at him, trying to come up with a reason why an attorney would be looking for her.

"Porter or Potter?" Dry Vagina asked. "Because Potter would make more sense."

He looked pained. "I get that a lot, but it's Porter."

"How do you know my name?" Quinn asked.

"Look, can we just . . ." He gestured to a small table off to the side of the line.

Torn between curiosity and a healthy sense of survival, Quinn hesitated. "I'll be late for work."

"This will only take a minute."

Reluctantly, she stepped out of line and moved to the table. "You've got one minute."

He took a deep breath. "As I said, I'm an attorney. I located you through a mutual acquaintance."

"Who's that?"

"I'll get to her in a minute. She let me know I could find you here in the mornings rather than scare you by tracking you down at your place of residence. I'm from Wildstone, a small town about two hundred miles north. I'm here to give you news of an inheritance. It's important we talk about it because—"

"I've never even heard of Wildstone," Quinn said. "I certainly don't know anyone from there."

He nodded like he knew this. "We're a small coastal ranching town that sits in a bowl between the Pacific Coast and wine country. Maybe you should sit," he said quietly, and also very kindly she had to admit. "Because the rest of this is going to be a surprise."

"I don't like surprises," she said, "and you have thirty seconds left."

It was clear from his expression that he wasn't happy about having to go into the details in public, but as he was a stranger and maybe also a crackpot, too damn bad. He drew in a deep breath. "The person who left you this inheritance was your birth mother."

She stared at him and then slowly sank into the before-offered chair without looking, grateful it was right behind her. "You're mistaken," she finally managed, shaking her head. "I wasn't adopted."

He gave her a wan smile. "I'm really sorry to have to be the one to tell you this, but you were."

"I have parents," she said. "Lucinda and James Weller."

"They adopted you when you were two days old."

The shock of that reverberated through her body. "No," she whispered. Heart suddenly racing, palms clammy, she shook her head. "They would've told me. There's absolutely no way . . ."

"Again, I'm very sorry," Cliff said quietly. "But it's true. They adopted you from Carolyn Adams." He pulled a picture from his briefcase and pushed it across the table toward her.

And Quinn's heart stopped. Because Carolyn was the woman she'd met here in this very coffee shop.

Chapter 2

My mom always said that right before she died she wanted to swallow a bunch of popcorn kernels to make her cremation more interesting. She totally would've done it too, if she'd gotten the heads-up that her number had been picked.

—from "The Mixed-Up Files of Tilly Adams's Journal"

Quinn found herself sitting on the curb outside the coffee shop, staring blindly at her Lexus, the car her parents had given her last year even though she'd wanted something less expensive.

Her parents. Who might not really be her parents . . .

"Here," Cliff said, pushing a cup of cold water into her hands as he sat next to her. "Drink this."

She took the cup in two shaking hands and gulped down the water, wishing a little bit that it was vodka. "You're mistaken," she said again. "Carolyn was just a woman I met here. We spoke only a few times."

"Three." Cliff gazed at her sympathetically. "She told me about the visits. She always came here instead of your condo or work because it was a social setting and she felt she could approach you here. She'd come to get a peek at you whenever she could, born from the desperate curiosity of a woman who had haunting regrets."

Quinn shook her head, unable to descramble her brain. "I don't understand."

"She knew she was terminal," he said. "She had every intention of telling you all of this herself, but she ran out of time. And what she left behind is important because—"

"Wait." Quinn closed her eyes, just now realizing what he was telling her.

Carolyn was dead.

Cliff took the cup of water from her before she could drop it. "The funeral was a few days ago," he said quietly. "We really need to talk, Quinn. In Wildstone. There are things you don't know that you need to."

Quinn let out a sound that might have been a mirthless laugh or a half sob, she wasn't sure. She shook her head for what felt like the hundredth time in the past few minutes, but the cobwebby feeling didn't clear.

It couldn't be true, any of it. Harry Potter here was just a stalker, a good one. Or maybe a scammer. She hated to think that the nice woman she'd known could be a part of some kind of con, but she simply couldn't accept that her parents wouldn't have told her she'd been adopted. "I don't want any part of this." She stood up and a wave of dizziness hit her.

Cliff rose to his feet too and put his hand on her arm to steady her, looking at her with nothing but kindness and concern in his gaze. "Take my wand."

She focused in on him, expecting to see a lightning-bolt scar on his forehead. "What?"

"My card," he said, the furrow between his brows deepening with concern. "Take my card. Think about it and give me a call tomorrow so we can talk about the inheritance. We *really* need to talk about the inheritance, Quinn." He paused. "Are you going to be all right?"

"Yeah. Sure," she said and drove to work on autopilot, where she proceeded to spill things, plate the wrong entrées, make silly mistakes like using shallots instead of onions—

"What the hell's wrong with you?" Marcel demanded. "Get out of my kitchen until your head's screwed on straight!"

For once he was right. Her head was most definitely not screwed on straight.

They adopted you when you were two days old . . .

"Are you even listening to me?" Marcel yelled up at her. Up, because he was five feet two to her five feet seven, something that normally gave her great pleasure. "*Du flittchen,*" he muttered in disgust beneath his breath and the entire staff froze in the kitchen like deer in the headlights.

Slut.

Quinn set down her knife so she wasn't tempted to run him through as she turned to him. "*Schiebe ex,*" she said, which meant "shove it." It was the best she could do, at least in German. Pushing past him, she walked out of the kitchen.

"Where are you going?" he screamed after her. "You can't just leave!"

But leaving was exactly what she was doing.

Skye followed her outside. "Quinn? You okay? What's going on?"

"You've got to go back in there before he gets mad at you too," Quinn said.

Skye shrugged. "He was born mad. Talk to me."

So Quinn told her what had happened at the coffee shop, and Skye just stared at her. "Shut the front door."

"I've got to go. I need to talk to my parents," Quinn said.

"Uh, yeah you do."

From inside they could hear Marcel yelling for Skye, who squeezed Quinn's hand. "Call me."

Quinn promised she would and gave her a quick hug. Then she headed toward her car, pulling out her cell phone to call her boss, Chef Wade.

Chef Wade never wasted words. He answered with, "Talk."

"I need to leave early," Quinn said. "I'm so sorry for the short notice, but there's . . . an emergency. Marcel's here. He's got things under control." By being a tyrannical asshole, but that was another story.

"What's wrong?" he asked, voice softening with concern, as he was a longtime friend of her parents.

"Nothing I can't handle," she promised and hoped that was true. She disconnected and drove straight to her parents' house.

Her mom and dad were in the living room in front of their lit gas fireplace, sharing a drink. Yes, it was 3 P.M. in April in L.A., which meant the air conditioner was on full blast, but her mom liked her alcohol with ambience.

"Darling," her mom said, smiling as she stood in welcome. "Such a lovely surprise. Where's Brock?"

"I'm alone." Quinn didn't bother to address—for the thousandth time—that she didn't spend nearly as much time with Brock as they seemed to hope. "I met someone today."

Her mom looked dismayed. "Other than Brock? But what will people think?"

"Mom . . ." Quinn pressed her fingertips into her eye sockets to ward off an eye twitch. "I keep telling you, Brock and I aren't together like that anymore."

"Right *now* you mean," she said. "Right?"

A conversation she didn't have the strength for. "The man I met today had an interesting story to tell me." Her breath caught. "He said that I'm adopted."

Twin looks of shock and guilt slid over her parents' faces like matching masks and reality hit Quinn smack in the face. "Oh my God." She staggered to the couch opposite them and sank to it, staring at them. "Oh my God, it's not a story. It's true."

At the awkward beat of utter silence, Quinn stood back up and headed straight to the kitchen. She needed alcohol or sugar, stat. Thank Toll House, she found some ready-made cookie dough in the fridge. Her mom didn't bake. For that matter, neither did Quinn. She loved to cook and she was good at it, but for whatever reason, baking skills eluded her.

She was stuffing spoonfuls of dough into her mouth when her parents—who were apparently *not* her parents at all—appeared in the doorway. It was the most disorienting thing she'd ever experienced, looking at them and realizing her life was forever changed, that the very foundation of her entire world had crumbled. "It's day one of my new raw food diet," she said inanely.

Her parents exchanged a concerned look. "We need to talk," her dad said solemnly.

Little late for that . . .

"Honey," her mom said earnestly. Quinn turned to her hopefully.

"If you eat that whole package, it's the equivalent of forty-eight cookies."

Quinn blinked. "Are you kidding me?"

Her dad sighed and leaned onto the island between them. He

nudged the block of knives out of her reach and said, "We never expected you to find out."

"Okay," she said, absorbing that with a nod. "Wow." She scooped up the last of the dough.

Her mom opened her mouth but nothing came out of it because Quinn jabbed a finger at her. Then she popped the last bite in, chewed, and licked her thumb before taking a deep breath. "Why?" she finally asked, suitably sugared up. "Why didn't you just tell me? People are adopted all the time. What possible reason could you have for keeping it a secret?"

"Because I wanted you to be mine," her mom whispered, her eyes soft and, dammit, a little damp.

Her dad slid an arm around her mom's waist. "It wasn't important to us *how* we got you," he said. "We wanted a baby, and we couldn't have our own."

Quinn sucked in a breath. "Beth," she said through a throat blocked by what felt like a regulation football. "*Was she adopted too?*"

Her mom shook her head. "No. We'd been trying for years before we were told we couldn't have our own. So we set an adoption in motion. When you came along, we were so happy, just completely over the moon." She stopped and drew a deep breath, as if reliving the joy. "But then the unbelievable happened. When you were four months old, I learned I was pregnant." She put a hand to her chest. "I'm more grateful to Carolyn for you than you could ever know," she said fiercely. "Because we were twice blessed. But . . ." She looked to Quinn's dad.

"But," he continued on for her, "Carolyn signed a confidentiality agreement. We could sue her for discussing the adoption. She had no right."

"Too late," Quinn said quietly. "She's dead. And apparently she left me some sort of an inheritance."

"That doesn't make any sense," her mom said. "She had nothing of worth to speak of."

"I was so shocked I didn't ask for details," Quinn said. Details Cliff had tried to give her. She hugged herself, feeling a little sick from the dough.

Or her life. "So . . . were you sorry you'd adopted me once Beth came along?" she asked.

"Oh my God, no." Her mom came around the island and took Quinn's hands in her own. "*No*," she said again more firmly. "It was a happy accident. The truth is, we didn't want to take away from *either* of you, so we just kept it quiet. It didn't matter to us, and I know this is asking a lot, but I wish it wouldn't matter to you."

Her dad nodded his agreement on that.

But Quinn didn't know how to make it not matter. She didn't know what to feel, not about the adoption, the devastating betrayal, or the fact that she and Beth had never been sisters at all. She let out a breath and took a step away from them. "I need to think."

"It doesn't matter," her mom said. "None of this matters."

"Mom, how can you say that?"

"Because we love you. Maybe we were wrong to not have told you about being adopted, and I'm sorry you found out in such a shocking manner, but we've never thought of you as anything but a real daughter. Ever."

This brought a huge lump to Quinn's throat so all she could do was nod.

"Now," her mom said, tears shimmering brilliantly in her own eyes as well as she patted Quinn on the arm. "Let's just look forward, to you marrying Brock and getting on with your lovely life."

Quinn closed her eyes. "I'm not getting married to Brock. And even if I wanted to, how could I?" she asked. "I don't even know who I am anymore."

"Okay," her dad said. "That seems a little dramatic."

Quinn let out a low laugh. "You're right. It is. And now I'm going to take my dramatic ass home. I need some time."

"Time?" Her mom exchanged another worried look with her dad. "But you're still coming over next weekend for dinner, right? Say Saturday night . . . seven o'clock? On the dot? And you'll text me once you get here, before you come in?"

Quinn had gotten to the door. She turned around to find them standing in the same position at the island, looking shocked at her unusual temper tantrum. "Let me get this straight. You can't keep my surprise party a secret, but you were able to keep my adoption one?"

Her mom bit her lower lip. "I don't know what you mean about a surprise party."

With another low, mirthless laugh, Quinn walked out. She drove home to the quiet little condo she was mortgaged to the eyeballs for and stared at herself in the bathroom mirror. She was in shock. And adrift. And . . . sad. Angry too . . . and so much more.

It was shocking for more than one reason, not the least of which was that she felt more emotion right this minute than she'd felt in two years.

She'd meant it when she'd told Cliff that she didn't want anything to do with any inheritance, especially not from someone who'd apparently thrown her away without so much as looking back.

Not that she was happy with her parents right now either. They should've told her the truth a long time ago. Instead they'd hidden it and even now had tried to underplay everything, encouraging her to get on with her nice, comfortable life.

But it suddenly didn't feel so nice or comfortable at all.

Feeling shockingly alone, she looked at her phone. She wanted to call Beth. God, how she wanted that, but instead she called Brock.

"Hey," he said when he picked up, his voice brisk and rushed. "I'm in a meeting. Leave a message and I'll get right back to you."

His voice mail. Disappointment washing over her, she tried to tell herself she was fine, she didn't need anyone. But her heart was racing and it didn't seem to fit in her rib cage anymore. *Everything* felt tight and she couldn't breathe because she had no one else left to call.

Well, except one person.

Harry Potter, aka Cliff Porter.

Chapter 3

I'd give up being a bitch, but I'm not a quitter.

—from "The Mixed-Up Files of Tilly Adams's Journal"

Mick Hennessey stood on the sand dunes, the evening sun still strong enough to beat down on his head, the waves crashing over the shore loud enough to drown out his own thoughts.

Which was just as well since they weren't good.

He'd grown up here in Wildstone, which was literally an old wild, wild west town that sat in a bowl between the mid-California coast and the rolling hills that lined that coast.

He no longer lived here, but his mom had needed him, so he was back.

Temporarily.

Which didn't stop him from feeling like a worthless kid all over again in spite of the fact that he'd worked his ass off to make something of himself.

Wildstone had done the same, several times over in fact. In

the 1890s, it had been nothing more than a clapboard sidewalk and a row of saloons and whorehouses, supported by local silver mines and logging mills. In the mid 1900s, the town had attempted to legitimize itself and had done away with most of the whorehouses—though the saloons had stubbornly remained. Then the county had discovered wine making and ranching, and the hills had become dotted with wineries and ranches. In the 1970s, the bad economy had forced Wildstone to put on yet another hat, and for a while the town fathers had played up their infamous past, marketing the place as a wild west ghost town, using the historic downtown buildings to do so, claiming them haunted to gather interest.

Mostly the only people who'd taken note were ghost hunters, although Mick's own mother still swore that her shed was haunted.

In the 1980s, surfers had found the little-known beaches to be perfect, and so Wildstone had added tourism to the roster, pulling in vacationers. Ten years ago they'd been in the running to make the list of California's Top-Ten Best-Kept Secrets.

They'd come in at number eleven and hadn't been featured. Without that boost, Wildstone's economy had continued to suffer beyond the recession.

It was still struggling.

Mick found the place as constricting and stifling as his bullheaded father, so he'd fled the minute he'd graduated from high school. He'd spent almost no time here in the years since, and had been a happier man for it.

Until his dad had stroked out on the throne early one morning four months ago.

Coop whined and Mick looked down at the twelve-year-old golden retriever, ball in his mouth. Coop panted happily and dropped the ball at Mick's feet, his rheumy brown eyes ever hopeful.

Mick shook his head. "Last time I threw it, you decided you didn't mean it."

Coop gave a talkative "woo woo woo."

Translation: *Mick was full of shit.* "I had to go get it myself," he reminded the dog. "Remember that?"

This bought him another "woo woo woo."

"Okay, okay." Mick picked up the ball, and because there was a lot of old-man dog pride on the line here, he gave it a dramatic throw, making sure it went only about twenty feet.

Coop gave an energetic leap. A single energetic leap. After that, he eyeballed the sea of sand ahead of him, huffed out a sigh, and sat. Then he craned his big, fuzzy golden head and gave Mick a sad-eyed look.

"Are you kidding me?" Mick asked him.

Coop lay down, set his head on his front paws, and stared forlornly out at the ball that his brain wanted to chase but his sore joints and tired body wouldn't allow. It was a daily reminder for the dog, who in his own mind clearly wasn't elderly, forgetful, or more than half deaf. Nope, in Coop's opinion, he was still a rambunctious, energetic puppy.

Mick blew out a sigh and fetched the damn ball. When he came back, the dog sat up, eyes bright, tongue lolling.

"Not a chance," Mick said on a laugh. "I'm not throwing it again. This was about your exercise, not mine. I already had my run today."

A Lexus pulled up. A woman sat behind the wheel and stared out at the dunes and the ocean. All Mick could see of her was a cloud of whiskey-colored waves of hair and a pale face. She stared at the water and then set her head to the steering wheel and banged it a few times.

Then, head still down, she went utterly still.

Coop whined about the ball and nudged Mick's knee, eyes pleading.

With a head shake, Mick threw the ball five feet.

Coop happily pounced on it.

While his dog pranced around proudly, ball in his mouth, Mick turned back to the car. The woman hadn't moved. Had she knocked herself out? Was she still breathing? "What do you think?" he asked Coop. "Stay out of it, or ask her if she's okay?"

Coop, who'd never been impressed by a single one of the women in Mick's social life, yawned.

"Right," he said. "Stay out of it."

But the woman suddenly sat up straight and fumbled her way out of the car, falling to her knees on the rough gravelly asphalt, gulping in air like she was suffocating.

Realizing she was hyperventilating, Mick rushed to her and crouched at her side, having to push Coop back from making her acquaintance—which he tended to do with a rude nose push to the crotch. "Stay," he ordered and looked the woman over.

Young. Late twenties maybe. Definitely having a panic attack of some kind. Not touching her, he spoke quietly and calmly. "Take a deep breath through your nose."

She had to quiet herself to hear him, but she did as he said. She took a deep breath, shuddery as it was.

"Good," he said, still holding Coop back from trying to say hello. "*Stay.*"

"What?" she gasped.

"Sorry, not you. My nosy-ass dog. Keep breathing. That's it," he said when she worked at it.

When she had it under control, she met his gaze, her own eyes hooded and clearly embarrassed. "I'm sorry."

"Don't be."

Coop, tired of being held back, shoved his big old head between them and licked her from chin to forehead. Mick palmed the dog's face and pushed his head away from the woman whose shoulders were now shaking.

Aw, hell. He patted his pockets—for what, he had no idea. It wasn't like he carried tissues or napkins on him to offer her. He rose to his feet to go search the truck, which was when she lifted her face and he saw that she was shaking with laughter, not tears.

She was laughing at his ridiculous dog.

Then she ran a hand down Coop's back and that was it. The dog fell in love, sliding bonelessly to the ground to roll over, exposing his belly and all his manly bits—well, the bits he still had after the vet had finished with him years and years ago now.

"Ignore him," Mick said and offered her a hand to pull her up to her feet.

Instead, she bent over Coop, stroking his belly. "What a good boy," she murmured softly. "You're just the sweetest thing, aren't you?"

Coop ate it up, sighing in utter bliss, and . . . farted.

"Sorry," Mick said, fanning the air with his hand. "He's old."

Coop sent him a reproachful look and then went back to smiling at the woman, who laughed softly and kissed his dog right on the snout. "Don't worry about it," she whispered. "You're still the sweetest thing. Yes, you are."

Coop agreed with an ongoing tail wag, stirring up the sand.

The woman stood on her own and sighed before meeting Mick's eyes. "Thanks."

"You okay?"

"Always."

He arched a brow and she shrugged. "Sometimes you have to fake it until you make it, you know?"

As he did indeed know, he nodded.

"And sometimes in the faking, I panic." She looked away, taking in the now-setting sun. "What you saw was just a long overdue panic attack, but I've got it handled now." She bent and kissed Coop again, on top of his head this time. "And thanks to you too," she whispered. Then she got into her car and drove off.

Sitting at his feet, Coop watched her go and let out a soft whine.

Mick, who at the ripe old age of thirty-two was far too jaded and cynical to whine after a woman, opened the door to the truck. "Can you make it?"

Coop tap-danced on his paws like he was going to jump, but didn't. Instead he whined at Mick.

"You don't want to even try?"

The dog took a step toward the truck as if to jump, but limped now as he looked back at Mick.

Mick sighed and picked up the hundred-and-fifty-pound oaf. "You're going on a diet," he said and buckled Coop in.

An hour later, Mick stood in the garage of his childhood home, trying to shrug off his frustration. Hard to do when just being here exhumed all his deeply buried resentments.

There were tools, boxes of decades-old crap, outdated cans of dried-up paint stacked high, and pretty much every garden hose his dad had ever bought, despite half of them being cracked or riddled with holes. The old man hadn't thrown a single thing away in all the years he'd lived here.

And now Mick was stuck with straightening out every mess the guy had left, including his sorry finances.

Mick kicked aside a tarp and found a stack of kindling for the woodstove they'd had in the living room—twenty years ago. It had long ago been converted to gas and he'd bet that under the wood lived a very large, very fat family of field mice who probably spent their days wreaking havoc in the walls.

Perfect.

"Honey? Where are you?"

The sound of his mom's voice flashed him back to when he'd been twelve, hiding out in here, stealing materials for the bike track he'd built in the field behind the house, complete with the ramps and jumps he'd used to shatter his collarbone with that summer.

"Micky?"

With a grimace for the nickname he hated almost as much as this house, he called out to her. "In the garage."

Audra Hennessey appeared in the opened door holding two tall glasses of what he knew to be her fresh lemonade. Hers would be liberally laced with her *also* homemade moonshine.

She'd been working hard at pickling her internal organs for a couple of months now. Four, to be exact.

She handed him a glass and Coop lifted his big, heavy head from the nap he'd been taking on a pile of old rags. He gave a soft "wuff" in happiness and staggered to his feet. This took him a minute because his hips were really bothering him today, but he shook it off and trotted over to greet the love of his life.

Mick's mom's face lit up as well. "Oh look at you, my handsome boy!" She pulled a doggy treat from her pocket. "Don't tell your daddy," she whispered. "He thinks you're getting fat."

"He *is* getting fat," Mick said as Coop wolfed the treat down without so much as tasting it.

Coop slid him a look.

Mick shook his head. "The vet said you had to lose ten pounds, man. Don't blame me."

Mick's mom squatted down and gave Coop a big hug, whispering in his ear that she'd made dinner and saved him some.

Mick gave up. He couldn't win all the battles. Plus, it was good to see her smiling. Between his father's death and his sister Wendy's vanishing act, she'd had it rough.

"Watch out," he said, dragging a heavy box of crap to the driveway, tossing it into the back of his dad's old truck, which Mick had been driving around while in town so he could dump the trash at the end of the day and also pick up supplies as needed.

She looked at the big pile of things in the driveway that Mick still had to discard, more stuff he'd dragged out of the garage to get to the dump, and frowned. "That's my old rocking chair," she said.

"*Old* being the key word."

"I want it back, Mick."

"Mom, it's broken beyond repair." He nudged it with his toe and another rung from the armrest fell off. "See? And admit it, you'd completely forgotten about the thing until you saw it just now."

"Not true," she said. "I know more than you give me credit for."

He set his empty glass down to take her gently by the shoulders. She was frail, and he hated that. He turned her around to face him, looking up at him with dark brown eyes identical to his own. "I want you to tell me—without looking," he said, "which stuff in that pile are things you want to keep."

She bit her lower lip, trying to hide a smile.

"Just one thing, Mom," he said, and had to laugh when she rolled her eyes.

"You always were too smart for your own good," she said. "An answer for everything. No wonder you and your dad never got along."

True story. Mick had been born with an insatiable curiosity. He'd questioned everything, and his dad, a manual laborer all his life with only an eighth-grade education, hadn't had the answers, which had brought out his temper, hating that Mick's questions made him feel small. Adding to the unpinned grenade was the fact that his dad always had to be right.

"*All* of these things are memories to me," his mom said, looking around them. "I know you don't understand that because, like Wendy, you were always so unhappy here."

"Wendy was born unhappy," he said and she smiled sadly because it was true. Wendy had always had big plans. She'd wanted to be an esthetician, so Mick had sent her to school. Twice. Neither time had stuck. Her latest plan was to become rich and famous, and Mick wished her nothing but good luck on that. "And I wasn't *always* unhappy."

"When?" she asked with a hopefulness that stabbed him in the chest. "When were you happy here?"

He slung an arm around her. "When you baked strawberry pies."

She snorted and pushed him away. "I made those pies to sell at the farmers' market and you'd steal them. You were always hungry. A bottomless pit." And then, as if the memories were all too much, her smile faded and suddenly she looked every bit of her sixty years as she sipped her "lemonade." Her eyes were too glassy and she was flushed.

"Mom," he said quietly. "This is all too much for you. Running the house by yourself, keeping it and the yard up. I want you to reconsider—"

"No," she said. "I don't want to sell and move."

Mick lived and worked in San Francisco, two and a half hours north. The commute to check in on her every week since his dad's death was starting to hurt his business. He was a structural engineer in a firm with three partners, although he'd recently turned his attention to buying up properties and leasing them out to a wide assortment of businesses. But even without his crazy-busy schedule, the five-hour weekly round-trip to Wildstone was killing him.

When he was in town, he stayed at the Wild West B & B, a property he was actively looking at buying since the owners were in financial trouble. Mick's mom wanted him to stay here in his old bedroom, but luckily for him it was still stuffed to the gills with more old stuff he hadn't gotten to yet.

His mom was a *Hoarders* episode waiting to happen.

Normally, he came on the weekends, but he was staying all week to expedite necessary renovations on the house. "The guys I hired to haul some of this stuff away should've been here today."

She bit her lower lip.

"What?" he asked.

"They showed up a little while ago and I turned them away. I don't need help," she said when he groaned. "I've got you."

"Mom." He rubbed his temples, but it didn't ease the headache. "It took me three weeks to get them here."

She crossed her arms, her face set. "I didn't like the look of them."

He had to laugh, but honestly there was no way he was going to even try to squash her 'tude. His dad has been a stern and dominating force that Mick had never managed to get along with. But if his mom wanted to grow a backbone at her age, he was all for it. "Fine," he said. "You win. You're never going to be serious about selling this place anyway."

"Now you're catching on." She patted him on the cheek. "I love it here, honey. I just wish you loved it here too." She paused, waiting for his reaction.

But he couldn't give her the one she wanted.

She sighed. "You spent the last two weekends renovating my kitchen, and you know what? I think you secretly enjoyed it. You handled it far more capably than I could ever have imagined."

"Guess the old man taught me something after all, huh?"

Her smile faded and he felt like an asshole.

"You're not being fair," she said quietly. "Yes, he was tough and demanding, but it's not like you suffered for it. Look how well you turned out."

Still sticking up for the bastard.

"He was hard on you," she said, "because he saw your potential early on."

If his dad had seen Mick's potential, this was news to him. All he could remember was being refused every request to do anything, even though he'd been a decent kid who'd stayed out of trouble.

His mom looked at the shovel and rake hanging from hooks on the wall. Beside them were painted outlines of other tools that were now either lying on the floor or missing entirely, and she smiled sadly. "I'm surprised you haven't painted over those outlines."

Mick shrugged. He was trying to do things methodically and not let his emotions get the best him. "I've got to clear things out before I can paint." But the truth was, he couldn't wait to obliterate the physical proof of his father's need for complete control. He straightened and felt the ache in his back and shoulders from the work. "I'm going to knock off for the day. I want to go shower."

"It's ridiculous, you coming from San Francisco so often and staying at the Wild West B and B instead of here."

The Wild West B & B was so named because it had been there since the sidewalks were clapboard. It was rumored to be haunted, something he was certain the owners perpetuated to bring in business.

"You know you could move your office here," his mom said. "Wildstone could use a man like you. You belong here, Mick."

But that was just it. He didn't.

And he never had.

Chapter 4

Sometimes my life feels like a test I didn't study for.

—from "The Mixed-Up Files of Tilly Adams's Journal"

After the humiliating panic attack on the beach in front of the dark-haired, dark-eyed, apparently unflappable stranger and his big, adorable dog, Quinn drove away just far enough that she couldn't be seen by said unflappable stranger and adorable dog before she pulled over again to gather herself.

Probably an impossible task.

It hurt to think her birth mom had lived only two hundred miles north of her and she'd never known. And what about her birth father? Who was he? Did she have grandparents? Aunts? Uncles? Anyone else?

Why hadn't she thought to ask Harry Potter?

She pulled back out into the street, and her GPS—programmed to find the town of Wildstone—wasn't sure what to do with itself now that they were here. "In half a mile turn right," it intoned in an irritated female voice that insinuated Quinn was an idiot.

Once she'd attempted to change the voice to male. She'd been hoping for an Aussie or British accent. Unfortunately, her tech skills didn't extend that far and she'd ended up with this very stern, disapproving female voice.

But she turned right. Mostly because it felt good not to think.

"At the intersection, turn left."

Quinn flicked a gaze to her silent phone. It was silent because it was off. She'd gotten in her car and driven here without telling anyone. Well, except Cliff, who'd seemed hugely relieved to hear she was on her way. He'd made an appointment to see her first thing tomorrow morning.

But in the end, she hadn't waited for morning to make the drive. She was here and lead sat heavy in her gut with panic clogging her throat again, making it hard to breathe. Her head pounded in a way that was reminiscent of the night Beth had died, leaving Quinn alone and adrift and devastated without her best friend and confidante.

She missed the intersection.

"Recalculating," the GPS said, judgment heavy in her tone.

Quinn reached out and turned the app off. In blissful silence, she pulled into a gas station and filled up on both gas and snacks. When she dumped her loot on the counter to pay, the clerk raised a brow. "Skipped dinner, huh? That's rough."

She'd stopped an hour ago and grabbed a sandwich that had served as her meal, which meant that this was actually dinner number two—not something she wanted to admit. "Yeah," she said. "Real rough. Do you know of any good hotels in town?"

He grinned. "Hotels? No."

"Motels?"

"Sure. There's the Wild West B and B just up the street. It's only two point five stars but it's haunted, which is cool."

Uh-huh. Thirty minutes later Quinn had checked into the place that claimed it was a "slice of heaven."

She stood in the middle of her tiny room—which, for the record, was *not* exactly a slice of heaven—and looked around. The lower half of the walls were lined with wood that had come from fencing slats, the upper walls covered in floral print wallpaper that instantly brought to mind the old, wild west. The furniture looked like pieces from a wagon, and the room was decorated with flowers in rustic milk cans and wanted posters on the walls, all dated around 1900. Cheesy but cute.

The walls were clearly thin, as sound carried like nobody's business. She could hear the bathroom sink dripping and the couple in the next room arguing.

"You're watching TV?" a woman yelled. "We've got my mom watching the kids for a whole night and you're watching baseball?"

"It's the playoffs," a man said.

"I can't believe I wore my fun underwear for this!"

Quinn remoted the TV on and turned up the volume to give them some privacy and also to distract her from the drip, drip, dripping coming from the bathroom. She moved to the closet, which was a pretty antique armoire. It squeaked ominously as she opened it and peered into the dark cabinet.

Spooky, she decided, and shut it again. Besides, she wasn't staying long enough to unpack. She wanted to go to sleep, then wake up and meet with Cliff in the morning for some answers to her questions. Then she was out.

Too keyed up to hit the sack, she sat on the bed and read the B & B's brochure, which playfully warned her about their ghost. Apparently in 1892, this building had been a saloon and the madam had been murdered here. Hmm. Not exactly a good bedtime story.

Tossing the brochure aside, she looked around for a coffeemaker.

The fact that there wasn't one nearly brought on another panic attack.

Next, she opened her laptop, where she came up against another problem. No Wi-Fi. She called the front desk and asked about it, and was laughed right off the phone.

Fine. She'd take a bath and soak her problems away. It might take all night but it was worth a try. Except . . .

She stifled a scream and jumped out of the bathroom.

There was a bug with a whole lot of legs in the tub.

She felt the panic creeping in on her again, a big, fat knot in her throat, blocking her air pipe because everyone knew that bugs traveled in packs. Only the stupid ones got caught. The smart ones lay in wait for her to go to sleep so they could attack.

On shaky legs, she sank to the bed and then plopped back to stare up at the ceiling. Exhaustion, probably nerve based, crept in on her and she lay there thinking that maybe what she needed more than anything was a drink. A stiff one.

She closed her eyes and had actually started to drift off, but there was that drip, drip, dripping.

And God knew how many bugs were mobilizing . . .

Jerking upright, she grabbed her phone. She knew it made her seem weak, but she was going to call Brock. She needed to let him know she'd run away anyway, but . . . oh yeah—no service. She moved around the room, holding up her phone like she was making an offering to the cell-service god.

Nothing.

This was crazy. It was the twenty-first century, who didn't have service? But hold on . . . at the window, she caught a flicker of a single bar. *Gotcha.* Dragging the lone chair over to the window, she stood on it, keeping the phone held up high.

Two whole bars.

Score!

Standing there carefully balanced on the chair, with her head, arm, and phone hanging out the window, she hit Brock's number.

It rang three times before he picked up, sounding winded. "Busy," he said. "I'll call you back—"

"Brock, wait!"

"Okay," he said, sounding surprised at her vehemence. "What's the matter?"

"Did you read my texts?"

There was a pause. "Hang on," he said and she rolled her eyes.

She'd sent him a series of texts telling him her entire sordid, woeful tale and he hadn't even read them. That was Brock.

He came back. "Holy shit," he said.

"Yeah. So . . . I'm in Wildstone."

"*What?*"

"I sort of drove up here earlier today," she said.

"You just up and drove there? By yourself? What the hell for?"

She let out a mirthless laugh. "Did you not understand the texts?"

"I understood them, but, Quinn, your family, your *real* family, is here in L.A., including me. We have that stupid fancy work dinner to go to tomorrow night, and you promised to be my plus one and hang all over me like I'm the best thing since streaming."

She actually pulled her phone away from her face and stared at it, nearly falling out the window in the process. "I don't think you're listening. I'm not Quinn Weller!"

He sighed. "Babe, you are. You're Quinn Weller to the bone."

"Don't you get it? It's like I've been living my life from chapter two of my own story! I missed chapter one entirely! *And* the prologue!"

"You can't let this derail you," he said. "And if you'd waited until after that work party I've got to attend, I'd have gone with you."

No, he wouldn't have. The only thing that Brock ever left L.A. for was work, and only when he had to. "Would you still feel this way if this was you and your parents we were talking about?" she asked. "And *your* adoption?"

Brock laughed softly. "You mean Mr. and Mrs. Robot? I used to *dream* of being adopted."

She closed her eyes. "Yeah, well, I didn't."

He sighed. "I know, Q. And I'm sorry, they should've told you, but it doesn't change anything about who you are. It doesn't. You're still smart, funny, and . . . amazing."

That was sweet and she started to tell him so when he spoke again.

"Now get your cute ass home," he said. "I need you here."

"I'm not—" she started, but he was already gone, either dumped by her barely there service or because he'd disconnected.

She'd started to pull herself back in the window where she was precariously perched, but she caught sight of a guy getting out of an old beater truck filled with tools parked right in front of the office. The maintenance guy. But hold the phone—she recognized the long denim-covered legs and the big old retriever.

It was her mysterious panic-attack rescuer. "Hey," she called down to him.

He stopped on the curb beneath a lamppost and looked up at her, his expression shielded by the ambient lighting.

"Hi," she said, possibly never so happy to see someone in her life. "Remember me?"

His lips quirked.

Yep. He remembered her all right. "I've got a problem," she said.

His smile faded. "You okay?"

She exhaled, feeling like an idiot. "There's a big bug in my tub and the sink is dripping. Do you have time to help or are you off the clock?"

He studied her for a beat. "I'll grab some tools and be right up," he finally said.

She watched him stride off. Maybe she couldn't find her feels, but apparently she could still appreciate a nice ass.

Good to know.

Five minutes later there was a simple, firm knock at her door. She opened it and stood back to let him in, but he remained on his side of the doorway, toolbox in hand.

"I'm Mick Hennessey," he said.

Great, but she had no time for introductions. *Bug in her tub!* "Nice to formally meet you, Mick, but . . ." She pointed to the bathroom.

With a mock salute, he ambled in there.

Quinn remained right where she was, counting off the seconds while she heard nothing. "Did you get him?" she finally called out.

"The bug?" he asked.

"No, the president of the United States! *Yes,* the bug!"

The only response was the sound of the toilet flushing and she panicked. "You squished him first, right?"

Mick stuck his head out of the bathroom and flashed her a

smile. "Worried he's going to swim his way back up and bite you on the—"

"*No!*" *Yes . . .*

He vanished back into the bathroom. Quinn heard some other sounds that were hopefully related to him working on the sink. Unable to stop herself, she made her way over there and peered in. "Where's your dog?"

"Coop? With my mom. She lives here in town and made stew. Apparently, I don't rate on the same scale as beef stew." He was on his back, head and shoulders wedged beneath the sink, legs bent at the knees because he was longer than the bathroom. He wore a T-shirt advertising some pub in San Francisco named O'Riley's, that had risen up, revealing his low-slung jeans and some impressive abs, including those V muscles that made women so stupid. "Can you fix it?" she asked.

His hands looked confident working the wrench before he pulled his head from beneath the sink and sent her a slow smile.

At the barely recognizable flutter low in Quinn's belly, and also decidedly south of her belly, she froze in shock. She'd felt next to nothing for a very long time, but it hadn't been so long that she couldn't place this for what it was.

Lust.

She staggered out of the bathroom to get a grip. But there was no grip to be had. With no idea of what was happening, or why now, she moved to her suitcase on the bed just to keep herself busy. She'd come here to Wildstone on mindless adrenaline, not planning on staying past her tomorrow's morning meeting.

But suddenly she realized that what she really needed was time to process her new reality. Pulling her suitcase across the bed toward her, she entered the code to unlock it and . . . nothing happened. It wouldn't open. She tried again.

Still nothing.

Out of patience, she tossed the suitcase hard to the floor and tried again.

No go.

"Dammit!" She kicked it a few times and that's when it happened.

A buzzing.

From inside her suitcase.

She stared at it in growing horror because it was her electric toothbrush, it *had* to be, but it sure sounded a whole lot like—

"Your vibrator's batteries are going to die."

This from Captain Helpful, who was leaning casually against the doorjamb of the bathroom, looking amused again.

"It's my toothbrush!" she said. "I swear it."

"You're blushing." He smiled. "Cute."

Appalled, she tried again to open the suitcase, while it just kept buzzing like her toothbrush was having a seizure. Grinding her back teeth into powder, she kicked the suitcase again for good measure.

The buzzing got louder.

Mick let out a low—and sexy—laugh. Damn him.

Unbelievable. Desperate, she got on top of the suitcase and jumped up and down. This didn't stop the buzzing but it did burst the thing open, and when she hopped off, her stuff got flung far and wide. Clothes, bathroom stuff, the birth control pills she took to control cramps since she sure as hell wasn't having any sex . . . everything *except* the toothbrush.

"Oh my God," she said, scrambling through it all to find the damn thing—which of course, thank you, laws of Newton—was still buzzing. When she finally wrapped her fingers around it, she lifted it high and blew a strand of hair from her now-sweaty face. "See?" she asked triumphantly. "*Not* a vibrator."

Mick, still watching the Quinn Show, smiled. "Smart to pack multipurpose items."

She pointed at him, not in enough control of herself to speak.

He laughed. "Bad day, huh?"

She blew out a sigh and tossed the toothbrush back into her suitcase. "You have no idea."

"Try me."

And maybe because when she looked into his eyes she saw nothing but a genuine curiosity—among other things—she actually said it all out loud. "I had unwelcome news, a fight with my family, a long drive, and I can't get my phone to work unless I'm hanging out the window." She paused. "I might be more than a little unhinged."

"That's allowed sometimes, you know."

"Yeah." Mostly she was hurt on top of hurt, lonely, unnerved, and . . . not herself. Which really wasn't surprising given that she literally didn't know who she even was.

"Well, at least the bug's gone and the sink's handled." He pushed off from the doorway and started across the room to leave. "'Night. Oh, and ignore any nighttime creaking."

"Creaking?" she asked his broad back. "You mean like . . . ghostly creaking?"

He flashed a grin back her way. "I mean the old building creaks as it settles."

Or that.

"You could always use the toothbrush as a vibrator to help you relax enough to sleep."

Luckily for him, he shut the door immediately after saying this, so she didn't get the chance to kill him. She took a deep breath and then took a long hot bath in her bug-less tub. And no, she didn't use the toothbrush as a vibrator . . . but she thought about it. Instead, she watched some worthless TV, ate the secret stash of chocolate she kept in her purse, and then hit the sack.

There she lay, the endless questions once again swirling around in her head.

Why hadn't Carolyn said something to her sooner?

How many other secrets had she taken with her to her grave?

Acutely and painfully aware that all of it was more than likely to remain a mystery, she sighed, flipped over, and tried to go to sleep.

It was a long time coming . . .

Chapter 5

Whenever I used to feel powerless, Mom would say to remind myself that a single one of my turds could shut down an entire water park.

—from "The Mixed-Up Files of Tilly Adams's Journal"

Psst. Quinn, wake up."

Quinn stretched, opened her eyes, and then gasped at the sight of Beth sitting crossed-legged at the foot of the bed in a cute white sundress, sipping one of her beloved iced teas. Quinn rubbed her eyes, but her sister—her *dead* sister—was still there. "I'm dreaming," she said. "It was the piece of chocolate before bed."

"Actually, you ate *all* the pieces of chocolate," Beth said.

Quinn didn't take her eyes off Beth, afraid she'd vanish. "I don't understand," she whispered. "Where did you come from?"

"The TARDIS slash wardrobe," Beth said and gestured over her shoulder at the innocuous piece of furniture. "Nice hair, by the way."

Quinn reached up and felt her hair, which was definitely not anywhere even *near* the vicinity of "nice."

"You haven't been using that oil treatment I gave you," Beth chided.

"I know, I haven't used it since you—"

"Bit the bucket?" Beth nodded sympathetically and drank some more tea. "I hated going out like that. But let's face it, if it had to be my time, going instantly in a car accident is the way to do it. One minute I was driving, singing along to One Direction—I really miss them, by the way—and the next I was gone."

"Because you took your eyes off the road to mess with your phone and wrapped yourself around a tree," Quinn said. Maybe yelled. "And One Direction broke up!"

"Well, that sucks." Beth's brown eyes, so different from Quinn's own deep blue—how had she never questioned that before?—held hers. "But honestly? It was my time, Quinn. And do you know whose time it isn't? *Yours.*"

"Okay, that's it." Quinn pinched herself. "Ow!" She blinked, but Beth was still there. "If I felt that," she said slowly, "then I'm not dreaming this, right?"

Beth's image shimmered as she gave a small smile. "I've gotta go. Get over yourself and go get what's rightfully yours." She began to fade away, but then came back. "Oh, and also the hot guy!"

And then she was gone.

"Wait!" Quinn cried and leaped forward. She fell off the bed and scrambled to her feet, turning in a circle to search every nook and cranny. But the room was empty. She moved to the wardrobe, took a deep breath, and yanked it open.

Also empty.

Her sister was gone.

And it was morning.

She dropped back to the bed and shoved her hair out of her face. "You're losing it."

Her phone rang and she nearly jumped out of her skin. She had service? Since when?

"Darling," her mom said when she'd answered. "Where are you?"

Barely able to hear her, Quinn moved to the window and stuck her head out for better reception. She'd texted both of her parents when she'd arrived last night, but she dutifully repeated herself. "Wildstone."

"Good God, Quinn."

"I had to do this."

"When are you coming back?"

"Soon." The parking lot was busy, but there was no sign of Mick, the hot maintenance guy. For the best because, well, her hair. "I'll let you know."

There was a long pause. "Honey . . . you know we didn't mean to hurt you."

"I know. I'm just confused."

"Well, come home so you can get unconfused."

"Soon," she promised. "I've gotta go. Love you, Mom." And then she disconnected.

A minute later she got a text.

MOM:

Forgot to tell you something! Yesterday at the grocery store, I stood in line with the nicest man. Harvard. Lawyer. I showed him your picture and gave him your number.

QUINN:

Mom, you can't just give my number out to strangers!

MOM:

HARVARD.

Annoyed and tired, but far too keyed up to go back to bed, Quinn showered—with an eye peeled for bugs—dressed, and headed out.

Downstairs in the main entry there was a buffet setup. Loosely. There was coffee and a choice of doughnuts. She took two with her to her car.

For her, the good, ol' US of A had always consisted of Los Angeles, New York, and San Francisco, with nothing in between except a nap at thirty-five thousand feet. She realized that probably made her a city snob, but the truth was, she just didn't know anything different.

But California's midcoastal area took her breath away. Endless green rolling hills, lined with gorgeous old oak trees, dotted with ranches scattered far and wide.

Wildstone itself wasn't much more than a few streets of historic downtown buildings filled with a mix of both old and new shops: an art gallery, a handmade-jewelry store, an ice-cream parlor, a hair salon, a bar and grill, a general store. Several of the storefronts were vacant. She could see that they were trying to lure in tourists, but they had a ways to go.

Since her appointment with Cliff wasn't for another hour, she took a few side streets and found an old café named Caro's. It was kind of cute despite the fact that it was located in the middle of absolutely nowhere. But what got her out of the car was her growling tummy. The doughnuts hadn't really done it for her.

To her dismay, the place was closed.

Damn. Back in her car, she programmed Cliff's address into

the bitchy GPS and ended up parked in front of a small, older house sitting on the edge of town. A discreet plaque read: CLIFFORD PORTER, ATTORNEY AT LAW.

Quinn was a little early, but the receptionist was there. A distracted-looking woman in her early twenties wearing a headset, she held up a finger while she glared at her printer—which was blinking but not printing. "Dammit," she said and slapped it around a little.

It still didn't print.

"It knows you're in a hurry," Quinn said. "They can smell fear."

"Bastard." The woman pulled off her headset and sighed. "Sorry, I was in class. Online Psychology. It sucked." She shut her laptop and shook it off. "Okay. Switching hats from prelaw student to lawyer receptionist now."

Quinn smiled. "Good morning."

"Well, if it was a *good* morning, I'd be on a South Pacific island being massaged by Tom Hardy. But that's another story. I'm Kelly, how can I help you?"

"I'm here to see Mr. Porter," Quinn said. "I'm—"

"*Quinn*," Kelly said, giving her the once-over although her eyes remained warm and friendly. "Nice to meet you. Cliff had to run a quick errand, but make yourself at home in his office, he'll be right back."

Cliff's office was small but neat. The walls were dedicated to pictures, some of them going back decades. One had Quinn stopping in her tracks and leaning in closer. It looked like a recent pic of herself and Cliff—except it couldn't be, for two reasons. One, he was looking at her with familiarity and so much love it took her breath away. And two, the date on the print was 1996, when Quinn would have been . . . ten.

"It's your mom," Cliff said, coming into the office.

Still unable to think of the woman she'd known only as Carolyn as her mother, Quinn turned to face him. "And . . . your dad?" she guessed.

Cliff smiled. "They were close. I took over his law practice when he retired a few years back."

Quinn stilled. "Oh my God. Are we . . . brother and sister?"

His smile widened. "No. Dad loved your mom though. But then again, most men did."

Quinn looked at the picture again, honing in on Carolyn's younger, happier face. "She didn't love him back?"

Cliff came to her side and eyed the picture as well. "She wasn't one to be tied down."

"Just knocked up then?"

Cliff met her gaze. "I take it you're curious about your father."

"To say the least. I have less than zero information. Did you know him?"

"Not personally," Cliff said. "His name is Eric Madden. He's a professional bull rider, or was until his age caught up with him. He still lives on the circuit, but he's their traveling chef now. He rarely comes through town anymore, if at all."

Quinn's legs felt a little wobbly and she staggered back to a chair and sat heavily. "A chef."

"Yes." Cliff poured her a glass of water. "I'm guessing that hits a little close to home. I'm sorry. He was contacted about Carolyn's death, but he didn't respond. In any case, I'm very glad you changed your mind about coming to Wildstone to discuss the estate and your inheritance. There are decisions to be made."

"I don't want to get ahead of myself," she cautioned. "This is a fact-finding mission only."

"Fair enough." He pulled out a file. "Here's Carolyn's will. Her assets include some property. Everything gets passed to the heirs."

Quinn's head jerked up. "Heirs? As in plural?"

"Yes. It's what I've been trying to tell you." He paused and there was a quiet empathy in his gaze. "You have a sister, Quinn, born from the same parents you were. Her name is Tilly. She's fifteen and I just brought her here; she's outside, waiting to meet you."

Quinn stared at him, trying to take in the words through the bomb he'd just dropped. She had a sister.

She'd *had* a sister.

She'd lost that sister.

And now she had another.

Her head spun in circles and she had absolutely no idea how to land on any of the emotions racing through her at the speed of light. Rising to her feet, she headed to the door.

"Quinn—"

Ignoring Cliff, she strode out into the main room and turned in a slow circle. It was empty.

Kelly burst in the front door, looking breathless. She put a hand to her heart and gulped in air. "That girl can run." She met Quinn's gaze. "I'm sorry. Tilly didn't take to the news of a sister very well. She's gone."

I'm sorry. She's gone . . .

Those four words were a terrifying, horrifying, nightmare-inducing repeat of what she'd been told the night of Beth's accident, when she'd stood in the ER staring in shock at the doctor.

I'm sorry. She's gone . . .

"Gone?" Quinn repeated past a clogged throat.

Kelly nodded. "She's faster than I am. Plus she can climb a tree and I can't, so—"

"Which tree?"

"What?"

"*Which tree did she climb*?" Quinn asked with urgency.

"The park at the end of our street has a grove of oaks on the far side of the play set, and one of them has a huge tree house where some of the teens stash stuff and hang out," Kelly said. "She's—"

Quinn was out the door.

She made it to the park before having to stop and bend over at the waist to gasp in air. She needed to get to a damn gym.

When she found the play set, she eyed the huge grove of oaks. Great. She moved in closer and stopped to listen.

Nothing but the buzz of what she sincerely hoped weren't bees. "Hello?" she called.

There was a loaded silence and then . . . "Go away."

Quinn took a deep breath and told herself that this was her sister. Her blood sister. She and Beth had been . . . well, everything to each other, *everything*, and Quinn missed her like she'd miss a limb. But after her death, Quinn had purposely backed away from any sort of emotional attachments because she couldn't open up her heart like that again, she just couldn't.

But Tilly hadn't asked to lose her mom, to be left alone in the world. The ground had been ripped from beneath her feet, and much as Quinn wanted to run, she couldn't. She located the tree with the tree house and moved beneath it. No ladder. Of course not, that would've made things easy and heaven forbid anything be easy. "I'm Quinn," she said to the tree.

"I know who you are. Go away."

She could. It would certainly be the easy thing to do. She could turn on her heel, walk away, return to L.A., and never look back. She would once again step onto the hamster wheel and run in place in her little rut, ordering the same coffee every day, getting in the same fight with Marcel every day, never looking up.

And she almost did just that.

But she'd already lost one sister to a tragedy. She didn't want to lose another to cowardice. So she stopped herself and looked up, where she could see a red sneaker, laces hanging loose and untied. She followed the line of sight to a pair of jeans, a far-too-small tank top, and a face that looked startlingly like her own. Defiant and mad as hell at the world.

"Just go," that face said. "You know you want to."

Quinn certainly hadn't known she had another sister, but Tilly was just as surprised.

And unhappy about it.

Added to that was the fact that the girl was grieving, something Quinn knew a little too much about. So she drew in a deep breath and said, "I'm not leaving. At least not yet."

Chapter 6

I wouldn't mind someone looking at
me the way I look at pizza.

—from "The Mixed-Up Files of Tilly Adams's Journal"

To say that Tilly had had a bad day, a bad week, a bad month was an understatement. But as she stared down from the tree house, looking into a face that so resembled her own, somehow, in spite of not being able to breathe, she managed to find her voice. "I don't need you," she said, hating that she sounded thin and quivery, like she'd been crying.

She had not been crying.

At least not that she would admit to.

She hadn't been in the tree house in a while. Not since she'd gone through a rough patch at school when the girls had been bitches and the teachers jerks, and her mom had been on her about her grades, and all she'd wanted to do was make herself invisible. But no matter how much she'd wished for superpowers, including invisibility, they'd never come.

So she came here to vanish. The tree itself was tall and stable, and it always protected her. She'd named it Kevin.

Kevin had come through for her more than anyone else, with the exception of her mom.

The first time she'd sat up here, her mom had freaked out and called the cops to report her missing. When they'd found her, her mom had gotten a ladder and climbed up to the tree house, and with tears in her eyes she'd said, "Don't fly away from me yet, darling, I'm not ready."

After that, Tilly always had told her mom whenever she'd needed to be invisible and her mom had understood.

But now she was gone. There'd been no one left to give a shit if she disappeared or not. Especially not Quinn, a mysterious sister she hadn't even known about. "I don't need you," she repeated.

"Well, that's fair," Quinn said. "I don't like to need anyone either. You going to come down so we can talk?"

"No."

"Is there a ladder?"

"It rotted."

"Okay then." And to Tilly's shock, Quinn inhaled deeply and then began to climb the tree herself. "Yikes, they're some seriously gigantor ants."

"And killer squirrels," Tilly said.

Maybe two whole feet off the ground, Quinn froze, looking terrified. "Killer squirrels?"

"They throw acorns with deadly accuracy," Tilly said. "And the kamikaze blue jays are vicious, so watch out."

Quinn searched the tree with concern, making Tilly laugh

for the first time in a long time. "Are you afraid of squirrels and blue jays?"

"Of course not," Quinn said. "I'm afraid of killer squirrels and kamikaze blue jays. In fact, there's a squirrel staring at me right now with beady, shifty little eyes."

"City girl."

Something buzzed on Quinn's phone. Tilly's eyebrows went up when Quinn ignored it.

"It's just a notification telling me that my friend Skye played her turn at Words With Friends," Quinn said.

"Words With Friends?"

"It's a game. A fun one. Maybe we could play sometime."

"I thought only old people played Words With Friends."

Quinn snorted. "I probably should've told you, insulting me only tends to make me try harder." And with that, she began climbing the tree again, muttering something about ruts and routines, and how she'd totally gotten off the hamster wheel, thank you very much.

Tilly craned her neck to watch, fascinated in spite of herself.

"Oh shit," Quinn said, first when she snagged her pants on a branch and ripped them, and again when she ran into a spiderweb with her face and tried to break-dance while hanging out of a tree.

Tilly heard herself laugh again.

Quinn blew out a breath and gave up about ten feet below Tilly—at a whopping five feet off the ground. But still, she supposed it was pretty good for an old chick.

Quinn looked up. "Listen, this isn't exactly the ideal way to meet you, but it's all we've got. So . . . hi." She paused. "I take it you didn't know about me either."

Tilly couldn't hold back her surprise. "Wait—*you* didn't know about *me*?"

"I didn't even know I was adopted until Cliff found me to tell me about your mom's death." Quinn paused, her eyes warm. "I'm really sorry about that, Tilly."

Because it put a pit in her gut and blocked the air in her throat to think about it, Tilly could only shrug, like no big deal, when it was a huge big deal. The biggest deal ever.

"Cliff said she'd planned to tell you," Quinn said. "And me too. She just didn't get the chance."

Great, and now her eyes were burning. Refusing to cry, Tilly pulled out her phone for a diversion. And of course, the one time she didn't have any texts . . . Out of desperation, she opened Snapchat. She had three friends. Katie snapped daily pics of her stupid cat in baby clothes. And then there was Melanie's close-up selfies that all looked the same with her ridiculous, overglossed pout.

Dylan didn't Snapchat at all.

Terrific. She'd actually rather be in school taking her biology exam and she hated biology.

Hated.

Hated.

Hated.

But this was worse. Her mom had told Tilly about the cancer three months ago but had neglected to mention being terminal. Or that Tilly had a sister. And then there was the biggie—she'd up and *died*. It wasn't fair. Any of it. She wanted, *needed*, everyone to just go the hell away and leave her alone.

She switched over to Instagram, but that was equally unsatisfying. Still, she went through the motions of thumbing along and was doing a great job of ignoring Quinn when she caught sight of a post from one of her mom's friends. It was a throwback picture of the two women together, beaming wide.

She had to close her eyes, but the image of her mom's coffin being lowered into the ground still came.

"Tilly—"

"You really didn't know about me either?" she asked, eyes still closed.

"No. If I had . . ."

Tilly opened her eyes and met Quinn's matching deep blue ones, wanting to hear . . . well, she wasn't sure. Something to make her feel better. "What?" she asked. "What would you have done?"

Quinn opened her mouth but then closed it with a helpless shake of her head, like she wasn't sure.

"So you came here now to what, then?" Tilly asked. "Appease your curiosity? Well, you've done that. So I guess I'll be seeing you around sometime. Or whatever."

"Tilly." Quinn's voice sounded as unsure as Tilly felt. "I'm in uncharted waters here too. But we can at least try, can't we? It's never too late to make up for lost time."

But it was. The past couldn't be changed. Her mom was dead and going to stay that way. She looked at her phone again, opening Facebook because she was that desperate for a distraction, even though no one she knew used FB anymore except old people. "I've gotta get back to school."

"I'll drive you."

"No, it's not far," Tilly said. "I'll walk."

Quinn looked hurt at that and Tilly told herself she didn't care.

"How about I pick you up after school?" Quinn asked. "I could take you to dinner."

"I've got dinner plans."

"Breakfast before school tomorrow then," Quinn said with

enough hope in her voice that it almost hurt to listen to her. "Before I go back to L.A."

Right, because Quinn wasn't here to stay, just to get a good look at the freak show. That worked for Tilly because she didn't want to do this, didn't want to feel good about anything, even finding a sister, which she'd always secretly wished for.

Quinn started to say something else but a bee dive-bombed and she squeaked instead, and began waving wildly at the air with her free hand. "*Ohmigod!*"

"Stop moving," Tilly said. "It won't bother you if you just ignore it."

"I can't, I'm allergic!" She let go of her death grip on her branch and used both hands now to shoo the bee. "*Ouch!*" she yelped and slapped at her forehead. "I'm hit, I'm hit!"

"Hey," Tilly said. "Careful, you're going to fall out of the—"

Quinn fell out of the tree. Since she hadn't gotten very far up there, she didn't have all that far to go, but she hit the ground hard and lay still.

Tilly stared down at her, looking for a sign of life. "You okay?"

No answer. No movement either, and Tilly's heart just about stopped. "Quinn?"

Quinn's eyes were open, staring blindly at the sky. Then her mouth moved a little. Kinda like a fish who'd just flopped out of its tank and needed to get back in the water.

"Shit," Tilly said. "Damn. Fuck . . ." *Nice going, you get a sister and kill her all in the same day.* She came out of the tree house, slid down the tree trunk, and then jumped, landing next to Quinn's prone body. "Hey. Hey, you all right?"

More nothing from Quinn, although her fingers twitched.

"Okay, I'm calling 911," Tilly said and pulled out her phone. She'd never done this before, but the dispatcher was calm and that helped. She gave their location and then bent over Quinn again. "An ambulance is coming."

Quinn's fingers were still moving, like she was trying to get something out of her pocket.

"Please say something," Tilly begged. "Did you break your neck?" Then she realized there was a big red dot in the middle of Quinn's forehead.

She really had been stung by the bee.

Quinn managed to pull whatever she'd been looking for from her pocket. "Open it," she wheezed.

Tilly stared down at the tampon-size cylinder with a bright orange cap.

"It's an EpiPen." Quinn's voice sounded strangled, like she couldn't get enough air.

And Tilly remembered her sister's earlier words. She was allergic to bees. Tilly took the EpiPen and stared at it. "What do I do?"

Quinn was working the button and zipper of her jeans, then struggling with pushing them down her thighs past a pair of Wonder Woman undies.

Then she grabbed the EpiPen back and stabbed herself in the thigh with it.

Tilly had to close her eyes because needles weirded her out, but almost immediately she could hear the difference in Quinn's breathing. Which made her realize Quinn had been wheezing for air because her throat had started to close up. "Oh my God." She leaned over Quinn. "Are you okay?"

"I will be," she said thickly, like her tongue was swollen. "If you help me get my pants up before anyone gets here."

"Too late." Cliff crouched at their side, lending his hands to the cause.

Tilly would have been mortified—*Wonder Woman? Really?*—but Quinn just laughed a little.

"Better than my Hello Kitty thong, I guess," she said.

"Seriously," Tilly said. "You should stop talking."

The ambulance whipped into the park, lights flashing, sirens wailing.

"We don't get a lot of action here," Cliff said apologetically.

"But I'm fine," Quinn was still saying thirty minutes later at the hospital.

She wasn't fine. Anyone could see that she felt like she'd been hit by a Mack truck and she was still having the shakes from the letdown after the huge adrenaline rush of the EpiPen injection.

Tilly stood at her side, half out of worry for the woman she was determined to hate with all her being since it was the only thing that deflected the pain of her mom being gone, and half because if she'd gone back to school, she'd have had to take the dreaded biology test. "You really okay?"

Quinn looked touched at the question. "Other than a killer headache, I'm really okay."

When Quinn was finally cleared to go several hours later, Cliff gave them a ride, taking Tilly straight to school, just in time for last period—biology. Damn. She turned to Quinn. "Thanks for not dying."

"Thanks for helping me to not die."

Tilly grimaced with guilt. She hadn't helped. In fact, she'd caused this mess.

"Not your fault," Quinn said, apparently reading her mind.

But it sure felt like Tilly's fault. And there was something else too. She really wanted to hold on to the ball of resentment regarding Quinn's existence, but it had melted away in the face of the sheer terror of the past few hours.

"Who are you staying with?" Quinn asked. "Who's taking care of you?"

"A friend," Tilly said as vaguely as she could while trying to sound earnest enough that Quinn wouldn't dig, which was the last thing she needed.

Quinn looked at her for a long moment and Tilly did her best to look innocent. And happy. Which was a huge stretch.

"Can I see you again before I leave?" Quinn asked. "If not tonight, then for breakfast before school?"

Right. A reminder that Quinn was leaving. "Maybe," she said. "If you promise not to fall out of a tree and need 911 again."

Quinn gave her a small smile. "I'll do my best."

Chapter 7

There are three stages of life:
1. Birth.
2. WHAT THE HELL IS THIS?
3. Death.

—from "The Mixed-Up Files of Tilly Adams's Journal"

Quinn watched Tilly walk into the high school and sighed. "That went well."

Cliff was driving calmly. "It's not as bad as you think."

"How do you figure? Because I chased her through a park and up a tree like a stalker, and instead of becoming sisters, I made a fool of myself, got stung by a bee, fell out of the tree, and scared her half to death."

"You got her out of her own head," Cliff said. "You made her see that she's not alone. She had to help you, and *that*, whether you realize it or not, bonded you two in a way that a scheduled sit-down in my office never could have."

Quinn blew out a breath. "Do you know a lot about teenage girls?"

"Know? Yes. Understand? No." He shrugged. "I've got sisters. Tilly's taking your mom's death hard, and she wasn't ready to meet you."

Well, that made two of them. "She said she's staying with a friend. Why not other family? Grandparents, aunts, uncles, cousins . . . ?" She trailed off when Cliff shook his head.

"There are no other blood relatives," he said. "Both your parents were only children."

So much to process. "So which friend is she with and is she okay there?"

"She's staying with Carolyn's next-door neighbor and ex-boyfriend Chuck. He watches after her and always has. He has guardianship."

Quinn stared at Cliff. "Are you telling me that Carolyn left guardianship of her daughter to an *ex*-boyfriend? For God's sake, she's not a coin collection or a piece of art."

"No, she's not," Cliff agreed. "Carolyn was . . . complicated. She loved Tilly very much and was painfully aware the girl didn't have a lot of choices if something were to happen to her. When she got her diagnosis, she knew she had to make some decisions, but she thought she had time." Cliff shook his head. "Turns out that time was the one thing she didn't have."

"So she didn't have a will? I mean, even a note would be welcome. Like, 'Hey, Quinn, long time no see but here's the thing—I'm dying and I'm going to leave some stuff in your lap, including a sister. Love, your real mom.'"

"She was working on all of that but no one could rush her. And she did have a will, but it wasn't updated," Cliff said. "It leaves everything to you and Tilly. What it doesn't do is outline care for Tilly in the case of her being a minor when Carolyn passed."

Quinn let out a shocked, dismayed breath. "Pretty big oversight, wouldn't you say?"

"Like I said, she was working on that; there weren't many options. She couldn't leave Tilly's care to you when she had no relationship with you or any idea if you'd be a good choice. Chuck was her only option."

Quinn made a noise that she hoped spoke of her horror, disgust, and frustration.

"It's not as out there as you think," Cliff said. "Chuck's taken care of Tilly plenty of times before, such as when Carolyn had her cancer treatments. They're well acquainted. I'll also say that you could remedy the situation by taking over the guardianship. Chuck would be more than okay with that."

Quinn turned her head and met his gaze. His expression told her that he wasn't playing on her sympathy. He was being genuine and just doing his job. "Tilly doesn't want anything to do with me," she said.

"She's a teenager, Quinn. By very definition, she doesn't want anything to do with anyone who's not also a teenager. You could change the course of her life."

But could she? Her job was two hundred miles away. As was her condo and the only friends and family she'd ever known. So no, she couldn't see how to remedy this.

"How's your head?" Cliff asked.

"Messed up."

"I meant the bee sting, but good to know where you're at."

Oh. Right. She laughed a little and touched the swollen spot smack dab in the center of her forehead, the one that looked like a big, fat, stress zit. It hurt.

She'd spent a lot of time lately being numb but that was wearing off like a Novocain shot. None of it felt real right now. She felt like she was watching a movie of her own life. Too bad she couldn't just get up and walk out. "I need to think."

"Of course." Cliff pulled into the Wild West B & B parking lot and turned to her. "You should know that the property mentioned in the will is to be divided equally between you and Tilly. There's a small café and a house. Both need some work." He showed her a pic on his phone and she stared at Caro's Café, realizing it was the one she'd driven by that morning. "It's closed."

"Ever since Carolyn's death," Cliff said. "It should be reopened, both for the money it generates and for the townspeople who miss the food. Maybe you'd consider relocating here . . ."

Quinn shook her head. Not going to happen. In spite of her anger, and the feeling of betrayal and the unhappy surprise of her adoption, her life really was in L.A. "I'm going home, Cliff."

"Today?"

"I'd planned on it."

Cliff didn't say anything to this, clearly disappointed. And hey, he wasn't the only one. She was plenty disappointed in herself too. "But I asked Tilly if I could see her again tomorrow." Something she hadn't yet shared with Brock, her parents, or her boss . . . None of whom were going to appreciate that decision. Her real world, her life, was waiting for her three hours south of here.

Or not waiting, as the case might be. She had no idea how Wade was going to react to her needing another day off, though she was pretty sure how Brock and her parents were going to react.

"Another night is a good start," Cliff said. "You can sleep on everything."

Head spinning, Quinn headed to her room with the sporadic cell phone reception, leaky bathroom sink, surprise bugs, and maybe a ghost, and flopped onto the bed.

"It's unbelievable, all of it!" Beth said excitedly from her perch on the TV. As in *on* the TV, and since it was a flat screen, this was quite the feat.

"Are you serious?" Quinn asked, a hand to her suddenly pounding heart.

"Tilly's lovely!"

"Tilly's *angry*."

"That too," Beth said with sympathy. "Something I know you understand."

Quinn looked at Beth and felt her heart pinch. "You're wearing my sweater."

"Well, I did steal it all those years ago to do just that," Beth said. "And anyway, it looks better on me."

This is just a figment of your imagination, Quinn told herself. That or she was stroking out.

But regardless, it was such a Beth thing to say, she felt herself laugh. Two years and she'd never missed Beth more than she did right this very minute. "Are you not the least bit threatened by the knowledge that you and I are no longer blood sisters?"

Beth's smile faded. "Quinn," she said with a terrifying gentleness. "I don't give a shit about blood. You are, and always will be, my sister. Heart and soul." She shimmered and started to fade. "You've got another chance here. Let her in. Let someone in . . ."

And then she was gone.

"Dammit! Next time I get to die first and haunt your ass!" Quinn yelled and then she blew out a breath and looked around. Turned out, living in a haunted B & B and being pestered by her dead sister made her hungry. She had to stand on a chair near the window again to get enough reception to see what kind of food one might be able to get delivered in Wildstone.

The answer was simple. Nothing. One could get nothing delivered in Wildstone.

Which made it official. She was on Mars. Still standing on the chair, leaning precariously out the window for reception, she caught sight of sexy Mick Hennessey walking across the parking lot again, so there was that at least. The day wasn't a complete disaster.

Coop was at his side. The dog was on a leash but holding the end of it in his own mouth. Mick, looking good in dark sunglasses, another pair of jeans, and a T-shirt stretched enticingly taut over his broad shoulders, glanced up. When he saw her, he pushed the sunglasses to the top of his head and their gazes locked.

For a single beat, her heart did something other than ache for a change. It skipped. She shook her head at herself. Why in the world was her heart reacting now, after all this time? And why not with Brock, who although they'd backed off from a relationship, she still felt comfortable with?

Why did it have to be a perfect stranger instead? It made no sense. Especially since she hadn't felt a thing in two years, but whenever this man looked at her, the ensuing zap was like sticking her finger in a light socket.

Mick vanished around the corner of the building and out of sight and Quinn let out a breath, grateful that he was smarter than she.

Two minutes later, there was a knock at the door. She hesitated, then put her face to the peephole hoping Beth had ordered her a pizza from the afterlife.

But it wasn't pizza.

It was Coop.

And his human, Mick.

When she opened the door, Coop sat on his haunches, dropped the leash from his mouth, and panted a smile up at her.

Mick didn't pant or smile, but he did hand her a Verizon Jetpak. "My password is CoopForPresident101," he said. "Caps on the first letter of each word. It'll get you the Internet without putting your life in mortal jeopardy by hanging out the window."

Quinn patted Coop on the head and stared at the Jetpak, moved by Mick's generosity. "That's . . . way too kind of you."

Coop leaned against her with his considerable girth, nearly knocking her over. Mick nudged him aside. "You should have it in case of another emergency," he said.

"Another emergency?"

He eyed the huge red mark on her forehead, which she sincerely hoped by now looked more like a bee sting than a humongous zit. "News travels fast in Wildstone," he said.

"How?" she asked baffled. "How does news travel without the Internet?"

He smiled. "You don't need the Internet in a town like this." He nodded to the Jetpack. "Hold on to that until you leave."

The gesture was the kindest thing anyone had done for her in recent memory and she felt her throat tighten. Clearly she was an inch away from losing her collective shit. Refusing to let it happen in front of this man—*again*—she found a nod. "Thanks."

He nodded and looked at his now-sleeping, and already snoring, dog. "Coop. We're out."

Coop didn't budge.

"There's no takeout here in Wildstone," Quinn said, suddenly not wanting him to leave.

"No drive-throughs either. If you're looking for food, there's the Whiskey River. It's a bar and grill and is usually open by . . ." He looked at his watch. "Now."

"Usually?"

He gave a low laugh. "Well, it's Wildstone, so time's always a little fluid. But it's five o'clock, so you've got a shot."

"It's not five, it can't be, I just got here and it was only two."

Mick gave her an odd look. "Maybe you napped."

Quinn looked at the bed, which did indeed have a Quinn-size indentation on the covers.

Had she dreamed Beth's visit or was she losing her mind?

"You okay?" he asked.

"Yeah." She shrugged it off. She considered offering to buy him a drink to thank him for his thoughtfulness, wondering if he found her even half as irresistibly attractive as she found him. But before she could say anything, he stepped back with a nod and vanished down the hall.

So much for being irresistible.

When she was alone, she used the Jetpak to check her phone. She had three voice mails. One from Skye saying, "Call me when you're home to catch up."

The next was from her parents—who were baffled that she still wasn't on her way home, and then Brock—baffled and rounding the corner into irritation.

Figuring texts would be better than calls, she texted Skye and Brock, letting them know she'd be staying in Wildstone another night. And then her mom and dad on a group text that didn't go over quite as smoothly as she'd hoped.

QUINN:

Nobody panic, but I'm staying another night.

DAD:

Did you check the oil in your car?

MOM:

Don't pay any attention to your father. If you check the oil yourself, you'll get it on your clothes. Ask someone at the gas station to do it for you. Do you have enough money? Maybe we should drive up.

QUINN:

I'll check the oil and I have enough money. Don't make the drive, I'm fine. We're fine. I'm sorry I had a freak-out, I was just shocked. I'm processing.

MOM:

Can you process here, with us? Because we understand the freak-out. We do. I get that our decision to not tell you some things was . . . questionable . . . but can you accept that at the time of your adoption, all we knew was that we loved you like you were ours. Period. And maybe we've been overprotective of that but nothing's changed. We still love you like you're ours. Because you are.

DAD:

What your mom said.

QUINN:

I love you both. I'll call soon.

MOM:

Tomorrow. You'll call tomorrow.

QUINN:

I'll call tomorrow.

And she would. She needed to remember that she wasn't the only one who'd lost Beth. So she got that they didn't want to lose her too. Not that they would. She just needed a minute to rebuild some trust.

Maybe a few minutes.

Next, she called Chef Wade and chewed on her nails waiting for him to pick up, trying to figure out how to keep her job from two hundred miles away.

Chef Wade didn't pick up.

Not a good sign. She left an awkward voice-mail message and hoped like hell he wasn't about to fire her.

As she disconnected, Brock called.

"What do you mean you're not coming back yet?" he asked.

"It's about my sister—"

"Beth?"

"Tilly."

"The fifteen-year-old you told me about in your texts? What about her?"

"She's so . . . alone."

"Yeah and that sucks. I feel bad for the kid but . . . wait. Are you about to tell me you're going to bring her home with you?"

"Would that be so shocking?"

He chuckled a little at that. "Hell, yes. Did you forget that you're afraid of kids?"

"No, I'm afraid of your twin two-year-old nephews," she corrected. "They're crazy." But it was true, she couldn't imagine anything more terrifying than taking Tilly on, taking all of this on. But nor could she see herself just walking away either.

"Teenagers are a whole different species," Brock said.

"And?"

"And it's your call, but I'm game."

"Game as in . . ."

"Anything that gets you back to the land of the living, back into a relationship."

"You're game," she repeated, stunned. "To get back into a relationship."

"Yes," he said. "But fair warning in the interest of honesty, I've been sowing my oats. You'd need to give me a minute to clear my deck." He paused. "Or two. Tops."

She waited for the pain of his sexual escapades to hit, but before it could, he went on. "Look, babe," he said, voice more serious now. "Honestly? I've been hoping for something to come along and snap you out of it."

"Hoping," she said carefully. "While screwing everything that moves?"

"Well, not *everything*. And my point is that I'm here for you, whatever you want. Just come back."

To L.A. Where her life was.

It was a reasonable suggestion. But Tilly was *here* and Quinn didn't see her up and moving to L.A. in the middle of a school year.

"What if I stayed here awhile?" she asked. She couldn't even believe the question popped out of her mouth.

On Brock's part, there was such a long silence that she pulled the phone away from her ear and looked to make sure they were still connected. "Hello?"

"I'm here," he said. "How long is awhile?"

"I don't know." She shook her head, completely overwhelmed.

"Quinn," he said slowly, "our thing, you and me . . . it never involved leaving L.A."

Even though she knew this, her heart did a little squeeze. "First of all, I never said I was leaving L.A. And second of all . . . so I'm the One for you, but only if I agree to stay in L.A., on your terms?"

"I love you, Quinn. But I love my job too. It's very important to me. You know that."

She did. And she knew something else too. "I don't think this is going to work," she whispered.

There was a loaded silence. "So you're staying in Wildstone."

"No. *No,*" she said again, softer. "But that's not what I'm talking about. I don't like the ultimatum from you."

"That," he said. "Or you're looking for excuses, as you have been for two years."

She inhaled a long shuddery breath, looking for calm. And didn't find any. "I'm sorry if you feel like you've been waiting on me, but we never agreed to that. You know I've had a problem with emotions and feelings."

"Two years," he repeated.

"Stop. You have *not* been waiting around, pining for me, for that long. You've been . . . sowing your wild oats!"

"Quinn—"

"No." She knew that voice of his, that overly calm, reasonable tone, and she wasn't having any of it. "Maybe I need to sow mine. You ever think of that?"

He was silent for a beat, processing. Thinking.

Which she suddenly resented. "I've got to go."

"Don't do anything hasty, babe."

"Hello, have you met me?" she asked. "It took me a year to decide which condo I wanted to buy!"

"Uh-huh," he agreed. "And only an hour after receiving shocking news to jump into your car and drive three hours north of here without telling anyone."

She shook her head. "You're not understanding what's going on up here."

"Come home and tell me about it." There was a beep in her ear. "Shit," he said. "A call just came in that I have to take," he said, apology heavy in his voice. "We'll get back to this, okay?"

"Sure."

"Don't get pissy, like you don't care or feel anything, since it's clear you're back to doing both."

"I gotta go too," she said. "Bad connection." And she turned off the Jetpak and let the crappy Internet cut out on them.

But not before Chef Wade's text came through: no worries, Marcel's covering for you.

Not exactly music to her ears . . .

Chapter 8

Things that annoy me:
1. Feelings
2. People
3. Basically everything, I have no idea why I started a list . . .

—from "The Mixed-Up Files of Tilly Adams's Journal"

Fifteen minutes later Quinn was at the Whiskey River for a badly needed drink. She didn't imbibe much. First, she was a lightweight. And second, normally she preferred to eat her calories.

But her shitty week called for alcohol. Her gaze fell to the flyer on the bar touting the "Bartender's Special," so she ordered one of those.

"After the day you've had, good choice," the good-looking bartender said with a wink.

She resisted covering the large red bee sting she knew still stood out in the middle of her forehead and turned to take in the crowd.

The music was surprisingly good and she sat there absorbing the easy laughter and sounds of conversation around her. By the time the door opened and in walked no other than Mick Hennessey, maintenance guy, mind reader, and incredible Levi's filler, she was relaxed.

Or so she thought. Because from across the large room, Mick's gaze met hers and she stilled from the inside out, if that made any sense at all. It was the oddest thing.

The bartender greeted Mick with some complicated handshake followed by a back-slapping guy hug. "Beginning to look like you're sticking," the bartender said.

"No," Mick said. "Hell no."

The bartender grinned. "Ah, come on, man. You know you've missed us."

"Again, hell no."

"Take it back and first round's on me."

Mick slapped some bills on the bar and the bartender sighed dramatically. Mick's gaze locked on Quinn as he headed her way.

"Sticking?" she asked, admittedly curious about him.

He shrugged. "Long story."

"Yeah?"

"Yeah. And it's one I don't want to tell any more than you want someone to ask you about that sting on your forehead."

Touché. She lifted her drink in a silent toast.

He touched his beer bottle to her glass and said, "When I walked in, you were staring into the bottom of your drink like you were searching for the answers to the mysteries of the universe."

"There should be a warehouse where you could buy the answers," she said. "Preferably in Hawaii, 'cause that'd be nicer than, say, Toledo, you know?"

He studied her and then slowly nodded. "I do know. I also know that you could use some food."

What she could use was a night of wild, passionate, up-against-the-wall sex with a man who'd make her forget her upside-down life, but she managed to keep that thought to herself.

"Let's move to a table," he said, standing, looking . . . hell. Hot as sin and just as irresistible.

She bit her lower lip. "You should probably know something about me."

"I'm all ears."

"I'm not doing the whole guy thing right now."

"How about pizza?" he asked, cocking his head with a smile. "Are you doing the pizza thing?"

Dammit. The way to her heart was pizza. And maybe also that incredible smile he was sporting. "Sure," she said. *Stupid alcohol . . .*

He picked up his drink and hers, and gestured with a head nod to an empty table. The waitress came over with another round. "Bartender's Special," she said. "On the house. Tonight's a Red-Headed Slut. Boomer, he's the bartender, he said he could make you a Wallbanger if you'd rather. Or a Sex on the Beach." She shrugged when Quinn just stared at her. "It's Drink-a-Kink Night. Boomer takes his theme nights seriously. We've also got Angel's Tits and Slippery Nipples. Oh! And Bend-Over Shirleys, though I can't remember what's in those."

Mick craned his neck and looked at Boomer, behind the bar, who winked and gave him a thumbs-up.

"Good friend of yours?" Quinn asked dryly.

"Since kindergarten, but I'm still going to have to kill him."

She laughed. "I guess a little kink never hurt anyone."

"Exactly!" an elderly gentleman at the table on the other side of them said. "That's what I say too! And anyway, silk panties aren't a kink, they just feel good against the skin. Everyone knows that."

They toasted to silk panties and then ordered pizza. Quinn added a salad because something green would make her feel less guilty about the pizza. When it came, she ate the salad first and then inhaled her half of the loaded pizza.

"I'm impressed," he said. "When you ordered the salad, I got worried."

"You don't like salads?"

"I like girls who eat."

"Well, I do want to look good in a bikini this summer," she said. "But I also want to eat pizza. It's pretty unfair that I have to choose, but it is what it is."

"I'm betting you look sexy as hell in a bikini," he said.

This gave her a hot flash. But she decided to attribute it to the alcohol. She was now halfway through her second Bartender's Special and still had no idea what was in it, but it was delicious and had gone down smooth, so she kept sipping.

Mick, who was clearly smarter than she was because he'd had only one beer and had drunk only half of it, smiled. And just like that, something fluttered low in her belly.

"Are you flirting with me?" she asked.

"Trying. The question is, are you flirting back?"

She laughed and felt her face heat. "Maybe. But I don't want to be. It's . . . not a good time for me."

"Because you're not doing the whole guy thing right now," he said.

"I'm just a little bit . . . upside down at the moment, and not myself." She paused. "At all."

"So what brings you to Wildstone?" he asked, leaning in a bit to hear her answer. It wasn't just him making conversation, he was actually interested in what she had to say.

"I sort of ran away, actually," she admitted.

"And here I thought you were at the Wild West B and B because of the exemplary plumbing."

She snorted. Like actually snorted, and clapped a hand over her mouth in horror at the sound.

He smiled. "Loves pizza. Snorts when she laughs. Cute."

She felt the wide grin on her face. "I can also burp to the count of ten. Can't do the alphabet though. It's too long."

He laughed. "I can teach you." He tugged gently on a wayward wave of her hair. "You ever going to tell me more about the upside-down thing?"

She shook her head. "Definitely not."

"That bad, huh?"

"Let's just say that on a scale of mental breakdowns from Justin Bieber to Britney Spears, I think I'm about a Shia LaBeouf."

He gave a low laugh. "I bet I could make you feel better about your life."

"Yeah?" she asked with doubt. "Go for it."

"All right." He had a hand resting on his bottle of beer, his thumb taking lazy swipes at the condensation. He took another long pull and she watched his throat as he swallowed.

He was sporting at least a day's worth of stubble. Maybe two. All she knew was that when he rubbed a hand over his jaw, the ensuing sound made her mouth feel dry enough that she needed another sip of her drink.

"My dad died four months ago," he said, and she stilled, her gaze flying to his.

"He left my mom with a stack of bills," he went on, "and a house she needs to repair before she can sell or even refinance, and I'm the only one she has left to help her."

So she wasn't the only one facing a whole barrage of things she didn't know how to face. "I'm sorry," she said, reaching for his hand. "About all of it. You're an only child?"

"I've got a younger sister, but Wendy's in New York waitressing, waiting for her big break on Broadway." He shrugged. "She got out and stayed out." He looked into her eyes. "Now you."

She looked into his eyes. Dark brown. Gold flecks. She'd seen them cool and accessing. Amused. Now they'd warmed like melting chocolate. And she felt herself melt a little bit too. Damn. He wanted her to open up and she realized she was not authorized to make this decision while under the influence of alcohol.

"Excuse me a minute?" she asked and made her way down a hallway toward the restroom, where, once inside, she pulled out her phone and texted Skye.

QUINN:

So there's a guy.

SKYE:

And the problem is?

QUINN:

I can't remember. That's why I'm texting you.

SKYE:

Bring him into work so I can get a look at him. I'll let you know yea or nay.

QUINN:

Can't. I'm still in Wildstone.

SKYE:

Then yes. Hell, yes. You go for it. Out of town is like being in Vegas.

What happens in Vegas stays in Vegas. Bring me back a good story. Gotta go, Marcel is on a tear about the effing carrots.

Quinn shoved her phone away and made her way back to their table.

Mick greeted her with an easy smile, sitting there looking better than the pizza she'd just inhaled.

So what's the holdup? she asked herself. *You're leaving tomorrow, never to see him again, right?*

Right.

And as it turned out, he was a really good listener. Too good a listener because before she knew it, she'd told him about meeting Carolyn at the coffee shop in L.A., how she'd not known who the woman was until Cliff had shown up and told her, and that she'd been completely in the dark about Tilly.

And then she sat back and waited for him to have some variation on the same reactions her parents and Brock had given her.

But Mick took another pull from his beer and nodded. "You really have had a shitty week."

She found a laugh. She should have known he'd be different. "You could say that." She paused. "You don't think I'm a little nuts, or overreacting to all of this?"

"Don't ever ask someone that," he said. "Your reactions, your emotions, they're all your own. You don't need permission to have them." He gave her a small smile. "But for what it's worth, I think you're entitled to going more than a little nuts."

His eyes were deep, fathomless really, and full of easy affection, but also a good amount of trouble.

Run or stay? she asked herself, desperately unsure.

Stay, said her brain . . .

Run, said her feet.

Stay, said Beth.

Run, said Quinn's own good sense.

Mick lifted his beer and touched it to her glass. "To a better week this time around then, yeah?"

She looked into his mesmerizing eyes and nodded. "Yeah," she whispered, and just like that, her brain and Beth won the round.

Chapter 9

I wish everything was as easy as getting fat.

—from "The Mixed-Up Files of Tilly Adams's Journal"

Quinn looked down at her drink—which would be her third—and gently pushed it aside. It had been a long time since she'd indulged in more than a glass of wine. Long enough to forget how alcohol tended to make her tongue run away with her good sense. "I should go. I'm hoping to sleep through the ghost of Christmas Past tonight."

Mick looked amused. "You read the brochure, didn't you. It's just hype."

"Well, I was pretty sure," she said. "Until my sister showed up."

"Your sister came to Wildstone too?" he asked. "Where is she now?"

"Well, she's dead, so I'm thinking she's back in the haunted wardrobe."

Mick looked at her for a beat and then slid a big, warm hand over hers. "I'm sorry, Quinn."

A lot of people had said those two words to her. The words had never meant much but there was something about Mick's husky, low voice that reached her. Which in itself was so unsettling that she closed her eyes. "About my room being haunted?" she asked, trying to joke it away. "Or that I've clearly gone over the edge?"

She felt him shift closer and give her hand a gentle squeeze. Reluctantly she opened her eyes.

"About your sister being gone," he said quietly. "How long?"

"Two years." She looked away. "She was sort of my everything, so it's been a little rough."

"I can only imagine. And you've been seeing her?"

She blew out a breath and faced him again. "Yesterday afternoon she sat on top of the TV in a sweater she stole from me four years ago and told me it was time to get back to the land of the living, that I needed to stop not feeling." She snorted. "And that was when I was one hundred percent alcohol free."

"What did she mean, stop not feeling?"

He was holding eye contact so she did her best to do the same, but it was difficult. "I go through the motions but I haven't felt anything since losing her. Just . . . numbness. It makes the people in my life uncomfortable and unhappy, but I don't seem to care about that either. My parents try to understand, but most of my friends don't, except for Skye." She shook her head. "And Brock."

"Your . . . boyfriend?" Mick asked.

"Not since I made him give up on me. Am I rambling? It feels like I'm rambling."

"No," he said. "So about this Brock guy."

"We've been friends since kindergarten, but the truth is that I'm . . . broken," she admitted.

"You sure?"

When she slid him a dark look, he squeezed her hand again. "I ask because the woman I'm looking at, the one who drove two hundred miles to learn more about herself, doesn't seem broken to me. The woman I'm looking at seems like someone who feels so deeply maybe she's just a little scarred. And scared. But not broken."

She inhaled a shuddery breath and held it. "You don't understand."

"No, you're right," he said. "I've never experienced anything as unfair and soul destroying as losing a sibling. But, Quinn, you could've taken Tilly's rejection today and left. You didn't. That suggests you're feeling more than a little."

"She lost her mom."

He nodded. "And you understand that loss."

"Okay," she said, admitting he might be right. "So I can feel empathy. Sympathy. I'm talking about *other* feelings and emotions, things required to maintain any sort of a . . ." She paused and waved her hand to help her find the word. "Connection."

"For the record," he said, "are we talking about a sexual connection?"

She squirmed but couldn't look away. "Among other things."

"So you're saying you don't feel excited or aroused. Ever."

Well, she hadn't. Until yesterday when she'd reacted to his leanly muscled build like she'd never seen a man before. And at the thought, she squirmed again.

"Quinn." He ran a work-roughened finger along the palm of her hand and she got a full-body shiver. "Do you feel that?"

"Um," she said eloquently.

His eyes held her prisoner while her pulse raced and butterflies danced in her belly and at that realization, her palms went sweaty. She thought about lying but knew she couldn't sell it, not with how closely he was watching her, seeing her. "Okay, so I feel *something*," she managed. "I think maybe you just switched me back on."

He smiled and good lord, she nearly slid off her chair into a puddle of goo. She closed her eyes. "I'm really not much of a drinker."

She heard his soft chuckle and opened her eyes. He was looking at her mouth, so she felt it only fair game to look at his too. It was a good mouth, as far as they went. Nice lips. Sexy stubble. She imagined what it would feel like beneath her fingers and she realized her body was tensed, like anticipation tensed, and she shook her head with a little laugh and sat back, eyeing the last piece of pizza.

"It's got your name on it," he said.

"You sure?"

"Absolutely," he said. "Especially if you're going to moan again as you eat it."

"I didn't moan!"

"Like it was the last piece of pizza on earth," he said.

She rolled her eyes and took a bite and . . . crap. It took everything she had not to moan. "Show-off," she said around a full bite.

He just smiled.

Damn. Damn, she was feeling all sorts of things right now. She'd always assumed when that happened again, it would be with Brock. But Brock was out sowing his wild oats, something she'd never done.

Ever.

Not that it mattered. This wasn't about guilt or revenge, or anything like that. This was about *her*. About something she'd been missing without even realizing it.

Mick watched Quinn eat that piece of pizza like it was the best thing she'd ever tasted. Everything he'd seen of her, from watching her have a panic attack on the beach, to dropping to her knees to love up on his dog, to freaking out about a bug in the tub, to watching the grief in her gaze when she talked about her sister . . . it all suggested that she was a woman who lived life to its fullest and felt to her very core.

And she had no idea.

She'd been through hell and still wasn't fully back from the trip. He got that. But she was wrong about herself.

Her wild brunette waves were uncontained and her haunting blue eyes fully on the prize—that being the last of the pizza—and he couldn't tear his gaze away. It was crazy how much he was drawn to her, in a way he couldn't explain even to himself. Normally that alone would have him running for the door. But he didn't move.

When she caught him watching her, her smile warmed and she shifted in her seat, like maybe it was hard to hold the eye contact, but she still did.

And that's when he knew just how much trouble he was in. When it came to women, he typically didn't have a type. What tended to draw him in was an easy confidence and a sense of independence that said she wouldn't be looking for any sort of permanence from him.

With his life as insane as it had become, his business exploding in San Francisco, his dad passing, his mom needing him as much as she did, he had zero interest in another thing that tied him down.

Less than zero interest.

Especially one in Wildstone. He'd worked his ass off to get out, needing to be away from his dad's heavy rule and a town that had felt claustrophobic. He'd gotten good grades, which had led to a scholarship, and on top of that he'd taken every odd job available to pay the rest of his way through college a hell of a long way away from here.

Did he have some regrets along the way? Sure. Had the end justified the means? Pretty much, though he would've been a lot more sure of that answer four months ago, before his dad had died. Spending time with his mom and cleaning out the old house had been screwing with his head.

And now there was Quinn, whose confidence seemed to have taken a hit. But she absolutely had a sense of independence, not to mention sweet curves, a sexy smile, and deep blue eyes that revealed a haunting vulnerability and a not-so-hidden pain.

Even so, she smiled at him, clearly boosted by the strength of Boomer's damn special, and he felt something warm deep down inside him. Her smile was warm and contagious, and it should've had him taking a big step back.

A big one.

Instead, watching her loosen up, listening to her talk, taking in the good humor and intelligence in her gaze, he felt himself wanting to go all in.

Good thing he was smarter than that.

Boomer came up to their table and handed Quinn another Bartender's Special.

"I didn't order this," she said.

He winked at her. "On the house."

"Oh boy. I'm not sure I need it."

"It's a thank-you for making this guy smile," Boomer said, jerking a thumb in Mick's direction. "Been a while since anyone in these parts saw that."

Mick squelched a grimace as Quinn looked at him.

He shook his head. "Don't listen to him."

Boomer grinned—the bastard—and sauntered off, mission accomplished. Meaning: trouble was brewing—Boomer's favorite pastime, as Mick knew all too well. So it was an especially good thing he wasn't going to let himself get drawn in.

No matter what.

"How long are you staying in Wildstone?" he asked.

"Until tomorrow. Tilly and I didn't exactly have a smooth introduction." She shook her head. "I've had enough regrets in my life. Leaving without seeing her again won't be one of them."

Mick caught sight of a familiar figure entering the bar—Lena, his old high school girlfriend—and acknowledged with an inward grimace that only in a town Wildstone's size would he run into everyone he knew while at the bar.

She was probably seeking out Boomer, her latest conquest. But then Lena's gaze locked on Mick and she headed right for him, a familiar gleam in her predatorial gaze.

"Excuse me a minute," he said to Quinn and stood up to ward Lena off, meeting her in between the bar and their table.

"Mick." She smiled. "Just the man I was looking for."

"Why?"

She laughed softly. "Well, it's a warm, gorgeous summer night and in case you've forgotten, you really know how to show a girl a good time on a night like this. How about we take a ride to Mercury Point?"

He had a lot of memories tied up in Mercury Point. The first time he'd gotten drunk. Or four-wheeling over the dunes. And then there'd been losing his virginity—to the tall, beautiful brunette standing in front of him.

Of course they'd also broken up there as well.

And gotten back together.

And broken up . . .

"You're with someone else now," he reminded her. "One of my oldest friends."

"Boomer and I aren't together," she said. "He said we couldn't be until I got my head on straight." She glanced over at the bar.

Mick did too and found Boomer watching them with an unreadable expression on his face before he turned away to serve a customer.

"I'm not going to let anyone tell me what to do," Lena said. "Even him. And anyway, my head *is* on straight."

Mick gave her a wry look and she rolled her eyes.

"It's on straight *now,* I mean," she said and sighed. "Look, I know I didn't do right by you, Mick. I'd like the chance to fix that."

He was assuming that "not doing right by him" was an acknowledgment of how she'd screwed around on him. And he was also assuming that since they hadn't talked in a while, plus the fact that she'd never tried to apologize to him before, she was only doing so now because people were already talking about him and Quinn. "It was a long time ago," he said.

"Doesn't have to be." Her gaze shifted to take in Quinn. "Your date needs a leave-in conditioner," she said. "And a good stylist."

"Good night, Lena." He turned to move back to Quinn but she'd gotten up and was moving to the door.

Lena smirked. "Must be losing your touch. I could give you a tutorial."

Ignoring her, he wound his way through the crowd, but Quinn was gone. Wanting to catch her before she drove off, he tried to toss some money to Boomer, who shook his head.

"She already got it, man."

To Mick's relief, he caught Quinn in the parking lot, leaning against her car, her thumbs moving furiously over the screen of her phone. When she saw him, she grimaced.

He lifted his hands and stayed out of her personal space. "Thought you could use a ride back to the B and B," he said.

"I'm not driving." She lifted her phone. "I'm trying to get an Uber."

He smiled. "How's that going?"

She sighed and slipped her phone into her pocket. "So Wildstone doesn't have drive-throughs, Thai takeout, *or* Uber? Seriously?"

"We have other things."

"Yes," she said. "Ghosts. Big bugs. Cute dogs. And girlfriends, apparently."

"Lena's not my girlfriend," he said. "She's Boomer's. Sort of." He shook his head. "It's complicated."

She didn't take her eyes off him. "But you've slept together."

He arched a brow.

"I'm sorry," she said, closing her eyes. "That was rude. There's a chemistry there, and a familiarity, that's all. You know what? Don't listen to me. My tongue's running the show and I think I'm just jealous at how everyone else seems to take life's shit in stride and keep going. I haven't learned that trick and I need to. And how to keep going, that is. Like the Energizer Bunny. Or my electric toothbrush. God." She pressed her hands to her face. "I really need to stop talking. Make me stop talking!"

He took her hand and tugged her to his truck.

"Wait," she said, putting a hand to his chest and fisting it in his shirt to hold him to her. "You're not a murderer or a rapist or anything like that, right?"

He lifted a hand. "Scout's honor."

"Were you a Boy Scout?"

Laughing a little at that because he'd been just about the furthest thing from a Boy Scout, he gently pushed her into the passenger seat and leaned in to buckle her seat belt, and suddenly their faces were an inch from each other. He heard her suck in a breath and he did the same.

Talk about chemistry.

"Mick?" she whispered.

"Yeah?"

"Are you feeling something?"

"You could say that," he murmured. "You?"

She licked her lips and he nearly groaned. "I think so," she whispered.

"That's good."

"Are you going to kiss me?"

He cupped her face, let his thumbs trace her jawbone, his fingers sinking into her silky waves. "No," he said quietly. "And not because I don't want to, but because when I do, I want to know you're ready. That you'll feel it."

She sighed. "Guys do whatever they want all the time, no emotions necessary. I want that skill." Another shaky breath escaped her, and since they were literally an inch apart, they shared air for a single heartbeat during which neither of them moved.

Her gaze dropped to his mouth. "Okay, so I'm definitely feeling things." She hesitated and then her hands came up to his chest. "Maybe we should test it out to be sure."

God, she was the sweetest temptation he'd ever met, and he wanted nothing more than to cover her mouth with his. Instead, he brushed his mouth to her cheek.

"Please, Mick," she whispered, her exhale warming his throat. He loved the "please," and he wanted to do just that more than anything. But when she tried to turn her head into his, to line up their mouths, he gently tightened his grip, dragging his mouth along her smooth skin instead, making his way to her ear.

"Not yet," he whispered, letting his lips brush over her earlobe and the sensitive skin beneath it.

She moaned and clutched him. "Why not?"

It took every ounce of control he had to lift his head and meet her gaze. "Because I want to make sure you're really with me, that you're feeling everything I'm feeling. That there'll be no doubt, no regrets."

"You sure have a lot of requirements."

He laughed. And she was right, it was all big talk for a guy who didn't do relationships anymore. Still, he forced himself to step back and shut the passenger door.

As he rounded the hood to the driver's side, he tried to remind himself of all the reasons she was a bad idea. He lived two hundred miles away and he was hoping to move his mom up by him and never come back here. Not to mention that Quinn lived an equal two hundred miles in the opposite direction and she was in a deeply vulnerable place. No way would he even think about taking advantage of that.

But when he slid behind the wheel and their eyes locked, he realized that while his mind could stand firm, the rest of his body wasn't on board with the in-control program.

Chapter 10

Olympic events I could compete in:
-Extreme lurking
-Marathon sleeping
-Rhythmic eating
-Freeestyle complaining

—from "The Mixed-Up Files of Tilly Adams's Journal"

The drive to the B & B was quiet but not uncomfortable. In fact, Quinn felt a flash of disappointment that the evening was over as soon as she and Mick got out. Being back meant facing her hot mess of a life and she wasn't ready. So she stood still and tipped her head to take in the view.

She wasn't sure what was happening to her. Maybe the domino effects of Carolyn's dying had kick-started her emotions again, at least the simple ones like lust and anger and frustration.

But things like sadness and grief and love . . . those she'd shoved so deep she didn't know how to access them anymore.

Basically, she was an emotional idiot.

She distracted herself from that knowledge with the scenery. Wildstone at night was an experience. There were no streetlights. No billboards, and with the exception of the bar, the sidewalks apparently rolled up at eight o'clock. There was nothing to detract from the inky night shining with the brilliance of so many stars it looked like a velvet blanket scattered with diamonds.

"It's . . . wow," she breathed as wind rustled through the trees, crickets doing their song and dance, and she thought maybe she could also hear the distant sound of the tide pounding the shore. When she inhaled deeply, it smelled like one of those woodsy outdoor candles she loved. "Wildstone at night is incredible."

Mick took her hand in his and let out a low laugh, his head tipped back as well. "Yeah. I guess I forget what it's like."

"How?" she asked, awed. "How can you forget?"

He shook his head, making her even more curious.

"How long since you moved away?" she asked.

"I left after I graduated from high school and didn't come back much until four months ago."

When his dad had died. She turned and took in his profile. He was good, he didn't give much away. The tall stance, the broad shoulders capable of holding the weight of mountains . . . he could hide in plain sight. "Do you miss him?"

He let out a low, mirthless laugh and met her gaze. "We didn't do well together. But I miss him for my mom. She loved that heartless bastard." He led her toward her room. With the open hallways empty, it felt like they were alone on the planet as they walked, and at her door she turned to him.

Sexy, alpha, quiet-but-most-definitely-not-shy Mick Hennessey. "Thanks," she said softly.

He nudged a wayward strand of hair from her forehead, curling it behind her ear, his finger brushing the shell of her ear. "Anytime."

"I didn't mean for the ride," she said.

"Again," he said. "Anytime."

His voice was deep and rich. Went down as smoothly as her alcohol had. And damn, but she'd enjoyed herself tonight. No way around that. Mick was an unusual man. No hidden agenda. No complications. Easy to be with, so damn easy, and suddenly, standing in the moonlight in front of him, she needed more of all of that, along with a chance to forget, even if only for a little bit.

She'd had no idea how much she'd shut herself off, shut herself down, but a few hours in his company and suddenly she was aching for things she'd long ago forgotten about. Aching to be held, touched . . .

"Quinn."

His tone held a warning. Like he knew what she was thinking and it was a bad idea. Well, of course it was a bad idea. But she realized that wasn't going to stop her. Was it? She looked past his broad shoulders to the rising moon. "Today sucked golf balls," she said. "Until you. You said you wanted to see me feel something." She looked at him, into his dark eyes. "Well, I'm standing here, feeling plenty."

His expression was strained. "I'm into that, believe me. But I'm trying like hell to be the good guy here. I need you to go inside and lock the door behind you to keep out of trouble."

"I thought Wildstone was safe."

"It is. The trouble isn't going to come from the unknown. It's going to come from me. Go, Quinn. Now. And lock your door."

She stared up at him, mesmerized by the thought of him being trouble, images going through her head of him proving it to her, all of them involving little to no clothing and a bed.

Or not a bed . . .

Watching her face, maybe reading her mind, Mick groaned. Pretty sure he was about to retreat, she fisted her hands in his shirt and tugged. Given the solidness to his build, she knew she couldn't have budged him unless he wanted to be budged, but he obligingly stepped in close. Now they were chest to chest, toe to toe, the heat of his body instantly enveloping her even as her body shivered in anticipation. She went up on tiptoe and brushed her lips over his, feeling a rush of long-forgotten pleasure as desire went skittering through her. Desire, and a yearning so strong she moaned with it.

So did he. His hands went to her hips, gripping hard as they stared at each other for one breathless beat. Then he lowered his head and kissed her, a slow, melting nuzzle of lips that was at once both perfect and not nearly enough, and she moaned again. Mick murmured something wordless and sexy, and he slid his hands to her jaw to hold her head in place, keeping her steady as he kissed her again, light at first, until she squirmed against him for still more, and then it was an explosion of want and hunger and hard need.

She was pressed between his body and the door and trying to climb him like a tree when he pulled back and pressed his forehead to hers, breathing hard.

"You're going inside," he said, his voice not so smooth now, but low and rough as sandpaper. "Alone."

Unable to speak, she nodded, but when she didn't, couldn't, move, he let out a half groan, half laugh. "Come on." Taking her key, he unlocked her door, flicked on the light, gave the room a cursory once-over before gently shoving her inside and shutting the door behind her.

"Lock it," he said from the other side of it.

Not that she was counting, but that was twice now he'd turned away for what she suspected was her own sake. She hit the lock and pressed her face against the peephole in time to watch him walk away.

QUINN DREAMED ABOUT star-filled skies and long, drugging kisses and woke up all erotically charged and achy. Someone had once told her that coming out of a period of extended grief felt like the aftermath of a root canal—everything got tingly as the feelings came back. But that wasn't it at all. Nope, it felt a lot less subtle than that, more like being hit by a freight train.

She called Cliff for Tilly's cell phone number.

"You staying?" he asked.

"Long enough to at least see her again. And to ask if she needs anything, and if we can keep in touch."

He was quiet for a beat. "Stay out of trees."

Right. She felt her forehead. The huge lump was gone. And she was breathing just fine. With the day's good news out of the way, she texted Tilly.

QUINN:

Breakfast?

TILLY:

I don't do breakfast.

QUINN:

Lunch?

TILLY:

Do you ever take no for an answer?

QUINN:

I was a pit bull in another life. So . . . lunch? Whatever you want. Except sushi. I know it's not cool, but I hate sushi.

TILLY:

It's cute that you think you could even get sushi in Wildstone. I'll meet you at the house at my lunch break. I need to pick up some stuff anyway.

Lunch it was. Quinn got up, showered, grabbed a big, fat jelly doughnut from the "buffet," and then looked at the clock. Still three hours before she'd see Tilly.

She went to the front desk, where surfer boy sat thumbing through his phone. "Do you think I could pay someone to take me to the Whiskey River to get my car?" she asked.

"No," he said, not looking up. "I mean yes, but no."

She put a hand over the screen of his phone and he yelped, pulling the phone free to stare at it. "Ah, man. You made me lose a life."

"Want to lose another?"

He sighed. "Your car's already here." He tossed a set of keys at her.

Hers.

"Who—" she started but the guy was back to his game, non-responsive. It didn't matter, she figured she knew who'd retrieved her car for her.

Mick.

Not knowing how to feel about that, being dangerously attracted to a man she hardly knew after going so long without being attracted to anyone at all, she got into her car.

She drove along the coast, mesmerized by the pounding surf, the small morning dots that were surfers, and then farther out, sailboats glinting on the water dusted with whitecaps. By the time she then turned inland again, she was smiling as she took in the wineries and ranches in the green rolling hills.

Smiling.

Back in town, she drove down the main drag, eyeing the hair salon. One glance in the rearview mirror at her crazy uncontrollable waves convinced her to stop. Maybe she could get help making a better impression on Tilly.

She took one step inside and stopped short. The woman behind the counter was none other than Lena, Mick's ex-girlfriend.

"Hi," the woman said, her mouth curved, eyes cynically amused. "You going to bring your other leg in and stop letting out all the bought air, or . . . ?"

Feeling silly, Quinn let the door shut behind her.

"There you go. Now, do you speak?" Lena asked.

Quinn narrowed her eyes. "Are you always so rude?"

"Yes, one hundred percent. It's called sarcasm and attitude, which are both so much cheaper than therapy and bail. What can I do for you?"

"I was thinking about having my hair done."

Lena looked at it critically. "Good decision, and I've got some time. My first client just canceled—got food poisoning and is in the hospital."

"Oh my God."

Lena shrugged. "No worries, she's evil to the bone, so she'll make it. Evil always does."

When Quinn just stared at her in horror, Lena smiled. "I'm kidding. It's my mom, she's not evil to the bone. Just halfway. And my next client isn't due for a while, so lucky you."

Oh boy. "How is this lucky me when you hate me?"

"Lucky because I'm the best," Lena said. "And I don't hate you. What I hate are men in flip-flops, slow drivers, and humidity. You, I just intensely dislike."

Quinn blinked.

"Look," Lena said, "you gotta know by now that not everyone's going to like you. Not everyone likes chocolate ice cream even though it's fucking delicious. What do you want done to your hair?"

"I need to impress someone."

"Mick isn't impressed by hair."

"Good to know," Quinn said dryly. "But I meant my sister. I need to somehow look cool and approachable."

"You mean not like the sort of woman who stalks people in trees and then falls out of them?"

Quinn sighed. "Yeah."

"That would take more time than I have, but I'll work around it. Sit. Your color makes you look pale. You need highlights, just a few foils."

"Uh—"

"Trust me."

"*Can* I trust you?" Quinn asked.

"Definitely not. So, would you say you're a go-with-the-flow kind of woman?"

Sure. She was totally a go-with-the-flow kind of person. As long as that flow was detail oriented, went according to plan, and had its own color-coded itinerary. "No."

"Hmm," Lena said, already working, getting out supplies. She was blessedly quiet for a few minutes. Then she said, out of the blue, "I liked Carolyn."

The abrupt change of topic startled Quinn.

"I'm pretty sure she's sitting on a cloud watching over everyone—like she did from down here," Lena said.

Quinn met her gaze, surprised by the unexpected warmth in Lena's. "She helped people?"

"Everyone," Lena said. "She's definitely up north, if you know what I mean." She smiled. "Not me though. When I die, I'm going to slam into hell, take off my bra, sit on Satan's lap, and say, 'Hi, honey, I'm home, what's the Wi-Fi password?'"

An hour and a half later Lena turned Quinn to face the mirror.

Quinn looked and barely squelched a startled scream. "Blue?" she managed to squeak out.

"Just a few streaks. You wanted to look cool and this is definitely that. And actually . . ." Lena artfully played with Quinn's hair. "Blue's a great color on you. I should've gone for obnoxious orange, but I was torn between my reputation for great hair and my need to make you look unappealing to Mick."

Quinn gaped at her. "I could complain to the owner here, you know that, right?"

"Go for it. You're speaking to her."

Quinn blinked at Lena and then stared at herself some more. There weren't many streaks of blue, a very select few actually, professionally placed and . . . damn. It totally made her complexion pop.

"You're welcome. That'll be eighty bucks."

Quinn paid her and started to head out, stopping to turn back. "Mick told me you and he were high school sweethearts."

"Did he?"

"Yes."

"Did he also tell you that I let him slip through my fingers once and I don't intend to do it again?" Lena asked.

"I thought you were with the bartender."

"Boomer?" Lena shrugged.

"Maybe he's your soul mate," Quinn said hopefully.

"I'm ninety-nine percent sure my soul mate is carbs. And anyway, me and Boomer are taking a break. The thing you should know is that I was Mick's first. And I intend to be his last."

Chapter 11

I want to be cuddled. But I also want to be left the hell alone. Being crazy is hard.

—from "The Mixed-Up Files of Tilly Adams's Journal"

Quinn knew she was early when she parked at Carolyn's property, but she'd wanted to check it out. She felt she needed to do this for Tilly's sake, who was now left with a wanderlust father who'd apparently never expressed interest in either of his two daughters, a closed-for-now café, and a not-so-slightly run-down house.

Clearly money had been a problem, and Quinn thought of the café's lost revenue. Not good. She walked around the back of the house and found . . . good God.

Chickens, all of them staring at her with beady black eyes and squawking in disapproval.

No one had told her there were chickens.

Her phone buzzed with an incoming text.

MOM:

Honey, did you get enough food for breakfast? Remember you get cranky if you don't eat.

Quinn pointed at the chickens. "Hear that? I get cranky if I don't eat. Don't test me." Then she texted her mom back, crossed her fingers, and lied through her teeth that she was eating super healthy.

MOM:

You never could lie very well . . .

Quinn rolled her eyes but also smiled. Love was a funny thing. You could get mad, hold a grudge, let it fester even, and then with one little sentence, forget all the bad for all the good.

The sound of voices brought Quinn to the front of the café. Three old guys stood there listening to a short, curvy woman with a booming voice and a German accent—which reminded her of Marcel.

The woman had a key, which she put into the lock to let herself in.

"Excuse me," Quinn called out.

The woman turned and sized up Quinn, and smiled. "Knew I'd see you sooner or later."

Quinn swiveled her head to look behind her, but nope, no one was there. "Me? You know who I am?"

"Quinn Weller," the woman said. "You're from L.A., which is proved by those blue streaks you've got in your hair."

Quinn lifted a hand and touched the strands in question with a grimace.

"I also know that you climbed a tree and then fell out of it and landed in the ER."

"Okay," Quinn said in her defense, "I was stung by a bee and I'm allergic. Or I wouldn't have fallen out of the tree."

"My point is that you must have known you're allergic, yes? It's bee season. Yet you tried to help soothe Tilly anyway." She paused. "That told me all I need to know about you. You're Carolyn's daughter. You were the one in the bar kissing Mick Hennessey last night."

Quinn blinked, stunned on so many levels. "How do you know all that?"

"Because I know everything."

"Well, your sources are off," Quinn said. "I wasn't kissing Mick Hennessey." *At the B&B, yes. Bar, no.*

The woman shrugged. "If I was skinny and looked like you, I'd kiss him too. As for me . . ." She nodded to the café. "I work here."

"Hasn't the café been closed since Carolyn's death?"

"Yes, but I came to check on the perishables and make sure everything is okay. I'd reopen, but I have no authority to do so."

"Do it anyway, Greta!" one of the old guys standing around said.

"Yeah," yelled another. "We're hungry!"

"My wife won't let me come home until noon," the third called out. "And the library says I can't come back anymore on account of when I read, I have to do it out loud to myself and they objected to my . . ." He did air quotes. "Content. They said I read too much porn, that I'm addicted."

"You are," old guy number two said.

"Hey, I could be addicted to drugs, you ever think of that?" he asked. "Do you realize how lucky you all are?"

Greta leveled a look at the old men and they shut up as if on cue. "Everyone zip it. Time to be on your best behavior." She pointed at Quinn. "We've got the new owner standing right here."

Everyone swiveled wide-eyed gazes her way and then started talking at once.

"Please open!"

"I'm starving."

"Can I use the bathroom? My prostrate ain't what it used to be."

Greta brought her fingers up to her lips and let out a piercing whistle. "*Silence.*"

The three old men fell silent.

Greta looked at Quinn expectantly.

Quinn wasn't happy about being called out, but she couldn't help but be curious. "I'd like to go in."

Greta opened the door for her and then followed her in. "It's nice to meet you. I'm Greta, by the way. I've worked for Carolyn the past twenty-plus years. She was the kindest woman I've ever known, cared for everyone in her circle."

A circle that hadn't included her own daughter, but hey, whatever, Quinn was over it.

Or at least working on being over it.

"You're from Germany," Quinn said, knowing that her German accent was the real thing compared to Marcel's fake one.

"I came here twenty-two years ago with my husband on a business trip of his," Greta said. "I had no English. We stopped here for lunch and he left to make a phone call. He never came back."

Quinn, who'd been staring at the old kitchen equipment—so old that it was a wonder anyone could cook anything decent with the antiquated appliances—turned to look at Greta in shock.

"I know," the forty-something woman said. "He was a *sohn von einem weibchen.*"

"Stupid head," Quinn translated loosely and for the first time in her life, she had something to be thankful to Marcel for.

"Yes." Greta looked impressed as she began to go through the storage bins with an eagle eye. "I had nowhere to go, no money, no place to stay. Carolyn took me in and gave me a job. I helped her cook. Or served. Whatever was needed. This place is a mess. It's good you're here, City Girl. We'll clean and reopen."

"She's not staying," Tilly said, having just arrived in the doorway. She looked at Quinn's hair and arched a brow. "Blue?"

"Don't ask."

"My friend did blue streaks once," Tilly shared. "She's on the swim team and the chlorine turned her hair from blue to pea green."

"Good thing I'm not a swimmer," Quinn said. "Can we go somewhere and talk?"

"Maybe. I've got to do homework first. I'll be back."

"But—"

But nothing because the girl was gone.

Quinn sighed and moved to check out the dining room. One wall was covered in corkboard. It was lined with a shelf upon which sat an old Polaroid camera. The board was filled with pics of Carolyn and her customers. Tilly was in there too. As was Greta, often arm in arm with another woman, the two of them in aprons with Carolyn. There were also reviews of the café, and a couple of award certificates as well. Just small-time regional stuff, not the awards and reviews Quinn was accustomed to seeing, but still. "Impressive," she said.

Greta smiled. "Carolyn would love you being here."

Quinn struggled with both resentment and nostalgia for her few conversations with Carolyn. She knew that much of the resentment came from how deeply hurt she was by the deception, but she found herself unable to quickly get over it. "How did you know who I was?"

"Easy." Greta came close and took Quinn's hands, smiling at her with a fondness Quinn had no idea how to accept. "Carolyn described you perfectly. She said you looked just like her, which is true. Although you don't have the fret lines between your eyes yet."

"Don't worry, they're coming."

Greta smiled. "She also said that you were smart, beautiful, and successful."

Quinn couldn't help but be fascinated in spite of herself. "She talked about me?"

"Oh yes. After each trip to L.A., she'd go on and on. Her entire face would be lit up for days." Greta's eyes went damp. "Truly," she said softly. "Your mum was the kindest woman I've ever known. It bothered her over the years, not knowing how you'd turned out."

But not enough to actually look for Quinn sooner. Because damn, it would have been nice to hear all of this from Carolyn herself.

"Hey!" This was followed by a knock on the front door. Old man number three. "We're starving. You opening or what?"

Greta looked at Quinn. "Can you really cook?"

"Yes."

"So . . . ?" Greta asked. "How about it? There're people who need the income, you know."

It shamed Quinn to realize she'd never even thought about that.

There was another knock, on the back door this time. The tall, dark-skinned woman from the photos with Carolyn and Greta. She walked in like she owned the place, her eyes on Greta, her jet-black hair in thick braids down her back, tied together with a colorful ribbon. "What is it, Greta?" she asked in a melodic, soft accent. Jamaican, maybe. "What's your emergency?"

"Other than you didn't return a single text?" Greta asked. "We talked about this, Trinee."

"No," Trinee said. "You talked about my dislike of cell phones. I listened. I did not agree. Why are you here bothering Carolyn's daughter?"

Did *everyone* know who she was?

"I miss my job," Greta said. "I miss being needed. I found out she was in town and I thought what the hell, go big or go home."

"You say that like going home is a bad thing," Trinee said. "I've been working my new job at the grocery store, which I hate. I don't want to go big. I want to go home. And I want to take a nap when I get there."

Greta tossed up her hands dramatically.

"You'll find another job, as I did," Trinee said. "Leave her alone, the girl doesn't need this right now." She then gathered up the full trash bin. "I'm taking this out, but I'll be back." She pointed at Greta. "And then we're going home."

"Hmph," Greta said.

Quinn smiled. "You two bicker like sisters."

"Or like an old married couple . . . ," Greta said and held up her hand with a pretty gold band on her ring finger.

"Oh," Quinn said. "I'm sorry. You got married again. That's lovely."

Greta snorted. "Not always. But we're happy. I'm happy. At least until she walks away like my first spouse did."

Trinee had come back into the kitchen, hands empty. She slipped her arms around Greta. "Never."

Quinn's heart sighed for them while aching for herself.

"Hey," someone called from out front. "You opening or what?"

Greta and Trinee looked at Quinn.

"How can we?" she asked. "We'd need fresh produce and meat and herbs . . ."

"Fresh nothing," Greta said, bustling around. "We've got an entire freezer full of stuff to use up. And we'll have eggs just as soon as someone goes and collects them. We could start with half days. Breakfast and lunch only. Dinners would have to wait until we're back on our feet."

Quinn literally didn't know what to say. She felt a responsibility to these people who needed their salaries but when she turned in a slow circle, taking the place in and looking for sanity, she failed to find it.

Tilly popped her head back in. "What's going on, did you reopen?" She looked . . . hopeful.

It shocked Quinn. As did the words that came out of her mouth. "Yes, but just as a trial," she said.

Greta grinned and unlocked the front door. The three old men came in. "Lou, Hank, and Big Hank," the oldest one said by way of introduction. "I'm Lou. That one's Big Hank." He jabbed a thumb at the shortest but widest one.

Big Hank stopped in front of Quinn and looked anxious. "You any good at cooking?"

"I'm a sous-chef at Amuse-Bouche," she said.

Everyone collectively blinked as one.

"It's a trendy, popular restaurant in L.A.," she said.

"Never heard of it," Big Hank said.

"Me either," Lou said. He was bald, his head shiny like a cue ball, although he did have a bunch of hair coming out of his ears.

"What the hell's a sous-chef?" Not-Big-Hank asked.

"Not sure, but it sounds fancy," Greta said. She tossed Quinn an apron. "Have at it, City Girl. It's all yours today. Make it easy for yourself and stick with the breakfast menu only. Pancakes, waffles, French toast, bacon, sausage, biscuits, eggs . . ."

Quinn shook her head. "I don't do that kind of cooking."

"What other kind is there?" Tilly asked.

Quinn shook out the apron. It read: WARNING! HOT STUFF COMING THROUGH. "I mostly handle the planning and directing of food preparation, supervise kitchen staff, take care of any problems that arise, that sort of thing."

Tilly didn't look impressed.

Neither did anyone else.

Big Hank turned to Greta, looking desperate now. "I'm *real* hungry," he said.

Greta took back the apron. "I'll make my famous pronto potato pancakes. I do it as a special once a week," she told Quinn.

Everyone groaned but when Greta whipped around to look, they all found something else to look at.

"We hate her pancakes," Trinee whispered to Quinn. "But no one'll say so and hurt her feelings."

Everyone looked pleadingly at Quinn.

Oh good God. And that's when she saw Trinee getting the baskets ready for the tables. "Wait! You can't just put out cold butter packets. And the crackers might be stale."

"Yes, because that's our problem right now," Trinee said. "No one at the stove cooking, but the crackers might be stale."

And so Quinn ended up in the kitchen learning a very important lesson—there was a huge difference between being able to cut up a carrot in two hundred different fancy ways and flipping pancakes fast enough to fulfill quick orders.

"Another short stack," Greta yelled at her thirty minutes later.

When Quinn hadn't been looking, the café had filled up. "It's going to take a few," she said. "I need to make more batter."

"The sign out front says we serve FAST," Greta said and clapped her hands. "Chop-chop. What the hell are you doing now?"

"Garnishing the plates," Quinn said. She hadn't found any fresh herbs but there'd been a bag of carrots, which she'd sliced up for a splash of color.

"She's cute," Trinee said. "Real cute. But she's not especially quick."

Quinn didn't even have time to roll her eyes because Trinee was bringing in the orders with alarming speed, stringing them up by her face. Which is how Quinn ended up burning a big pan of eggs. The last of their eggs, in fact.

"I thought you said you knew how to cook," Tilly said, sounding disappointed from her perch on the counter.

"I think that's a health hazard," Quinn said. "Get down."

"I think that burnt pan is the health hazard," Tilly said, waving a hand in front of her face.

"Tell us the truth, City Girl," Trinee said, hands on hips. "You just watch cooking shows and think you're a chef, right? Which one, *Cutthroat Kitchen*? *Iron Chef*?"

Lou poked his head into the kitchen. "You want me to take over? I cooked in the army for hundreds back in the day."

Quinn gritted her teeth. "I've got this." And she would get this. If it killed her.

"Great. But we're out of eggs." Greta shoved an empty basket in her hands. "Go get more."

"From the store, right?"

"Honey, we ain't got time for that," Trinee called in from the other room.

"The henhouse," Greta said. "Out back."

The words struck terror in Quinn's gut. "But . . ."

"The hens are just sitting in their laying boxes on their eggs," Greta said. "All you've got to do is shoo them."

Quinn looked at Tilly.

Tilly shrugged. "Don't ask me. The chickens were Mom's, not mine."

Fine. Two minutes later, Quinn stood staring at the hens, who were flapping their wings and making threatening noises. "Hey," she said. "This wasn't my idea."

A few of them ran right in her path and she nearly fell to her ass trying to get out of their way. "Stay cool," she told herself and headed to the boxes where the majority of the hens sat. "I just need the eggs, ladies, that's all."

Not a single hen left her perch, all of them mutinously holding guard.

Quinn did as Greta had suggested. She waved her hands and said, "Shoo!"

No one shooed. All of them stared at her with beady black eyes.

"Great." She drew in a breath and made eye contact with the hen closest to her. "Hi there. You're pretty, very pretty." She could see the smooth curve of an egg peeking out from beneath the bird. "And hey, I'm sure you're used to this, right? So you won't mind if I just . . ." She tried to pilfer the egg and the hen went batshit crazy, squawking and trying to peck Quinn's hand off.

Staying cool went out the window. Quinn screamed and ran. She got to the back door of the café and put her hand to her chest to keep her pounding heart inside. By some miracle she still had the basket in her hand.

Greta let her in and looked down at the empty basket.

Quinn gasped for air. "I barely got out with my life."

Greta rolled her eyes and pointed to Tilly. "Honey, you're up."

Tilly hopped off the counter.

"Wait a minute," Quinn said. "You know how to get eggs?"

"Duh."

"Why didn't you just do it in the first place?"

Tilly flashed a smile. "'Cause this was more fun."

A few minutes later she came back in, basket full of eggs. She handed them over. "Okay, so yeah. I gotta go now."

"Where?" Quinn asked.

"I take AP English and history classes at the community college in San Luis Obispo on Tuesdays and Wednesdays. I can't get them at my high school."

Damn. Impressive. "Okay," she said. "Maybe we can meet up later?"

"I'll be studying late. I guess I could wake up early if you want to do breakfast."

Quinn hadn't planned to stay another day. Her mother would threaten to send out the Coast Guard when she called to tell her. Brock . . . well, Brock was Brock. He'd get over it. But she wasn't so sure Chef Wade would, or that she'd even have a job to go home to. All of which weighed heavily on her mind, and yet her mouth, clearly not catching onto the reality raining down on her shoulders, said, "That'd be great," without permission or hesitation.

And then Tilly was gone and Quinn was back to work as a short-order cook. The demands were insane. She was trying to do four orders of eggs and two orders of French toast while simultaneously making up a new batch of pancakes when the toaster caught fire.

She unplugged it and put out the small flames before tipping her face up to the ceiling, speaking to whatever deity was listening. "Are you kidding me with today?"

That's when the smoke set off the fire alarm.

"Uh-oh," Not-Big-Hank said, poking his head into the kitchen, helpfully pointing to the fire alarm high on the wall.

"Shit!" Quinn climbed up on the counter and waved at the smoke alarm with her apron, trying to clear the smoke from it so it would shut up.

"That won't work," Greta said, hands on hips below her. "The firefighters will already be on their way."

"Oh my God. I'm so sorry."

"Don't be," Trinee said. "They're all really cute. What," she said to Greta's eye roll. "I'm a lesbian, I'm not dead."

The firefighters did indeed come.

So did the entire town, it seemed.

"It's all good," Trinee told a fretting Quinn. "Now everyone knows we're open for business. A lot cheaper than an ad."

Chapter 12

I'm just a girl, standing in front of a salad, asking it to be a doughnut.

—from "The Mixed-Up Files of Tilly Adams's Journal"

It was early evening when Quinn drove herself back to the B & B. Between yesterday's ER trip, failing to impress Tilly into wanting to be sisters, missing Beth, nearly setting the café on fire while cooking, no less, not hearing from Chef Wade about her extra days off—which meant she had no idea on the status of her employment—she was done in.

"Beth?" she whispered to the empty room.

Nothing.

She sighed. "Look, I need to see you."

More nothing.

Par for the course. She decided what she needed was a bath. She checked the tub carefully. No bugs. She started the water before realizing she had no bubble bath, so she dumped in some shampoo and called it good. She stripped and started to get into the tub and . . .

There was a big fat bug doing the doggie paddle in her fresh, bubbly water.

She shoved her clothes back on, missing a few key items like bra, undies, and socks, and ran out of her room, intending to go straight to the front desk to yell at someone. Halfway down the hallway she ran into a brick wall that turned out to have really great arms that surrounded her.

Mick.

"I like the blue," he said.

She'd forgotten all about the blue streaks in her hair and let out a watery laugh with her face pressed against his chest.

"Hey," he said and tipped her face up to his, his warm smile fading. "Tough day?"

"Yes. But that's another story." She pointed at her room. "It's in the tub."

He took her key and vanished inside.

Ever loyal, Coop went with him.

Quinn moved into the small courtyard, sat on a weathered Adirondack chair that gave her butt splinters, and stared up at the sky, looking for the answers to her universe.

None were forthcoming.

A few minutes later she felt Mick at her side. He was good, she hadn't even heard him coming. All she heard was Coop dropping to the ground with an "oomph."

"If you say the bug was small," she said, "I'm going to have to hurt you."

"I'm smarter than that."

She nodded and kept studying the sky because looking at him standing there, tall, strong, ready for anything, made her want things she tried really hard not to want anymore.

He dragged a chair close and sat. Face to the sky like herself, he leaned back, relaxed. "What's eating at you?"

"Oh. Well . . ." She closed her eyes. "Nothing." *Or you know, everything . . .*

"If you don't want to tell me, I get that, but you don't have to pretend to be fine when you're not."

She opened her eyes and found his right on hers, warm and accepting. No one in her world had ever been able to tell when she was upset or unsettled, or even completely off her rocker.

But this man, whom she'd known all of what, three days, could tell. "I'm not sure where to start."

"Does it have anything to do with setting the café on fire?"

"Hey, it was the toaster, not the café!" she exclaimed. "If you're going to listen to the gossip, at least get it straight."

His mouth quirked and he took her hand, his thumb stroking over her fingers. It was work roughened, with calluses, and gave her a full body shiver of the very best kind.

"It's about more than the toaster fire," he said.

She blew out a sigh. "I think Carolyn was hoping I'd stay and help Chuck take care of Tilly, a teenager who thinks I'm somehow responsible for every bad thing that's ever happened to her."

"I can sympathize," he said. "My sister's twenty-five going on fifteen. She and my mom have butted heads all their lives, so it's been mostly up to me to keep her on the straight and narrow. It's been hit or miss at best, which is not something I'm proud of."

He said this like it really got to him, and she tried to imagine how it would feel to have been responsible for Beth. The truth was, she and Beth had been equals, cohorts, partners in crime, and confidantes. "Did you give it your best shot?" she asked.

"Always."

"Then that's all you can ask of yourself, right?"

"Right." His mouth quirked again. "Are you listening to your own advice?"

She rolled her eyes, and because his nearness—not to mention the testosterone and pheromones coming off him in waves—was distracting her, she pulled her hand free. "I'm willing to do whatever needs to be done for Tilly. It's . . ." She could still see Beth's face as she'd looked sitting on the TV the other night. Carefree. Happy. At peace . . .

The opposite of how Quinn felt.

"I don't know if staying would even help her," she said. "I'm not sure I'm . . . enough."

"Quinn, her father walked off into the sunset and her mom's dead," he said. "She's got nothing. No ties, no blood looking out for her at all. Anything you do for her is far more than she has right now."

She stood up and walked to the end of the courtyard, taking in the inky black lines of the rolling hills in the distance. She felt Mick come up behind her.

"You said you were in a rut," he said softly, right at her backside, the heat of him warming her. "So why not try something new. Follow your heart and go for it."

The words drifted over her and made more sense than anything she could remember hearing.

Try something new.

Follow your heart and go for it . . .

"You're right," she said softly. And then she did just that, she tried something new. She turned, went up on her tiptoes, and kissed him. Her life was upside down and sideways. More than that, she was feeling way too much, and some of that seemed to be tied to him. So she pressed close and tried to convey that with her mouth, her body. When she stroked her tongue against his, he let out a rough groan and the sound ignited something long dead inside her.

More.

That was her only thought. She needed more, now. So she pulled back and looked at him. She wasn't the only one who was breathless, a fact that bolstered her courage. She took his hand and led him back to her room, where she nudged him inside and kicked the door closed. Once it was locked, she walked him straight to her bed.

"Quinn," he said quietly, with reluctance. "You've had a rough few days. I'm just here to help."

She kicked off her flip-flops. "Okay, so help. I need help having fun."

"I'd be taking advantage of you."

She pulled off her shirt and heard him suck in a breath at the realization that she wasn't wearing a bra. Turning to face him, she said, "You're not taking advantage. If Wildstone and everything in it is my storm cloud, you're the silver lining. Please, Mick. Stay?"

He let out a short breath and stepped into her, banding his arms around her. "I'm not one to argue with a beautiful woman."

"Glad to hear it. Consider it one of your best qualities. Even better than your ass."

He laughed and then so did she, but the breath shuddered out of her lungs when those big work-roughened hands slid up her torso and cupped her bare, aching breasts. Her hands got busy too, sliding inside his shirt, her fingers spreading wide over the smooth, hard planes of his back. He felt big and strong and warm, and she quivered with pleasure, nearly drowning in the unfamiliar sensations, like she was waking up from a long, dreamless sleep.

He cupped the back of her head and held her to him, lengthening and deepening their connection, lazily stroking his tongue to hers until her knees wobbled. "*Mick*."

"I know." But he didn't hurry, he just kept up the slow, teasing, taunting build, stroking those hands over her until she was whimpering and squirming against him for more.

When they finally broke apart to breathe, he pressed his forehead to hers. "Be sure, Quinn."

"I am." She tugged his shirt up, watching with hunger as he took over the task, pulling it over his head and letting it sail through the air behind him. "Now the rest," she said.

She'd meant his jeans but his hands went to hers. In a blink he had them unbuttoned. He crouched low, easily balanced on the balls of his feet as he slid the denim over her thighs, giving him a front-row view of what he unveiled.

His heartfelt groan told her he liked the commando situation. "I was in a hurry," she said breathlessly as his hands guided the jeans the rest of the way to the floor. His hands encircled her ankles and then slowly ran up her legs, past her knees, her thighs, not stopping until he ran out of leg. Not stopping then either, lingering to play.

"Mick—"

"Mmm," he said and she could feel his warm breath brush over her heated flesh, making her tremble, her toes already curling. He just continued his gentle torment, causing an onslaught of erotic need that swept over her. Literally. It had been so long since she'd allowed herself this pleasure, this need . . .

"I can't stand," she gasped as she burst and shuddered. Mick rose to his full height and lifted her up against him, fusing their mouths together. Her hands wound their way into his hair, holding him to her as she tried to get as close to him as possible.

Then she was in free fall to the bed . . .

He followed her down, divesting himself of his jeans as he did. Quinn grabbed for the covers but he caught her hand and kissed the palm. "You're beautiful," he said.

And she felt it. From the tips of her hair to her still-curled toes. She leaned over him to make him feel the same, brushing her mouth over a wide shoulder, a hard pec. She stopped at his abs and couldn't help but take a lick as she filled her hands with him.

His groan rumbled through her as he rolled her to her back, his mouth coming down on hers. He'd come up with a condom, which made him smarter than she was. He nudged her thighs apart and she eagerly made room, wrapping her legs around him as he filled her, locking her ankles behind his back to keep him right where she wanted him.

She was already chanting his name when he began to move, rolling his hips with purpose until they came together, even as they fell apart.

As simple and terrifying as that.

They lay there awhile, entangled on the trashed sheets. She'd opened the window earlier, and she could hear the lovely night sounds she'd forever associate with Wildstone. She could also hear the damn sink dripping again, which would drive her crazy. Later. For right now her brain was still nothing but a pleasure button, one that couldn't find annoyance or irritation to save its life.

It had been a long time, but she knew holy-cow sex when she had it, and it had been exactly what she needed. She opened her eyes to tell Mick so and found him watching her, a pensive look on his face. "Uh-oh," she said, suddenly feeling very naked. "Regrets already?"

"Hell no," he said.

There was something in his tone and eyes that she couldn't name, but it made her both yearn and feel uneasy at the same time. She knew this was a man she could fall for, if she let herself.

She wasn't going to let herself.

She couldn't even commit to brunch plans with her parents, much less a relationship. And more than that, aside from what had just happened, she wasn't ready to feel emotion again, of any kind. Just the thought made her panic.

Mick smoothed a fingertip over the furrow in her brow and smiled wryly. "Regrets already?" he murmured back to her.

She forced away whatever troubles were lurking on the horizon and smiled. "Hell no."

Chapter 13

There should be a weather app for people with social anxiety, like "Today life will be partly crowdy with a 70 percent chance of having to deal with people."

—from "The Mixed-Up Files of Tilly Adams's Journal"

The next morning, Mick woke up to numb extremities. He instantly saw the problem. Coop lay on his feet, Quinn on the rest of him. She'd fallen asleep in his arms muttering something about needing to get him to fix the damn dripping sink again, and he'd stilled as he'd realized.

She still thought he was the B & B handyman.

When she'd first assumed that on day one—four days ago now—he'd been amused. And intrigued. And then, let's face it, turned on by the bossy, cute, sexy woman sticking her head out her window, asking so sweetly if he could fix her shit.

The fact was, she'd been a welcome distraction from the hell he was in, being back in the town he hadn't been able to escape fast enough, having to deal with the mess his dad had left behind.

His problem, not hers.

And so was the fact that he'd misled her, no matter how unintentionally. Not that this mattered if this was truly just the "fun" she said she needed his help with, but he was beginning to get to know her now, and he also knew himself. Yeah, it *was* fun, a hell of a lot of fun. And the sex had been off the charts, but . . . it had also been more.

He'd just tell her the truth, that was all. He'd say: *So, by the way, funny story—I'm actually a structural engineer from the Bay Area, staying at this B and B, same as you, since it's the closest to my mom's house, where I really am a handyman.*

Just not a paid one.

Yep, he'd tell her the minute she woke up. She had a good sense of humor, it would be fine.

Coop lifted his head and yawned. And also farted. The dog jerked his head around and stared at his own ass in shock, even though this happened every day.

"Dude," Mick said and Coop sighed. Slowly, so slowly he might've been moving backward, he slid off the bed and plopped to the floor, like Mick had insulted him to the marrow.

Unable to help himself, Mick stroked a hand down Quinn's back and palmed her sweet ass. She stirred and stretched, and then froze for a beat before lifting her head.

Her face was adorably sleepy looking, her hair a wild, rioted mass of waves all over the place. She blinked once, slow as an owl, taking in their positions. "Forgot to warn you that I'm a bed hog," she murmured. "Sorry."

"Don't be." He paused. "Quinn."

"Uh-oh," she said, her eyes clearing a little bit. "That's a very serious tone." And this time when she tried to pull free, he let her. She sat up, tugging the sheet with her and stared down at him. "If you're going to tell me you've changed your mind about regrets, just keep it to yourself—"

"I'm an engineer," he said. "I run a structural engineering firm with three other partners in the Bay Area."

She stared at him. "What?"

He reached for her, but she scooted back. "Wait," she said, holding him off. "You told me you were the B and B maintenance guy. You lied to me?"

At her tone, Coop gave a low, worried "wuff."

"It's okay," Mick told him. "And no," he said to Quinn. "I didn't lie to you. I never said I was the B and B maintenance guy."

"Yes you did." She stared at him some more, thinking so hard her ears were smoking. "Oh my God," she whispered. "You're right, you didn't. I just assumed. And you let me." She scrambled off the bed, snatching the entire sheet as she did, wrapping it around herself like she was cold.

Or needed armor.

In any case, it left Mick bare-ass naked on the bed. He sat up and opened his mouth but she whirled on him, pointing a finger in his direction. "Why did you let me assume that?"

"A hot woman asks me for help?" he asked. "Are you kidding? I wouldn't have refused you. And to be clear, even if you weren't hot, I wouldn't have refused you."

She just narrowed her eyes. "*That's* your defense?"

"Well, you've got to admit," he said, "it's a little funny. Though the joke's really on me because I had no idea what I was doing under that sink, I just got lucky."

"It's still dripping," she pointed out.

"Yeah, see, my dad would've loved that. It proves him right, that I never listened. He tried to teach me everything he knew." He let out a low laugh. "And hey, it made me think of him fondly, which is a rarity, so that's actually a favor you did me."

"This isn't a joke, Mick." She closed her eyes. "Why were you always parked right out in front of the office, like you belong there?"

"Because besides staying here, I'm working with the owner, who wants to sell this place and lease it back."

She was holding tightly to the sheet. Coop moved close and leaned on her. She crouched down and hugged the dog. "What is it with my life?" she asked Coop. "Why is lying and deceiving me some kind of new trend? Or is it just that everyone thinks they can decide for me what I need to know and what I don't?"

Coop licked her chin in commiseration.

Understanding her reaction now, and also feeling like a complete asshole, Mick got out of the bed. "It wasn't like that, Quinn."

"No," she said quickly, holding up a hand to ward him off. She took another step back and caught her foot in the sheet.

Before she could go down, he caught her, all soft, warm curves he'd been hoping to get another taste of this morning, but she broke free. Sending him a scalding glance over her bare shoulder, she turned to look for her clothes, grabbing pieces as she came to them, yanking them on.

"Wuff," Coop said, clearly deeply concerned.

Quinn gave the dog another quick, soothing hug that Mick wished she'd bestow on him. Instead, she leveled him with a withering stare. "To be clear, this, between us, was just—" She jabbed a finger at the bed. "*That*. And it's done now. I'm done. We're done." Her phone rang and she snatched it up. "Hello." She paused, listening, giving him a moment to appreciate that she'd gotten her jeans up but not fastened, and her top only halfway on before she'd frozen in place. "You're kidding me." Another pause. "Oh for God's sake, yes, I'm coming." She disconnected, shoved the phone into her pocket, and to his disconcertion, finished dressing in two seconds, muttering something about "those effing chickens are going to effing kill me."

"What's wrong?" he asked, pulling on his clothes as well.

"My life."

"Quinn—"

She shoved her feet into her shoes. "The hens made a run for it."

"The what?"

"I know, right? But maybe they've got the right idea, running like hell." And then she was gone, slamming out of her own room.

Coop's expression said, *I can't believe how stupid you are.*

A fact Mick had to agree with.

IN TILLY'S WORLD, she was the caregiver. She'd taken care of her mom. The house. Her friends. Chuck. It was what she did.

She'd been taking care of her mom's chickens for years on top of everything else and she'd never once left the pen open. And she wouldn't have done it that morning either except Chuck's silly girlfriend had a silly hissy fit when Tilly had eaten the last two eggs—like there weren't more out back.

So Tilly had dragged herself out of bed half an hour before her usual time to stop the fighting that was coming through the thin walls.

"I didn't sign up for a teenager, Chuck!"

"She's a good kid. A really good kid."

"To you, maybe. But if it's not you, she's sullen as hell, and I think she stole a twenty from my wallet."

"Here's another twenty," Chuck said. "And she just lost her mom. She's earned the sullen . . ."

So yeah, Tilly had gone to the hen coop with a bad 'tude, and somehow she'd managed to leave the gate open. The stupid-ass chickens had escaped and were currently running around the yard acting like their heads had been cut off.

Which made it official—her life sucked. The chickens were out, she hated school, and her mom was gone. Her mom hadn't been perfect, but she'd been Tilly's. Now she had no one except a sister who couldn't wait to vanish.

Greta and Trinee had come out of the café to stare at the loose chickens, but were no help.

"Baby girl, there's no way on God's green earth I'm chasing chickens," Trinee said.

"And don't look at me," Greta added. "You think this body got its curves by running?"

"So to be clear," Tilly said, hands on hips, "no one's chasing the chickens?"

They both just looked at her.

Whatever. Mad at the world, Tilly had used the number she hadn't planned on ever using and called Quinn. "You said I could call you for anything . . ."

Five minutes later, Quinn's Lexus arrived. "What happened?" Quinn asked.

Tilly shrugged. "Someone let the chickens out."

"Who'd do such a thing?"

Tilly shrugged.

Quinn watched all the chickens losing their collective shit. "So . . . what do we do now?"

"I don't know," Tilly said. "Catch them?"

"Oh my God. *How?*"

Tilly didn't have to fully fake the quaver in her voice. "They were my mom's pets. We have to get them."

"Okay." Quinn seemed to gather herself and reached out to squeeze Tilly's hand. "Of course. We'll get them."

And then to Tilly's utter shock, Quinn inhaled deep, like she was searching for courage, and then began to run after the loose chickens.

Cars on the street stopped to watch, proving there wasn't a lot to do in Wildstone. From one of the cars, Lena got out and came to stand next to Tilly, a wide grin on her face as she sipped on a to-go coffee.

"I was working on my bookkeeping," she said. "This is much more fun."

Tilly, starting to feel a little guilty, chewed on her lower lip. She'd made a few motions to help but mostly she'd been caught up in the amusement of watching Quinn.

Sweating, breathless, Quinn stopped in the middle of the yard and put her hands on her hips. "How about a little help?"

Lena lifted her cup. "First I drink the coffee. *Then* I do the things. But only when I'm *paid* for the things . . ."

Quinn rolled her eyes and looked at Tilly.

Tilly went back at it with Quinn. And when Quinn actually caught a chicken, she flashed a triumphant grin Tilly's way—and then the chicken squawked and emitted a long stream of poop. Right down the front of Quinn's shirt.

Lena leaned in with her phone and took a pic. "For Instagram," she said. "Also, I don't know if you noticed, but you smell like shit."

"Thanks for the tact."

"Honey, tact is for people who aren't witty enough to be sarcastic."

Lou popped outside, holding the Polaroid camera. He lifted it to his face and peered through the lens in her direction.

Quinn pointed at him. "Don't you even think about—"

He snapped the pic of her and two seconds later it rolled out of the camera. He waved it in the air and grinned. "For the wall."

"Perfect," Quinn muttered, and to Tilly's surprise, forged on.

When she caught another chicken, she thrust it into Tilly's hands. "Either you help," Quinn said to Lena, "or I'll go swimming until my hair is green and tell everyone it's your fault."

The threat was pretty impressive, Tilly had to admit, and she got much more serious about helping. Five minutes later they'd caught every last wayward chicken.

Quinn blew a strand of hair out of her sweaty face. "Thanks for the assist," Quinn said dryly to Lena.

"I never run. Well, unless running out of fucks count."

"Hey, watch the language. Impressionable kid sister aboard."

Tilly objected to this. "I'm neither impressionable nor your kid sister."

Quinn straightened and looked at her. "Maybe you're right on the impressionable part, but whether you like it or not we *are* sisters."

For the record, Tilly *didn't* like it. She didn't like anything anymore and she didn't know what to do about it. She was stuck, literally stuck, and it made her feel like her insides were a tornado hell-bent on self-destruction. "You can go back to L.A. now," she said. "You know you want to."

"What about what you want?" Quinn asked. "You really want me to just walk away?"

"It's not like we're family," Tilly said.

"We *are* family, and if you need proof, you need only say so and I'll get it for you."

Tilly stared at her, irrationally angry and unable to control herself. "I'd rather have no sister at all." She wished the words back right after they'd escaped but she just let them hang in the air.

Quinn stepped up to her, chicken shit on her boobs and all. "I've already lost one sister," she said, voice quavery, like she was really, *really* mad. "A sister of my heart, and I'd give anything, *anything at all*, including my own life, to have her back. The same, I imagine, as how you feel about your mom. So I'm going to hope that what you just said isn't really true, Tilly, because trust me, having no sister at all sucks."

And then Quinn did what Tilly had thought she'd wanted—she walked away.

Chapter 14

Luckily even the worst days only have twenty-four hours.

—from "The Mixed-Up Files of Tilly Adams's Journal"

Quinn left, desperate to get away before she cried in front of everyone and made a fool of herself. She headed for the B & B, giving Cliff a call as she did. "Can you set it up so the café stays open to generate money for Tilly, and also to keep the people who work there employed?"

"You're leaving," he said.

She blew out a breath. "It's complicated. My job, my parents . . ."

"You already have a full life. Believe me, I get it."

Why didn't that make her feel any better? "Can you manage the café business?" she asked again.

"Absolutely."

One relief anyway.

"I'm sorry I can't stay," she said. "But Tilly isn't interested, and

I can't see how to make it work if she doesn't want to. You sure she's okay with the neighbor?"

"Yes."

It was all she could do at this point. Back at the B & B, she got into the shower to get rid of both the chicken poop and the crazy morning.

"Hey," Beth said.

Quinn let out a startled scream and dropped the shampoo bottle on her toe. "Fuck, shit, damn . . ."

Beth, sitting on the countertop, rolled her eyes and then studied her own reflection in the foggy mirror, messing with her hair. "Think I should put in some blue streaks of my own?" she asked Quinn.

Quinn was still hopping on her one good foot, holding her throbbing toes. "What are you doing here, and why won't you ever come when I call for you?"

Beth turned to her, her brown eyes serious. Calm. Loving. "It's not all about you, Quinn." She started to shimmer.

"Wait! Don't you dare leave—"

But Beth was gone. "Dammit!" Was she hallucinating or had Beth really been there? She stared down at her foot. Her toe was swollen and already turning black and blue. With a sigh, she picked up the shampoo bottle and went back to her shower.

It's not all about you, Quinn . . .

She got out of the shower and left the bathroom to stare at her suitcase, opened on the floor, a haphazard mess. She could shove it all in and close it up and be on the road in five minutes.

"Stop running, Quinn."

She closed her eyes at Beth's voice. "I'm not running. Everything I know is in L.A."

"Not anymore. You wanted off the hamster wheel, you wanted to feel again. So do it."

Quinn opened her eyes and turned to look at the TV.

No Beth.

Quinn was alone in the room, which meant she really was going crazy. Admittedly, not a far trip.

"You're looking to go back to the land of not feeling, because it's easier," Beth said from atop the armoire.

Quinn put a hand to her racing heart. "You're not being helpful." She scrubbed a hand over her face and when she dropped it, Beth was gone.

"Dammit!"

But Beth was right. She *was* running, or thinking of it anyway. Running from the reality that everything she thought she knew of herself was no longer true, running from having a sister who hated her, running from having a pretty severe overreaction with Mick that morning, which—if she was being honest with herself—she was feeling deeply embarrassed about.

Not that it mattered. She'd decreed herself and Mick done.

Just as Tilly had made the same decree about herself and Quinn.

At least the café was open again. And yeah, she was disappointed about how it had gone here in Wildstone, but her life really was in L.A. She couldn't turn her back on her parents simply because they'd made a mistake.

And as if she'd conjured them up, her phone buzzed, an incoming call from her dad.

"How's it going, honey, you on your way home yet?" he asked.

She'd talked to her mom earlier so the urgency in his voice stopped her heart. "No— Is everything okay?"

"So have you checked your oil yet?"

She let out a shaky breath as her chest tightened in a good way now. Her mom showed love with food and gifts. Her dad showed love by caring about her car. "Yes, Dad. The oil's good."

"The fluids?"

They'd already lost one daughter and they were worried they were about to lose their other one too. Which wasn't going to happen. She drew in a deep breath. "All good, Dad," she said, her voice a little thick. "Promise."

"How's Tilly?" her mom asked, clearly standing right next to her dad.

"She's . . ." Hurt, pissy, sullen, and more emo than Quinn had ever managed on a bad day. "Great."

Her mom laughed softly. "People used to ask me how you were at that age and you know what I told them?"

"What?"

"That you were a shithead."

Quinn found a laugh. "I was."

"You were. But I think you were that way because you knew no matter what you did, you had someone to catch you."

Quinn's smile faded. "I know."

"This girl, she doesn't."

"I know that too."

"You'll figure it all out, sweetheart," her mom said. "We have faith in you."

It shouldn't surprise Quinn how much she was learning about herself through this whole thing. Or that she was coming to appreciate her parents more than she ever had before, which was making her realize something else.

She wanted more than what she had with Brock. She wanted what her parents had.

No settling for her. "Mom?"

"Yes?"

"I love you. I love you both."

Now her mom's voice was thick too. "Love you too."

"I love you too," Beth murmured. "Btdubs."

Quinn drew in a deep breath and turned to the armoire.

No Beth.

"Mom? Dad? I've gotta go. I'll call you back later." She disconnected and took a few deep breaths.

Because she got it now, what Beth had been trying to tell her. Whether Tilly wanted to acknowledge her or not was secondary to the fact that Quinn was all Tilly had. Period.

And more than that, running wasn't the answer. This decision was big and it needed to be decided carefully and thoughtfully, with Tilly's best interests at heart, not Quinn's. She needed to give Tilly one more chance to say she wanted or needed Quinn's help, in any capacity.

"Bet you enjoy being right on this one," she muttered to the empty room, and she'd have sworn she heard the soft, musical sound of Beth's pleased laughter.

MICK HATED HOW the morning had gone down with Quinn. Being with her had been the best thing to happen to him in a damn long time and he'd messed that up.

Even worse, he had no idea how to fix it. All he knew was that being here in Wildstone this week was taking a toll on him. He needed to get back to the Bay Area for mental health.

His.

But he couldn't do that until he finished up at his mom's house. To that end, he stopped at the hardware store.

The place was empty as he and Coop walked in.

"Mick Hennessey," came a hoarse old voice. Lonnie Rodriquez, the owner. "Long time no see."

Mick had gone to school with Lonnie's son. "How's Cruz?"

Lonnie shook his head. "Having a hard time. He's been working here at the store, but I can't always afford him. I thought he'd take over when I retire, but there's no business. Might have to close up shop."

This wasn't the first time Mick had heard this complaint. Wildstone's local business owners had been hoping tourism would keep them alive, but nothing was being done to promote the town.

"I saw the new construction going on downtown," Mick said. "A hotel. Are they ordering their building supplies through you?"

Lonnie scoffed. "That job's being done by an outside contractor. So are the two other new construction sites. No one's hired a single local. Things aren't like they used to be, Mick."

Mick didn't think that was necessarily a bad thing, but he did find it odd that the city had accepted bids from outside companies without demanding they at least offer some kind of employment to the depressed town. "Why isn't anyone doing anything about it?"

Lonnie shook his head. "How can we when our own city manager is the one breaking all his promises to local business owners?"

Mick had no love for city manager Tom Nichols, who happened to be Boomer's father. Years ago when Mick and Boomer had been in school together and Boomer had been getting into trouble left and right, Mick had worked his ass off to keep his best friend on the straight and narrow. He'd dragged Boomer's sorry, wasted ass home from parties, forced him out from behind the wheel when he'd wanted to drive, stopped him from doing all sorts of stupid shit whenever he could.

Tom knew this, but he'd always somehow resented Mick's actions instead of appreciating the help, which was proved in their senior year when Boomer had pulled an *especially* stupid prank. He'd gone joyriding in a cop car and gotten caught because his wingman—Mick—had been stuck at home when his dad had refused to let him out that night.

Someone had told on Boomer, and when the cops came to his door, Tom flashed the city manager charm and . . . told the cops it had been Mick to sneak out, not Boomer.

Mick's dad had bought the bullshit story about him sneaking out and had nearly killed him.

So while he was sympathetic to the local business owners for having to deal with a shady city manager, he was also happy to say that the guy was no longer his problem.

He left the hardware store and hit the lumberyard to replace some baseboards in the house, and it was practically a wash and repeat of his experience at the hardware store. Rick Espy, the owner, was angry and worried. Mick wanted to be unaffected but Wildstone was still home to his mom, so on some level he cared whether he wanted to or not.

After, Mick sat in his dad's old truck with Coop's heavy head on his thigh and pulled out his phone to call Colin, a friend and an ex-cop turned private investigator. Mick used Colin's services at work, occasionally hiring him to check into potential problems. "I'm looking at some properties in Wildstone," he said. "Need you to do your thing. Something's going on."

"It's Wildstone," Colin said. "The whole town's insane."

"Something more than the usual insanity. Something financial."

"Great, digging through financials," Colin said dryly. "My favorite."

"You'll feel better when you send me a big, fat bill and you know it."

Now there was a smile in Colin's voice. "Yeah, I do like that part."

Mick disconnected and took the supplies to his mom's. He lifted Coop out first to save the old guy's hips. Then he unloaded the supplies. By the time he was done, he was hot and tired and . . . off.

Always sensing his moods, Coop pressed against him, drooling on his leg. Mick crouched down to hug his big, silly dog and got licked from chin to forehead for his efforts. When Coop slithered boneless to the ground for a full belly rub, Mick of course obeyed, smiling as Coop's tail thumped the dirt like a drum while he writhed in ecstasy. When Mick stopped, Coop took Mick's entire wrist in his soft mouth and gave a tug.

More.

With a low laugh, Mick obliged, watching as a truck made its way up the drive, parking next to his.

Boomer got out and Coop promptly abandoned Mick to welcome the newcomer with a nose to the crotch.

"The goods, man, watch the goods," Boomer chuckled and pushed Coop away before looking at Mick. "Wow," he said. "You're still here. A whole, what, six days in a row? That's some kind of a record, isn't it?"

They hadn't seen each other or spoken since the other night at the Whiskey River, and not for the first time since Boomer and Lena had been on/off/on again, it was awkward between them. "I'm trying to get out of here, believe me," Mick said.

"A certain brunette holding you back?"

"It's got nothing to do with Quinn." At least not anymore. Mick carried the new paint to the garage. Boomer and Coop followed. "It's my mom and this damn money pit of a house," he said. "There's still a lot to do, including painting this nightmare of a garage."

"Hey, I remember that one," Boomer said, pointing to the painted white outline of a missing hammer. "We took it the night of our senior prank. You nearly had a coronary when we lost it, remember? You made us stop and buy a new one, and your dad knew the difference." He laughed. "Christ, we were blockheads back then."

Mick laughed too, and that felt good between them, but Mick's good humor faded as he looked around. "What I remember is my dad having a fit when things didn't get put away in the exact right spot. I can't wait to paint over these outlines."

Boomer shook his head. "Hell, my dad would've thought he'd died and gone to heaven if he'd had a son like you instead of the fucked-up, used-up sometimes mechanic, sometimes bartender he got." He gave Mick a sheepish look. "How many times did you drive my drunk ass home and sneak me into my own bedroom?"

"I didn't keep count." As for Boomer's dad preferring Mick, that was a laugh. He still burned remembering needing a written recommendation to submit to colleges. He'd gone to Tom, a pillar of the community, and been turned down flat.

Something Mick had never told Boomer.

"So if it's not Quinn holding you here, then what?" Boomer asked. "You nostalgic for the old days?"

Mick snorted.

"Hey, we had some good times."

"Name one that didn't end with you in some sort of trouble," Mick said.

"How about that time we both raced that very truck . . ."

Boomer pointed to Mick's dad's truck. "Up at Bliss Flats. We won a hundred bucks."

Mick let out a low laugh. "We got pulled over on the way home because you were waving an open beer out the window. We both nearly got arrested and I wasn't allowed to drive for the rest of the year."

"I drove you wherever you needed to go," Boomer said.

That much was true. But Mick still had no idea why Boomer had stuck around Wildstone and he studied his longtime friend. Boomer had always been lean, but he was almost gaunt now, and looked exhausted. "What's going on with you?"

Boomer shrugged.

When Mick had gone off to college, Boomer had found trouble taking on a couple of side jobs that were a little too far to the left of legal, such as selling prescription drugs like Percocet. That, along with an alcohol addiction, had led to several rehab stints. The latest had been two years ago and as far as Mick knew, he was holding strong. But the fact that he was working as a bartender, along with playing some sort of cat-and-mouse game with Lena—Queen of Eating Men Up and Spitting Them Out—meant he'd set himself up for certain failure. "You okay?"

"Terrific," Boomer said with only a shadow of his former bravado.

Dammit. "And . . . you're sure you know what you're doing?"

Boomer smirked. "I was born knowing what I was doing."

"I meant with Lena, you jackass."

Boomer's smile faded. "Knew we'd get to that." He lifted a hand. "Let's hear it. You still want Lena for yourself, is that it?"

"She cheated on me," Mick said. "With you."

"I was drunk and stupid, and you and I already had this fight—ten years ago."

"I know and I don't care about any of that," Mick said, and he didn't. "I just want to make sure you know what you're doing now. Ten years later."

"Fuck no, I don't know what I'm doing." Boomer let out a mirthless laugh. "I'm keeping my head above water, that's what I'm doing. It's a sink or swim world, and I'm doing my best."

"And Lena's your best?" Mick asked.

Boomer blew out a sigh. "Look, for what it's worth, I love her. But we're not together, we never have been, not in the way you're thinking. And anyway, I told her I couldn't do this anymore, whatever 'this' was, until she settled on just one guy—me."

"And she said?"

"She walked off into the sunset." Boomer shrugged. "Last I saw her was the other night when she was sniffing around you again."

Mick shook his head. "I'm not planning on going there."

Boomer paused. "I think I hear a *but* on the end of that sentence."

"*But* . . . I hope you don't either," Mick said. "And not because I want her, but because you have your sobriety to protect, which you're already straining by working at the bar."

Boomer's eyes shuttered and he stepped back. "Looks like we both have shit to figure out." He headed to his truck.

"Boomer."

Boomer lifted a hand, but still got into his truck and drove off, leaving Mick eating his dust.

QUINN DECIDED THE thing to do was to try to talk to Tilly. She parked behind the café, in front of Carolyn's house. She knew Tilly was staying with a next-door neighbor, but she had no idea which one.

Getting out of the car, her attention was immediately drawn to the house to the right of Carolyn's, where a woman who was dressed like her job might be a stripper came out the front door. In five-inch FMPs she got into a little beater of car, and with a puff of smoke out of the exhaust pipe, ripped down the street and vanished.

Okay, then. Quinn turned to the house to the left of Carolyn's. There were two guys in the yard, no shirts on, fit and tan and gardening. "Hi," one of them called out with a wave. "Can we help you?"

The other one straightened and slid his hand into the first guy's. "You're Quinn."

She sighed and they laughed. "Wildstone takes a while to get used to," one said. "I'm Jared and this is Hutch. We were just rearranging the garden a little bit to make room for some more tomatoes. Carolyn loved them. We're going to miss her, and we're very sorry for your loss."

"Thank you," she said. "It's nice to meet you. I'm looking for Tilly. Have you seen her?"

"Other side," Jared said. "She's staying with Chuck, though she does come over for pizza night. She's a meat lover."

"Like me," Hutch said and smiled. "Jared here is a veggie lover."

Quinn hesitated. "I just saw a woman coming from that house."

"FMPs? Tiny dress? That'll be Kendall," Jared said. "Chuck's renter. She's an exotic dancer."

Quinn turned to Chuck's house and thought she caught a quick peek of Tilly looking out the window. "Thanks," she said and headed over there.

No one answered her knock.

Quinn was back in her car trying to figure out her next move when Chuck's garage door went up and a truck pulled out. An older man sat behind the wheel, with Tilly in the passenger seat. Quinn rushed out of her car and waved at them.

The truck didn't stop.

Quinn ran to the driveway and blocked the truck, gesturing for Tilly to roll down her window.

Tilly rolled her eyes but did it.

"Why aren't you in school?" Quinn asked.

"It's a minimum day. Heading to the racetrack day."

Quinn looked at Chuck, who didn't speak. "Okay," she said to Tilly. "Look me in the eyes and tell me you're good. That you don't want me to stick around for you."

"I'm good," Tilly said without blinking or batting an eye. "I don't want you to stick around for me."

The man said nothing and the second Quinn backed up, they drove off.

Chapter 15

My mom used to say it's easy to love someone when they're at their best, loving them at their worst is the true trick.

—from "The Mixed-Up Files of Tilly Adams's Journal"

It was afternoon by the time Quinn walked into Cliff's office. She found him leaning back against his desk eating the hugest bowl of Cap'n Crunch she'd ever seen. The empty box lay on its side like the dead next to him.

"Life hack," he said. "So your cereal doesn't get stale, you eat the whole box."

She found a laugh but sobered quickly. "As the only sane person I know in this whole godforsaken town, *please* tell me why Tilly is living with Chuck, whose girlfriend is a stripper—excuse me, exotic dancer—and he takes Tilly out of school to go to the racetrack."

Cliff shoved some more cereal in, his eyes hooded. Which was interesting, because though she didn't know him well, she sensed he was honest to the core.

"Look," she said. "It's obvious you have a good idea of what's going on here."

"Carolyn trusted Chuck, enough to know he'd take care of Tilly with or without the compensation she set up from her small estate—"

"*He's being paid?*"

"But I can tell you," he went on, "that he moonlights at the track as a janitor and Tilly helps him sometimes. His mom's in the late stages of Alzheimer's in a nursing home and it's expensive. Also Kendall, the dancer, rents a room at Chuck's. She didn't start out as his girlfriend, although that seems to be changing." He paused. "What you have to understand is that Carolyn trusted Chuck with Tilly. Again, you could consider taking over—"

"She won't have me."

"You're sure about that?"

"One hundred percent." And with nothing to keep her here in Wildstone, it was time to go home.

Tomorrow morning, she told herself. On the off chance that Tilly changed her mind, she would stay until morning before heading out.

THAT NIGHT TILLY was in her "bedroom" at Chuck's house, which was really the laundry room with a futon shoved in it. She had her phone plugged in and was on Hulu with Cliff's password. She had the volume up so she couldn't hear Chuck snoring.

But at least he was sleeping. The poor guy was an insomniac. She'd made him some Sleepytime tea, which he swore helped him. Of course the liberal dollop he added from whatever was in his flask was the real magical element.

Kendall hadn't gone to bed yet; she was in the living room practicing dance moves, making the house shake when she leaped across the floor.

Tilly sighed and tossed and turned some more, stilling at a sudden ping of a rock on her window. Before she could get up, the window slid open and Dylan's long, lanky body climbed in.

Her best friend in the entire world had a fat lip and a black eye.

"I told you to keep this locked," he said. He was pissed.

And hurt.

Tilly drew him down to her bed to take care of him, like she did every time his asshole dad beat on him. She cupped his face, her eyes filling when she saw what had been done to him this time. "I want to kill him," she whispered.

"Shh," he said and closed his eyes. "But if he touches my mom again, I'll kill him myself."

Fear for him made her legs wobble. His dad didn't live with Dylan and his mom, he'd been kicked out of the house several years back and now lived two towns over in Paso Robles. Whenever he came to "visit," aka steal money from Dylan's mom, Dylan did his best to draw his attention away from her.

Brave. And terrifying.

She got up and slinked into the kitchen so Kendall wouldn't hear. Like she'd notice anything anyway with her Beats headphones on as she writhed against the floor.

Tilly grabbed an ice pack, and then on second thought also peanut butter and jelly, and went back to her room.

Dylan hadn't moved.

He was a year older than she was, a grade ahead of her, and on a different planet when it came to life experiences. He ran with a fast crowd and wouldn't let her hang with them.

"You still have a shot at a good life," he always said when she asked. "I'm not going to fuck it up for you."

She sat crossed-legged on the bed at his side and gently laid the ice pack over his eye.

He hissed in a breath and she laid a hand on his chest. He remained still but the steady beat of his heart reassured her. And something else, something that was her own little secret.

Whenever she was close to him like this, she felt warm. Hot, even. And tight, like her skin had shrunk and her body didn't fit inside it.

She sighed, hating this big, fat crush she had on him. If he knew, he'd vanish from her life. She knew it, so she kept her damn infatuation to herself. "Hungry?"

Eyes still closed, his lips curved. "Always."

She laughed a little. This wasn't a lie, the guy was truly always starving, like he was hollow on the inside and nothing could fill him up.

She reached across Dylan for the pack of crackers she had on her nightstand. Her arm brushed his and she felt a tingle make its way through her body. "Here," she said, dipping the cracker first into the peanut butter and then the jelly, and holding it out to him.

He opened his eyes and then smiled. "PB and J for dinner."

"Is there anything better?"

"No." He sat up gingerly enough that she worried he'd been hurt elsewhere as well, but when he saw the look on her face, his eyes went dark. "Don't," he said and took the cracker, shoving the whole thing in his mouth.

"But—"

"Not talking about it, Tee."

They dipped crackers into the peanut butter and jelly until they were both full. Actually, she got full right away but she didn't want him to stop until he was full as well, so she totally overate.

And then had to open the top button on her jeans.

After, Dylan pulled her down with him to the bed again and closed his eyes. She thought that she couldn't think of another place she'd rather be. She wanted them to grow up and still do this, still be like this. She'd be an artist and he'd be . . . "Dylan?" she whispered.

"Yeah?"

"What do you want to be when you get older?"

"Alive."

Her heart pinched. "I mean as a job."

His hand squeezed hers. "It doesn't matter," he said a little dully.

She knew what that meant. He didn't see himself making it out, and that made her so sad that she couldn't speak for a long moment.

As if he knew he'd brought her down, he stirred himself and changed the subject. "Did you finish your biology homework?"

"Shh," she said. "I'm sleeping."

"Tee."

"You can help me tomorrow," she murmured softly, letting herself relax against him, purposely letting him think she was exhausted.

She felt when the tension finally left him and he fell asleep. Only then did she allow her eyes to close. She was comfortable and she should've been thrilled because she never slept as well as she did when he was in her bed. But worry for him kept her up long after he'd drifted off.

Worry for him, and also guilt. She'd been a jerk to Quinn today and she hated that. But she had to get rid of her, had to chase her away. Because one, Quinn would never stay in Wildstone. She was city through and through. So if for some reason, out of guilt, she decided to take on guardianship of Tilly and then left . . .

Well, then Tilly would have to leave Wildstone as well.

And that wasn't going to happen. She didn't know that Chuck could be on his own, even with Kendall around. And then there was Dylan. He needed her. They both did. She had to stay and take care of them, and tightening her arm around Dylan's chest, she snuggled in closer.

Nope, she wasn't leaving. Ever.

NOTHING HAPPENED THAT night. Quinn didn't hear from Tilly. Or Mick.

Or Beth . . .

The next morning she texted Tilly: You need anything, anything at all, you call me. Day or night.

She didn't text Mick. Instead, she packed up and checked out of the Wild West B & B . . . and found him in the parking lot.

He was slouched against her car, arms folded over his strong chest, dark lenses covering his eyes, and just looking at him had all her good spots doing the happy dance.

He was turned away from her, looking at Coop, who was sitting at the base of a huge oak tree, staring up at a squirrel.

The dog gave one low, rough bark.

"No," Mick said. Then more quietly, "We talked about this. Squirrels are not your friend, man. You got beaned in the head last time, remember? Hard enough to rattle half the thoughts right out of your head."

Coop heaved out a sigh and lay down, but he kept his eyes on the prize.

Mick's eyes locked in on Quinn, the expression in them matching Coop's as he kept the squirrel in sight.

Grim determination.

Quinn's feet faltered. What to do? Be a grown-up? Or run like hell? She blew out a breath and walked up to him.

His lips quirked slightly, like maybe he'd sensed her inner civil war. Then he pushed the sunglasses to the top of his head. "Hey," he said.

"Hey yourself," she said. He seemed impossibly large and unyielding. And slightly wary.

Although she'd never tell him so, she thought maybe she liked him best this way, a little worn and rough around the edges.

He was so different from any man she'd ever met.

"So about yesterday," she murmured and then hesitated, biting her lower lip. "I might've overreacted."

"And I might've been a dumbass."

A small smiled escaped her. "Were you waiting for me?" she asked. "Because I thought I was pretty forceful about us being done." She let her voice hold a playful note as she tried to convey that she realized she'd been a complete bitch.

Mick grabbed the ends of her scarf and reeled her in, looking into her eyes. "I should've left things alone, let you go back to L.A. in peace. It would've made things easier."

"But . . . you couldn't do it?" she asked.

"I could." There was no sign of amusement now. "Discipline runs deep, Quinn. And you'd definitely be better off without me. But . . ." He shook his head. "I kept picturing the look on your face yesterday morning. I hurt you, and I couldn't leave it like that."

"Consider it forgotten," she said, and meant it. "No hard feelings."

His phone rang and he ignored it, just staring at her.

"What?" she asked.

"I'm leaving too," he said.

"Oh." She nodded and did her best to shrug off any disappointment. He was going home and she'd be doing the same, and they might not see each other again. "Then I'm glad I got to see you before you left," she said, managing to sound completely fine with this good-bye.

But she wasn't fine. Not even close. "Good-bye, Mick."

Still holding the ends of her scarf, he lowered his head and kissed her. Soft at first, and then with heat and purpose so that she was breathless by the time he pulled back.

And so was he.

"Bye, Quinn," he said quietly, and then he and Coop were gone.

She told herself she was fine with that. Hell, she'd said so many good-byes lately, she was a pro.

Chapter 16

Are you there, God? It's me, what the actual fuck?

—from "The Mixed-Up Files of Tilly Adams's Journal"

It took Quinn two days of being back in L.A. to realize that Beth wasn't going to show up on her TV, or from inside her closet, or anywhere in her condo.

It made her ache deep in her heart.

It took another two days to unpack from Wildstone, but once she did, she realized she still had the Jetpack Mick had loaned her. She scrolled through her contacts to his name and stared at it a moment, her entire body softening as she remembered how she'd felt through the hours of the night they'd spent together in her bed. And her shower. And on the chair . . .

She heard a soft laugh and realized it was her own as something popped into her mind and it was unnerving.

She'd been frustrated over the lack of Internet service in Wildstone and Mick had done something about it for her.

Just because he could.

She stared at the Jetpack, uncomfortably aware of how often things had been handed to her in her narrow world. Her adopted parents had done that for her. Been there. Always and without fail, even after Cliff had shown up and pulled the rug out from beneath all of their feet. In fact, her mom had been helicopter parenting since she'd gotten home, showing up with flowers and soup—the only thing her mom could cook, and by cook she meant heat up—like Quinn had been through an illness.

Smothering was how she showed love, and right now, Quinn would take it.

Because she was lucky. So lucky. Who did Tilly have other than her mom's attorney and a neighbor?

No one but Quinn.

At that thought, she tried calling her again and got sent right to voice mail.

Right.

Message received.

So she texted Mick.

QUINN:

Just found your Jetpack. Oops.

MICK:

Maybe you stole it as an excuse to text me.

QUINN:

You wish.

MICK:

I do wish. I wish hard. Hey, how do you tell the difference between a snowman and a snowwoman?

QUINN:

I don't know, how?

MICK:

Snow balls.

Quinn stared at her screen and found herself laughing out loud. He was ridiculous and she told him so.

And thus began an ongoing texting conversation sharing stupid jokes back and forth, him from the Bay Area and her from L.A. Lots of physical distance, lots of sexy, light texts.

Right up her emotionally stunted alley.

Over the next week they continued in that vein and his stupid jokes became the highlights of her days.

As everything else began to unravel, so did work. It was crazy busy. That was nothing new, and in fact, in many ways she'd always loved that. Preparing food for people in a hot kitchen under pressure and coming through . . . that fueled her.

Being frozen out by Marcel and the staff he'd managed to turn against her in the time she'd been gone, not so much.

"Don't pay any attention to them," Skye said. "They just know that he has Chef Wade's ear, so they're afraid to cross him. Tell me about your men."

"My men?"

"Brock and Mick."

"There's nothing to tell," Quinn said. "They're both past tense."

"I knew Brock was, but Mick too?"

"Yeah."

"Dammit," Skye said. "Did he keep his Tinder app? Play Pokémon in the middle of dinner? Like his car better than you? What?"

Quinn choked out a laugh. "None of those things. I like him. I like him a lot. It's me. I'm not . . . a whole lot of fun."

"That's ridiculous," Skye said. "You're lots of fun. But I get it. I mean, my post-college life's a lot less Beyoncé than I'd planned."

Quinn thought about that and at the end of a particularly insane shift, she finally put her finger on the problem. She hadn't realized just how much she *hadn't* been feeling, but being back in L.A. was like watching a movie of her life, without sound.

In other words, the job was just a job.

Her condo was just a condo.

As for her parents, they were thrilled she was back. Her mom had suggested more than once that she go get Tilly and move her to L.A., that she and her dad would help Quinn raise her.

But Quinn knew Tilly wouldn't be happy here, not the way Quinn was. And truthfully, Quinn loved L.A., she did, but being here felt a little bit like wearing a pair of jeans that no longer quite fit.

Quinn was pragmatic enough to realize she had to forgive herself for moving on the best she could after Beth's death. But it turned out she couldn't forgive herself for something else—walking away from Tilly.

Not that Tilly cared, from all the response she'd gotten to her calls and texts, which made the small, nagging thought that kept popping into Quinn's head all the more ridiculous, but it wouldn't go away.

The thought that kept whispering in her ear that maybe, just maybe, she should be the one watching over Tilly.

As if that would ever happen. Resorting to calling Cliff for intel, Quinn was somewhat reassured by the news that Tilly was the same, bad 'tude and all.

And then there was Brock. He brought Thai takeout one night, which was unusual because he wasn't crazy about Thai.

"You're buttering me up for something," she said, digging in.

The flash of guilt on his face said she'd hit it right on the head and she set down her food. "What?"

"It's a surprise," he said, flashing that smile she'd rarely if ever been able to resist.

"I've had more than a few of those lately." No longer amused, she just looked at him. "What is it, Brock?"

His smile had faded. "I'm sorry. I said that without thinking. Come here."

She resisted, but he pulled her in for a warm hug anyway, and she found herself relaxing into him.

"I just wanted to make sure we were okay," he said. "You've been different since Wildstone." He stroked a hand down her hair. "What's wrong, Quinn?"

She let out a mirthless laugh. "What's wrong? Are you kidding me?"

"You chose to come back," he said. "I figured that meant you'd made peace with it."

"I came back because I wasn't needed in Wildstone, and also because I thought my life was here."

"It is," he said. "You've got a great job that you love in spite of Marcel the Shit, and parents who'd do anything for you."

Except be honest . . .

"And you have me," he said.

She met his gaze.

"You do," he said. "I'd do anything for you, surely the past twenty years have told you that."

"Yes, and I for you," she said.

"Then come with me to London. That's what I wanted to talk to you about. I've got a work trip. I'll be there for two weeks, but we could extend it another week and take some time off."

"London," she repeated.

"You'll love London."

She was sure. But though it had only been a week since she'd been home, she was fighting the urge to go back to Wildstone. She wanted to check on Tilly. She wanted to see if Greta and Trinee were doing okay with the café, or if they needed help.

Brock cupped her face. "Think I lost you there for a beat. Where did you go?"

Wildstone . . . "I just got back, Brock. I need to stay at work, not ask for more time off. Chef Wade isn't super happy with me right now. I'm afraid I'll lose the job."

His eyes dialed into frustrated. "You know you could get your parents to talk to him, they're good friends. They could get you the time off if you wanted."

She stared at him, disappointed that he didn't get it. "I don't want to ask my parents to talk to my boss, Brock. Would *you* do that?"

He grimaced and stood up. "Look, I get it. You got your world rocked. But so did I, Quinn. Beth died and I lost you. I miss you, dammit. I'm no longer important to you."

"Okay, that's not fair," she said quietly. "You're one of the most important people in my life. But it can't always be about you and your schedule. You travel all the time, and I'm supposed to just drop everything if you happen to need a plus one?"

"Yes, that's what we do. Or did."

"You could take the blonde I saw you with on your brother's Instagram," she suggested.

He sighed and looked down at his shoes. She had no idea if he was struggling with the urge to strangle her, or laugh. When he lifted his head, his eyes were smiling but his mouth was serious. "You're still my favorite."

She smiled back, relieved they weren't going to fight. "Good to know."

"Quinn." He stepped close and pulled her into him. Cupping her jaw he brushed his mouth over hers.

She stilled, willing herself to feel something, the shockingly sensual, erotic explosion of lust she'd experienced in Mick's arms, or even just a flash of the long-lost spark she'd once had with Brock.

Neither happened.

He pulled back. "You're not coming to London, are you?"

Her heart squeezed. "No," she whispered.

"Fine. But this isn't over, Quinn. I won't let it be. Go sow your wild oats too, babe. Then we'll regroup."

She could still feel Mick's hard, tough body holding hers down on the bed, moving against her in a way that had driven her crazy, along with his mouth whispering dirty hot nothings in her ear . . .

He hadn't felt like a wild oat.

Brock was looking at her oddly. "Or maybe you've already done so."

She wouldn't lie, but if he wanted answers, she didn't have them. "I don't know what I'm doing."

He hesitated and then he pulled her in and kissed her.

And then he was gone.

The new theme of her life, apparently . . .

THAT NIGHT, TILLY stood at her bedroom window, staring out into the night wishing Dylan would materialize.

He didn't.

But that wasn't what scared her. She hadn't seen him all week.

She'd called and texted until she had a blister on her finger and finally, he'd texted her back.

TILLY, STOP. WE CAN'T BE FRIENDS ANYMORE.

We can't be anything.

Don't call or text me again.

She stared down at her phone in shock and disbelief. Pain sliced through her and she actually had to sink to the floor because her legs wouldn't hold her up.

We can't be friends anymore . . .

She pressed her fist against the ache in her chest. Since when weren't they friends? Something was wrong, she was sure of it, and what told her so, more than his harsh text, was that he hadn't been in school. He was a smart guy and knew his only ticket out of this town was grades, which would hopefully equal a scholarship.

He'd never miss school, not on purpose anyway.

She'd burned the mac and cheese she cooked Chuck for dinner because she was so distracted and worried.

And freaked.

Where was he? Was he okay?

"What's your problem tonight?" Chuck asked.

"No problem. I'm going out," she said.

"Out where?"

She wanted to catch a bus to Paso Robles, where Dylan's dad lived and see if Dylan was there. She had to know if he was okay. "Just to the movies with friends."

"You're in danger of failing science," he said. "Stay home and study to bring your grade up."

She stood up. "I saved my money to go tonight."

"And I said no."

"You're not my mom," she said, and horrified at the words she'd just flung at him, she covered her mouth.

They stared at each other.

Finally Chuck sighed and set his spoon down.

Oh great. He was going to tell her a story, and his stories were long. Days long. But all she could think about was Dylan—not that she could tell Chuck that because he hated Dylan, said he was a bad influence on her.

"Your mom and I," Chuck said slowly. "We . . ."

God. *Please don't tell me about your sex life with my mom . . .*

"I loved her. And you're a part of her, you know?"

Dammit. Dammit, her throat tightened. "Chuck—"

"But this isn't about me, Tilly. It's about you. You need to get back into your schoolwork."

Like she cared about that. Her mom was dead. She was living on a futon. Her best friend in the whole world had vanished . . . "I'm going to the movies, Chuck."

"No way in hell."

She walked away and tried to slam herself into her room but she'd slammed into it one too many times and the doorjamb was warped. The door *couldn't* slam. She had to turn back to even shut it, and then managed to catch her shirt so she had to open it yet again.

Chuck stood there, eyes flashing with temper. "Don't slam my doors."

Compounding her errors—hey, look at her with the big words, take *that* school!—she shut it on his nose.

Then she sat on her bed and waited. It didn't take long. When Chuck got stressed, which was all the time, his choice of an antianxiety med was alcohol. In forty minutes, he would put away a six-pack and be snoring on the couch, louder than the TV.

She watched an episode of *Say Yes to the Dress,* checked her watch, and peeked beyond her door.

Yep, Chuck was out.

Tilly nodded to herself and tiptoed out the front door, stopping to cover him with a blanket first.

Chapter 17

Mom used to tell me not to worry when people didn't get me—people throw rocks at things that shine.

—from "The Mixed-Up Files of Tilly Adams's Journal"

On Saturday night, Quinn walked in on her own surprise party. She blamed herself really. For one thing she'd been trying not to remember today was the day she turned thirty. And for another, she'd forgotten what her mom was up to and she'd been tricky enough to call Quinn at the last minute and ask to borrow her blender.

Quinn tried to be gracious as she made the rounds, tried not to look into the faces of her parents' friends and wonder how many of them knew she'd been adopted. It wasn't healthy, but that didn't stop her. She finally managed to escape to the kitchen, where she went straight to the fridge but . . . no cookie dough.

Damn.

Skye—who moonlighted as a most excellent caterer—came

into the room carrying trays. "Hey, birthday girl. How's it going?" She slapped Quinn's hand from rearranging the serving platters of hors d'oeuvres. "And stop that. You're not working tonight. Where's Brock?"

"London."

"And Mick?" Skye asked. "Anything more from sexy Mick?"

When Quinn didn't answer, Skye bumped her hip to hers. "Oh, come on. I've got zero men and zero prospects. I've gotta live vicariously through your thrilling life with two hot men."

Quinn let out a long breath. "You'd be vastly disappointed to know I've messed everything up."

"Okay, I get that, but you know what? You can also *un*-mess it up."

Quinn nodded and then shook her head.

Skye nodded. "You can, Q."

"It's not that easy."

"Well of course not," Skye said. "Or I'd have two hot men too."

Quinn sighed. "I need outta here."

"Not going to happen. Your mom's got eyes on the exits."

"Please let me help you," Quinn begged. "I desperately need something to do other than think."

Skye looked around them dramatically, like she was about to reveal a state secret. "Okay, listen. I'm going back out there, but I didn't plate the smoked-paprika deviled eggs yet. So if they were to be magically done by the egg fairy while I was gone, I'd be ever so grateful."

Quinn was the grateful one and she jumped on the chance to work alone in the kitchen. She messed around with her plating technique, popped a deviled egg into her mouth, and let Skye's words of wisdom replay in her head.

You can un-mess it up . . .

Skye was right, so she ate another egg, pulled out her phone, and texted Mick.

QUINN:

So what do you do when you're not rescuing crazy women in a B & B?

MICK:

Right now I'm doing some research on purchasing a B & B before it goes under.

QUINN:

Because . . . ?

MICK:

Because it's a cool old building, and also it's rumored there's a really great ghost living there.

QUINN:

You're buying the Wild West B & B?

MICK:

Thinking about it. Now you.

QUINN:

Aren't you supposed to ask what I'm wearing, not what I'm doing?

MICK:

I stand corrected. What are you wearing? In detail, please.

QUINN:

Subject change. Tell me something else about you.

MICK:

I'm wearing a T-shirt and jeans, that's it.

QUINN:

Commando?

MICK:

It's laundry day.

She was laughing when her phone buzzed again, a call this time, just as her mom came into the kitchen.

"Quinn, honey, get off your phone. Come enjoy the party, people are expecting to see you."

But Quinn was looking at her screen. Cliff. Why was Cliff calling?

"Sorry to bother you," he said when she answered, "but we've got a problem. Tilly's run away."

Chapter 18

There are people my age competing at the Olympics and I still try to enter Walmart through the exit-only door.

—from "The Mixed-Up Files of Tilly Adams's Journal"

Quinn's first reaction at Cliff's phone call was guilt. Leaving Wildstone was one thing. But leaving Tilly in a situation she hadn't felt good about was another.

And she'd left anyway.

Try as she might, Quinn couldn't shake the image of the defiant look Tilly had flashed her the last time she'd seen her.

She'd been letting her emotions rule. That's what fifteen-year-olds did.

Quinn should've ignored the bad attitude and stood her ground. Instead she'd thought only of her comfortable, easy life here, where she had people who loved and cared about her and no real difficult decisions to face.

Having no idea how she could possibly help, only knowing that she had to try, she grabbed her purse to head out.

"Where are you going?" her mom asked.

"Tilly's run away. I have to go see if I can help."

"Oh no," her mom breathed. "Have you tried calling her?"

"For days. She's not really on the Quinn train right now."

Her mom nodded. "Teenagers aren't ever on the adulting train."

Quinn met her gaze, remembering all the times she'd freaked out and worried her parents when she'd been fifteen. "I have the sudden urge to say I'm sorry to you. For everything."

Her mom smiled and patted her on the cheek. "And someday Tilly will do the same. But you won't need to hear it because you'll already know she's sorry."

Quinn felt her heart squeeze with love, regret . . . "Mom."

She smiled. "Go. Drive safe, it's late and you've got three hours on the road ahead of you."

"I'll be okay." She wasn't happy with some of the decisions she'd made. She couldn't change that, but she sure as hell could change how she did things going forward. Staying here and letting other people worry about Tilly would add a layer of shame she didn't want to face. It was time to grow up, without the safety net.

Chef Wade came into the kitchen behind her mom, who'd invited him. "What's wrong?" he asked.

"I'm sorry," Quinn said. "I know I just asked for time off but I have to go back to Wildstone."

Wade looked torn. He exchanged a look with her mom before saying, "It's okay, Quinn. It's not a problem."

Quinn hesitated, dividing a glance between them. "Okay, what am I missing?"

"Nothing," her mom said.

Quinn looked at Wade.

Who sighed. "Your mother and I disagree on employee management."

Quinn blinked. "No disrespect intended, but what does it matter what my mom thinks on this subject?"

"Because she and your dad are my silent partners. They own half the restaurant." He looked at Quinn, whose mouth had fallen open in shock. "You didn't know?" He watched as she turned to her mom in shock. "You didn't know," he murmured. "Christ. I'm sorry."

"No," Quinn said with what she hoped was admirable patience. "Don't be sorry. This is something I *should've* known, say back when I clearly got the job because of it." Mortified, and too emotional to even ask if she had any real cooking talent at all, she turned to go.

"Quinn," her mom said.

Quinn whipped back around. Wade had slipped out to give them privacy and her mom stood there wringing her hands. "Are you kidding me?" Quinn asked.

"I didn't know how to tell you."

Quinn tossed up her hands and headed to the door.

"Please don't go like this. We need to talk about it."

"This problem is going to have to get in line," Quinn said grimly and walked out. She went straight to her condo, quickly packed a bag, and then hit the highway.

On a whim, Tilly went to Dylan's mom's house first. When she answered the door, she told Tilly that Dylan had just left.

Tilly's gaze strayed to the woman's fat lip.

"Not Dylan's doing," she said softly, tears in her voice.

Which meant that Dylan's dad had been here and there'd been another fight. Tilly froze, remembering what Dylan had promised the last time—that he'd kill the guy if he laid another finger on his mom.

Panic nearly choked her.

Ten minutes later she was on a bus heading toward Dylan's dad's house, the address written on a piece of paper clutched in her hand. Half an hour later, she stood in front of a small ranch house. It was run-down, but there was a lot of acreage. She could smell cattle and heard mooing off in the distance.

The house wasn't close to any others, which didn't feel like a good thing. She could hear yelling from inside, and then the sounds of something crashing and breaking, and she ran to the front door.

It was locked.

Heart racing, she pounded on it. "Dylan!"

No answer. But she could still hear shouting inside, so she hurried around the side of the house to the back. There was a patio and a slider, which slid right open under her hand. She stepped into a living room, lit only by the spill of lights from a bedroom down the hall, from which the sounds of a fight drew her.

Heart lodged in her throat, she looked around for something to protect herself with. Nothing. She glanced down at her hands and realized she was still clutching the soda bottle she'd bought while waiting for her bus.

The hallway ended all too fast and then she stood in the doorway of a bedroom. Dylan was in the corner, down like he'd just fallen, blood coming from his nose and mouth, one eye swollen nearly shut, shirt ripped, watching a man twice his size come at him.

Chapter 19

Having plans sounds like a good idea—until you have to put on clothes and leave your house.

—from "The Mixed-Up Files of Tilly Adams's Journal"

It was midnight by the time Quinn arrived in Wildstone. The café was closed, but by some miracle, Greta and Trinee were inside, planning menus for the following week. They were relieved to see her. Cliff had called them looking for Tilly, and unable to sleep, they'd come here.

"Neither of us has seen her for several days," Greta said worriedly.

Not good.

Quinn tried Chuck's house next. He took a while to answer the door and when he did, he looked sheepish and upset.

"I have no idea where she went," he said. "She told me she wanted to go to the movies and I said no way. I feel asleep on the couch and when I woke up, she was gone."

"And she wasn't at the movies?"

"No," he said. "When I woke up and found her gone, I went to the movie theater. She wasn't there."

"Where else would she go?" she asked.

He shrugged. "She's a good kid. She's never done anything like this."

"She was staying with you by choice," Quinn said. "Why would she leave?"

His gaze skittered away. "I don't know."

Quinn didn't believe him, but there was nothing she could do about that. She left and went to Cliff's office, somehow not surprised to see him through the window, at his desk, head bent to his laptop, thick-rimmed glasses slipping down his nose as he pecked at the keyboard. When she knocked at the locked door, he pushed his glasses back high on his nose and came to the door.

"Quinn," he said in his usual unflappable manner. "You drove up. And quickly." He gestured her in. "Can I get you anything?"

"An arrest warrant for Chuck."

Okay, *that* flapped him. "For what?"

"For being a dumbass who didn't keep track of my sister."

They stared at each other, Cliff thinking God knew what, Quinn a little shocked at the emotions barreling through her. "What are my rights when it comes to Tilly?" she asked.

"None," Cliff said. "Unless you were to take guardianship. Which, honestly, I think Chuck would be fine with."

Was she ready for that step? Hell no, but that wasn't what stopped her. What did was Tilly and *her* wishes.

The kid had lived fifteen years without knowing of Quinn's existence. Her dad had long ago walked, she'd lost her mom, she'd had to move in with a neighbor and in the process had lost a good part of her childhood to circumstances. Quinn refused to force her into a guardianship she wouldn't want. "I can't," she said quietly.

Cliff looked at her for a long beat and then turned to his drawer, pulling out a sealed envelope. "It's a letter from Carolyn."

"To me?"

"Yes."

"Why now?" Quinn asked, taking the envelope but not opening it.

"It was your mom's instructions to give this to you if you showed no interest in staying here in Wildstone to form a relationship with Tilly."

Quinn stared down at the envelope, irritation overcoming her. This felt an awful lot like manipulation, and she'd had just about enough of that for a lifetime, thank you very much. She shoved the envelope in her purse for later. "We need to call the police."

"Already done," Cliff said. "Our local sheriff knows the situation and he's got an eye out. But at the moment, it appears that she told her caretaker she was going to the movies, and being that she's fifteen, probably ended up at a party she wasn't supposed to attend. Teens are prone to meltdowns, Tilly included, so as hard as it is to hear this, no one is especially alarmed. Especially since she's only been missing a matter of hours."

Quinn drove to the B & B and checked in. She could've stayed at Carolyn's house, but she didn't feel right about doing that without Tilly's permission, as it was far more her house than Quinn's.

By this time it was one in the morning and, stick a fork in her, she was done. A few hours of sleep, she told herself, and then she'd get back out there and retrace Tilly's steps.

But instead of undressing and climbing in bed, she stood in the middle of the room feeling helpless. Feeling horribly out of her depth and out of her comfort zone. Hell, she thought, thinking about how she was still stinging from discovering her parents owned half the restaurant where she worked, she didn't even know what her comfort zone was anymore.

"It's me," Beth said. Clear as day. "I'm your comfort zone." She was back on the TV, this time in Quinn's favorite sandals, eating a bowl of ice cream.

"Where've you been?" Quinn demanded. "I kept waiting for you to come visit when I was home in L.A."

Beth just smiled and ate her ice cream.

"The least you could've done was bring some for me."

"Maybe next time." Beth's mouth was curved, but her eyes were serious. "You're okay, you know."

"Am I? Because I'm talking to my dead sister in the middle of the night."

There was a knock at her door and Quinn nearly jumped out of her own skin. She glanced back at Beth, but she was gone. Shaking her head at herself, she looked through the peephole.

Mick held up a brown bag that smelled amazing. "Food," he said. "And—"

And nothing because she yanked the door open and walked right into his arms, never more happy to see anyone in her life.

"Is this because I brought you food?" he asked, setting the food down and pulling her in close, wrapping her up in his warm, strong grip that felt like her only anchor in a world gone crazy. "Yes," she said and burrowed in, desperate for comfort, which he offered in spades.

With a low, wordless murmur of reassurance, he nudged them both inside, kicked the door shut and locked it, all without losing contact. "Who were you talking to?"

She lifted her head and looked at him. "You heard voices?"

"Just yours."

She sighed. "I was talking to Beth."

He gave her a long once-over but didn't tell her that was ridiculous. "Any word on Tilly?"

"No. How did you hear?"

"It's Wildstone," he said. "The Twitter account sends out texts from the police scans. It's almost always about a drunken brawl or a bunch of deer eating someone's crops. But tonight it was about Tilly."

Quinn thought of how in L.A. a missing teen wouldn't even have caused anyone to blink. Chalk one up on the pro column for Wildstone . . . Then she blinked. "So you saw it and drove down from the Bay Area?"

He lifted a shoulder. "Thought you might need some help."

"You knew I'd come."

"Of course."

Of course. She let out a low laugh. Seemed he knew her even better than she knew herself.

"You should eat," he said, mouth against hers. "You need—"

"*This*," she said. Turned out adrenaline and fear could be its own kind of foreplay, and this was one of those times. "I need you."

When he opened his mouth to speak, probably to gently push her away, she put her fingers over his mouth. "It's my birthday," she admitted. "Or was until an hour ago. I want you to be my present."

Their gazes met. He hadn't shaved that morning, maybe not the morning before either, and there was a darkness to his gaze that suggested she wasn't the only one spiraling.

But he shed his sweatshirt and boots without another word and helped her do the same. Then he stripped the rest of his clothing off, making her realize three things. One, he wasn't remotely shy about being naked. Two, he had no reason to be. And three, he still took her breath away.

She must have made some sort of sound of approval because he smiled and then divested her of the rest of her clothing as well. And then he tumbled her to the bed.

She snuggled in close, trying to climb him like a tree, desperate for the contact. His arms closed hard around her as a groan rumbled up from deep in his throat. "Missed this, Quinn. Missed you." Then he rolled her to her back and kissed her until she clung to him before working his way down her body, down every single inch, so that by the time he got to her personal favorite inch, she was more than halfway gone. He easily nudged her over, and then after protecting them both with a condom, sank into her, taking her outside herself, to a place where there was nothing but this. Him.

Them.

In hindsight, Tilly would've said she wasn't good in an emergency of any sort. She tended to panic first, think later. And in a way, that's just what she did at Dylan's dad's house. She panicked. Didn't think. And hit the man over the head with her glass soda bottle.

He went down like a sack of rocks.

"Dylan," she said on a sob as her legs finally gave way. "Oh my God." Her vision wavered.

When she blinked the cobwebs clear, she was outside, Dylan tugging her down the street. A hundred yards from the house, he finally stopped.

Trembling all over, she sank to the wild grass. Dylan did too, on his knees in front of her, still bleeding and looking pissed.

"I told you to stay away," he said grimly. "I told you I didn't need you or your help."

"But you did need me," she said and reached out to touch the cut over his eye.

He flinched away. "How did you get here?"

"Bus."

"Christ," he muttered and swiped his arm over his bleeding lip. "You're going to have to go back the same way, and do it now in case anyone calls the cops."

"Dylan—"

"Now, Tilly. Go now."

"Why?" She gasped and covered her mouth. "Omigod. Did I kill him?"

"No." He pulled her up to her feet and gave her a little push. "You were never here, got it?"

"But . . ."

"No, Tilly, for once in your fucking life, listen. I know you have a crush on me, but I'm wrong for you. All wrong. And I'm always going to be wrong for you." His gaze was fiercely intense, and scared her.

She shook her head vehemently. "Dylan—"

"I'm seeing someone else, Tilly, okay? I'm going to handle this, but you've got to go and don't look back." He turned her away from him and gave her another push. "You don't know me and I don't know you. We're not friends anymore. And remember, *you were never here*."

Her heart had stopped. Just stopped as his words messed with her head. *Seeing someone else . . . They weren't friends anymore . . .*

Fear and hurt filled her, consumed her. She couldn't leave

him. "I can't, Dylan. I can't just leave you to take the blame—" She whirled back to him—but he was gone.

Having no idea what to do or who to call, she pulled out her phone and stared at it.

You need anything, anything at all, you call me. Day or night.

Tilly let out a shaky breath and hoped that Quinn had meant it as she hit her number.

She didn't know what she expected to happen. She'd ignored all of Quinn's calls and texts, not to mention Quinn was still in L.A., a lifetime and a galaxy away from here—

"Tilly," Quinn answered, sounding worried and yet somehow relieved at the same time. "Are you all right?"

Was she? She thought about the one time she'd asked Quinn that and she'd said, "Always." It had stuck with her, that dogged determination, and even, she could admit, impressed her. "Always," she tried to say but nothing came out.

"Tilly?" Quinn's voice was tight. "You there?"

"Yes."

"*Are you all right?*"

"Always," Tilly whispered.

"You don't sound all right. Talk to me."

Where did she start? Her mom had died. She'd had to leave the only home she'd ever known. Dylan, who was supposed to be her best friend, had pushed her out of his life and she had no one left to turn to. A sob escaped and she put her hand over her mouth to keep the next one in.

"Where are you?" Quinn demanded quietly.

"Paso Robles," Tilly said. "I . . . need you."

"I'm twenty minutes away, getting into my car now. Are you safe?"

"How are you going to get here in twenty minutes?" Tilly asked, confused. "A spaceship?"

"When you turned up missing, Cliff called me. I drove up to Wildstone."

Tilly was stunned at the realization that her sister had done such a thing.

Stunned and . . . grateful beyond measure.

"Are you safe?" Quinn repeated, and Tilly could hear a car door slam and an engine kick over.

Quinn, backing up her promises with actions . . . "I think so."

"Good. Stay that way."

Chapter 20

Becoming an adult is a lot like when you're trying to get one ice cube from a cup into your mouth and they all fall on your face.

—from "The Mixed-Up Files of Tilly Adams's Journal"

Mick drove, for which Quinn was grateful. By the time they got to Paso Robles, Tilly had walked the few blocks to a convenience store and was sitting on the curb, looking pissed off.

Quinn jumped out of Mick's truck and ran to her, looking her over carefully. No outward injuries, none that were obvious anyway. She stepped into the girl to pull her in close in a hug, but Tilly took a big step back.

"I changed my mind about needing a ride," she said, apparently having found her bad 'tude.

Or maybe she'd been alone just long enough to realize she was in trouble and didn't want to explain it. "What happened?" Quinn asked.

"Long story." Tilly turned to walk away but Quinn caught her hand.

And held on when Tilly tried to tug free. "Let me go."

"Soon as you tell me what the hell is going on."

"Nothing's going on! I don't need you!"

"Tilly, it's two in the morning. You've been missing for hours."

"Like anyone cares."

"*I* care," Quinn said. From the corner of her eye she could see that Mick had parked the truck and gotten out. He was leaning back against it, giving them privacy but watching closely.

"Is there a problem here?" This was asked by the store clerk, who'd poked his head out of the store. "What's going on?"

"This woman is stalking me," Tilly said, jabbing a finger at Quinn.

The store clerk pulled out his cell phone. "I'm calling the cops."

"*No!*" both Tilly and Quinn said in unison.

Look at that, the first thing they'd ever agreed on.

"I'm her sister," Quinn told the guy. "And her legal guardian. We're just having a family disagreement."

The clerk looked reluctant to believe her.

Tilly looked stunned.

"I can give you the name and number of our attorney," Quinn said. "You can call and verify this with him."

The guy looked at Tilly. "Is this true?"

Quinn held her breath, because it *was* true—well, except for the legal guardian thing. But to her shock, Tilly didn't call her out. Instead, she nodded.

"It's true," she said.

Looking annoyed, the clerk went back inside.

They got into Mick's truck. Mick got in as well, not saying

anything, for which Quinn was hugely grateful. She called Cliff. "I've got her safe and sound," she said.

"Bring her here," Cliff said. "To my office. We can talk and make our next move."

"It's the middle of the night," Quinn said.

"You've got a better idea?"

Good point. "We'll be there." She disconnected and turned to Tilly. "What brought you to Paso Robles?"

"A friend," Tilly said. "He was in trouble."

"He?"

"Dylan." She closed her eyes, looking so much younger than her fifteen years all of a sudden. "My best friend. But he walked away from me and just left me there."

Quinn's heart split in two. Just cracked wide open and exposed itself. "I'm sorry," she said softly.

"He's been pushing me away, acting mean, but I thought it was because of all he was going through."

"If it has tires or testicles, it's gonna give you trouble," Quinn said without thinking, repeating Skye's favorite mantra.

Mick's eyebrows shot up an inch.

Tilly looked at her as well. "Please never say testicles again." She paused. "And you lied to that clerk. You're not my legal guardian. Which I'm glad about, 'cause maybe I don't want to live with you either."

"Maybe?" Quinn asked. "I thought it was a *for sure* you don't want to live with me." She liked the maybe. It meant there was a chance . . .

"Whatever," Tilly said, and worked at trying to swipe away some of the makeup that had pooled beneath her eyes, giving her a raccoon look. She'd worn a lot of makeup tonight, unlike any other time Quinn had seen her.

"I never saw Carolyn wear any makeup," Quinn said. "Did she mind when you did?"

Tilly stopped running her fingers beneath her eyes and stared at her. "You saw our mom what, once?"

The barb stung, but she'd just referred to Carolyn as "our mom," so Quinn let it go. "To be clear, you're saying you didn't run away, you were just going after your friend Dylan?"

Tilly hesitated a beat too long, a look of vulnerability flashing on her face before she morphed back into the tough-girl act, which haunted Quinn.

"Tilly," she said gently. "I thought you were happy at Chuck's."

"I was happy before my mom died."

Quinn's heart squeezed and she started to speak, but Tilly cut her off. "Don't even try to tell me that time heals all wounds," she said, arms crossed tightly over her skinny form, face turned to the window now. "Because people who say that are full of shit."

Something else they agreed on. Look at that. "I get that," she said.

"How could you? You've never been in my shoes. You've never had—literally—no one and nothing to your name. You've got a fancy car, a fancy job, and probably a fancy boyfriend too."

Quinn, exhausted after the scene at her parents' house, the long drive, the worry and fear for the teenager who hated her, felt something snap inside her head. "You really think you're the only one who's ever been hurt or disappointed?"

"The only one in this truck at least."

Quinn stared at her in disbelief. "Hello, dead sister, remember? And Carolyn gave me away at birth, like yesterday's trash. So please, say again that you're the only one hurting here."

Tilly blinked, like maybe she was possibly looking at it from

Quinn's perspective for the first time, and then retreated into silence.

At the moment, Quinn would take it.

Mick drove them straight to Cliff's office. Quinn was surprised to see Chuck waiting in the reception area as well, face pressed to the window, looking out into the night.

When they walked in the office, Chuck moved past Quinn, exchanging a look with her that she couldn't translate, and went straight to Tilly. "You okay?" he asked.

Tilly, staring at her shoes, nodded.

He let out a shaky breath. "Good. But Christ, Tilly. You can't just sneak out like that. You just can't." He put a hand on his chest. "My ticker can't take it."

"I expected to be back before you woke up," Tilly muttered. "I didn't mean to worry you."

More words than she'd ever managed to string together for Quinn and she watched them, wondering at their relationship. The clear concern, and even affection, in Chuck's voice surprised her.

"What's that shit all on your face?" he asked.

Tilly huffed out a sigh and glanced at Quinn. "Nothing."

"Bullshit. It's makeup. Your mom didn't allow you to do that, why would you think I would?"

Score another point for the man, Quinn thought, starting to look at him in a whole new light.

"Okay," Cliff said. "Let's get to the heart of the matter. Have plans changed for Tilly's guardianship?"

Feeling reluctant to discuss this in front of Tilly, Quinn turned to the girl. "Can you give us a minute?"

"Why? So you can admit to Cliff that you lied about being my legal guardian to the store clerk tonight?"

Cliff looked at Quinn.

"She wasn't exactly planning to come peacefully," Quinn said.

"So she *lied*," Tilly said again. "And used swear words too. Pretty sure if the question is who's qualified to be my guardian, a judge might frown upon those things."

"I'm your only relative willing to step up," Quinn said.

Tilly took a peek at Chuck.

He shrugged.

"Okay, what?" Quinn asked. "What's going on that I don't know about?"

"Chuck's my uncle," Tilly said. Paused. "Kinda."

Both Cliff and Quinn turned to Chuck in unison.

He lifted his hands. "Carolyn sometimes called me that because I was around when the kid was little. A lot. You all know we . . ." He glanced at Tilly and grimaced. "Look, go wait outside, would ya?"

Tilly crossed her arms.

"Now," Chuck said.

Tilly narrowed her eyes, but huffed out a breath and headed to the door.

"And don't vanish again or I'll take your damn phone!"

Tilly slammed the door behind her.

"We've been over this, you and I," Chuck said to Cliff and then turned to Quinn. "Carolyn and I go way back. To before your good-for-nothing, dickheaded, self-centered prick of a father came along. She chose him and I forgave her." He paused. "Twice. But the fact is that she trusted me with Tilly. Temporarily."

"Temporarily?" Quinn asked.

"I never wanted kids and she knew that. I still don't want kids, and she knew that too. But in this case, she didn't have a choice.

There was no one else to watch over Tilly. And we've done fine. Better than fine. I'm happy to take care of her."

"I can take care of myself!" Tilly yelled through the door. "I don't need anyone to do it! Especially *her*, since she ran away back to L.A. after the thought of being my guardian traumatized her so deeply!"

The *her* in question took umbrage at this. "I left because you'd made it clear you weren't interested," Quinn yelled at the door and took a deep breath. She was incredibly aware of Mick quietly standing there, listening to all of this, which should have embarrassed her but instead, she felt his strength and calm and took some of it in for herself. "And also because I was scared," she admitted to Tilly. Hell, holding back from the girl was only making things worse. Might as well lay it all on the line.

"Maybe if we all just calm down," Cliff said.

"I am calm!" Tilly yelled.

"A hint about women," Mick said to Cliff. "Never in the history of all history has telling a woman to calm down ever calmed one down."

"And *that's* sexist!" Tilly said through the door.

"She's right," Quinn said, and blew out a sigh. There was really only one thing to do here and she knew it. The thing was, she might be a complete hot mess at the moment but she wasn't, and never had been, selfish. Beth was gone and there was nothing she could do about that.

But Tilly wasn't gone. She was right here, scared, alone, and pissy as hell.

And Quinn wanted, *needed* to do the right thing for her, even if that meant putting her L.A. life on hold, including jeopardizing the job she'd thought she'd loved above all else. "How about a trial period?" she asked, thinking that it might actually reassure Tilly if nothing was set in stone.

Cliff nodded his approval and opened the door.

Tilly, who'd had her ear to the door, nearly fell in.

Chuck snorted.

"What do you think of a trial period?" Cliff asked Tilly.

Tilly slid Quinn a dark look. "So she can decide she doesn't like me and then throw me out?"

"No," Quinn said quietly. "I don't throw people away."

Tilly stilled, staring at Quinn some more. Somber, and for once free of the cynicism she wore like a suit of armor. "For how long?"

"As long as you need."

Quinn felt Mick look at her in surprise, which she got. Only a week ago, she'd run away from here. Now she was offering to stay, temporarily anyway.

"Listen, it's late," Cliff said gently. "Or early, however you want to look at it." He looked at Tilly. "Since all of your stuff is already with Chuck, I don't see a need to move you to the B and B and then back to Carolyn's house, so how about you go home with Chuck for tonight. You get some sleep, wake up, and give you and her a shot." He looked at everyone. "Acceptable?"

Quinn nodded.

Chuck nodded.

Tilly didn't move.

Cliff put a hand on her shoulder. "Your call, Tilly. Your say."

"You can think about it," Quinn said. "If you want."

Tilly's gaze met hers. "Yeah. Okay. I'll think about it."

Quinn held out her pinkie. "Pinkie promise?"

Tilly rolled her eyes. "What is this, the nineties?" But she wrapped her pinkie in Quinn's—their first physical contact—and shook on it.

And that was that. Tilly left with Chuck. Quinn walked out into the night with Mick. He took her hand and pulled her in against him.

"Proud of you," he said.

Her throat tightened up and her eyes burned at the quietly spoken words that were like a balm to her churning gut.

Chapter 21

How am I supposed to make big decisions when I still have to sing the alphabet to myself to alphabetize stuff?

—from "The Mixed-Up Files of Tilly Adams's Journal"

Quinn walked through the café the next morning, still on the phone with her parents. They'd wanted to make sure she'd found Tilly, and then her mom had wanted to make sure Quinn understood the choices they'd made.

"It's not that we thought you couldn't get your own job, Quinn," her mom said. "It was nothing like that. We just wanted you to have the world."

Quinn rubbed the ache between her eyeballs. "I get it, Mom."

"So you're not mad anymore?"

"Are there any more surprises?"

"No," her mom said emphatically. "Promise."

Quinn sighed. "I'm not mad." She wasn't sure what she was. "But I'm at the café, I've gotta go."

"We love you," her mom said.

"Check your oil," her dad said.

Quinn choked out a laugh and disconnected, and as had become habit, she took a moment to look at the wall of pictures before she was discovered and hugged half to death by Trinee and Greta.

"I'm not going out to get you eggs, if that's what you're buttering me up for," Quinn said.

Greta snorted. "Still cynical as ever. Maybe we're just happy you've come back, City Girl, and proud of you for getting Tilly back safe and sound."

Was she cynical? she wondered as she took over cooking for Greta. She'd never thought about it before, but she supposed in a lot of ways, she was indeed very cynical.

Thirty minutes later, Trinee came into the kitchen looking harried. "People are complaining the food's coming out too slow. And they want to know why your pancakes are so flat."

Quinn gritted her teeth. She'd been whipping through batches of crepes, which Trinee had put up on the chalkboard out front as their surprise special. "Because they're not pancakes. They're crepes—as it says on the board."

"I told you that we're not fancy like that here," Greta said.

"Crepes don't have to be fancy."

Greta didn't look convinced. "Maybe you could just make them faster."

"Trying." And she was. But the truth was, she—they—needed help. "We need to put out an ad for another short-order cook."

Greta looked at her like Quinn had just asked her to stand on the highway, naked, holding one of those silly arrow signs.

Big Hank stuck his head into the kitchen. "Hey," he said to Quinn. "Nice job on the pancakes, but you could use a little more flour, I think."

She resisted smacking herself in the forehead with her spatula. "They're *crepes*."

"Carolyn used to put chocolate chip smiley faces on her pancakes," he said hopefully. "Did you know that?"

"I've heard that once or twice," she said dryly. Or a hundred times . . . "We were going for something a little healthier."

Trinee lifted her hands and shook her head as if to say not me . . .

Quinn rolled her eyes. "Fine. Tomorrow I'll . . ." She managed not to grind her teeth. "Use more flour and chocolate chips."

Big Hank beamed. "Atta girl."

Five minutes later, Lou popped his head in. "You going to cook every morning?" he asked hopefully.

"Do you like my cooking?" Quinn asked, surprised.

He held up his phone. "I just want to catch the firefighters coming in hot. I missed getting a video of it last time."

Trinee smacked him upside the head.

"Not funny yet?" he asked.

"Maybe next week," Trinee said.

Lou just winked at her. "Oh, and I wanted to tell you," he said to Quinn. "Big Hank told his doctor what you mentioned about his low energy maybe being an iron deficiency, and his doctor agreed. So now Not-Big-Hank wants you to come out to our table and tell him what's wrong with him too."

"Why?" she asked. "What's wrong with him?"

"Well . . ." Lou scratched his head and grimaced. "Let's put it this way. He can get to the batter box and swing, but he can't, er . . . make it home."

Quinn stared at him. "Tell me you're actually referring to baseball."

He grinned. "Can you come tell him what's wrong or what?"

"I can tell you what's wrong with *me*," she said. "And that's the fact that I now need therapy."

"Carolyn used to listen to our woes all day long," he said. "And she was good at the advice too."

"Yeah?" Quinn asked. "And what would she have told Not-Big-Hank?"

Lou laughed. "That if he was a few decades younger, she'd have taken him for a test drive to see what was wrong under his hood, if you know what I'm saying."

"Lou, I wish to God I *didn't* know what you were saying."

Greta and Trinee were cackling like hens by the time Lou went back to his table. "You think this is funny?" she asked.

"Honey," Trinee said. "Let's just say that the apple didn't fall far from the tree, and that we're blessed as blessed can be having you here."

Quinn's irritation immediately fled at the unexpected compliment and she realized something. It had been a rough few days, and she was still as messed up and confused inside as ever but . . .

No matter what went wrong here, everyone seemed to find a way to laugh about it. It was so different from what she had at Amuse-Bouche that it was like landing on another planet altogether.

What remained to be seen was how she felt about it.

Chuck came in to grab breakfast and popped his head into the kitchen. "So," he said.

"So." Quinn managed a smile. "How's our girl doing?"

"Okay, I think." He ran a hand over his head. A gesture that gave away his discomfort. "Look, we both know I'm not the greatest at this but I'm not going to turn her away if she wants to stay. Carolyn . . ." He stared at his shoes for a minute. "She meant a lot to me," he eventually said. "So if you've come around to wanting to keep Tilly, that's going to be up to you to coax her."

"I understand. I'm . . ." She shrugged with a little laugh. "Working on it. She's not easily . . . coaxable."

"Well, she is her mother's daughter." He let out a small smile. "Seems maybe you are too."

And then he was gone.

"You and Tilly are going to live together?" Trinee asked.

"For a trial period."

The two older women exchanged a long glance. "Told you," Greta said.

"What?" Quinn asked.

"Trinee owes me a hundred bucks," Greta said.

Quinn stared at them. "You had a bet on whether or not Tilly and I would forge a relationship?"

"No," Greta said. "We bet on which of us was right."

"Which is almost always me," Trinee said proudly.

"Ha," Greta said. "*Wrong . . .*"

An hour later, Quinn was relieved by Greta when things slowed down. She left the café, walking past the henhouse to stand in Carolyn's yard staring at the house.

This was it. Tilly's childhood home. Knowing that she and Tilly were going to give themselves a trial run here for a few days filled her with equal parts hope and terror.

She moved to the porch. The sun was slanting across the wood slats and Quinn sat on a bench next to the front door, tilting her head back for a long moment, letting the sun warm her.

Then she inhaled a deep breath and pulled Carolyn's letter from her pocket. She hadn't opened it yet, but it was time.

My darling Quinn,

I was so proud and overjoyed the first time I met you in the coffee bar. It was like all my prayers had been an-

swered to find you everything I'd hoped you'd be. You're generous and kind, smart and funny, and you took my breath away.

I know I have no right to say anything to you at all after all this time, but I want you to know I didn't give you up lightly, and I never stopped thinking of you. Never. Chalk up what happened to me being too young, too scared, and far too alone. I didn't have parental support and your dad, God bless him, loved the open road more than air itself.

Excuses, all of it. If I'd been stronger, or had the means to support you, things would have been different but that's no comfort now, I get that. I should have told you who I was when I first started talking to you. I get that too. It was hard not to, believe me. But there was so much more at stake than my own selfish happiness. I'd hoped for many more chats between us, but if you're reading this now, it means that's not meant to be. I'm sorry about that. But the timing needed to be right before I told you that you have a sister. I wanted to tell you that she's smart and kind like you, that she has a sassy mouth on her, but a heart as big as the moon. You don't know Tilly yet, but I hope you'll come to love her as I have loved both of you, and show her how to become beautiful in mind and spirit, just like her big sister.

I understand I have no right to ask this of you, but I'm asking anyway. Please. Please, Quinn, can you find it in your heart to be there for Tilly? She'll be angry and afraid, and she'll need you. I need you.

Love you, Quinn. Always have and always will.

Quinn set the letter in her lap and let her head fall back again, feeling the tears on her cheeks. She hadn't expected Carolyn's emotions to affect hers. Maybe it was her clear joy and pride over who Quinn had grown up to become, maybe it was the simple but powerful sense of sorrow and loss in the words, or the suspicious smudge spots on the paper that might've come from tears, she didn't know.

What she did know was that Carolyn had had a plan. Cancer had ruined that plan and taken her too soon.

Beth had had a plan too. A full life plan that involved mountain climbing and a guy to love her and babies . . . and most certainly not dying before she could fulfill all that. If she'd left Quinn a letter making a request of her, any request at all, Quinn would've done whatever she asked, or died trying.

So why was she hesitating to do this?

"You okay?"

She opened her eyes and found Mick standing there on the porch. "Yes."

Mick studied her and then set two cups down on the railing and crouched in front of her, putting a hand on her thigh. The touch grounded her as nothing else had. Slowly he reached up with his other hand, cupping her face, using the pad of his thumb to wipe away a tear she'd missed.

He'd gone back to the B & B with her last night. Or this morning, rather. He'd tucked her into bed, pulled her against his chest and had said, "Get some sleep," and she had.

He'd been gone when she'd woken up.

He handed her one of the cups and she took a sip, smiling at the first taste of the hot, strong coffee. "Not decaf," she said. "I could love you for that alone." Leaning in, she kissed him softly.

"That's for coming by to check on me." She kissed him again. Not as softly. "And that's for the caffeine."

"Remind me to bring you coffee every morning." He rose and pulled her to her feet. "You're going in?"

She looked at the house. "I'm going in." She took a deep breath. "I want to make sure there're no unhappy surprises in there for Tilly when she shows up."

"Want company?"

She'd expected to have to do this alone so she was pathetically grateful for his offer, because *not* alone would be so much better. "I already dragged you here from the Bay Area. Don't you have to work?"

"It can wait."

The house was small. Small kitchen, small living room, small bathrooms, all outdated but clean and neat. Better yet, there were no visible bugs and no dripping sinks, which meant it was a big step up from the B & B.

It was obvious which room was Tilly's and which had been Carolyn's. Tilly's room looked like a cyclone had gone through it. The floor was completely hidden beneath discarded clothing and God knew what else. The bed was unmade, the dresser drawers opened with clothes half in and half out.

In contrast, Carolyn's was neat as a pin and Quinn looked around with mixed feelings at the light oak furniture and white bedding and curtains. It suited the simple, smiling woman she'd last seen a month ago now, and brought back a few fond memories of laughing with her at the coffee shop.

The third room was smaller than Quinn's condo's walk-in closet and filled with sewing and boxes of craft stuff.

No bed.

Quinn figured she could clear out the room a little and sleep in here, maybe move some of the stuff to the attic, but she stopped herself midthought.

Moving in was temporary.

Very temporary.

She'd sleep on the couch for now. And if Tilly decided she wanted to have Quinn take on guardianship, they'd go to L.A. as soon as she could get Tilly to make that move.

Back in the kitchen, Quinn took in the table and mismatched chairs, the hanging pots and pans, the fridge dotted with magnets, the open cabinets filled with a variety of pottery dishes and jars for drinking glasses . . . and found herself aching. The sun beamed in through the window, casting the room in a golden glow, and she could easily picture Carolyn standing right here where Quinn stood, making dinner for herself and Tilly.

For two years now Quinn had been an utter pro at blocking out everything, but she was starting to feel like a dam that was slowly bursting apart at the seams, unable to control anything, much less her own destiny.

Mick met her gaze, his own softening. "You okay?"

"Am I doing enough?"

"You've already done so much."

She shook her head.

"You have," he said. "You came back. You went after Tilly when she needed you. Hell, you've put your life on hold to give her the time she needs to make a decision. Which, by the way, is a brave act all in itself."

She turned to him then and searched his gaze. "But will it reach her?"

He shook his head. "I don't know. You're the one of us who was an actual teenage girl. I watched my sister go through it, and

I certainly dated enough of them, but it seems to me most teenagers are actually insane. Like committable insane."

She found a laugh. "Are you saying that all of the girls in your past were crazy?"

He grimaced. "I should probably plead the fifth on that one."

But she was curious now. "What about the women?"

"What about them?"

"Well, for starters . . . have there been a lot?"

He rubbed a hand over his jaw and the ensuing sound of the stubble against his palm caused her to want to drop this conversation and maybe press up against him until he growled low in his throat like he sometimes did when she touched him.

"Define a lot," he finally said.

She rolled her eyes and turned away, but he caught her with a low laugh. "A lot might be an exaggeration. I've had several long-term relationships, if that answers your question, none of which worked out."

"Why not?"

He rubbed his jaw again, still studying her. "Either the timing was wrong for one of us, or one of us was the aforementioned crazy and . . ."

She cocked her head. "And what?"

"And she cheated on me."

She stared up at him. "Lena?" she guessed.

"It was a long time ago."

"If it helps, she seems pretty sorry," she said as diplomatically as she could.

He let out a low laugh and grabbed her hand, tugging her into him. "Are you campaigning for her now?"

"Hell no."

His eyes heated and he stepped into her, backing her into the kitchen counter, putting a hand on the tile on either side of her hips. "What *are* you campaigning for?"

She stopped breathing. "Are you asking me what I want?"

"Yes."

They looked at each other and then Mick's hands went from the tile to her hips, his fingers spread wide, his thumbs brushing beneath the hem of her shirt to graze along her bare skin.

"I want peace on earth and to end world hunger," she said, biting back a moan as his mouth settled at the crook of her neck. "I want my job to be more mine, not my parents'—I want—" She broke off to gasp when he nibbled his way along her collarbone and slid one of his denim-clad thighs between hers.

"What else?" he murmured against her skin.

"Um . . ." She struggled to breathe, much less think. "I want Tilly safe and happy, and I want her to like me—although I'm pretty sure that's a pipe dream." She clutched his shoulders, digging her fingers into him. "But what I really want is for you to take off your shirt so I can lick you like a lollipop."

Instead he pulled off her shirt. She got his shoved up and he had one hand inside her bra and another in her panties when her phone rang.

They both stilled.

She dropped her forehead to his chest, so hot and bothered she wanted to cry. "It might be important."

"I know." He pulled free and handed over her phone. "It's Tilly."

"You picking me up or what?" the teen asked.

"From where?" Quinn asked. "Aren't you right next door at Chuck's?"

"On Sundays I work half a day at the hospital reading to old people. I'm done now and it's too hot to walk home."

Quinn sighed and watched Mick pull his shirt back on. "I'll be right there." She disconnected and met Mick's gaze. "I feel like I should call my mom and apologize for ever being a teenager."

His eyes smiled, but his mouth remained serious as it brushed a kiss over hers. It was a really great kiss, but unlike the ones before it, it wasn't going anywhere.

"You've got this, Quinn," he said.

She appreciated the faith and could only hope he was even half right. She turned to the door, but he caught her. "I'm sorry but I've really got to—"

"Your shirt," he said and dropped it over her head, laughing at her.

"Gah!" She pulled her shirt back into place and wished she could screw her head into place as well.

Chapter 22

When kids scream in public, I always want to say you have no real problems, it should be ME screaming . . .

—from "The Mixed-Up Files of Tilly Adams's Journal"

Tilly walked out of the hospital and stopped short at the sight of Quinn right up front, waiting for her at the entrance. Great. Yeah, she'd called for a ride, but suddenly she wished she hadn't. "Anyone ever tell you that teenagers don't like to be picked up where anyone can see?" she asked when she got into the Lexus. "It makes us not cool."

Quinn's brows went up. "I can pretend not to like you, if that helps."

"Or you could just not talk to me. Can I drive?"

"Thought we weren't talking," Quinn said dryly.

Huh. Her sister was a smart-ass too. Guess they did have something in common after all. "I'd make an exception if you let me drive home," she said hopefully.

"Do I look like I just fell off a turnip truck?" Quinn asked.

"No, but you talk like you did."

Quinn pulled off an impressive eye roll. "Do you have a learner's permit?"

"Yes," Tilly said.

"That's a lie."

"How can you tell?"

Quinn smiled. "Practice. You're pretty good, but I'm better."

Tilly sighed. "You're going over the speed limit."

"Am not."

"Are too," Tilly said. "On this stretch of road, cattle and other livestock get loose sometimes. The county lowered the speed limit because people kept hitting cows and totaling their vehicles."

Quinn gaped at her. "Cows can total a car?"

"Well, duh."

"That's ridiculous, they're huge. How do people not see them from a mile away and steer accordingly?"

Tilly shrugged.

Quinn shook her head and let off the gas pedal a little bit but not quickly enough, because like clockwork, a cow ambled into the middle of the road right in front of them.

Quinn slammed on the brakes, which had them executing one perfect spin, directly into . . .

A mailbox.

"Omigod," Quinn gasped when the car shuddered to a sudden halt. "Are you okay?"

Tilly looked down at herself. "I think so." Craning her neck, she took in the back of the car, from which the mailbox proudly protruded. "But I think you just gave your car a colonoscopy without anesthesia."

Thirty minutes later, Quinn had talked to the owner of the

property and promised to replace the mailbox, and they were back on the road, none the worse for wear.

With the exception of the very large, mailbox-size dent in the back bumper.

"So," Tilly said casually. "People can see a cow from a mile away and steer accordingly?"

Quinn moaned. "I don't suppose you could forget that happened?"

"I don't suppose," Tilly said, suddenly feeling almost downright cheerful for a change.

TEN MINUTES LATER, they pulled up to the house and Tilly's momentary happiness faded behind a block of nerves and anxiety. "So what's the plan here?"

"The plan is our trial period." Quinn glanced over at her. "Don't panic on me, it's just temporary."

Tilly had no idea why that set her off so badly. Wait, yes, she did know. It was because she wanted Quinn to want her, dammit. "So you've said."

"I was just reiterating," Quinn said.

Yes, well, she'd reiterated it enough and Tilly had gotten the message, thank you very much. It was only temporary. It was just a trial period. She got it loud and clear—Quinn needed an out clause.

Tilly's entire life was an out clause. "What happens if it doesn't work out?" she asked.

Quinn looked at her again. "Let's hope it doesn't come to that."

"But what if it does?" she pressed, needing to know. What if Quinn decided she was too much trouble, like when a puppy became more annoying than cute? Would she get rid of Tilly?

Ship her off? Because she was tired of being an extra. Unwanted. A mouth to feed.

Quinn turned off her fancy-ass car and turned to Tilly. "You know," she said. "*You* may decide you don't like *me*. Maybe you'll think I'm a pain in the ass. It goes both ways, Tilly."

This surprised Tilly into momentary silence. "I already don't like you and think you're a pain in the ass," she finally said.

Quinn let out a low laugh. "Shock."

Their gazes met and Quinn snorted, and Tilly thought the sound so ridiculous that she snorted too, and just like that they were united in ridiculousness. But Tilly sobered quickly enough. She intended to stand firm on her Not-Liking-Quinn stance, but something was eating at her.

"What?" Quinn asked.

"I need to apologize to you about something," Tilly admitted, not happy about it but her mom had drummed in the point of basic kindness.

"For what, letting me catch all the chickens by myself?" Quinn asked. "For laughing at my underwear when I was in the throes of anaphylactic shock? For putting it out there on Instagram that I almost burned down the café? For—"

"No," Tilly said. Then winced. "Well, yes." She held her breath and looked at Quinn. "But most especially for making that crack about us not being sisters." She paused. "You really lost your sister?"

"One of them," Quinn said quietly and gave a very small smile. And then, as if she knew Tilly was hungry for more information but didn't want to ask for it, she went on. "Her name was Beth. She was eleven months younger than me, and my mom—" She stopped, gave another small smile. "—the mom who raised me, always said we were like twins. But it's not true. *Beth* was better than me at just about everything. She died unexpectedly in a car accident because she loved music and had to fiddle with the radio while she was driving and wrapped herself around a damn tree."

"You miss her," Tilly said softly.

"Very much." Quinn drew in a deep breath, her expression telling Tilly that it hurt to breathe while thinking of her loss, and for the first time, Tilly looked at her as a real person. With problems not all that different from what she was facing.

"Listen," Quinn said slowly. "I'm more than willing to give this a try, and I get that you have no reason to believe me or even trust me, but I want you to know I'm not quick to judge or get rid of people or things lightly."

Tilly wasn't ready to believe her, but she didn't really see an option other than to nod. Her phone buzzed with an incoming text and she looked at the screen.

Dylan.

She hadn't heard a single word from him since last night and it hurt deep in her chest to see his name. Unable to ignore him, she swiped her phone and read his text.

I'm sorry.

"So can we do this?" Quinn asked. "Can we go inside and . . ." She shrugged. "Do whatever normal families do?"

"What do normal families do?" Tilly asked as she texted Dylan back with: Are you okay?

Quinn let out a low laugh. "Honestly? I have no idea."

Tilly lifted her head from her phone. "What do you mean? You came from a normal family."

"You think so?" Quinn asked. "My adopted parents lied to me for thirty years. How is that normal?"

"You're *thirty*?" Tilly asked, shocked.

Quinn laughed a little. "You don't have to sound so horrified."

"I didn't realize you had one foot in the old people's home is all." Tilly looked down at her phone when it buzzed.

DYLAN:
I need another job to help my mom pay for the two windows my dad broke, but other than that I'm great.

Tilly looked up at Quinn. "Hey, do you think there're any job openings at the café?"

"Yeah, we're looking for a short-order cook. And Greta says we need a part-time table clearer for some evening and weekend shifts. Why?"

"Like a busboy?" she asked hopefully.

Quinn looked at her. "Or a busgirl."

Okay, so Quinn thought she was asking for herself and she maybe felt a twinge of guilt at that, but this was Dylan, and he needed her. "So can we tell Greta the position is filled?"

"How about a trial run?"

"What is it with you and trial runs?"

Quinn just looked at her and Tilly sighed. "Okay, fine. A trial run. On *everything*. Duly noted."

A few minutes later she and Quinn stood in the kitchen staring at the threadbare fridge that held some condiments, a container of expired lemonade, and a half-empty bottle of vodka in the freezer.

"My mom liked a little lemonade with her vodka at night," Tilly said. "It's a Lemon Drop, but she always called it a Lemon Ball. No idea why . . ." She saw the way Quinn looked a little horrified and felt the need to defend her mom. "She wasn't an alcoholic or anything."

"I didn't say she was."

"Good. 'Cause she wasn't. She just worked really hard . . ." Tilly felt her throat burn. Out of all the things she wished, one of them was that she could talk about her mom without wanting to cry. "She always said she wanted to give me the moon, but I didn't need the moon. She was everything I needed."

Quinn nodded, her own eyes looking suspiciously bright. "I know."

"She didn't even tell me she was terminal." Tilly turned away from the fridge. "If she had, then maybe I could have helped, or—"

"No, Tilly," Quinn said with such gentleness in her voice that Tilly had to close her eyes. "Nothing you could've done or said would have changed what happened." She paused, spoke carefully, like she knew the truth of the words deep in her gut. "Some people aren't meant to stay in your life. But that doesn't mean you can't carry a piece of them in your heart."

Tilly refused to be moved. Or at least to admit it. "Whatever, it's over now." She opened the cupboards. "People helped clean out everything in here when I had to move to Chuck's so that nothing would go bad. Which leaves us with saltines."

"I could go to the store, stock up, and make us something," Quinn said, still way too gently for Tilly's comfort.

"I don't need charity."

"I didn't say you did. It's merely an alternative to saltines."

"I like saltines," Tilly said. Actually, she hated saltines. But hell if she was going to admit it. "There's also peanut butter and jelly."

"And you'd rather eat PB and J and saltines than have me cook us something?" Quinn asked.

"Yes."

"Fine. Works for me."

Tilly craned her neck and eyeballed Quinn for sarcasm but didn't see any. She'd only been kidding, and maybe testing Quinn just a little bit because she knew Quinn came from a different world. Where jeans didn't come from Walmart and food came cooked all fancy. Normally Tilly would just walk over to the café and Greta or Trinee would load her up with enough food to take home for Chuck too. "You want peanut butter and jelly on crackers," she said, heavy on the doubt.

"Why not?" Quinn asked. "You do."

"Have you ever actually had peanut butter and jelly on crackers for a meal before?"

Quinn laughed ruefully. "No. But to be fair, that's because I do a lot of cooking."

"You cook," Tilly repeated, also doubtfully.

"It's my job. I'm a sous-chef at a restaurant in L.A. called Amuse-Bouche."

"Sounds hoity-toity."

"It is. And my co-sous-chef is a complete asshole. But I still love it."

"When I say asshole at school, I get detention."

Quinn winced. "Who did you call an asshole?"

"Evan. He's a dickwad, cheater asswipe in my math class who copies off me because he's stupid."

Quinn raised a brow. "Maybe we should start a swear jar."

"For you?"

"For both of us. It'd keep you out of detention, even if the dickwad asswipe is an asshole."

Tilly didn't want to admit it out loud but she was pretty impressed with Quinn's potty mouth.

They had peanut butter and jelly on stale saltines in front of a TV marathon of *Friends*.

"I used to have a thing for Joey," Quinn said after a few episodes.

"Ew. He's old," Tilly said, even though she'd always had a thing for Joey too.

Quinn sighed.

Three episodes in, Dylan texted Tilly to meet him at the park so they could do homework. Her heart started pounding because he wasn't sounding like a guy who'd told her they were no longer friends. It was further proof that he'd only told her that to get her to leave last night before she got hurt, and she quickly stood up. "I'm going out."

"Where to?" Quinn asked.

"A party."

"You're fifteen," Quinn said.

"It's not like it's going to be at a strip club or anything like that."

"So where *will* it be?" Quinn asked.

"I don't know yet."

"How long will you be gone?"

"I don't know that either."

"Uh-huh." Quinn was looking unimpressed. "Who are you going with?"

Tilly shrugged.

"Gee, Tilly, I'm starting to feel pretty stupid for overreacting . . ."

Tilly blew out a sigh. "A friend needs help with homework."

"Have that friend come here."

"We're going to meet at the park."

"Or *here*."

Tilly stared at Quinn, using her best resting bitch face.

Quinn gave it right back to her.

Tilly blew out a sigh. "Fine, whatever." And she stormed off to her room, and for good measure, slammed the door. Two seconds later she got a text.

QUINN:

One time when I was fifteen and I slammed my door, my dad took the door off the hinges. Just FYI.

Tilly laughed in spite of herself. She didn't answer. In fact, she deleted the text. But she was still half smiling when she climbed out her window and went to the park to meet Dylan.

He was a lone dark shadow sitting on a swing, his foot down and anchoring him to the sand beneath.

Feeling shaky with relief, Tilly sat next to him. She wanted to soak him up, but instead mirrored his position, head tipped back, staring at the stars.

"Tilly . . ." He blew out a sigh and she heard him shift and felt the weight of his gaze. She didn't look. She was very busy counting the stars.

"Tilly," he said again, voice low. Tense. Anguished. "I'm sorry."

Her heart squeezed. Dammit.

"I hate that you saw me like that," he said roughly. "I hate . . ." He paused and when he spoke, the words sounded like he had to drag them over shards of glass. "I hate that you know what my life's like."

Now her heart seemed swollen, unable to fit in her rib cage, and she turned to him, reaching out for his hand.

He hesitated and then took it in his bigger, callused one.

"And I hate it for you," she whispered.

They sat like that for a long time, just watching the sky.

"I've got to go," she finally said reluctantly, wanting to get back before Quinn found her missing and called in the Coast Guard.

"My sister . . ." She paused, shocked by those two words she'd just uttered. *Her sister.* God. Crazy. "She doesn't know I left."

Dylan nodded. "I'll walk you back."

They stood and walked through the grass and stopped short at the lone car in the parking lot, lights off, engine running.

It was a Lexus, Quinn behind the wheel. She got out of the car. "Hi," she said. "How did the homework go?"

Chapter 23

Stu(dying)
Stu(died)
Coincidence? I think not.

—from "The Mixed-Up Files of Tilly Adams's Journal"

Quinn looked at the tall, lanky kid standing next to Tilly and had to sigh. "Dylan, I presume?"

He nodded and upped her opinion of him when he shook her hand, held eye contact, and said, "It was my fault. I needed to apologize to her."

"For?"

Tilly shifted. "Dylan, no. You don't have to—"

"For letting her put herself in danger for me when she came out to my dad's house last night," Dylan said over Tilly.

Quinn looked at her sister.

Tilly looked right back at her. "I'd do it again," she said with such fierceness that Quinn knew she was missing more than a few pieces of this puzzle. She took in the fading bruise on Dylan's face and filled in some of those pieces herself.

She drove them all to Carolyn's house and waited inside while they said their good-byes, because Dylan insisted on walking home from there. When Tilly finally came in, she had a chip on her shoulder the size of the planet.

"Don't start," Tilly said.

"You could've just told me the truth about who you were meeting."

"Right. And you'd have let me go?"

"Well, you'll never know now, will you?" Quinn asked.

Tilly tossed up her hands and went to her room, once again slamming the door.

Good times.

But they were both in the same house, relatively unscathed, so Quinn decided to consider Day One a success. She fell onto the couch, exhausted, and looked at her phone when it vibrated with an incoming text.

MICK:

What are you up to?

QUINN:

Aren't you supposed to ask what I'm wearing?

MICK:

I should've let you lead. Yes, what are you wearing?

QUINN:

Far too many clothes. You know, I don't think I'm going to like being thirty.

MICK:

I could show you otherwise.

She had no doubt . . . He was a great distraction, one she dreamed of regularly. But he was also something else. He was dangerous to her heart and soul, and she knew it. She didn't have the capacity to give a relationship with him what it deserved, and more than that, she didn't want to.

Or, more accurately, she was working on not wanting to.

The next morning, Quinn took Tilly to school and then went over to the café. Greta was in the kitchen waving a frying pan and swearing in German, giving Quinn a bad flashback to Marcel.

"How can I help?" Quinn asked.

Greta gave her a long look. "Well, let's see, I can't send you out for eggs because you'll cry, and I don't dare ask you to go check the garden for fresh tomatoes because you're allergic to bees, so—"

"Greta," Trinee said from the other side of the counter. "I told you to drink your damn coffee before you try to masquerade as a human."

"Fine." Greta sniffed. "I'm sorry," she said to Quinn. "She's right. I need caffeine."

"Go take a break," Quinn said. "I'll bring you a coffee."

"That'd be super," Greta said gratefully. "I'll also take scrambled eggs, crispy bacon, crispy hash browns, and sourdough toast. Oh, and don't bother with any of that ridiculous garnish."

"You mean fruit?" Quinn asked dryly.

"That," Greta said.

Quinn went to work, shocked by the sheer number of people who showed up for breakfast. "Where do all these people come from every day?" she asked in amazement to a running-harried Trinee.

"Truckers, ranchers, surfers, tourists," she said, picking up her table's food. "We get 'em all."

It amazed Quinn. The place was run on a shoestring budget with antiquated equipment and—in her opinion—an antiquated menu, and yet it was widely beloved.

And then there was the other thing. She'd never worked harder in any kitchen than she had in this one on the few times she'd been cooking here, but . . . it was something she'd never expected—satisfying.

There was a knock at the back door and Quinn turned to see Dylan standing there. "Hey," she said. "What's up? Tilly okay?"

"Yeah," he said, shoving his hands into his pockets. "Or I think so. I haven't seen her today. I have one less class than she does."

"Okay," Quinn said and paused. "Are you hungry? Do you need breakfast?"

Dylan's eyes moved hungrily to the range. "I'm here to start work," he said, surprising her.

"Um . . . what?"

His gaze slid to hers. "Tilly told me I start work today. The busboy position. It's still open?"

Quinn blinked as she realized she'd once again been bamboozled by a far-too-sharp fifteen-year-old. If only the girl used her powers for good . . . "I thought the job was for Tilly."

"I've bussed before, I've got experience."

Trinee shoved her head in from the dining room and yelled, "I need some damn help out here, the crowd's getting restless and I can't do it all by my damn self."

Quinn turned to Dylan. "It's an insane asylum. Why would you want to work here?"

He looked at the stove and then met her gaze again. "I've always been pretty passionate about not starving to death."

Her heart squeezed hard. Dammit. She was so used to not feeling a single thing. And now here she was feeling . . . everything. All the damn time. Before she knew it, she'd probably be crying at tampon commercials. "Welcome aboard," she said, and insisted he eat a large plate of food she made up for him before he went to work.

He inhaled every bite and that tugged at her heart too.

When the crowd finally thinned several hours later, she stepped out into the dining room and to her surprise, the patrons applauded.

Okay, so it was mostly the geriatric crowd: Lou, Hank, and Big Hank, but still. Laughing, she took a bow.

"Hey, nice job," Lou called out. "You didn't get stung by a bee, beaten up by a chicken, or need an ambulance or fire truck today."

She took another bow and when she straightened, caught sight of the tall, handsome man walking into the place, hair wind tousled, dark lenses covering his eyes.

Mick.

Her silly heart skipped a damn beat as he pushed the glasses to the top of his head and sought out her gaze. "Thought you could use a lift."

"A lift?" she asked.

His mouth was solemn and serious, but there was something much lighter and amused in his gaze. "Yeah. To the thing," he said meaningfully.

Her entire body quivered in anticipation. "Oh, that's right," she said, untying her apron. "The *thing*. Give me a sec."

She whirled and rushed into the kitchen, tossing her apron aside.

Greta and Trinee stood there side by side, brows up. "The thing?" Greta asked. "What is this thing?"

Quinn tried to be cool, but let's face it, she'd never been cool a day in her life. Worse, she couldn't control her sudden smile. "Oh, it's just a thing."

Trinee gave Gerta a knowing glance. "Uh-huh. When you and I go to a"—she used air quotes—"'thing,' I smile like that too."

Five minutes later, Mick had Quinn in his car, heading up the highway along the coast. He had a million other things he should be doing, but he didn't care. He had the windows down, the ocean breeze blowing in, stirring Quinn's hair, teasing him with the scent of her shampoo.

"I've never seen you drive anything but a truck," she said.

"The truck's my dad's. I usually drive it in Wildstone when I'm working at the house because it's more convenient for hauling materials. And also because Coop likes it better than this."

Quinn looked at the dog in the rearview mirror. "He doesn't seem to be having a problem enjoying himself."

And true enough, Coop had his entire head out the window, eyes and jowls flattened back by the wind, making him look like an alien.

Quinn laughed, and Mick discovered he liked the sound of that almost as much as he liked the scent of her hair. But he knew what he liked even more than both of those things, and that was the taste of her.

To that end, he pulled off the highway and drove them along a private road up the bluffs and stopped facing the ocean.

"Wow," Quinn said, sounding awed. "What a gorgeous view. Where are we?"

"This property used to be a small, local family-run winery. It's thirty acres of dust crop now, with several run-down buildings."

"They went bankrupt?"

"They were headed that way," he said. "They started some renovations that the city objected to and they got their permits rescinded. But they were already tens of thousands of dollars into the renovations. They were going to have to declare bankruptcy."

"How awful for them."

"Yeah. Then the vultures descended with ridiculously low-ball offers."

She stared at him. "And you . . . did something. To help . . . Yeah," she said, studying him, cocking her head to do it too.

It was pretty fucking sexy. And cute. "I bought the place."

"Not for an undercut price," she said, sounding so sure of him that it did something to his gut.

"I always pay fair market value," he said. "Only part of the reason that the city manager isn't happy with me."

"Why would he care?"

"He's the main vulture." Colin had called him with the news. It seemed that Wildstone's city manager might be taking kickbacks from outside builders and businesses—at the expense of the locals. "He likes to use his position and power to learn which properties are in trouble, and then he does his best to make it worse for them, and when they're at rock bottom he comes in and buys for pennies on the dollar."

"Isn't that illegal?"

"If he's caught at it."

"So you're going to run a winery," she said, looking at him like he was some kind of hero instead of just a solid businessman.

"No," he said. "I'm going to fund the renovations and then the original owners are going to lease it back and run it." Without the heavy mortgage and the second and third loans they'd had out on the place, which had been running them into the ground.

They were good people who'd run into bad times, but the bottom line was that the property was a good investment for him, one of several he'd made over the past year.

"You know them?" Quinn asked.

"Everyone knows everyone out here, at least loosely."

"Hmm," she said and kept watching him.

"What?"

"I think it's cute that you bought this land to keep a local winery intact."

"And because it's a win-win for me," he repeated.

"I still think it's pretty damn sweet of you." She paused. "Or are you one of those guys who think sweet threatens his . . ." She gestured to his crotch.

He grinned. "I'm willing to go with sweet if that turns you on."

Her gaze dropped to his mouth as she licked her own lips. "Is this where we get to the . . . *thing*?"

In answer, he scooted his seat back as far as it would go and hauled her over the console and into his lap so that she was straddling him.

Coop gave one happy bark, excited at the possibility of a wrestle session. Mick reached back and opened the car door. The dog hopped out, happily loping along the bluffs, nose down, taking in all the scents.

"He won't wander off?" Quinn asked, worriedly watching him go.

He cupped her face and turned it back to his. "Not even if I wanted him to. Where were we?"

She smiled and wiggled a little bit, causing him to groan. He slipped his fingers into her hair and pulled her mouth down to his.

Sweet turned to scorching when she melted against him. It awed him, and it turned him on like nothing else, and he knew he was going to take what she was willingly giving him, keep her for as long as she allowed, and maybe, if his luck held, it'd be a long time before she wrenched his heart out and walked away.

He slid one hand up her shirt, the other in her pants, and she whispered his name, her voice a breathy, desperate whisper. The tension in her changed when he found the right spot and he felt her go utterly still, like she didn't want to misdirect or distract him. But he could read her like he could his own soul. He knew exactly what she wanted, what she needed. "I've got you, Quinn."

She clung to him, a few wayward strands of hair slipping into her face, her fingers digging into his shoulders as she came apart. After, she sagged against him, nestling in close, and he savored that, wondering, as he always did, if this time would be their last.

Then she lifted her head with a smile and met his gaze as she ran her fingers down his chest, pushing up the hem of his T-shirt to open his jeans. A minute later she had him in her hot little hands and he knew he wasn't going to last all that long when his phone, which had slipped out of his pocket and landed on the seat at his thigh, went off with an incoming text.

The screen ID said: MOM. He closed his eyes and felt Quinn's silky hair brush over his abs.

"I think your mom's—"

"Ignore it," he said, his hand gently fisting in her hair.

She dropped to her knees between his and had her mouth just below his belly button, heading for his favorite body part when his phone went off again—a call this time.

Quinn's soft exhale brushed over him and he groaned.

"Maybe it's important," she whispered.

He blew out another breath, and eyes still locked on Quinn's, he picked up the phone. "Everything okay?" he asked in lieu of a greeting.

"Well, what kind of a hello is that?" his mom asked. "Of course I'm all right, why wouldn't I be?"

"Is it Wendy?" he asked. "Have you heard from her?"

"Actually, yes. She's still in New York and she says she's doing great and that she'll return your texts and calls soon."

Uh-huh. More like she'll do so when she ran out of money . . .

"But that's not why I'm calling," his mom said. "I need you to come over."

"I can be there later tonight—"

"I was hoping for now, honey. What's got you so busy you don't have any time for me?"

"Mom." Mick let out a low laugh and rubbed his forehead. "I'm . . ." He met Quinn's still languorous, still hungry expression. "Busy."

"Well, get unbusy and hurry," she said and disconnected.

He stared at his phone.

"She okay?" Quinn asked.

"She needs my help with something." He paused. "She hung up on me. She's never hung up on me."

"Does she live close by?"

"Yes, actually, only a few miles from here."

Quinn sat up, and to his sexual frustration, climbed back into the passenger seat and put herself back together. "Let's go make sure she's okay."

"We?"

She looked at him. "Well, you're already almost there, right? I can wait in the car, if that's what you're worried about."

She thought he didn't want her to go. Which was more than a little true, but not for the reason she believed. His mom didn't have much of an inner filter and he held no illusions of even trying to control the things she might say. "It's fine." He started the car and opened the door to whistle for Coop.

When they pulled up to his mom's house a few minutes later, she was sitting on the porch in one of the two chairs. The other chair was filled by . . .

Lena.

And to think he'd been worried about what his mom might say. He parked and just looked at the porch.

"What's going on?" Quinn asked.

"I don't know," he said. But he was pretty sure he wasn't going to like it. He got out of the car and was grateful for small favors when Quinn didn't follow.

He walked up to the house and looked at Lena and then his mom. "What's up?"

Lena stood up. "I asked your mom to call you out here so we could talk. About us."

"Lena, there is no us."

"But there could be an us," she said. "I know it. Your mom knows it. The whole town knows it—"

"Lena." Christ. He didn't want to be doing this, but he especially didn't want to be doing this with Quinn right there. Were his car windows down? Yeah, perfect. They were. And then there was his mom sitting there soaking up every little thing, hopeful, eternally hopeful, for grandchildren.

"I just don't know where we went wrong," Lena said.

He snorted and turned back to his car but Lena ran down the steps and put her hand on his arm.

"Stop this," he said quietly, for her ears only. "Before I say something that hurts and embarrasses you. What we had when we were kids is long over and you know it. You also know why."

"I apologized for that," she said. "It should be like a juvenile court record—expunged."

"I agree, and I've forgiven you if that's what you're looking for. But we were kids and I no longer—"

"Don't say you don't have feelings for me, Mick. I can feel that you do. I'll show you." She went up on tiptoe and brushed her mouth across his.

Two things happened simultaneously. One, Mick took a step back. Two, a truck pulled up. And before Mick knew it, he was being cold-cocked right in the jaw.

He hit the ground and blinked up at a furious Boomer bending over him. "What the—"

"Get up, you two-timing hypocrite," Boomer snarled and then dove on him.

They rolled in the dirt. Mick got a good shot in before they were stopped by two blurs who came from opposite sides to pull them apart.

Quinn and Lena.

Quinn put her hands on Mick's chest. "You good?"

He swiped at his bloody lip. "Yeah."

She pushed his hair from his forehead, looked him over, and then nodded.

Lena was faced off with Boomer, hands on her hips. "What the hell are you doing here?"

Boomer swiped at his own bloody lip. "What do you think?"

Lena stared at him. "You dumped me, remember?"

"I said you needed to make some changes. I didn't mean to go after your damn ex and my best friend! Jesus, Lena."

"You need to make up your damn mind," she said.

"Don't you mean you need to make up your damn mind?" Boomer demanded incredulously.

"You're both insane," Mick said.

Boomer gave him a long, considering look and Mick gave it right back to him. He was pissed enough to go another round, no problem.

But then Quinn gave him a shove in his chest much in the same way Lena did with Boomer. In fact, Lena pushed Boomer toward his truck. "Go," she said.

"I'll go when you go."

She blew out a breath and climbed into his truck—leaving her car—and gave Boomer a "get the hell in here too" look.

Boomer got behind the wheel and peeled out, not looking back.

Mick's mom brought Mick and Quinn inside. She introduced herself to Quinn and then went straight to her liquor cabinet and pulled out a bottle that looked identical to the one on the table, with the exception that this one was full. She handed it to Quinn.

"What's this?" she asked.

"My secret recipe."

"Pretty color," Quinn said, holding the bottle up to the light and admiring it.

Mick, still pissed off, found a rough laugh. "Don't let the color fool you. It's moonshine."

"For the rough days," his mom said.

"For every day then," Quinn said.

Chapter 24

I've learned that you can't make everyone happy, you're not a bowl of ice cream.

—from "The Mixed-Up Files of Tilly Adams's Journal"

After the "thing" and Mick's and Boomer's fight, Quinn went back to the café to help close up for the day. Dylan was there, and he'd turned out to be a diligent and hard worker, helping Greta and Trinee like he'd been there forever. She already couldn't remember what they'd done without him.

She was in the kitchen making a shopping list when there was yet another knock at the back door. *What now?* she thought and turned to look.

"You've got to be kidding me," she said.

Lena lifted a basket. "I've got something for Greta."

"Let me repeat," Quinn said. "You've got to be kidding me."

"Actually," Lena said. "I rarely kid."

Greta came into the kitchen and gestured Lena in, excitedly peering into the basket. "Is that what I think it is?"

"My homemade honey-ginger tea for your sister," Lena said. "You said it helped her asthma, so I brewed up some more for you to send to her."

"Brewed in your caldron, you mean?" Quinn asked politely.

Dylan, from where he stood at the sink doing dishes, snorted, but when Quinn looked at him, he was head down, concentrating on his task.

Greta took in Lena and Quinn with narrowed eyes. "If I leave the two of you alone in the kitchen, you're not going to have a fistfight like your boys did, right?"

Lena grinned. "I don't know. It's been a long time since I had a good fight."

Quinn rolled her eyes. "We'll be fine," she told Greta.

When they were alone, Lena's smile fell from her face. "So. About before."

"You mean when you tried to cajole Mick back to you by getting his mom involved?" Quinn asked. "Romantic, by the way."

"Hey, romantic is long, slow walks down every aisle at Target." Lena put her hands on her hips. "Now are you going to back off Mick or not?"

"Not."

"I'm going to be honest with you," Lena said. "You're a real pain in my ass."

"I'm not going to exchange blows with you in the dirt," Quinn said.

Lena's mouth quirked. "Good, because your skinny ass would lose."

Quinn sighed. "So where do we go from here?"

"Well, we start with you giving him up."

Quinn laughed, but sobered when she realized Lena was serious. "He's not mine to give up, Lena."

Lena looked happy at that, and Quinn shook her head. "Look, I don't know what you think's going on between him and me, and I'm not going to discuss it with you, but Mick's a big boy. You can't manipulate him into wanting you."

"I don't have to," Lena said. "He just needs to be reminded of how good it was back then, before I messed it up."

Quinn set down her pad of paper. It was that or smack herself in the head with it. Repeatedly. "Everyone makes mistakes, Lena."

"Exactly."

"Sometimes all that's left to do is learn from them and move on."

Lena looked at her for a long minute. "You're talking about Boomer."

"I saw how he looked at you," Quinn said. "I think he loves you. And I saw how you looked at him when he stood up after the fight. You were worried about him. He's important to you."

Lena's smug smile slipped. "Mick's important to me too, always has been. And not that this is any of your business but I recently figured something out . . . I need him."

"Why?"

"Because when I was with him . . . that was the last time my life worked."

Before Quinn could figure out a response to that, Lena was gone.

"There's a big difference between want and need," she muttered to herself, picking her pad and pen back up. "I mean, I *want* a bikini body, but I *need* chicken nuggets."

The next morning was a wash and repeat of the morning before, meaning Quinn woke up and got Tilly moving. Not an easy prospect, the girl liked her sleep, a lot.

She dropped Tilly off at school. Well, correction, she dropped Tilly off at the corner of the school, where she walked in because, oh yeah, she was embarrassed to be seen with Quinn.

After a shift at the café that was just as crazy as any other but thankfully minus the fire department, Quinn was back at the house. She was in the middle of stocking the fridge so they wouldn't have to continue to eat PB and J and crackers when her phone rang.

She'd already spoken to Chef Wade, her parents, and Brock. None of those phone calls had been easy since she'd had to admit that she had no idea how long she was going to be here in Wildstone. She'd also spoken to Skye, who'd made plans to drive up on her next day off to visit.

But the call wasn't from her parents, Brock, or Skye.

It was Cliff.

"What now?" Quinn answered with her heart in her throat. Tilly was still at school, at least as far as she knew.

"Just calling to see how it's going," he said.

"Would you believe that I have absolutely no idea?" She cocked her head, because wait a minute . . . she could hear the chickens. They were making noise, a *lot* of noise, much more than usual. And how weird was it that she could tell it was different from their regular clucking? She moved to the back door and peered out.

There was a cat ogling the hens. She could see the poor thing looked scrawny as hell, but that didn't mean she wanted it to feast on the hens.

"Just remember that Tilly doesn't deal well with authority," Cliff said.

"Gee, Cliff, that's brand-new information."

He chuckled. "Just be clear with your expectations and give her guidelines."

"I hear you," Quinn said, stepping out onto the porch. "But I'm not a miracle worker."

"If you need anything, you know where to find me," he said.

"Okay, but I've got a question—what if I'm the one who needs guidelines?" she asked but Cliff was already gone.

She shoved the phone into her pocket and crouched down. "Here, kitty kitty," she said and held out a hand to the cat eyeing the hens.

It was brown. Or maybe just dirty. Its fur stuck up in clumps, like it was too much for it to keep up with.

She—Quinn thought the cat seemed like a she—craned her neck and gave Quinn a level look through one good eye. Her other was at half-mast, giving her a somewhat inebriated expression that showed no fear but a lot of attitude.

"Don't tell me," she said. "You're fifteen too."

The ragamuffin cat dismissed her and turned back to the hens, who were still squawking like mad.

"Zip it," Quinn told the chickens. "If you'd just shut the hell up, I'd get her out of here."

The cat sat, tucking her tail around her body like she was a queen, clearly having no interest in going anywhere.

"Sorry," Quinn said. "But you're going to have to shoo."

The cat didn't shoo. Or take her eyes off the hens. Correction, her one good eye, which Quinn had a feeling wasn't all that good.

"Does everyone on the planet walk all over you?" a female voice asked.

Quinn sighed and turned to face Lena. "What *now*?"

"I forgot that I needed more eggs. Carolyn always let me take whatever I needed."

"Do you cook?"

"If offering people gum is cooking, then yes, I cook," Lena said and shrugged. "I use the eggs in some of my spa stuff. I supplied Carolyn with face cream that she lived by. You could use some of it, by the way, you're way too dry in your T-zone. You're going to wrinkle up like a dried-apple doll in no time."

"I'll keep that in mind." Quinn looked at the hens, who were still extremely worked up. She gestured for Lena to go ahead because there was no way in hell those chickens were going to let her take any eggs, and maybe this made her a bad person but she really needed some entertainment right about now.

But Lena moved into the pen and proceeded to get the eggs like a beast, moving fast and efficiently without a single problem.

"Seriously?" Quinn asked her. "You can't be bad at anything?"

Lena smiled. "Nope." She came out and eyed the cat. "Who's that?"

"No idea." Quinn looked over at the neighbor's house but neither Jared nor Hutch was in their yard, which was meticulous and perfectly kept up. There was no way that they owned an elderly cat they'd leave to fend for itself, half starved.

So Quinn scooped up the cat and headed to Chuck's house. He didn't answer, but Kendall—dressed to the nines in a dress that couldn't be more than three square inches—did. Her lip curled back at the sight of the cat.

"Who's that?" she asked.

"I was going to ask you the same question," Quinn said. "Is she yours? Or Chuck's?"

"Ew, not mine," she said. "I hate cats and Chuck's allergic."

Quinn walked back to Lena and set the cat down. They both took in the cat's raggedy fur and the fact that one eye sloped funny. "She's half starved," Quinn said.

"She's feral," Lena said. "And I think she's really old too. Probably mean. I'd be careful—"

Quinn looked at the cat. "You hungry? Wanna come inside for some food?"

As if the cat spoke English, she stood up and headed for the back door like she owned the joint.

Lena arched a brow.

Quinn, feeling triumphant for once, followed the cat, who'd stopped on the porch.

Quinn opened the door but the cat didn't budge.

Leaving the cat there, Quinn poured a small bowl of milk and set it down on the kitchen floor.

The cat hesitated and swiveled her one good eye to Lena.

Lena raised her hands. "Just standing here."

The cat walked past Lena into the kitchen and sniffed the bowl. Then she stuck her paw in it.

"Your cat needs the short bus," Lena said.

"I don't think she sees well, I think she's looking to see where the milk begins."

Even testing with her paw first, the cat still leaned in too far, got milk up her nose, and sneezed, blowing drops of milk. When she was done with that, she began to lap with a distinct lack of daintiness at the bowl, splattering milk everywhere. When she'd finished the bowl, she sat back and looked up at Quinn.

"She looks drunk," Lena said.

"She's cute."

Lena snorted. "If you keep her, she's going to tell all her friends, and by this time tomorrow you'll have a hundred wild cats and we'll all be calling you the cat lady." Lena paused. "On the other hand, keep her. Keep them all. It'll make you look crazy and I know Mick isn't into crazy."

Quinn, short on patience on the best of days, of which this wasn't one, crossed her arms. "He dated *you*, didn't he?"

For the first time since she'd stepped onto Carolyn's property, Lena smiled. "You know, it's really a shame we're sworn enemies."

Quinn sat on the kitchen floor, hoping the cat would come to her. "And why exactly do we have to be sworn enemies?"

The cat eyeballed her, consideringly.

Lena huffed out a sigh and sat on the floor too. "We're sworn enemies because you're sleeping with the guy I want to marry. Cat, don't go to her, come to me."

The cat climbed into Quinn's lap and Quinn felt her heart squeeze when she then rubbed her head against Quinn's shirt. "Ha. She likes me."

"She's marking you, making you her bitch."

Quinn rolled her eyes.

"Don't think I didn't notice that you didn't deny you're sleeping with Mick."

"It's none of your business," Quinn said. "And anyway, you had your chance."

Lena deflated a little, and Quinn realized this wasn't a joke or a game.

"I was young and stupid—emphasis on stupid," Lena admitted. "But Mick was so serious back then. I didn't realize it, but he had his hands full keeping Boomer out of trouble and giving school everything he had so he could get out of here, away from his hard-ass dad and everything. He was ridiculously responsible, and I mistook that for being too good for me." She shrugged. "So I did what I always do and self-destructed my happiness."

Quinn didn't want to buy into this story, but she couldn't help but feel sympathetic. "Have you tried stopping the pattern?"

"Unsuccessfully. The guy I was seeing before Boomer stole money from me." She shrugged at Quinn's sympathetic look. "So I bought a car for a couple of hundred bucks, registered it in his name, then parked it at LAX and racked up four hundred and fifty-nine parking tickets for him, totaling fifty grand."

Quinn blinked. "Actually, that's pretty brilliant."

"Not crazy?"

"Oh definitely crazy," Quinn said. "But crazy brilliant." She reached up to the counter where she'd left Mick's mom's moonshine and offered it to Lena.

"I'm good but you go right ahead."

Quinn's first sip was nearly her last. Fire burned a hole down her windpipe and her eyes were streaming by the time she managed to stop coughing.

Lena grinned. "Lightweight."

"Shut up. And for the record, you're *still* sabotaging your happiness. You've got a great guy waiting for you to grow up, but instead you're chasing a unicorn."

"Unicorn? You think Mick's a unicorn?"

"I know it." By now she'd had two more sips of the moonshine—which no longer burned at all, and in fact went down nice and smooth—and she had a little trouble counting off points on her fingers. "He's hot. He's employed. And he doesn't seem bothered by baggage. Lots and lots of baggage . . ." She sighed and hugged her newfound companion.

The cat allowed it for about three seconds and then gently sank her teeth into Quinn's hand, not breaking the skin but letting her know she meant business.

Quinn let go of her and the cat turned in a tight circle in

Quinn's lap three times and then plopped down with little to no grace and closed her eyes.

"So if I'm sabotaging my happiness with Boomer," Lena said, "maybe you're sabotaging Mick's happiness by getting in our way. You ever think of that?"

"You know, I liked it better when we didn't speak," Quinn said and Lena let out a low laugh in clear agreement.

To Quinn's surprise, she laughed a little too. Like Tilly, like the damn café and the people in it, like *everything* in Wildstone, everyone and everything here had all become little strings on her heart.

And she had no idea what to do with that.

Chapter 25

How come being fifteen isn't nearly as fun as it is on TV?

—from "The Mixed-Up Files of Tilly Adams's Journal"

After Lena left, Quinn took the bottle of moonshine and walked down the hallway.

The cat followed her around like a puppy. Lena had been right, the one droopy eye gave her a distinctively inebriated look. Her fur was still all clumped and matted, like maybe bathing herself took too much effort, and Quinn wanted to bathe and groom her badly, but one problem at a time.

She eyed the bedrooms and stretched the kink out of her neck. "I'm not sure how long I'm staying," she told the cat, who seemed interested in all she had to say. "But I refuse to sleep another night on that couch."

The craft room was smaller than the closet in her condo. Her first choice would be to take Carolyn's bigger room, but she didn't want to do that to Tilly.

Taking another sip of moonshine for fortification, she rolled up her sleeves and went to work, moving the sewing and boxes of craft stuff all against one wall so that she could move the old twin bed she'd seen in the garage into this room. There was a tiny desk with two drawers, one locked, one not. In the unlocked drawer was only one item.

A key.

It unlocked the first drawer, where she found a small journal. She opened it up and recognized Carolyn's writing from the letter she'd received. Another sip from the moonshine bolstered her courage as she opened the book and began to read.

Was told I was terminal today. Didn't see that coming. When I was little, I used to pretend I was Superwoman, with powers to transport myself from place to place. Right now I'd settle for the superpower to go back in time and make some badly needed changes.

I know I'm contractually barred from searching out the daughter I gave up for adoption. I get it. But what are they going to do? I'm dying, for crap's sake.

It was a mistake to agree to stay away from her but I can't regret anything I did back then as it was all for the sake of my baby girl. I wanted her to have a better life than I could give her. At barely eighteen, I wasn't equipped to handle myself, much less an infant. Hell, I couldn't have committed to a dentist's appointment, much less to raising a kid.

But oh how I wish I'd been stronger. That I'd not let her go. That I'd not signed away all my rights to her.

When Tilly came along so many years later, I expected some of the guilt to dissipate. Instead, it got worse. Because in spite of all my concerns about raising a child, Tilly and I did okay.

Better than okay.

All of which only makes the ache for Quinn worse. I failed her, and I can't live with that.

So . . . I searched for her, and what I found was far more than I deserved. I found a smart, kind, generous woman, and I couldn't be more proud of what she's made of herself and who she's become, in spite of her dubious beginnings.

The sound of Quinn's cell phone ringing from the kitchen where she'd left it had her jerking back to the present. Realizing her cheeks were wet, she swiped at the tears and stood up, reeling.

The journal echoed what Greta had told her. What the letter from Cliff had told her. There was a lot more, but she carefully slid the journal into the drawer, relocking it.

Then she took another sip of the moonshine—or two—before running into the kitchen to grab her phone.

The ID screen read: THE-GUY-I-LIKE-I-REALLY-REALLY-LIKE. In spite of herself, she had to laugh because damn, Tilly was good. That girl was way too smart for her grades and her own good. "Hello?" she asked, breathless from the journal, her mad dash to the kitchen, the moonshine . . . her life.

There was a beat of silence. Then Mick's deep, familiar voice, the one that made her nipples hard, said, "You okay?"

"You ask me that a lot. I might look fragile but I'm not."

"I already know that. And I ask because I like to know."

There'd been a part of her, deep, deep down, that had gone cold when she'd learned about being given up at birth. She was coming to terms with it, all of it, she really was. But that spot inside her had remained cold.

But ever since she'd met Mick, he'd been slowly defrosting it, warming her from the inside out.

"How about dinner tonight?" he asked.

"Like a date?"

"Unless you can figure out how to have dinner over the phone, yeah. A date."

She looked at the cat, who'd followed her into the kitchen.

"Mew," the cat said politely but definitely with a question on the end of it, like "Are you going to feed me or what?"

"Quinn?" Mick asked.

"Dinner sounds good," she said, and then remembered she'd have Tilly at home later, after her AP course at a local city college. And she wasn't sure she was ready to try and handle both him and Tilly at the same time. "Can we make it an early dinner? Or a late lunch?"

"Sure. When?"

"Now?" she asked. "And maybe it can be the kind of late lunch/early dinner you bring here to the house?"

"Okay," he said, easy as always. "What would you like?"

"Mew," the cat said politely.

Quinn looked down and met her one good eye. "Something a cat would eat."

There was a beat of silence. "What?"

"Don't ask." She disconnected and looked at the cat, who came closer, walking in a way that seemed like she might be tip-toeing. Dust danced away from her fur, floating through the air like . . . "Tinkerbell," she said.

The cat didn't seem impressed.

"Too girly?" Quinn asked.

"Mew."

"Okay, how about just Tink? It's a perfect name for such a beautiful cat."

Apparently the cat agreed because she wound herself around Quinn's feet and then nudged the empty milk bowl for more.

MICK AND COOP arrived twenty-five minutes later with a bag of groceries. "Hi!" Quinn said enthusiastically.

Mick gave her an odd look.

"What's the matter?" she asked, hoping she didn't have the same inebriated expression that Tink did.

"You're all flushed." He looked around and saw the moonshine, now missing a third of its contents, and burst out laughing.

"In my defense," she said, lifting her chin, "I was left unsupervised."

He ran a finger along her temple, tucking a stray strand of hair behind her ear, giving her a delicious all-over body shiver. "Want to talk about it?" he asked, voice silky. Sexy.

She closed her eyes and leaned into him, pressing her face into his throat, inhaling the sexy, comforting scent of him. "I don't know."

And here was the difference between him and . . . well, everyone else she'd ever known. He didn't push. He didn't poke or prod. He didn't cajole, demand, question.

He just let her be.

"I'm worried," she finally admitted.

"About?"

"Everything!" She sighed. "There's a boy . . ."

"I'm hoping the rest of that sentence is 'and his name is Mick.'"

She laughed. "I'm talking about Tilly. I'm stressing over how much a fifteen-year-old old knows about sex. I went online and tried to research—" She stopped talking when she felt his chest and arms shake.

He was laughing at her.

"How is this funny?" she asked. "I mean, do I have The Talk with her about boys being one big walking, talking blob of testosterone or not?"

"You're asking me? I'm one of those blobs of testosterone."

No kidding.

"You're doing great with her," he said. "Just have a frank talk, let her know you're there for her, and tell her to try to hold off at least another year before she goes for it. Guys don't know what they're doing when they're that age."

She gave him a speculative look. "Do you know now?"

"Come here and I'll show you."

She hesitated, not because she didn't want to jump him, but because she did want that. Bad.

He must have seen that all over her face because he gave her a slow, wicked smile and a finger crook.

When she just returned his smile, he reached out and snagged her by the hips, hauling her into him.

No longer hesitating, because after all, she'd just gotten exactly what she wanted, she snuggled in.

He fisted a hand in her hair and gently tugged her head back, studying her face.

She did her best to look one, sober, and two, like the best thing he'd never had but wanted.

Again he gave her that slow smile, the one that melted her bones away.

"You want me," he said.

She lifted a shoulder. "Maybe."

"Maybe? Quinn, the last time we were together, you climbed me like a tree."

"I did not." She totally had. "Maybe I just don't remember because it was over so fast . . ."

He laughed and then kissed her until she was breathless and clutching at him. "You're going to take that back when I'm done with you," he promised and she shivered with anticipation.

"Thought you were hungry," she said, already breathless as she ran her hands down the hard muscles of his back, touching as much of him as she could.

His hands were busy too, sliding up and down her back, making her heart thump.

"I *am* hungry," he said, grazing his teeth over her skin, taking a sexy bite of her throat, her shoulder, nudging her clothes aside, baring her to his gaze. "Just not for food."

His mouth came down on hers and she quivered as he curled an arm around her, nudged her thighs farther apart to fit between them. They moved wider of their own accord as he put on a condom and started to slide into her.

She was already gasping his name as he slid in deep. "Oh my God, Mick."

"I hope that's 'Oh my God don't stop.'" His low, husky voice washed over her as he drove himself deeper into her.

"Definitely don't stop," she managed, crossing her ankles behind him to keep him right where he was.

Don't stop.

Ever . . .

Which was a terrifying thought for someone whose world had spun out of control and into orbit with no landing in sight.

"Quinn."

She opened her eyes and looked at him, into his fathomless

dark eyes, and suddenly she felt anchored, and she clutched at him, shocked by how much she needed this, needed him.

"Stay with me," he said, and she knew he meant right now, in the moment. He couldn't possibly mean more, but she lifted up to kiss him, accepting.

Whatever it was he was giving her, a piece of him, all of him . . .

With a growl, he rolled his hips into hers with purpose, and they came together, even as they fell apart.

An hour later, Mick met Quinn's gaze.

She gave him a dopey smile. "Okay, I take it back. You're not fast. You're . . ."

He raised a brow.

"Disturbingly perfect."

Feeling suitably smug, he sat up on the couch and found a cat staring at him. An old, ratty-looking cat with only one good eye. "Uh, Quinn? There's a cat staring at me."

"That's Tink. Short for Tinkerbell. She's visiting."

Okay. Mick cracked his aching neck. "Tell me you're not sleeping on this couch."

"I'm working on turning the craft room into a bedroom." She sat up with a groan. Naked. He loved the view.

"I've cleared some space in it for the spare bed I found in the garage," she said.

Mick went out to the garage to check on the bed and found a family of field mice enjoying the hell out of the box spring. "You're not using that bed," he told Quinn, coming back in from the garage.

"Why?"

"Do you really want to know?"

She searched his gaze and then shook her head. "Nope."

"Give me half an hour, I'll be back with what you need." He gestured to the bottle of moonshine. "Maybe save the rest for another day."

"Why?"

"Because I've got additional plans for you," he said, amused to see her bite her lower lip in anticipation even as she blushed.

He was driving his dad's truck today and he was glad for that as he headed out to the one furniture store in the area that he knew of. He hadn't been by for years and hoped it was still there.

He got lucky. And it turned out the guy who now owned the place, Tyler Coronado, had dated Mick's sister way back when. Mick picked out a full-size mattress with a pretty wood frame for a screaming deal. "Good prices," he said.

Tyler sighed. "Going-out-of-business prices. I'm selling the property. I've slashed everything so I don't have to find storage."

"Sorry to hear that," Mick said.

"Wildstone's circling the drain, man. Not many of the small business owners think they can hold out for much longer."

"What's being done?" Mick asked.

"Nothing," Tyler said with disgust. "Seems certain officials keep getting richer, while the rest of us get poorer. Not that any of us can afford the legal battle."

When Mick left, he sat in the parking lot and sent off an e-mail to Colin, asking him to look into which specific business properties in town were in the most immediate danger of going under. He couldn't easily step in, as he was stretched thin now, but neither did he want to stand by and watch someone sink.

Half an hour later he and Coop were back at the house standing at the front door and staring down at Quinn's newest guard cat.

"Mew," the cat said, sitting smack in the center of the doorway, making no move to let Mick or Coop get by her.

Coop, normally a lover of people and all other creatures, whined, his ears down in a submissive pose.

Tink stared up at him from her one good eye, clearly in charge here.

"What do you think, buddy?" he asked Coop.

Coop—ears still low—slowly lay down, never taking his eyes off the cat.

Mick laughed softly. "She's harmless, bud. Look." He crouched down low and held out his hand.

The cat sniffed at it. Seemed to accept him. So he tried to pet her and . . . she sank her teeth into him.

"Jesus." He snatched his hand back.

Coop gave him a look like *and here I thought you were the smart one.*

Quinn came up behind the cat, wearing a white sundress, no shoes, no makeup, hair down and wild, and a soft smile. "My boys are back."

Coop perked right up.

So did Mick.

He rose to his feet, his eyes on hers. Leaning in past his silly dog and the Gestapo cat, he kissed her. Soft at first, and then when she made a soft little sound of acquiescence, he deepened their connection, feeling the stress of the day float away, feeling everything float away but the taste of her.

Smiling, she pulled back. "Thanks for the bed. Come on in."

Both man and dog looked down at the cat.

"It's okay, Tink," she said. "They're with me."

The cat didn't budge or take her eyes off them, and both man and dog hesitated.

"Come here, pretty girl," Quinn said and scooped up the cat. And just like that, the fierce-looking cat went boneless and set her head on Quinn's shoulder.

"Aw, isn't she sweet?" Quinn asked and turned away to lead them into the house as over her shoulder, Tink sent them both the evil eye.

"Sweet," Mick repeated and exchanged a wary glance with Coop as they followed.

Chapter 26

I miss when I was little and I didn't worry about grades, clothes, my weight, if someone liked me, or if my mom was going to up and die on me.

—from "The Mixed-Up Files of Tilly Adams's Journal"

It took negotiation and strategy to maneuver and then wrestle the new bed down the narrow hallway and into the tiny craft room. By the time they got the bed set up, Quinn felt like she'd just gone to the gym. "Not sure how I can thank you," she said.

He just smiled. "I've got a few ideas." He pulled her into him. "You're all sweaty." His voice made "sweaty" sound like the sexiest condition on earth.

She was breathless again. Still. He had her all worked up. "And you're all . . . hard."

"Watching you swear while working your ass off to get the bed in here turned me on."

Pleased laughter bubbled up in her chest. “Everything turns you on.”

“Actually, it’s you. You turn me on.” And then he tumbled her to the mattress, tucking her beneath him, pressing her into the bed as he made himself at home between her legs.

And quite possibly in her heart.

For her AP classes, Tilly was bussed with other kids from her high school to the city college and back. As she got off the bus at the end of her day, she looked around for Dylan.

Sometimes he came out to meet her off the bus and he’d walk her home. Sometimes they stopped for snacks at the convenience store first and went to the tree house.

Those were her favorite afternoons.

But he’d been busy lately. Too busy for her. Working, she knew, not messing around, but she missed him.

She missed a lot of things . . .

Because she was pouting and concentrating on her pity party for one, she didn’t pay attention and got caught by her home ec teacher, wanting to talk to her about her grades.

“I know you’ve had a hard time, Tilly,” Mrs. Bazio said. “And I’m prepared to give you some leniency because of that, but if you’re not careful you’re going to fail home ec and I know you don’t want that.”

Really? ’Cause maybe she *did* totally want that . . .

“If I offer you extra credit, are you going to try?” Mrs. Bazio asked.

She said yes. Actually, her mouth had said yes. Her brain, numb, hadn’t given a shit.

She turned and looked around for Quinn’s car. She didn’t have to look hard, the pretty Lexus stuck out like a sore thumb.

Quinn had parked facing away from the school under an oak tree, probably for the shade from the setting sun. But the joke was on Quinn because there was a reason no one parked there. The tree dropped acorns, which were sticky and a bitch to get off vehicles. The windows were down, all four of them, and at first Tilly thought her sister had her radio turned up, but realized she was just on the phone via her Bluetooth.

"My London trip's been postponed," a guy said, "and my sister's birthday party is this weekend. She was hoping for some of your spicy-chicken lettuce wraps, which you love to make almost as much as you love to come to my family's parties."

"I do love to make spicy-chicken lettuce wraps," Quinn said with a smile in her voice. She was both on her phone and thumbing through it at the same time. "And I also love to visit your family parties."

"You know we consider you one of us," he said fondly. "Although I'm pretty sure they're still hoping you show up with a diamond on your finger."

Quinn made a sound of regret. "Brock—"

"Look, I'm not trying to start a fight. I'm just letting you know, reminding you, that they love you."

"I know," Quinn said, suddenly sounding sad. "And it means a lot to me that they love me like their own, given that at the moment I'm feeling like I belong nowhere and to no one."

Tilly stilled. If she'd wanted proof that she was completely alone, here it was. Not even her sister considered her *real* family.

"Come back to L.A., Quinn," the guy said quietly, and there was something in his voice, something warm and coaxing, making Tilly realize that whoever this Brock was, Quinn meant a lot to him.

"And God help us all," he said, "but my dad found the karaoke machine, the one that we hid at the last party, so—"

"Brock."

He stopped talking. Blew out a breath. "You're not coming, are you?"

"I can't."

"It's still five days away, Q. How much longer are you going to stay up there?"

Quinn seemed to hold her breath at that one.

And there behind the car, Tilly did the same. *Yes, Quinn, just how long are you going to stay here and play house before you run back home and forget all about me?*

"Good question," Quinn finally said.

Tilly still wasn't breathing. She needed more. Except that when she got it, she wished she could unhear it.

"It's Tilly," Quinn said.

Tilly tried to keep holding her breath, but she couldn't, she had to gulp in air.

"You could just make the decision for her," Brock said.

"What, and drag her to L.A. kicking and screaming? How do you think that'll go?"

Nothing from the Brock dude on that.

"No, really, Brock," Quinn said. "I'm asking. Because I've no idea, okay? I'm out of my depth and out of my comfort zone. In fact, I'm so far out of my comfort zone I can't even see the zone."

"Quinn—"

"Do you think I don't want to come home? Because I do, badly. But I can't, okay? Not yet. I'm not going to just leave her here."

Tilly took a step back, and then another. No one was making any decisions for her, *no one.* Nor would she be dragged to L.A. Her heart was pounding so hard that at first she didn't register the fact that Quinn had gotten out of her car and waved at her, clearly completely unaware that Tilly had just overheard her.

"Come on," Quinn said, smiling like she was Tilly's friend. "What took you so long?"

Tilly got into the car and stared out her passenger window.

"Well hi to you too," Quinn said.

"Can you just drive?" Tilly knew she was being a complete bag of dicks but she couldn't muster up the capacity to care.

Quinn sighed and started the car. Tilly didn't pay any attention to where they were going until Quinn turned off the car and she realized they were at the beach.

Since it was dusk, cloudy, and barely seventy degrees, there wasn't another person in sight. Quinn pulled out her keys, grabbed a bag, and got out of the car. Without looking back, she started walking down to the water.

Tilly let out a rude sound of disbelief. Who did she think she was, just walking away like that without a word? And why would she assume Tilly even wanted to come here? She sat there stewing in her own negativity for a few more minutes, amusing herself by making a list of everything she hated.

The beach.
Her sister.
Her mom.
Chuck.
Cliff.
Girls who selfied all day long.
Girls with perfect hair.
Science.
Cooking.
Mrs. Bazio.

After a few minutes she ran out of things to hate and she got bored. She could barely see Quinn now, she'd sat on the sand, close to the water. Which was dumb because the tide was going to start rising and she'd ruin her really cute sandals.

"Dammit," Tilly said to the car and got out. She walked to where Quinn sat staring out at the water. "You're going to get wet."

Quinn shrugged.

She looked . . . sad. Like, really sad. Tilly sighed again and sat at her side. She played with the sand, running it through her fingers, letting the sound of the pounding surf ease her busy mind. "Do you miss L.A.?" she finally asked Quinn.

"Some."

Tilly's stomach hurt at that. As soon as Quinn decided she missed L.A. enough, she'd be gone. "What's your life there like?"

Quinn looked surprised at the question. "Well . . . I work a lot."

"At the fancy restaurant."

"It's fancy on the outside, yeah," Quinn said. "But on the inside, it's not nearly as nice as the café."

Tilly snorted. "Right."

"I meant on the *inside*, inside," Quinn said and put her hand to her heart. "The feeling you get standing in the kitchen there is very different from the feeling you get standing inside Caro's Café."

"Probably because there's no Greta yelling at you."

Quinn laughed at that. Laughed until she snorted and then laughed some more. The kind of laugh that might really be crying, and Tilly's heart felt tight. "I'm sorry," she finally said. "I'm sorry that my mom gave you away." She shook her head. "I don't get it, to be honest. She wasn't like that."

Quinn nodded but didn't say anything.

After sitting in silence for several minutes, listening and watching the waves, Tilly admitted something else that had been bothering her. "I'm mad at her too."

Quinn turned her head and met her gaze. "For what?"

"Dying."

Quinn let out a breath and reached for Tilly's hand.

"And for not telling me as soon as she knew she was sick," Tilly added. "For not telling me about you." She shrugged. "For a lot of things, I guess." She put her free hand to her chest. "I'm so angry it hurts."

Quinn squeezed her fingers gently. "She really had planned to tell you about me. Cliff told me that, and he seems like a man who values the truth."

Tilly swiped angrily at the few tears that had leaked out. "Or a man who just wants to smooth things over."

Quinn turned back to the water. "And Chuck? He's really a good guy?"

"Yeah." Tilly shrugged. "He's not my dad or anything but . . . well, he's been more of a dad than anyone else, I guess."

They stared at each other.

"Did you know him?" Quinn asked. "Our dad?"

Tilly felt an unwanted but undeniable tug of affection for this person she'd thought she hated, who was in the same boat she was. "I saw him once. He came to visit Mom. When he realized I was there, he took off."

"Maybe it was your sunny sweet nature," Quinn said.

Tilly, appreciating the dark humor, found a laugh. "No doubt."

They fell silent again. Quinn went through her bag and came up with two wrapped sandwiches. Grilled turkey from the café.

"Wow, Greta's getting better," Tilly said, munching hers.

"They're mine." Quinn lifted a shoulder. "I bought avocados. Greta was horrified."

Tilly laughed. "It's a kick-ass sandwich. You should add it to the menu."

Quinn looked pleased. "Yeah?"

"Yeah." She sighed. "I'm failing home ec. Specifically the baking part of home ec."

Quinn blinked at her and then laughed.

"Not funny," Tilly said. "If I fail, I have to take Mrs. Bazio for another whole semester and I'd rather—"

She broke off.

Because she'd been about to say she'd rather die.

But suddenly, that saying was no longer funny.

Quinn's smile faded. "I can help you. Not fail. Even though I suck at baking too."

Tilly met her gaze. "You do?"

"So much suckage, I can't even tell you."

Tilly laughed a little at this odd thing they had in common.

They were silent some more. No sounds other than the relentless waves crashing onto the sand and seagulls making sweeps to see if there were any leftovers.

"So can we put an end to this trial period?" Quinn asked after a long time. "Will you accept me as your guardian?"

Tilly hesitated. She didn't hate Quinn anymore, but she was pretty certain her sister wouldn't be sticking around Wildstone. The fact was, staying at Chuck's wasn't all that bad, and she had no rules there. Or very few.

She could tell Quinn would have a lot of rules.

The way Tilly figured it, she'd do better with Chuck until she turned eighteen, because if Quinn left, Tilly could get stuck in foster care and she didn't want that. "I think Chuck needs the money. So I was thinking . . . maybe I could float back and forth."

Quinn slid her a look. "So you can avoid any sort of real authority?"

Busted. "I wouldn't stay with him every night or anything, but he needs me to help him cook and stuff sometimes."

"Tilly," Quinn said gently. "It's his job to take care of you, not the other way around."

"Yeah, well, not everyone is good at that."

Quinn sighed. "Let's see how it goes. You've got to stay honest with me, okay?"

"Okay, and on the subject of honesty, I'm going camping tomorrow night with my friend Katie and her parents."

"Says who?"

Tilly sighed. "You going to be difficult about this too?"

"Maybe. I'm pretty good at it." Quinn looked at her. "What would your mom have said about the camping?"

Tilly went back to playing with the sand. "My mom knew Katie and her mom. She'd have had no problem with it. But it's no big deal, I'm not sure I want to go anyway."

"Why not?"

Tilly hesitated.

"Because you're not really going camping?" Quinn asked.

"No, it's really a camping trip, jeez!" Tilly had to laugh. "Suspicious much?"

"Hello, remember the park?" Quinn asked. "But do go on."

Tilly watched the sand sift through her fingers, catching the sunlight, looking like a million little crystals. Her mom had loved this beach. "I'm pretty sure the trip was planned just to cheer me up and get me away for a night, but Katie won't admit to it."

Quinn studied her for a long beat.

"What?" Tilly asked.

"I'm just wondering if I was ever this present and mature at your age. I'm pretty sure I wasn't." She sighed. "Honestly? It's up to you if you want to go or not, but whatever your decision, I'm trusting you, so don't blow it."

"No pressure or anything."

Quinn smiled. "Welcome to adulting. It sucks, by the way."

Tilly was starting to get that.

"And this reminds me," Quinn said. "I need a schedule of your normal routine, including the racetrack."

"I've only done that a few times," Tilly admitted. "Chuck needed the help because his back hurt. Also I'm good at picking winners. He uses the winnings to help keep paying his mom's bills."

"He shouldn't take you gambling, Tilly."

"Right," she said. "And my dad shouldn't have walked away from me before I was born. And my mom shouldn't have lied to me. And while we're on things that aren't fair, I'm only five foot two, but everyone else in the family is at least five foot seven, you included. I mean, what if I'd wanted to play volleyball?"

"Do you?"

She shuddered. "God, no. The girls on the team are total bitches." She sighed. "He's a cowboy, you know."

"Who?"

"Our dad." She felt Quinn turn to her, but she didn't look. Just kept playing with the sand. "On the rodeo circuit. Mom loved him." She paused. "I think about him sometimes. Wonder if he thinks about me. Us."

"I asked Cliff about him," Quinn said. "He gave up parental rights to each of us."

Tilly had dropped her head to her bent knees and turned only her face to look at Quinn. "Think he's ever regretted that?"

"I don't know."

But Quinn had hesitated in telling Tilly that she *did* know, or at least suspected that no, their father had never regretted his decision. But what if? What if he did? Tilly wondered. And what if they contacted him and he showed up and admitted he did? What if he wanted to stay and be with them? Would it fill the little tiny hole deep inside Tilly that had been there ever since she'd been old enough to understand he'd walked away from her?

And was this how Quinn felt about their mom? The thought stopped her in her tracks, brought her out of herself and reminded her that . . . she wasn't the only person who'd been abandoned.

Only Quinn had it double-fold.

"We should e-mail him," Tilly said. "Ask him if he's interested in seeing us."

Quinn didn't look as if this seemed like a good idea but she didn't say so. "Is that what you want to do?"

No, what Tilly wanted to do was have her mom back. But other than that, then . . . "Yes," she said softly.

Quinn nodded. "Okay. But not e-mail. We'll do it certified mail so we can see when he gets it. I think Cliff probably has an address for him."

Tilly nodded too, confident that their dad would get the letter, realize his daughters needed him, and he'd drop everything and come home. Because that's what dads did. Well, at least that's what they did in the movies and on TV. She had no other frame of reference, but she wanted to believe.

Chapter 27

I'm never sure if I actually have free time or if I'm just forgetting everything I'm supposed to be doing.

—from "The Mixed-Up Files of Tilly Adams's Journal"

They wrote the letter as soon as they got back. Quinn had mixed feelings about it but it seemed to give Tilly some peace, so there was that.

Then Quinn sat at the kitchen table to go through her bank account and make sure some bills got paid. Her bank account balance wasn't happy.

She was draining her funds at an alarming rate.

There were solutions. She could use a credit card. She could borrow money.

Neither appealed.

She could sell her expensive car, the one she'd never felt comfortable with in the first place, and use the money to make improvements in the café and house. In the meantime, she could use Carolyn's old Bronco, or buy herself something small and cheap.

Thinking it was a great idea and as good a place to start as any, she did some research on pricing, and listed the car online.

She and Tilly were standing in the kitchen arguing over dinner when her phone buzzed with an incoming FaceTime call from her parents.

"Oh, crap," Quinn said, not sure any of them were ready for this, a "family" video call.

"Are they mean?" Tilly asked.

It was that which decided Quinn. "No. The opposite. Brace yourself," she warned.

"For what?"

"My mom. She asks a lot of questions but she's all heart, so grin and bear it." She hit answer and her parents' faces, way too close to her mom's phone, came into focus, large pores and all. "Hey," Quinn said. "Before you start on the inquisition, Tilly's here."

Her parents both immediately beamed. "Show me!" her mom demanded.

Quinn turned to Tilly, who was standing on the other side of the kitchen shaking her head and miming a finger across her throat.

Quinn merely walked over there with the phone, went shoulder to shoulder with Tilly, and smiled into the screen. "Here she is. Fifteen in all her glory. Tilly, meet my mom, Lucinda, and my dad, James."

"Oh, honey," her mom said to Tilly, bringing trembling fingers up to her mouth as her eyes filled. "You look just like my baby! Which makes you also my baby! You're both too thin.

What have you been eating? Are you getting to bed early enough? If you're like Quinn, you're absolutely not. That girl used to sneak out and—"

"Mom," Quinn said on a laugh. "I'm trying to curtail the sneaking-out thing . . ."

Her mom smiled. "Ah. Karma has come around to bite you on the tush. About time." She looked at Tilly. "You doing okay, do you need anything? I've been dying to come up, but Quinn thought I'd overwhelm you, which is ridiculous."

Tilly looked at Quinn.

Quinn looked at her right back, daring her to misbehave.

Then Tilly smiled the sweetest smile Quinn had ever seen. "It's so nice to meet you," she said kindly. Kindly! "Quinn's mean, keeping you away. You should come visit sometime."

Her mom beamed.

Quinn groaned.

"We can't wait to do that!" her mom said. "In the meantime, you keep Quinn in line, you hear me?"

Tilly laughed in genuine delight while Quinn groaned again. "Oh, I will absolutely keep her in line," Tilly promised.

Looking thrilled at having a coconspirator, her mom smiled. "Good. Now what can you tell me about this Mick—"

"Mom, we've got to go. Love you," Quinn said and disconnected.

"You hung up on your mom. That's bad karma." Tilly, looking smug, went to the fridge. "They're very nice."

"Uh-huh. Don't snack, let's eat a real meal."

"So you can tell your mom you're taking good care of me?"

"I am taking good care of you."

They were arguing over dinner choices when someone knocked on the front door.

The cat, who'd been sitting near Quinn's feet as was her habit, bolted. Tink didn't like visitors.

Quinn opened the door to Coop and Mick. Mick held a casserole dish that smelled amazing and she fell a little bit in love.

"Wuff," Coop said and nudged his big head into Quinn's hand. She dropped to her knees and gave him a proper hug, for which she was rewarded with a face lick from chin to forehead. She laughed and stood up.

Mick smiled. "He took my move." But he leaned in and kissed her too.

"If it helps," she whispered against his mouth. "I like your move better."

"Good to know. My mom cooked something for you and Tilly."

"It smells like heaven," she said.

"Meat loaf, potatoes, and green beans."

"Comfort food," Quinn said with a smile.

"Or a heart attack in a pan," Mick said. "Whichever works for you."

The three of them sat and ate together—with Coop beneath the table lying in wait for scraps—talking, and even laughing. Until Tilly dropped a bomb.

"Are you two going to sleep together tonight?" she asked.

Quinn choked on a green bean.

Mick patted her on the back and handed her over a glass of water. When she finally collected herself, Quinn looked at Tilly. "Of course not."

"Because you two never sleep together, right?" Tilly rolled her eyes. "I'm fifteen, you know. Not five." She stood up and gathered the plates. "I'm just asking if you could not make a lot of noise so I don't have to keep the TV up loud."

Quinn was horrified. "Is that what you have to do at Chuck's?"

"Not every night," she said. "Sometimes he's too tired and Kendall sleeps in her own bedroom."

Good God.

Quinn tried to kick Mick out as soon as possible after that, but the man—as she'd already learned in bed—couldn't be rushed. First they did dishes. Then they had to go for ice cream because apparently Tilly couldn't go on without ice cream. Then they walked Coop around the block to do his business, which since he was like his master and couldn't be rushed, took a while.

When they came back, Tilly plopped herself down on the center of the sofa and proceeded to flip through the channels on the TV with the same intensity and concentration that a brain surgeon might show in the operating room. Certainly more intensity and concentration than she showed for her homework.

Or cleaning her room.

Or washing dishes . . .

Mick sat down next to her. Quinn tried to catch his gaze but he ignored her. She finally gave up and joined them, staring over Tilly's head at Mick. He wasn't afraid of bugs, women who saw ghosts, fistfights with his best friend, or going up against the city manager. And now he wasn't afraid of teenage girls either. Who was he, Superman?

Tilly had pulled up Hulu and was staring in horror at the history. "*Say Yes to the Dress*?" She jabbed a finger at the screen and then looked at Quinn.

"Are you Hulu judging?" Quinn asked.

"Oh my God, yes!"

Quinn squirmed and very purposely didn't look at Mick. "When I clean, I watch wedding shows. So what?"

"So you might want to seek help for that," Tilly said. "There's nothing new to watch."

"We could watch a movie," Mick said. "I brought a couple." He tossed a few on the coffee table.

Tilly snorted. "DVDs," she mused disdainfully.

"Got popcorn?" Mick asked, unruffled by the teen 'tude.

Coop's ears perked up at the word *popcorn*.

"Yeah," Tilly said, her ears perking up too. "We've got popcorn."

And then to Quinn's shock—they'd all eaten dinner, even had seconds, and then ice cream—Mick and Tilly inhaled popcorn while watching one of the DVDs—that they agreed on without argument.

When a kissing scene came on at the very end of the movie, Mick playfully reached out and covered Tilly's "tender" eyes.

"Fine by me," Tilly said. "Old people kissing is gross."

Mick got up and pulled Quinn to her feet and then kissed her right in front of Tilly.

"Ohmigod," Tilly moaned, covering her own eyes now. "*Gross.*"

"Deal with it," he said. He gave Quinn one more smooch and then headed to the door. "'Night, ladies."

Quinn followed him, shutting the door behind her. "What was that?" she asked.

"Me saying good night?"

"No, it was you making it clear we're a thing."

He looked at her, his amusement fading. "Actually, given what we talked about, your concerns about Tilly, it was me trying to show her that good guys do exist—as well as good relationships."

She stared at him, her belly pinched as an irrational fear gutted her. "But you and I aren't—"

He arched a brow.

"I mean . . ." She trailed off, unsure of herself, in uncharted territory. "We started off just as fun. We both said that."

"Yes," he agreed. "And it was fun, a hell of a lot of fun. Still is. It's also evolved into something more over the past month." He let out a mirthless laugh. "Which you obviously noticed or you wouldn't be freaking out right now over a perfectly great evening that didn't end badly."

"Are you suggesting I need drama in my life?"

"I'm suggesting you're scared."

Her heart was pounding against her ribs now. Because he was right. She was scared, scared he was going to want to define what they had, put a label on them, when she didn't even know who she was. And the thought of coming up with one made her feel anxious enough for a stroke. Why were they doing this? Why couldn't they just leave a good thing alone? "I've got to go in."

"Okay," he said, nodding his head like he wasn't surprised, and she felt like a coward. He started to go and then paused and looked right into her heart and soul with those deep, melting chocolate eyes. "Being scared is one thing, and in a lot of cases, it's smart. Probably in this case, it's smart. But if you're looking for an excuse to not have a relationship, it's fine. Just own it."

Her chest ached. "It's just that my life, it's . . . complicated."

"And?" he asked, not impressed. "Because everyone's is, Quinn. Mine included. But one thing I know, it's too short to be with someone who doesn't know if she wants me."

"I don't know what I want," she admitted.

He looked at her for a long moment, disappointment etched into his face as he nodded. "Can't fight that. You know how to get hold of me if you figure it out."

And then he and Coop were gone.

Quinn stared after the taillights of his truck, standing there long after they'd vanished. Finally she walked inside, feeling like she was clinging to the edge of a cliff with no safety net. In 150-mile-per-hour winds. With blocks of cement on her feet . . .

Tilly stood in the kitchen eating more ice cream right out of the container.

"He's very tall. Mick."

"Yes," Quinn managed.

"And he thinks he's funny," Tilly said, obviously having no idea that Quinn's entire world felt like it was shrinking in on her.

"Yes. He does think he's funny."

Another silence, and then Tilly said, "But he's okay, I guess. For a guy."

He was. And Quinn liked him. Way too much, clearly, as she'd just let her overwhelming feelings and emotions destroy everything.

Guess Lena wasn't the only one who could self-destruct her own happiness.

"What's your problem?" Tilly asked.

"I'm . . . not sure Mick and I are together like you think."

"Why not?"

Yeah, Quinn, why not? "Because he . . . likes me," she said. "A lot. And I . . ."

Tilly raised a brow.

"I'm not ready for that."

Tilly's eyes shuttered. "So you're, what, moving on? My mom did that too, you know. Hurt the people who loved her. Who's next? Me?"

"Tilly, no—"

But Tilly walked out of the kitchen and a moment later her bedroom door shut, hard.

Quinn walked around shutting off lights, getting ready for bed, and . . . tripped over Tink.

"Mew."

"Hey," Quinn said. "You done hiding?"

With no one around, the cat seemed to have let down her guard-dog stance. She looked somehow smaller, quieter.

Lonely.

Dammit. Quinn picked her up and the thing went completely boneless. She also shed enough fur to make a pillow. Quinn looked down at her black T-shirt, now streaked with brown hair, and sighed.

Tink sighed too and cuddled in more, pressing her face in the crook of Quinn's neck and then there was a sort of rumbling sound, like a motor starting up far, far away, one that hadn't been used in a long time and was maybe rusty. And about to break down.

Tink was purring.

"Glad you approve," Quinn said past a thick throat. "Right now you just might be the only one who does."

Tink purred some more.

"I'm really screwing things up," Quinn admitted into the fur. "Bad."

Tink nuzzled in a little, drooling on Quinn's neck.

"If only life came with an instruction manual. Then I could just look up all the right answers." She sighed and hugged the damn cat. "You're a good listener." Carefully, she set down the cat. "But it's time for bed." She opened the back door for Tink.

But with her ruffled head and tail high, the cat turned and headed down the hall instead.

"Uh—"

Tink jumped onto Quinn's new bed. And didn't quite make

it. Halfway up, she clung to the side of the mattress by her claws, having to make an effort to climb the rest of the way. At the top, she seemed quite pleased with herself, and also exhausted. She plopped down and began kneading the blanket like she was making biscuits.

At least one of them felt comfortable in her own skin.

THE REST OF the week both flew by and crawled. Quinn and Tilly—and Tilly and the cat—were all in some sort of uneasy alliance, a temporary one.

The story of her life lately.

They did find a routine—of sorts. Quinn and Tilly always got up early and went to the café, where Tilly got the eggs and Quinn cooked.

Then Tilly went off to school and Quinn stayed to cook through the lunch crowd. Quinn heard a lot of things at the café, learning more about the people in Wildstone than she'd ever wanted to know. Things like the fact that Big Hank had been married four times—to twins, and each had dumped him twice. Also, Cliff sometimes dated Lena's sister, who, apparently, was not crazy. Oh, and Carolyn had also dated Lou's second cousin's best friend's brother, who was the owner of the Whiskey River, and that she had a sandwich named after her there.

But most interestingly, she heard rumblings of Mick going toe to toe with the city manager—who was, as it turned out—Boomer's dad. There was a city meeting in a few days, and some of the old-timers were gleefully looking forward to watching Mick give the city manager an "ass whooping."

"It's not a wrestling match," Quinn said, hoping to get them to change the subject.

"No," Lou said. "It's going to be better."

This worried Quinn. From what she'd heard of the city manager, he wouldn't take anything Mick dished up lying down. When she got a quick break, she called Lena.

"You ready for me to fix your hair again?" Lena asked.

"Ha-ha, and no. I want to know what's going on with Mick and Boomer's dad."

Lena was silent for a beat. "Why?"

"Because you're mean and a little bit crazy, but you're also a solid judge of character."

Lena snorted. "Flattery will get you everywhere."

"It's not flattery," Quinn said. "It's the truth."

"Huh," Lena said with what sounded like grudging respect. "Okay. So about Boomer's dad. He's a complete asshat."

That's what Quinn was afraid of. "What will happen if Mick goes up against him publicly?"

"Whatever he can get away with," Lena said. "But don't worry, you can count on me."

"What— What does that even mean?"

But Lena had disconnected.

After school, Tilly called, checking in as Quinn had made her promise to do. Neither of them had talked about what would happen when school let out in a few weeks.

"How you doing?" Quinn asked.

"Heard you screwed up with Mick."

"You heard that at school?" Quinn asked, horrified.

"So it's true?" Tilly asked, sounding oddly disappointed.

"Only a little bit," Quinn said and tried to put on a good, brave front. "But look, I'm fine, okay? And we don't need a man anyway."

"Well, duh."

Quinn disconnected and sighed. She and Mick were . . . she

had no idea. She'd heard from Greta, who'd heard from his mom that he was back in the Bay Area.

Living his *not*-temporary life.

And he was doing it without her, because she hadn't straightened out her head, and in fact, had no idea what her life was even going to look like past this week.

On Saturday morning, Quinn woke up to some clattering in the kitchen. She moved down the hall, yawning. "What's going on?"

Tilly came out of the kitchen, holding her backpack, wearing a frown.

"What?" Quinn asked.

"I tracked our certified letter to Dad. It was delivered on Thursday."

"Okay," Quinn said. "And . . . ?"

"And he hasn't answered."

Quinn sighed. She'd been afraid of this. "We don't know that he will."

"I do. I know that he isn't going to."

"Tilly—"

"No, I get it. Message received loud and clear, right?"

"It was a long shot," Quinn said quietly.

"Yeah. I get it. My entire life is a long shot. Whatever." She pretended to shrug it off with the talent only a teenager could and turned away. She was wearing cutoff jeans, a tank top, and a backpack and Quinn pointed at her. "Where are you going?"

"Camping with Katie and her parents, remember?"

"Are you going to promise not to run away again? Because I don't want to chase you through the woods where there are probably bears and Big Foot and stuff."

Tilly laughed, and the sound was so unusual and nice that Quinn smiled too as she realized that sisters, whether by heart or by blood, were to be cherished for as long as you had them in your life.

"You're such a city girl," Tilly said. "And no, I'm not planning to run away while camping."

The qualifier didn't escape Quinn, but she'd take what she could get. "You going to be okay out there?"

"We're camping on the bluffs over the water."

"Same question," Quinn said.

Tilly nodded. "Yeah. I'm going to be fine."

"So you'll come back in one piece?"

"Sure. Whatever."

"Wow," Quinn said dryly. "Look at us having a bonding moment."

Tilly rolled her eyes. "Long as it doesn't come with a hug."

"Oh, but it does." Quinn lifted her arms and walked toward her sister like Frankenstein.

Tilly snorted and backed up.

"Ah, come on," Quinn said, following. "Hug me."

"No way!" Tilly dodged Quinn, but was at least laughing a little as she did so.

"Come on, we're doing so well."

"Yeah, well, don't get cocky," Tilly said. "Teenage girls are unpredictable."

"No kidding. I was one, you know."

"A million years ago, maybe," Tilly said.

"Yuck it up, Funny Girl. But one day you'll be on the wrong side of thirty and—"

"I didn't realize people lived that long."

"Okay, that's it," Quinn said and hugged her. And then when Tilly was squealing and trying to escape, she kissed her face all over.

Tilly finally gave up fighting it and sighed. "You're so weird."

"I know," Quinn whispered, and she held on tight.

So did Tilly.

Chapter 28

If thought bubbles appeared above my head, I'd be so screwed.

—from "The Mixed-Up Files of Tilly Adams's Journal"

Mick had been back in San Francisco a week, working his ass off. When he wasn't busy working his ass off, he slept. Or tried to.

It was crazy to him that after spending most of his life dreaming about getting out of Wildstone, all he wanted to do now was go back.

He'd known he was in deep with Quinn. He just hadn't realized exactly how deep, or that she'd stayed in the shallow end of the pool. He understood it, he did. She'd been hit hard by life several times over and she honestly believed she couldn't let herself love again.

But getting that and accepting that were two entirely different things. He knew it was probably foolish, not to mention stupid on his part, to think he could just be patient with her and wait her out.

But that's exactly what his plan was because when he was with her, he felt more alive, more happy, more . . . everything than he'd been in a long time.

And he wasn't ready to walk away from that.

But she needed space, and that he could do. At least he thought so, until he saw her ad to sell her car.

She needed money. He hated the thought. Thinking a text would be less likely to freak her out, he went with that.

MICK:

Hey.

QUINN:

Hey! Heard you were in SF.

MICK:

Yeah. Working. How are you?

QUINN:

You already know the answer to that. Screwed up.

MICK:

Knowing it is half the battle. You're selling your car?

QUINN:

How did you hear that . . . ?

MICK:

It's Wildstone. Do you need money?

QUINN:

No! Well, yes, but I'm fine.

MICK:

Quinn.

QUINN:

I want to make some home improvements, and I want to do it on my own. And I thought we weren't speaking.

MICK:

We're speaking. For future reference, we're always speaking. If you won't take money from me, then take a loan.

QUINN:

Sweet, but no thank you. I've got this.

MICK:

I'm the furthest thing from sweet you've ever seen and if you'd get over your fear of letting go, you'd let me prove it to you.

She sent him back an emoji of a laughing, smiling face and a blue heart. He had no idea why it was blue and not red, but he'd take it.

After Quinn drove Tilly to her friend's house for camping and met the parentals, she worked the breakfast shift at the café.

Greta took one look at her and did a double take. "You back together with Mick?"

Quinn blinked. "Um, what?"

"You're smiling."

"Grinning from ear to ear, actually," Trinee said, coming into the kitchen.

Quinn turned and eyeballed her reflection in the steel refrigerator door. Yep. She was grinning from ear to ear. It'd been Mick's texts.

She missed him.

"Maybe I'm just smiling because it's a nice day out," she said.

"Maybe," Greta said. "But I wouldn't mind having a smile like that."

"Later," Trinee promised her with a wink.

Quinn finished up her shift by two in the afternoon. In hindsight, with Tilly gone she should've gone home to L.A. for an overnight visit. She wasn't sure what it said about her that she hadn't even thought about it.

But then Skye blew her away by showing up to surprise her.

With her parents.

It was the very best kind of surprise.

Her parents were so disappointed to miss seeing Tilly—and meeting Mick—but they were happy to see where Quinn was staying. "It's beautiful here," her mom said.

"Not a bad place to build a life," her dad said.

Her mom took his hand, and looking both happy and a little bit sad, nodded. "I'm so proud of you, Quinn," she said quietly. "So happy to see you being so strong and building yourself a life, one that wasn't handed to you."

"Mom." Quinn hugged her, realizing that no matter how overprotective they'd been at times, they really did love her. They loved her every bit as much as they had Beth.

Which she also realized meant she could love Tilly every bit as much as she'd loved Beth too. "I want you to know that I'm grateful for everything you and Dad gave me. I should say that more."

Her mom nodded and squeezed her tight. Then she pulled free, swiped her tears from her face, and said, "I want to see the chickens."

So they visited the evil chickens.

And no surprise, Tink loved her mom. The cat rubbed herself all over her mom's black pants, leaving behind some brown fur clumps.

"It's okay," her mom said, much to Quinn's and her dad's shock. The woman felt faint if she found so much as a stray thread on her clothes. "She's a sweet thing."

Quinn watched her mom pet Tink. "Careful, Mom. You can pet her twice, but on the third time she's going to bite you."

Her mom stroked Tink a third time and . . . Tink's eyes drifted shut in bliss.

Quinn just shook her head.

The four of them went to the Whiskey River for dinner and the Bartender's Special. They laughed, talked, laughed some more, and when it was time for Skye and Quinn's parents to leave, they all hugged good-bye.

"You should stay for a couple of days," Quinn said, not wanting to let them go. "Or at least stay the night since it's so late and it's a long drive."

"Your dad has a golf game tomorrow."

"It's a tournament," her dad said. "I'm finally going to kick Ted's ass."

Ted was the district attorney, and they'd been battling it out on the course for years.

Her dad pointed at her. "Check your car fluids."

Quinn let out a low laugh and nodded as her heart tightened. "I will."

"I have to work tomorrow anyway," Skye said. "I don't want to come into Marcel's crosshairs." She paused and met Quinn's gaze. "I didn't want to ruin our day, but I don't feel right not telling you. Word is Chef Wade's looking for a new sous-chef."

It was a direct hit to the gut. But she didn't blame him. Not in the least. "It's okay," she told Skye. "It's going to be okay." Somehow . . .

Skye smiled and nodded, but she didn't look like she was sure.

Which was fair because Quinn wasn't sure either.

Quinn didn't sleep well. Correction: at all. She was worried about her job. Worried about whether Tilly was okay while camping. Worried about how much time she spent thinking about

Mick . . . She'd held back with him because they didn't have a future.

But was she doing the right thing?

"No," Beth said. "You're not doing the right thing at all. But please, carry on as you will, like you always do."

Quinn nearly leaped out of her skin. She flipped on the light and found Beth sitting on the end of her bed. "*Jesus.*"

Beth smiled. "The answer is still no. But don't let that stop you. You're the most stubborn woman I've ever met, and you'll figure it out eventually. Hopefully."

"What?" Quinn demanded. "*What* will I figure out?"

But of course, Beth was gone. "Dammit!" she yelled. "I really hate it when you do that!"

"Mew."

Tink was perched on top of the extra pillow. The cat came and went, but mostly came, staying near Quinn as often as possible.

Tink stood up, stretched, and made herself comfortable—*on* Quinn.

They cuddled through the rest of the night. The next morning, Quinn woke up and called Chef Wade. Yes, he was thinking he needed to hire someone, and she absolutely 100 percent understood. She had mixed feelings about her job in the first place. But . . . she wasn't ready to let go of it. She told him school would be out in two weeks and that if he hadn't found someone to replace her by then, she'd love to come back. And stay.

He was so hugely relieved by that, she utterly believed him when he told her he didn't want anyone else and that they could make do until she returned.

With that weight off her chest, she once again worked at the café and then went back to Carolyn's house and tried to take simple pleasure in the small changes she'd made, removing some of the clutter to the attic, clearing out a little bit more from the craft room to make her feel more at home.

She eyed the small desk and gave in to temptation, unlocking it and removing Carolyn's journal.

Tilly came home smiling today.

Smiling.

She got a B in her history class, and after the struggle she's had over grades for the past several years before we discovered she was dyslexic, this is a miracle.

Of course we owe it all to Dylan, who tutors her as often as he can, which is less now since his parents' messy divorce. Tilly took that hard.

And then came my diagnosis, which she took even harder.

She's had so much to deal with, so very much, that I don't have the heart to tell her just how bad it is.

People leave her; her father, Dylan, and now, though she doesn't yet know it, me.

I'm so scared for her. Terrified, really. So much so that I'm willing to do something I promised I wouldn't.

I'm going to find Quinn.

Quinn slowly shut the journal. So now she had the answer to the question of why Carolyn had come looking for her.

She'd needed someone to look after Tilly.

However Quinn felt about that, the fact remained that without her, Tilly was far too alone. She blew out a breath and put the journal back, shutting the drawer a little harder than necessary.

She headed through the house to the living room, Tink on her heels.

The sun beat in windows that were old and not dual paned, so the house was hot. The air conditioner had apparently gone on the fritz a long time ago. A fast, cheap fix would be some quality window shades to keep out the afternoon sun. Then there was the fact that of the two bathrooms, only one shower worked, and that one only trickled out tepid water.

She missed hot water. A lot.

The dishwasher was broken. And so was the lock on the back door. The list went on and on.

Whether they kept this house and rented it out, or sold it and the café, either way there needed to be some serious upgrades. Before they left for L.A., which they still needed to talk about.

The problem about fixing the house was money. Chef Wade paid her decently—when she was working there, that is. But the pay scale at the café wasn't exactly comparable and she was wracking up her own personal bills, including the last of her school debt. Her parents had offered to pay her school loans off several times, but it had been a point of pride with her.

She'd wanted to do something for herself.

She wouldn't ask them for help with this. She couldn't.

Which meant it was time for some tough decisions. She'd just lowered the price on her car in her ad when the front door slammed.

Quinn turned and looked at Tilly as she stepped into the living room. She wondered when would be the right time to bring up the whole moving to L.A. thing when school got out. Now?

The girl was subdued, standing there clutching a backpack and a big paper bag with clothes in it, looking . . . hollow.

Okay, so maybe they wouldn't talk about L.A. right now . . . maybe after a tub of ice cream. "How was camping?"

"It was camping," Tilly said. She looked around, eyes sharp.

Quinn had barely changed anything in the entire house; most of the changes had occurred only in the craft room. The only thing that she'd done out here was add a plant to the coffee table.

And a cat.

Tilly's glare zoomed in on the plant and narrowed. "What did you do in here?"

"Added a plant."

"You also stacked up the magazines."

"Yes," Quinn said, setting down Tink. "When I dusted."

Tilly looked at the cat.

Tink looked back, seeming as displeased by this new intrusion as the teenager herself.

"The stray's still here," Tilly said.

"Yes, and she's good at it, she hasn't strayed at all," Quinn quipped.

And speaking of that, neither had Tilly. She'd made sure she had the option to stay here or at Chuck's and yet from the day Quinn had started sleeping here, Tilly had done the same.

Surely Quinn could take some comfort in that.

"Mom didn't like cats, you know," Tilly said.

Quinn refrained from pointing out that no, she didn't know. "She's homeless. And her name is Tink."

Tilly stared at the cat some more.

The cat continued to stare back.

Bitchy teen versus bitchy cat in a standoff. Quinn wondered how long it could possibly go on. Who'd lose patience first?

Turned out it was her. "So . . . you going to tell me about camping or not?"

Tilly lifted a shoulder. "It was hot, dusty, and there were huge spiders in the bathrooms. Whatever."

"Okay then. So a good time was had by all."

Tilly rolled her eyes and headed toward the hall, slowing because the cat was in her way.

Another showdown began, and tired of it, Quinn moved in and picked up the cat.

Tink immediately went boneless in her arms, setting her head on Quinn's shoulder and snuggling in.

Quinn's heart did a slow melt as she hugged the skinny cat, who was less skinny now after a week of Quinn feeding her regularly. "She'll warm up to you," she murmured as Tilly vanished down the hall. "Probably we should give her a little space right now—"

"*What the hell*?" came Tilly's unhappy voice.

Still holding Tink, Quinn moved down the hall to find Tilly standing in the middle of the craft room staring at the room like a bomb had gone off.

"I was tripping over boxes getting in and out of bed," Quinn said. "I simply pushed some stuff over to make more room."

"You moved my mom's things."

"No, I purposely left your mom's bedroom alone. I just moved some of the craft and sewing stuff—"

"You had no right!"

"Tilly—"

"Some of that stuff was mine, did you think of that?" Tilly asked, voice raised but also quavering, like she was near tears.

"Honey, listen," Quinn said, "I didn't throw anything away, not a single thing. I just piled some of it up a little bit and put a few things in the attic—"

"The attic? There're mice in the attic!"

"Tilly—"

But the girl was gone, running down the hall to her room, where she—shocker—slammed the door hard enough to rattle the windows and every thought in Quinn's head.

Okay, so maybe a tub of ice cream wasn't going to do it either.

"Well," she said to Tink. "That went well." She'd hoped to show Tilly her mom's journal, but instead, knowing the teen needed some space, she worked on her laptop in the kitchen.

No offers on the car ad.

No sexy texts from Mick.

She checked in at home. Her parents were fine. Brock was still in London and sounded in his element. Skye told her Marcel horror stories.

When Tilly didn't come out, Quinn left a note on the kitchen table that she'd be back in time to cook dinner and got into her car.

Fifteen minutes later she was on the bluffs that she'd visited her first day in Wildstone. She kicked off her shoes and climbed down to walk along the shore. It was foggy and she felt like she was alone in the world.

Except she wasn't. A lone figure came out of the fog. Quinn sighed, more than a little irritated to have her solitude disturbed, especially by Lena.

Who looked no less thrilled than she.

"What are you doing?" Quinn asked, sounding as grumpy as Tilly and Tink. It must be contagious. "Don't tell me you're out here exercising."

Lena smiled. "The first time I see a jogger smiling, I'll consider taking it up. I'm just walking off some tension before I end up in jail for murder one."

"Who're you looking to kill?"

Lena just looked at her.

Quinn choked out a laugh. "Right. Me. Got it."

Lena sighed. "Okay, not you. Life."

"Join the club. But just remember that if you go to jail for murder, I don't think you get a full range of hair products in there."

Lena shuddered. "People would see my roots. Can you imagine?"

"This from the woman who gave me blue highlights."

Lena looked over her hair, coming close to do so, having no compunction about putting her hands in it to check it over. "And they still look fucking fantastic on you too. Bitch."

Quinn sighed and sat on the sand. When Lena didn't sit, she craned her neck, shielding her eyes from the setting sun with her hand. "You joining me or not?"

"Why would I?"

"Because like it or not, you need a friend. And so do I."

Lena hesitated. "I'm not very good at being a friend."

"Just sit."

"I'm wearing linen."

"Fine," Quinn said. "Suit yourself. But I was going to open up to you and whine, and make you feel really good about yourself."

"Well, hell, if you're going to make me feel good about myself . . ." Lena gingerly sat, carefully brushing off her hands. "Go ahead. Compliment me."

Quinn laughed. "Compliment you? Are you serious? You hijacked my hair, have used every opportunity to make fun of me, and you actively tried to steal away the guy I was seeing . . ."

"You said you were going to make me feel good about myself—Wait. *Was?* Did Mick dump you on your annoyingly great ass?"

"I dumped him," Quinn said miserably. "But it was totally accidental."

Lena stared at her and then tipped her head back and laughed.

"It gets worse," Quinn said miserably. "I'm blowing it with Tilly. If you know anything about teenage girls, now is the time to tell me. All advice is welcome."

"Tell her to use condoms, don't be stupid enough to get knocked up, and don't get fat," Lena said. "There's time for all that later, like when you're old. Or dead."

"Wow," Quinn said. "You're right. You're really bad at this."

"Hey, those golden tidbits came straight from my mom when I was a teenager." She went back to staring at Quinn's hair. "You really should reconsider using that deep-oil conditioner I wanted you to buy."

"It was a million dollars."

"*Forty* dollars," Lena said. "And worth every penny. You're as frizzy as a squirrel on a rainy day."

"Gee, thanks."

"You're not telling people I did your hair, are you?"

Quinn sighed.

Lena was quiet for a moment. "So you're really not seeing Mick anymore?"

"I'm not sure." Quinn turned and met Lena's gaze. "Besides, what does it matter? You were going after him whether I was or wasn't."

Lena let out a low, mirthless laugh. "Come on," she said. "We both know I don't have a shot as long as you're in the room."

"I still don't understand why you're not with Boomer, who clearly loves and adores you."

"I have my reasons."

"Such as you enjoy sabotaging your own happiness?"

Lena stared out at the water for a long time. "I'm an alcoholic," she said quietly. "Recovering, but still. Boomer runs a bar and he . . ." She shook her head.

"What?"

"He has a problem. With alcohol. He's gone to rehab in the

past, but it didn't stick. He says he wasn't ready then but . . . I can't . . ." She shook her head. "He's a bad influence on me."

Quinn felt a wave of genuine sympathy roll over her. "Can he get help?"

"Of course he can. The question is *will he*, and the answer is no, at least not for me."

"You've talked to him?" Quinn asked.

Lena just looked out at the water.

"You haven't talked to him," Quinn said.

"Look, if a guy can't read my mind and figure out my admittedly mercurial moods, then he's not for me."

"You're scared," Quinn said. Marveled. "Holy shit, who would've guessed that the badass Lena is running scared?"

"Shut up," Lena said without much heat.

Which meant she was right. "So what's this thing with Mick then? Just a way to make Boomer feel jealous so he'll kick it into gear?"

"Maybe I'm trying to save Mick from making a mistake with a spoiled city girl."

"Okay. Good talk." Quinn stood up, brushed herself off, and turned toward her car.

"*Now who's chicken?*"

"Still you!" Quinn yelled back. "Talk to Boomer!"

MICK CAME BACK into Wildstone on Monday for the night's bimonthly city council meeting. It turned out to be a crowded affair. There wasn't a lot to do here at night. Drinking at the Whiskey River, making out on the dunes, hitting the occasional moonlight surf contest . . . and going to Wildstone city council meetings.

Just about everyone in town was there. His mom. Lena. Greta and Trinee.

But not Quinn, which he knew because he searched the crowd. He didn't acknowledge the disappointment. She wouldn't be here, of course she wouldn't, she wasn't staying in town.

He did enjoy the surprise on city manager Tom Nichols's face when he spotted Mick in the audience.

The meeting droned on, but when the time was appropriate and people were allowed to speak or ask questions, Mick stood up. He asked several questions, all pertaining to the outside contracting of construction projects and other jobs.

"This isn't the time or place—" Tom began, but several other people stood up to join Mick, including some of the local businessmen Mick had been talking to: Lonnie and Cruz Rodriguez, Rick Espy, and Tyler Coronado, among others.

"Isn't it?" Lonnie Rodriguez asked. "I've been asking you all year and got nowhere."

More people stood up, and as the attendees got riled up and more assertive, their city manager got less polite. The mayor, Camille Olsen, an elected official in her last term, tried to restore order and failed, finally gesturing for Mick to go on and finish with his question.

"We'd like specifics for what's being done to attract visitors and boost the local economy," he said.

This was followed by a lot of vocal agreement. Everyone wanted to know what was being done.

"How is this your business?" Tom asked. "You don't even live here anymore."

"He bought property," Lonnie Rodriguez said. "Mine and the winery. And maybe the B and B too, so it's very much his business."

Mick knew better than to think anything could remain quiet in Wildstone, but he wasn't thrilled about this public statement of his business dealings. Everyone, including his mom, was suddenly looking at him, reading too much into it. "I'm not a local anymore," he emphasized. "But I do have a vested interest, same as everyone else."

Tom spouted some well-worded verbiage that didn't really answer anything, and right after that the mayor took back control and closed the meeting.

Afterward, Mick's mom hugged him. "Why didn't you tell me you'd bought property here in Wildstone?" she asked, looking thrilled.

"I didn't want you to make too much of it."

"Too late," she said, smiling big.

Mick drove her home and then, feeling restless, he took to the streets again. He ended up at the bluffs with Coop and was watching the waves by moonlight when a figure came close and sat next to him.

Quinn.

Chapter 29

I hate the feeling when you're sad and you have no idea why but you just are.

—from "The Mixed-Up Files of Tilly Adams's Journal"

Quinn had been quietly walking the bluffs, taking in the night and trying to clear her head when she'd seen Mick and Coop arrive.

Coop bounded over to her, all floppy ears, excited drool, and wide smile.

His owner was more subdued, but there was a light in his eyes that said he was just as excited to see her as Coop, and something went a little squishy in her chest.

Coop climbed into her arms and sat himself on her lap like he'd been born there, and just panted happily.

Mick shook his head at his dog. "What are you doing here?"

"I come here sometimes," she said. "When I need to think. It was my first stop in Wildstone, if you'll remember."

"I remember."

She smiled. Her panic attack at being here seemed so long ago now. "It's my spot."

"We have the same spot." He looked at her. "It's good to see you."

"You too. You've been avoiding me."

"Giving you time to think," he said.

Her heart melted and she leaned into him, setting her head on his shoulder. "I missed you," she said softly, and felt his arm come around her.

"Missed you too," he said in a voice that told her he meant it.

She was quiet for a moment, and so was he. Then she said, "According to the gossip mill, you're moving home to Wildstone and you're still buying up properties."

He snorted. "Don't believe everything you hear. In fact, don't believe anything you hear."

"But you did buy some properties when they were in trouble."

"Because they were a good, solid investment," he said.

Her smile was wry. "In Wildstone? I think we both know that's not necessarily true. Maybe you were meant to come back here." She paused. "And stay."

"I bought these properties because I hate how the town is being managed and I don't want to see good people go down. But that doesn't mean I'm going to be a local—something you of all people should understand. You're staying here for now but you're temporary too."

True. "It's hard to make any kind of personal decision because I'm making it for two."

"Is it?" he asked. "Or is the hard part following your heart when you no longer trust it?"

Her gaze flew to his as she felt the words echo deep in her heart.

"Quinn," he said with such terrifying gentleness that her throat burned. "You've gone a long time without letting your heart rule."

"Two years," she whispered back.

"You're fighting your own nature."

"Which is what?" she asked, and she wasn't kidding. She really wanted to know.

He nudged Coop out of her lap.

Coop snorted his displeasure but turned in a circle and plopped at their feet.

Mick moved in, holding Quinn's gaze. "To feel," he said quietly. "You're fighting your own nature to feel."

Oh, God. That was true too. She'd held back her emotions and she'd gotten good at it, but ever since coming to Wildstone, it had been nothing but a flood of feels.

"You've also held back your own nature to love," he said.

She stared at him, her heart pounding. "How do you know?"

"Because I know you. Or I'm starting to. I've seen you with Greta and Trinee, and the café you thought you didn't want. I've seen you with Tilly, and no matter what she throws at you, trying desperately to prove she doesn't need you or anyone, you keep your patience."

"She's my sister," Quinn said. "And the café is, *was*, Carolyn's." She hesitated. "My mom's."

"And Lena?" he asked. "You've gathered her in too, like one of your chickens. What's your excuse for caring about her?"

Dammit.

He laughed softly. "Let yourself go, Quinn. Let it happen. It's okay to love this place and everyone in it."

And you, she wondered. *Is it okay to let myself love you as well?* But she knew the answer to that. It wasn't okay. But looking into his eyes, seeing the easy attraction, she told herself it was okay to stay in the moment and enjoy this for as long as she could.

To that end, she stood and kicked off her shoes as her fingers went to the button on her jeans.

Coop lifted his big head and gave one excited bark. His humans were on the move!

Mick raised a brow at Quinn.

"It's hot," she said. "And my brain's tired of thinking. I'm going for a swim." She wriggled out of her jeans while he watched, eyes hot now.

"This swim," he said. "Is it a solo swim?"

"Only if you're slow." She pulled off her top and turned to the water, but before she'd taken a single step, she was lifted into the air and thrown over Mick's shoulder.

"It's not me who's slow," he said and dove into the water with her.

The following Saturday morning, Quinn stood in Carolyn's kitchen wearing nothing but Mick's T-shirt, undies, and some whisker burns. Tilly had spent the night at Katie's, and Quinn had had a sleepover of her own.

Later, after Tilly came home, she was going to have the let's-move-to-L.A.-and-make-this-real conversation.

She was nervous as hell about that.

But it was time. Past time . . .

The hens were very busy clucking and muttering among themselves. Such a simple life, she thought, and yet . . . it felt right. She'd been fighting that for a while, but she couldn't deny the truth.

She was happy here. She would definitely miss being here, including the sexy, six-foot, naked guy she'd left in her bed.

The knock on the front door surprised her and she looked

down at herself. Definitely needed more clothes on before answering. Dodging out of the kitchen, she stopped short in the living room, staring in shock out the window that ran alongside the front door.

It was Brock.

Before she could think it through, she pulled the door open. "What are you—"

He hauled her into him and kissed her.

She was so shocked she froze in place as his arms tightened on her so that they were pressed up against each other in a familiar way that once upon a time had both comforted her and turned her on.

It did neither now.

She took a big step back and shook her head at him, and then realized that Mick had come into the living room.

When she'd left him flat on his back, spread-eagled on her bed, he'd been sated, boneless, and practically purring. He'd certainly been relaxed.

He wasn't relaxed now. In nothing but unbuttoned jeans, he stood there with a carefully blank look on his face, tension radiating from him.

Not sure how much he'd seen, Quinn decided to deal with one problem at a time and turned on Brock. "What are you doing here?"

"Thought I'd visit my fiancée." He said this with his eyes locked on Mick. "I'd ask you the same question but I think it's pretty obvious what you're doing."

Resisting the urge to tug Mick's shirt down lower on her thighs, she shook her head. "I thought you were in London."

"I'm back. Surprise."

"Mick," she said with what she felt was remarkable restraint, "this is Brock. Who is *not* my fiancé. And also knows how I feel about surprises." She gave Brock a long look. "Brock, this is Mick."

The men stared at each other. Neither spoke. Awkward didn't even begin to cover it.

Quinn's dad wasn't a quiet man. When her dad got angry, he blew his lid so everyone knew it. Brock was very much the same. And those were the only two real relationships she'd ever had with the male species.

Mick was nothing like either of them. He was . . . stoic. When angry, he got quiet. She had no experience with this and had no idea how to defuse the situation. The only thing she could think of was that she had to get rid of Brock so she could explain things to Mick, but she knew Brock wasn't going anywhere until she made him. "Brock," she said. "We need to talk."

"I agree," he said.

She nodded and turned to Mick. "Can we have a minute?"

For a single heartbeat, Mick remained still, his body language carefully neutral, calm even. Then he gave her a single nod and turned away, giving a low whistle for Coop, who'd been sleeping on the living room rug.

Quinn assumed Mick would go back into her bedroom, or maybe the kitchen. Instead he walked—still shirtless and barefoot—right out the front door, Coop at his heels.

He must've had his keys in his pocket because he headed to his truck and drove off, leaving a small cloud of dust thanks to the dry weather, and a big hole in her heart.

"Fiancée?" she asked Brock, pissed off. "*Seriously?*"

"Hey, you once made a promise to marry me if we were both single when we hit forty."

"You know neither of us meant that!"

He blew out a sigh. "I want to mean it, does that count?"

She shook her head in temper and whipped around, heading to her bedroom.

"Where are you going?"

"For pants!"

"Don't do that on my account."

"Brock?"

"Yeah?"

"Shut up." She shoved herself into a pair of jeans and moved back to the living room.

"So who is he?" he asked.

"None of your business."

"Come on," he said. "I've got eyes in my head. He's someone to you."

"More than a wild oat," she agreed, and that it was true no longer surprised her. "He's an engineer from the Bay Area. He doesn't live here either, his mom does. He's helping her remodel her house and then he's out."

Brock took this in. "So . . . you've once again got yourself an out clause? Nicely done, Q."

Not a can of worms she intended to open, not with him. "Why are you here, Brock? The truth."

He ran a hand over his head and gave her a sheepish grin. "I came because your mom pleaded with me to talk some sense into you, but somehow when you opened the door and I saw your wild oat standing behind you with that bite mark on his neck, I talked myself into fighting for you instead."

Oh dear God. She'd left a bite mark on Mick? "You're not the fighting type."

"Yeah, the urge was temporary," Brock admitted. "I mean when the guy opened the door minus his shirt and with you in it, the first thing I felt was jealous."

"So that's why you kissed me."

He nodded. "But then you didn't respond to it and I felt . . ."

She raised a brow.

"Relief."

She smacked him in the chest and he let out an "oof" and caught her hand in his as he flashed her a grin, which slowly faded. "I know I've hurt you. I was an ass to not hold on to you harder."

"Not all your fault," she said. "Not nearly."

"No hard feelings?"

"Never," she said and walked into his arms. They hugged hard and Quinn spent a moment grieving for what would never be: having Beth alive to grow old with, having Brock as her "maybe," and . . . a life in L.A.

Because she got it now, 100 percent. She hadn't spoken to Tilly about leaving Wildstone for L.A. because . . .

She didn't want to go.

She wanted this life.

She wanted Tilly in this life.

And she also wanted Mick.

"About effing time," Beth said, laughter in her voice.

Quinn looked behind her but there was no Beth. Except for in her own head.

Brock pulled back, his face full of affection and regret. "I do love you, Quinn."

"I know," she said. "I love you too."

In what was actually the most tender moment they'd ever had, he leaned in and kissed her softly. "Want to go get something to eat?"

"I know you just drove three hours to get here," she said. "But I have something I really need to do."

Brock gave her a small smile. "A half-naked, pissed-off dude in a truck?"

"Yeah."

Twenty minutes later, Quinn located Mick standing in his dad's garage, hands on his hips. When he was tired, he wore the look he had now. Wary, as if maybe he couldn't count on his normal sharp instincts to function well enough on autopilot.

Although she wouldn't tell him so, she liked him best this way, a little worn and weary, a little rough around the edges. He was so different from any man she'd ever met. "Hey," she said.

He glanced over at her and didn't say a word. Nor did he give away any of his thoughts, though she figured he was angry. He'd found shoes and a shirt, and appeared to be getting ready to paint.

"I'm sorry about earlier," she said, coming into the garage. "I didn't know he was coming, or that he'd say he was my fiancé. He thought he was being funny."

"Did he."

Quinn moved to his side and met his gaze. Definitely angry. "I'm sorry," she said again. "I could've handled that better. It's just that Brock and I go way back, we've been friends forever."

"Friends. And lovers," he said. "He's the one you broke up with after . . ."

". . . Beth's death." She nodded. "Yeah. That's him. But we aren't sleeping together."

"That kiss said otherwise."

She sighed. "He did that to piss you off. It didn't mean anything. We broke up *years* ago."

"Two," he said. "And you're missing my point. You were with him until your world caved in, and then you two fell apart. Not because you fell out of love, but because you felt you couldn't love."

"No," she said, shaking her head. "You're reading this wrong. My relationship with him has no bearing on the one between you and me."

He nodded. "Yeah, see, I'm not sure you understand what constitutes a relationship. You're either in or you're out with someone, Quinn. I thought after the other night on the bluffs . . ." He shook his head. "Never mind."

"Look," she said, starting to panic that she was messing this up. "Whatever you think you saw between me and Brock, you're wrong."

"Maybe. Or maybe I was wrong about what's happening between us." And with that, he began to paint, dipping the roller brush into the tray, carefully and methodically painting the wall in front of him, his broad shoulders stretching taut the seams of his T-shirt.

Quinn watched his effortless movements for a long moment but he didn't look at her again. She found her temper at that. No, he wasn't wrong about what had been happening between them, but she didn't know what she was doing. She needed help because she was . . . lost. But hell no would she ask, so she spun on a heel and walked away.

And he let her.

Chapter 30

Anyone who doesn't agree that leggings are pants can physically fight me. I'll win because I have a full range of motion due to the fact that I'm wearing leggings as pants.

—from "The Mixed-Up Files of Tilly Adams's Journal"

Mick stood in his dad's garage, heart thudding dully, unable to think straight. Okay, yes, it had been sheer, stupid bruised ego that had let her walk away. The truth was that Quinn had been up front about her inability to love him. If his feelings had started to change—which, given the sharp pain in his chest, they had—that was all on him.

Not her.

As was the fact that he'd let those feelings take root, deep root. He'd dropped his walls. Been a long time since he'd let that happen. And that made him an idiot. He set down the paint roller and stood there, Coop at his feet, both of them staring at the wall he hadn't yet covered, the one with the damn white outlines of the still-missing tools.

Mick's dad had been controlling as hell, and as a result, Mick had made it a point to never tell people what to do with their lives, including their love lives.

So he hadn't been about to start with Quinn. She was a big girl. She either wanted him for keeps or she didn't.

And hell.

She clearly didn't.

Which was undoubtedly for the best and meant that she was smarter than he was. His life was far from here and far from her. It had also been a long time since he'd had anything more than casual, and he wasn't about to start with a woman he couldn't see when he wanted to see her. In his experience, absence didn't make the heart grow fonder. Absence made people do stupid things.

Like cheat.

"There you are," his mom said, stepping into the garage. Coop gave a low, excited "wuff."

"I heard you drive up," she said while simultaneously hugging Coop, "but then you vanished." She beamed up at Mick. "I'm so happy about what you're doing in Wildstone."

"Mom." He took her hands, which were fluttering around in excitement. "It's not what you think."

"You bought into local businesses," she said. "Because your town's in trouble. Promises have been broken, but you're trying to help. You care about Wildstone, and because of that you're going to stay—"

"I bought them because I care about the local businesses being squeezed out by a city manager who should be protecting this town, not taking kickbacks from outsiders while squelching businesses who've been here for decades. It's all just business to me."

"Of course it's not just business or you'd have done this anywhere *but* Wildstone." Her eyes got misty. "I'm so proud of you, Mick. You're the sweetest thing."

"Mom, I'm leasing back to the original owners and making money off them."

"*And* smart," she said. "Sweet and smart."

He had to laugh. "Don't you think you're a little biased?"

She sipped from her mason jar and just smiled at him.

"You're not drinking straight-up moonshine at . . ." He looked at his phone. "Ten A.M."

"Of course not," she said. "I've got ice cubes in it."

He sighed. "You know you got Quinn toasted with that stuff."

This gave his mom a big laugh. "I like her."

"You like everyone."

"I like her," she repeated. "For *you*."

"Again," he said with a small laugh, "you like everyone for me."

"I do not."

"Really? Because in the not so distant past you've tried to set me up with your mail carrier, a perfect stranger at the gas station, and let's not forget my ex."

"In my defense, the woman getting gas had a nice smile. You could've done worse for yourself."

Mick tossed up his hands. "I give up."

"You deserve a good woman," she said. "And since you've been in no hurry to find your own, I stepped up to help you. It's what a good mom does."

Mick snorted.

"And anyway, I backed off as soon as I realized you'd found someone on your own."

"Quinn is not mine."

"Why not?" she asked. "She makes you smile. She also makes you laugh. And she keeps you coming back to Wildstone—and don't think that didn't hurt at first, since I couldn't manage that feat myself, but I've made my peace with it. And I love her for it."

He could see the look in her eyes, the I'm-wanting-grandchildren look, and he shook his head at her. "I like her too, Mom, but that's not what this is between us. I'm pretty sure she's out of here as soon as Tilly's out of school."

"Nonsense. That girl was made for this town. She's sweet and kind and caring, and better yet, she's smart as hell and fiercely protective of those she loves."

"And how do you know all of that?" Mick said, amused in spite of himself.

"Because she's here in Wildstone, isn't she? Out of her element and away from her world, which might as well be on a different planet, all to take care of a sister she didn't even know she had and certainly has no obligation to. How many people do you know who'd do that?"

"We're changing the subject now," he said.

"Fine." Hand on Coop's big head, she looked around. "So what are you doing out here? After you had your worker bees sneak in here last week when I was out getting my hair done, I thought the work was finished. You got rid of all my things."

"Not your things, Mom. Just the crap."

"I know," she said. "They took it to the thrift shop on Fourth."

He gave her a long look. "And how do you know that?"

"Because Sally, who's worked there for forty years, called to tell me."

"Mom." He scrubbed a hand down his face. "Tell me you didn't go buy your crap back."

"Okay, I won't tell you. Just don't look in the shed," was her parting shot as she left.

"Shit." He shoved his fingers in his hair and turned in a slow circle.

"Looking a little crazy today."

He turned back to the door and found Boomer standing there, looking unsure of his welcome. "Crazy doesn't begin to cover it."

Coop, who'd used up his store of energy on Mick's mom, didn't get up to greet Boomer. He just thumped his tail on the dusty garage floor a few times.

"We going to fight again?" Mick asked curiously.

"We could." Boomer came closer, revealing the faint markings of a black eye. "But I gotta warn you," he said. "I just drank a protein shake so I've got an unfair advantage."

Mick laughed.

Boomer smiled ruefully and bent to love up on Coop. "Don't get too full of yourself. I bruise like a peach."

Mick rubbed his still-aching jaw. "If it helps, your right hook's stronger than it used to be."

Boomer snorted and then sobered as he rose back to his feet. "Look, man, I've fucked some things up. Lots of things."

Mick's smile faded. The last time Boomer had started a conversation in this way, he'd just come off a three-day bender, during which time he'd trashed his car, his relationships, and his entire life. He'd ended up in rehab. "You're not just talking about you and me," Mick said.

"No."

"Or Lena."

"No."

Mick met his gaze. "Tell me."

Boomer turned to the garage wall with the white outlines.

"I'm surprised after all this time you still haven't painted over those."

Mick took a good look at them, realizing that his original perspective was changing. His dad had done his best to be efficient. It hadn't been a personal attack on Mick. Hell, in his job, Mick was all about efficiency and expediency, so he should get it. "I'd *planned* on painting over them."

"But . . . ?" Boomer asked.

But . . . he was experiencing some surprising revelations about his dad and everything he thought he knew about his childhood. His dad had been far from perfect, but the man had truly believed he'd been doing his job as a father.

Unlike Tom, who'd purposely, almost happily, screwed up his only son, leaving Boomer tumbling in the wind.

Boomer looked amused. "You want to leave the outlines?"

"I want to not resent them," Mick corrected.

Boomer laughed ruefully. "We're both fucked up in a big way. Good thing we don't have kids. Neither of us knows shit about being a good dad."

"Maybe we'll do better," Mick said.

"Are you seriously telling me you want kids after all we went through?"

Mick shrugged. The truth was, he'd never given it much serious thought until recently.

Very recently.

Such as last night while holding a sleepy, practically purring Quinn in his arms, thinking he'd be happy doing so every single night for the rest of his life.

"Look at you," Boomer said. "Growing up." His smile faded. "I guess it's time for both of us to do so. I'm going to rehab, Mick."

"I know."

"I'm going to be gone for ninety days and I want to know if when I get back we could start over."

"No," Mick said.

Boomer's smile dropped.

"There's no need to start over," Mick said. "Because we're still friends."

Chapter 31

Potato chips always remind me that there are good things in this world.

—from "The Mixed-Up Files of Tilly Adams's Journal"

Quinn was in the café kitchen, trying not to pay attention to how heavy her heart felt about Mick letting her walk away.

You're either in or out with someone . . .

She had a pit in her gut. Because why couldn't she just tell him? Why couldn't she just say I'm in, like *all the way* in? Why did she have to push him away?

Feeling sick about her seeming inability to follow her heart, she looked out the window.

Lena pulled up and headed toward the chicken coop. Quinn called out, "Hey, grab us some too, would you?"

Lena shrugged like the motion required almost too much energy. Quinn watched her and told herself not to do it. Don't interfere. Don't ask her what's wrong.

But she called Greta in to take over and went out back. "You okay?" Quinn asked.

"Sure," Lena said.

Quinn had her hands on her hips. "Okay, now you're scaring me. No sassy comebacks. No sarcasm. What's wrong?"

"Nothing."

"Spit it out."

"You know, your compassionate tone needs a little work." But Lena must not have been too offended because she sighed. "Not that you care," she said, "but it's my birthday tomorrow. My thirtieth." She said this like *thirtieth* was a bad word. "I'm single on my thirtieth birthday, which means my life is officially over."

"I hit thirty this year and I'm single," Quinn said, "and my life isn't over."

Lena gave her a sideways look. "You sure about that?"

Quinn had to bite her tongue. "Okay, listen. Come to the café tomorrow night. I'll make you dinner."

Lena shrugged.

"It's better than being alone, right?"

"I guess." Lena looked at her. "Why are you being so nice to me? Do I have something in my teeth and you feel sorry for me?"

"Why can't I just be a nice person?" Quinn asked.

Lena looked at her.

Quinn laughed. "Fine. My parents taught me to be nice first because you can always be mean later, but once you've been mean to someone, they won't believe the nice anymore. So be nice. Be nice until it's time to stop being nice. Then destroy them."

Lena stared at her and then grinned. "Damn. That's good. I should try that sometime."

"Maybe you can try it on me."

Lena shrugged. "Will there be cake?"

"Do you want there to be?"

"It's not a birthday without cake," Lena said.

"Fine," Quinn said, even though she was a crap baker. "There will be cake."

"With chocolate?"

"Sure," Quinn said. "With chocolate."

"And male strippers?"

"Definitely not," Quinn said.

"Well, I guess I can't have everything . . ."

TILLY WATCHED OUT the window until she saw Dylan show up for work. She'd texted him to come a little early but he hadn't. She had to be quick to catch him getting out of his car before he entered the café.

"Thought you'd come over and see me," she said.

"Can't. I've got work. And you have to study for finals this week."

"I'm taking a day off from studying," she said.

"No, you're not."

She stared at his back as he turned away, hurt to the core that he didn't want to be with her. "What do you care?"

He turned to face her again, eyes dark, expression dark. Hell, his life was dark. "You think I don't care?"

She swallowed as he strode back to her and glared down into her eyes. "I spend more time on your schoolwork than mine," he said. "I check on you every single night that I can get away. I'm working more hours than I have in a day so that after I give most of my pay to my mom to cover her rent, I can put a little bit away for a future that I'm not even sure exists."

Tilly felt her throat burn. "It does."

His face softened. "I'm going to go to work, Tee. And you're going to study. We need the money and the education."

She held her breath. "We?"

"Yeah." And then he did something he rarely did—he touched her. He cupped her face in his big, callused hands and dropped his forehead to hers. "It's all about the we," he murmured. "Don't ever think otherwise."

So Tilly went inside to study. After several hours of that, she got up and stood in the doorway of Quinn's room staring at her mom's things, now shoved against one wall.

A small part of her could admit she appreciated that Quinn hadn't thrown it all in the attic. Or in her mom's room. Instead she'd left the master bedroom completely alone.

Tilly knew she should be grateful but instead she just felt . . . sad. She didn't know why she'd lashed out at Quinn about the things she'd moved. The truth was, nothing in this sewing/craft room belonged to her. Not a single thing. She just hadn't wanted Quinn touching her mom's things.

Their mom's things . . .

Her feet took her over to the wall and she nudged a foot against a few boxes. There was one that looked like a small chest. She couldn't remember ever seeing it before. Dropping to her knees, she pulled the chest to her and opened it.

It was handmade baby clothes—crocheted booties, a small blanket, a lopsided sweater, all things her mom had made.

But not for her. She was sure of it. She had a box of some of her baby stuff and it was mostly hand-me-downs or from discount stores. In fact, her mom had never made her anything. She'd mended the holes in her jeans, but that was about it. She'd taught

Tilly to replace her own buttons, and that was the extent of the sewing that had gone on in this house.

Tilly explored the little clothes. The sweater had a homemade label on it.

MADE FOR . . .

And in that spot, someone had handwritten in a name.

Quinn.

These clothes had been made for Quinn, before she'd been born.

And given up.

Tilly shoved everything back in the box, and heart pounding funny and a sick feeling in her gut, took it to her room and shoved it under the bed where she kept her own, very private journal. She flopped onto the mattress and closed her eyes to think.

Sometime later, she came awake to her phone buzzing. Night had fallen and she had a text from Quinn: I turned off your light and left dinner for you in the fridge. Hitting the sack myself. Night.

Another text came in, this one from Dylan.

Meet at the park?

Her heart did a little happy dance. Hell yes, she'd meet him in the park. She tiptoed out of the quiet house and made it to the park in a record-breaking three minutes.

The place was deserted. No one on the swings. So she walked past the swing set to their tree, and the tree house. In the dark, she could see the glow of a phone screen. She climbed up and found a tall, lanky figure sitting there and her pulse sped up even as her smile faded.

He was hiding from the world and that meant he was hurting.

She plopped down next to him. "Hey."

Dylan lay flat on his back and stared up at the stars. "Wouldn't mind being an astronaut."

Her heart caught. He had the grades for it. Or he would've had the grades for it if he hadn't had to work his ass off on top of school. "You could totally do it," she said, lying down next to him so that their arms brushed. She touched his fingers with hers. "You could do whatever you want."

He snorted and she wondered what had happened to upset him. She'd ask, but he wouldn't tell her so she did her best to look him over to see if he had new injuries. Thankfully, she didn't see any. "You can," she whispered. "Be an astronaut."

"Says who?"

"My mom." Her breath caught. "My mom always told me that."

He rolled to his side and propped his head up with his hand as he studied her in the dark. "She was trying to be nice," he said. "Nobody gets to do what they want. When school's out, I'm going to have to dig trenches for my dad."

He already worked as many hours a week as he could spare to help his mom cover expenses, she knew. And she hated that for him. "It's just for the summer. When you graduate, you can do whatever you want," she said.

"Don't be naive."

She pulled her fingers from his and sat up. She hated when he acted like he was so much older than she was. Hated when he made her feel like a stupid little kid. "I'm not naive." She pulled her knees in and pressed her forehead to them. "But sometimes, you just have to believe in something."

He blew out a sigh and sat up beside her. She felt his hand brush over her hair and wrap around her and he pulled her in closer. "I'm sorry, Tee. I'm an asshole."

"You're not." She turned her face to look up at him. "You aren't like your dad, Dylan."

His expression hardened at the thought. "And I'm never going to be."

"Good." She hesitated because he didn't like to be told what to do. Hated it actually, because so many of his choices had been taken from him. And she didn't want to make things worse but she really wanted to say something. "And just as you don't have to be the dick your dad is," she said carefully, "you also don't have to follow his chosen profession. You do whatever the hell you want to do. And you've got me at your back. You know I've been helping out at the café in the mornings and Quinn insists on paying me. I'm going to save every penny in case you need it. Do you hear me?"

A ghost of a smile twitched at his mouth. "I hear you. So do the people in China. But I'm not going to take your money, ever. I'm saving mine too, I'll be okay."

"So why would you go be a laborer when summer hits? Why wouldn't you do something you love? Like work at the rec center and help coach the little kids in baseball?" He'd been a baseball superstar until he'd had to quit the team for his job. "Or you could be a lifeguard. Lots of kids are doing that this summer and they're hiring."

"The class to become a certified lifeguard is three hundred bucks," he said. "The rec center won't hire me because I had to have a recommendation from my coach and the principal, and though the coach said I would be great in the job, the principal said I had a bad attitude and a temper."

This pissed her off. "That's not fair."

"I trashed his office when he accused me of stealing money from the cafeteria," he reminded her.

"Wrongly accused."

Dylan lifted a shoulder. Didn't matter. The damage was done. And now he would be digging ditches for his macho, sadistic father all summer and she'd be worried for him every single second of every single day.

"Did you study?" he asked.

In spite of wanting to cry, she smiled at him because he cared about her so much it hurt. "Yes."

"Good." He stood and pulled her up. "You've got to go home before you get in trouble."

She stood close to him, very close; the toes of their battered sneakers touched. But since he was so much taller than she was, that was about all that lined up and she *ached*, ached, to be as tall because then she could feel him, thigh to thigh, chest to chest. Her breathing hitched just thinking about it.

Kiss me, she wished with all her might. *Please for once, kiss me . . .*

And maybe it was her turn for a miracle because he did. He bent and kissed the top of her head.

"Dylan," she whispered with all the longing in her heart that felt like it might burst.

He stilled. "Tee—"

"Please?" she whispered, tipping back her head.

He groaned and crushed her to him. For the most perfect moment in all the moments of her entire life, he lowered his mouth to hers. Soft. Gentle. Patient.

But Tilly wasn't feeling any of those things, so she tugged him in even closer. Then, on a mission, she touched her tongue to his and . . . the kiss exploded.

It was like nothing she'd ever felt in her entire life as he hauled her in tight and kissed her deep. Her heart pounded, her skin felt too tight for her body, and she loved it.

But then he pulled away.

With a little mewl of protest, she tried to wrap herself around him, but he gripped her arms and held her off. "Tee. Tee, stop. We're not doing this."

"Why?" she demanded, and if he said it was because she was too young for him, she was going to—

"You deserve more."

"I don't. You're all I want," she told him with all the fierceness of her entire soul. "I love you, Dylan. You're mine, and you know what else? I'm yours."

He sucked in a hard breath and she realized he was shaking. Shaking with the effort to not kiss her again. Her hands came up to his chest and she fisted her fingers in his shirt, aching, aching . . . for more.

But it wasn't going to come because he gently wrapped his fingers around her wrists and brought her hands down and stepped back. "'Night, Tee."

"'Night," she whispered. Dammit. She took longer going home, dragging it out another good ten minutes, in spite of everything smiling to herself the whole time.

He'd finally kissed her! It had been a life-changing kiss, the kiss of all kisses, and no matter what he said, there'd be more.

Because he loved her too.

She knew that now, and because she did, she could wait for the rest.

She moved around back to the kitchen door, which was much quieter than the front door. Not wanting to wake up Quinn and alert her sister to the fact that she'd sneaked out, she quietly tiptoed in and . . .

Found Quinn leaning against the counter eating out of a gallon ice cream container with a wooden spoon.

Chapter 32

I made it through the day without beating anyone with a chair. I'd say my people skills are improving.

—from "The Mixed-Up Files of Tilly Adams's Journal"

Quinn had been up late, unable to sleep, wishing she'd talked to Tilly, wishing she wasn't such a big, fat chicken that she'd pushed Mick away instead of letting him know how she felt about him. The only thing she had going for her peace of mind was knowing Tilly was sleeping, safe in her bed.

Turns out, the joke was on her. She'd been halfway through a carton of ice cream when her sister had come sneaking in the back door and Quinn stared at her in shock. "What the hell?"

Tilly froze and then made a recovery attempt, taking her time shutting and locking the door.

Tink, sitting in the middle of the kitchen floor watching Quinn eat with the single-minded intensity only a cat could pull off, didn't even spare a glance at the teen.

But Quinn spared a glance. And a second. And a third as she visibly searched for signs of what Tilly had been doing.

What do you think she's doing, sneaking in at midnight with that guilty look all over her face? Don't you remember fifteen?

Tilly leaned over and peered into the ice-cream carton. "Hey, isn't that mine?"

"Nope, I ate yours yesterday. Let me repeat. What the hell?"

"I went to go see Dylan," Tilly said, sounding very fifteen. "He needed me."

"We've had this discussion, Tilly. You tell him to come here. I don't like you out at this hour alone. Hell, I didn't even know you were out. Do you have any idea what kind of trouble happens after midnight?"

"The same kind that happens at any other hour?" Tilly asked.

"Don't be a smart-ass." Quinn set down the ice cream. "I think we should have The Talk." And not the one that she'd hoped to have either.

"What talk?" Tilly asked suspiciously.

"You know, the birds and the bees."

Tilly looked horrified. "What century were you born in again?"

"I'm serious," Quinn said. "Do you know your options? Do you know that you don't have to do anything you don't want to do?"

Tilly closed her eyes. "I'm having a bad dream—"

"Speaking defensively is a sign that you're feeling pressured," Quinn said. "Never let a boy pressure you."

"Oh my God," Tilly groaned, covering her face.

"I'm serious." She paused. "Listen, I'm just going to come right out and ask you. Are you sexually active?"

"Let me repeat. Oh. My. God."

"It's a yes or no answer, Tilly."

Tilly sighed. "No," she said, looking so wistful that Quinn actually believed her.

"Okay," Quinn said, taking a breath for calm. "Can you promise to tell me before that changes so we can . . ." She felt ridiculous, but forged on. "Discuss your options?"

"I'll promise you whatever you want if you'll stop talking."

"You can't just sneak out, Tilly."

"And you can't tell me what to do."

"Actually, I can," Quinn said. "You're a minor."

Tilly sighed. "This sucks."

"You oughta try it from my side of the fence."

"I'd switch places with you in a heartbeat," Tilly said. "You've got it easy."

Quinn nearly choked on her laugh. "Anyone ever tell you to pick your battles? You don't have to show up to every argument you're invited to." She paused. "And you think I have it easy?"

"I know so," Tilly said.

"Then you have a deal."

"What?"

"You just said you'd switch places with me in a heartbeat," Quinn said. "Let's do it. Tomorrow you be me, and I'll be you."

Tilly stared at her. "But tomorrow's Sunday. I'm supposed to work the morning shift serving tables and you're in the back barking orders and cooking."

"Yeah. So?" Quinn asked.

"Fine. Whatever. If you don't care, neither do I." She shook Quinn's hand. "Deal. But just so you know, tomorrow you're going to tell me I was right, that you have it easy compared to me."

"Or," Quinn said. "You'll tell me that *I* was right. That your life doesn't suck nearly as bad as you think it does."

Tilly didn't look convinced. "So what now, we go to bed angry?"

"Never go to bed angry," Quinn said. "Stay awake and plot revenge."

THE NEXT MORNING they walked over to the café together and told everyone about how they were switching roles for the day.

Greta, Trinee, and Dylan stood there in morbid fascination as Tilly strapped on an apron and headed behind the stove.

"Uh," Dylan said. "Does anyone but me know that she burns water?"

Tilly jabbed a finger at Dylan, which Quinn presumed meant "Shut it!" Still, Quinn watched for another moment, suddenly torn, worried Tilly might burn herself or mess up on purpose to make a point. "Hey," she said. "If this is too much—"

"No." Tilly lifted her chin. "We made a deal. I get to be in charge and be bossy and all that."

"I'm not bossy," Quinn said.

Both Greta and Trinee snorted and Quinn gave them a "shut it" look.

Dylan studiously stared at his shoes, looking to be hiding what could have been either a grimace or a grin.

But at least they all zipped it.

"Okay, fine, I get it," Quinn said to Tilly. "You're in charge. But if you need a time-out, just say so, okay?"

"Piece of cake," the teen said. "And anyway, what are you doing standing around? The help doesn't stand around, they get out there and serve people. Go! Pour coffee, smile, and don't eat anything off the customers' plates, they frown on that."

Quinn opened her mouth and Tilly grinned. *Grinned.* With all her teeth and all her heart, and for a beat, she looked so young, so cute, so adorable and sweet that Quinn could only stare at her, unbearably moved.

"Go," Tilly said, shooing her along. "Oh wait! First we need fresh eggs."

Quinn's smile immediately drained away. "Oh no. Not me. I'm not going. Those chickens hate me."

"You backing out on our deal?"

Dammit. Quinn went out to the chickens, who got all ruffled up at the sight of her. "Oh, cool it," she said, hands on hips. "We're going to do this and we're all going to survive it."

Five minutes later she had a basket full of eggs and only one puncture wound.

Baby steps.

AN HOUR AND a half later, Quinn's arms were aching from carrying heavy trays and her back and feet were killing her. At a rare lull, she took a peek into the kitchen.

Tilly was flipping pancakes like she'd been born to the task, and Quinn had to admit she was feeling a little bit annoyed that the experiment, meant to make Tilly understand the difficulties of being an adult in charge, seemed to be backfiring. Spectacularly.

Then she caught sight of Trinee and Greta rushing around cooking everything else. "Hey," Quinn said. "That's cheating!"

"It's not cheating if you're the boss," Tilly said without looking up from the pancakes.

"You're not the boss."

"Today I am. You said so."

"No," Quinn said. "We're walking in each other's shoes, and I'm not the boss here."

Tilly looked confused. "Then who is?"

"We're *both* the boss," Quinn said. "Equally."

"You're just saying that because you don't want me to win," Tilly said.

"And that," Quinn agreed and Tilly snorted. It made Quinn smile. No one on the planet could make her as crazy or as amused as this girl.

Which was an odd and uncomfortable and kind of wonderful feeling all in one.

When the shift was finally over, Quinn and Tilly looked at each other. Quinn raised a brow. She happened to know that Tilly had indeed burned water, and that she couldn't have handled the shift without Dylan, Greta, and Trinee all sneaking time in the kitchen to save her cute little ass.

Tilly lifted a shoulder and rolled her eyes. "Fine. Your life sucks too. Happy?"

"Our lives don't suck," Quinn said. "But maybe we could each appreciate each other's role more."

"Hmm," Tilly said, noncommittal. "Sure. I guess."

Small favors . . . Quinn gathered Greta and Trinee and the rest of the staff. "I'd like to have a small surprise birthday party for Lena here tonight. She's turning thirty and she's sad," Quinn said. "Plus I need someone to make a cake. Chocolate. Anyone interested?"

"It's her thirty-first birthday," Greta said.

"She definitely said thirty," Quinn said.

"Well, of course she did, no one wants to admit to being thirty-one."

Quinn blinked. "You sure?"

"Yep. Unless last year's thirtieth roast she held for herself at the Whiskey River didn't happen."

Quinn sighed. "Okay, so she's pretending to still be thirty. So what?"

"I'd pretend to be twenty-seven," Tilly said. "'Cause thirty's old. Just sayin'."

Quinn did her best to ignore this. "We doing this or not?"

"Does this mean you're no longer fighting over that incredibly sexy package named Mick?" Trinee asked.

Quinn did her best not to react to that. "We're *not* fighting over a man." There was no way to explain that Lena really wanted Boomer, she just wanted him sober, and that Quinn had already blown it with Mick, so there was no fighting because she and Lena were both equal idiots. "She's sad and feeling alone on her birthday, which no one should feel." And okay, so she was projecting, sue her. "Look, are you guys going to help or what?"

They all stared at her as if she'd lost her mind. Then Greta tossed up her hands. "Fine. I'm in. And yeah, we'll bake the cake."

Quinn turned to Tilly, who gave an impressive eye roll, doing her best to remain sullen even though Quinn could tell she was into it. "If I have to," she said.

"Good. Text, e-mail, or call everyone you all know. Here, tonight. Lena's working until seven. Have everyone get here before then so we can surprise her."

An hour later her phone rang.

"So you finally lost it," Mick said.

"I lost it a long time ago," she said, trying to keep her voice steady at the shock waves his voice sent through her. She missed him. "So you'll have to be more specific than that."

He chuckled and the sound scraped at all her good spots and made her ache. "You're having a surprise birthday party for my ex."

Well, when he put it like that . . . "It's her birthday and she's alone and sad."

"She's alone and sad because she wants to be alone and sad. *If* she's even alone or sad. More likely, she's playing you."

"She's not," Quinn said. "She needs a friend and so do I."

Silence.

"Mick?"

"I'm here," he said. "I hope you know what you're doing."

"I do." Sort of. Or not at all . . . "I need you to get Boomer here."

"I'm not sure that's possible."

"Don't let him give up on her."

"Actually," he said, "that's exactly what he's *not* going to do, but he's got to go take care of some things first."

Quinn stilled. "Rehab?"

"How did you know?"

"Would you buy that I know everything?"

He laughed low in his throat, the sound sexy as hell.

"Has he left yet?" she asked.

"Tomorrow."

"Then bring him."

"I hope you know what you're doing," he said.

"Always," she said. *Or you know, never . . .*

"You sell your car yet?"

"No," she said. "I think the price is too high. I need to lower it so I can get renovation money."

"For the house and café," he said.

"Yes. I'd like to make some updates to the house especially."

Mick was quiet a minute. "Feels a little like you're looking to stay."

It was her turn to be quiet. "I'm thinking about it."

"For what it's worth, I think it's a great decision."

She drew in a deep, shaky breath. "So you'll come tonight?"

"If you want me to before I head out."

Her heart dropped. "Head out?"

"Back to the Bay Area."

Right. Just because a part of her brain was toying with staying in Wildstone didn't mean he was. He wouldn't. She knew that. "Yes, please," she said.

"Then I'll see you later."

When they disconnected she felt the oddest urge to call him back and . . . what? She had no idea. Hell, she just wanted to listen to him read the back of a cereal box.

She stared out the back window. From here she could see Jared and Hutch's yard. She knew now that they were married and in their midthirties.

And they were running around outside in bare feet with water pistols, soaking each other and laughing so hard they kept slipping. She stared at them and felt a yearning come over her so strong she had to sit down.

She'd spent a lot of time trying to make relationships perfect, when all that was really needed was someone who'd laugh with her for the rest of her life.

She was pretty sure that person was Mick.

Her phone buzzed again.

"Someone said you're having a party for your archnemesis," Cliff said.

Quinn blew out a breath and struggled to switch gears away from her staggering realization. "We came to a truce."

"Who got Mick?"

Quinn tipped her head back and stared at the ceiling. "It's not all about guys, you know."

There was a smile in Cliff's voice when he spoke. "I'm going to take this as a good sign that Wildstone's growing on you and you won't be leaving."

"I've been thinking about that. You want to scan and e-mail

me the guardianship papers to sign? I think she's almost convinced."

"Which she?" he teased. "You or her?"

She smiled. "Both." Or so she hoped . . .

By six o'clock that night, the café was filling up. She'd demanded that people come and . . . they did. Everyone in town it seemed. The place echoed with laughter and chatter and the scent of good food as people helped decorate. Even Tilly got into the spirit of things, stringing lights across the ceiling.

At seven, they all hid behind the counter. This was no easy feat and there were more than a few squabbles.

"Get off me!" Big Hank said to Not-Big-Hank.

"Why is your hand on my ass?" Greta asked Lou.

"That's not my hand . . ."

Which caused a tussle until Trinee put her fingers to her mouth and let out an ear-piercing whistle that had everyone shutting up.

"Better," she said.

Fifteen minutes later, there was still no sign of Lena, so Quinn went to the kitchen and called her. "Where are you?" she demanded.

"At home," Lena said. "In my pj's having a *Real Housewives* marathon with a pizza. Happy birthday to me."

Quinn pressed her fingers to her eye sockets. "You were supposed to come here at seven. To have dinner with me."

"Yeah," she said. "I'm tired. And coming down with a cold. So I'm not coming."

Dammit. "Listen to me," Quinn said. "I put together a party for you. It's supposed to be a surprise—"

"Oh, I know all about it."

Quinn pulled the phone from her ear and stared at it before bringing it back up. "If you knew, then why aren't you here?"

"I already told you," Lena said casually. "I don't want to. I'm not coming to a pity party."

"It's not a pity party!"

"Swear it," Lena said. "Swear that your plan wasn't to be nice to me because you felt sorry for me."

Quinn closed her eyes and counted to five. "How about I swear *not* to be nice to you?"

Lena paused. "That might work."

Quinn ground her back teeth into powder. "Okay, then I swear not to be nice to you. Now get your skinny ass dressed and down here right now or—"

"I'm going through a tunnel," Lena said. "About to lose reception—"

"Lena, I swear to God—"

Disconnect.

Quinn growled and texted her.

QUINN:

You'll never guess who just pulled into town for gas on his way home to Hollywood and needs a haircut from Wildstone's best hairdresser. I'm holding him hostage here. If you don't show up, I'll do his hair myself and tell him you trained me.

LENA:

You're such a bitch.

QUINN:

I come by it naturally. You've got ten minutes.

Quinn shoved her phone away and drew a deep breath for calm. It didn't work. She walked outside to draw in some better air. Still no calm to be had. She played a few games of Words With Friends—Skye was kicking her ass.

When she could breathe without chest pain, she moved around to the front of the café and found more people had arrived, including Mick if his dad's truck was any indication. All of which ensured that she was no better composed when she walked in the front door.

Everyone jumped up and yelled, "Surprise!" and "Happy birthday!" . . . until they saw it was her.

Quinn sighed. "Good news," she said. "We can eat the cake now."

Mick broke from the crowd and came to her, reaching for her hand and pulling her into him.

Her body went, like it was made to be pressed up against his.

"There's bad news and good news," he said.

Eyes closed, she snuggled in. She didn't care what it was, as long as he didn't let go. "Tell me."

When he didn't speak, she pulled back enough to meet his gaze. "Bad news first."

His mouth twitched, so she knew it couldn't be worse than being stood up by Lena.

"We already ate the cake," he said.

"And the good news?"

"I hid away a piece for you."

She stared up at him and it just popped out, utterly without conscious thought or guile. "God, I love you."

There was a beat of stunned disbelief on his part—and okay, on her part too because she had no idea where the words had come from. Horrified, she tried to pull free but Mick tightened his grip on her. "Quinn." His voice was low and gruff with some emotion she wasn't capable of translating at the moment.

"Hey, you two," Greta said, coming up to their side with Trinee. "We can always turn this party into my surprise party."

"Your birthday's not for two more months," Trinee said.

"So?"

"No one's stealing my party," Lena said from behind them as she walked into the café.

Not in pj's.

Not looking sick or tired.

In fact, she wore a killer dress and looked perfectly made up, not a hair out of place.

Quinn couldn't decide whether to strangle her or hug her. Scratch that. She didn't have the brain power for that, or anything beyond what she'd just said to Mick.

"So where is he?" Lena asked, looking around. "The Hollywood star who needs his hair done?"

"I lied," Quinn said.

Lena stared at her, the very slightest bit of admiration in her gaze. "I must say, as the queen of bullshitting, I respect what you've done. But also, I hate you."

"Right back at you," Quinn said.

Lena turned to the crowd. "What's a birthday girl got to do to get a piece of cake around here?"

They gave her the last piece of cake and poured drinks—apple cider in deference to Boomer's attendance—and when everyone had a glass, they lifted it in a toast but no one spoke. They all looked around at each other awkwardly.

No one had anything nice to say to the birthday girl.

Quinn hadn't seen this coming but she should have, so she drew in a deep breath to speak and . . . met Lena's dark and getting darker gaze, daring her to go back on her word.

I swear not to be nice to you.

Okay, then. Here went nothing. She cleared her throat. "When I came to Wildstone, Lena was one of the first people I met. She was . . ."

Lena's eyes narrowed dangerously.

". . . possibly the scariest woman I'd ever talked to," Quinn said, and everyone looked nervously at Lena to see how she'd take this.

Lena smiled.

Quinn lifted her glass a little bit higher. "She told me that the best things in life either make you fat, drunk, or pregnant . . ."

Everyone burst out laughing, including Lena.

"And," Quinn went on, "not to stroke her ego, but she's probably right."

"Always am," Lena said and toasted Quinn back, nodding her head in acceptance of the un-friend toast.

And thus cemented one of the oddest friendships Quinn had ever had. The oddest and yet the most real since Beth had been alive.

Chapter 33

No matter how much you eat, there's always room for dessert. Dessert doesn't go to the stomach, dessert goes to the heart. Learned that from my mom and it's true.

—from "The Mixed-Up Files of Tilly Adams's Journal"

That night Tilly was in bed, lights off, on her phone playing a game when she suddenly remembered the box she'd hidden under her bed. The one filled with the baby things her mom had made for Quinn before she'd given her up for adoption.

Guilt swamped her for keeping the box a secret, but her mom had made them, painstakingly, meticulously, and they'd clearly meant a lot to her. It was the one last little piece of her that Tilly had all to herself. God, she wanted her back, but more than that, she felt the clock ticking.

She was afraid.

She had no idea when her and Quinn's "trial" period was up and she refused to ask, but knew the end had to be barreling down on her and she had no idea how to stop it from coming. She was locked in anxiety over that when she heard a soft knock at the front door. She paused her game and cocked her head, hearing a low murmur of voices.

Quinn's.

And . . . Mick's.

Tilly tiptoed to her bedroom door and put her ear to it. Nothing. She couldn't hear a thing. Very quietly she cracked it open and . . .

The cat pushed her way in.

"Hey," Tilly whispered. "Get out."

Instead the scrawny old lady wound its way through her feet. "Mew."

Here was the thing. Tilly wasn't a fan of cats. They were bitchy and they thought they were the top tier of the food chain. Tink might've wormed her way into Quinn's heart, but as near as Tilly could tell, *everyone* wormed their way into Quinn's heart.

Tilly's own heart was much more discerning.

And impenetrable.

But not wanting to give away the fact that she was blatantly eavesdropping on Mick and Quinn, she picked up Tink and went nose to nose with her. "*Shh.*"

The cat stared at her from her one good eye, the other one doing its own thing, and the oddest thing happened.

She started to purr, a rough start-stop rumble, and then the cat did what Tilly had seen her do to Quinn—she set her cat head on Tilly's shoulder.

It was ridiculous. Clearly a blatant attempt to manipulate the stupid human, but Tilly fell for it hook, line, and sinker, hugging the cat a little tighter.

As meanwhile, in the hall, Quinn and Mick stared at each other, unaware of Tilly and Tink, their audience.

"Thought you were leaving," Quinn said quietly to Mick. "We said good-bye. Twice."

"We said a lot of things," Mick said cryptically, voice pitched so low that Tilly had to lean out into the dark hallway to hear. "But one thing neither of us mentioned is not wanting each other anymore."

Tilly rolled her eyes. "Cheesy," she mouthed to the cat, and then the traitor, who'd caught sight of her beloved Quinn, began wiggling to get to her.

"No," Tilly whispered. "Hold on, you're caught on my sweater—"

"*Mew!*"

And with that, Tink took a flying leap out of Tilly's arms, ripping her favorite sweater as she did, landing with a loud thump that rivaled an earthquake. The windows of the house practically shuddered.

Both Quinn and Mick, who were in an embrace by now and—*gross*—kissing with what looked like *way* too much tongue, turned in shock to stare at her.

"Hey," Tilly said, lifting her hands. "Don't look at me. For once I'm not the one sneaking around."

Quinn had backed away from Mick pretty quickly, but he was much slower to drop his hands from her. Tilly watched, amused, as Quinn pushed her hair back and looked guilty.

"Maybe we should have the birds and bees talk," Tilly said. "Do you know your options? Do you know that you don't have to do anything you don't want to do?"

Quinn rolled her eyes but also blushed. "Funny. And the difference is that I'm not fifteen."

"Right. You're forty."

"Thirty! And just barely!"

Tilly smiled. "Speaking defensively is a sign that you're feeling pressured. Don't ever let a boy pressure you."

"Oh my God," Quinn moaned, covering her face. "Tell me I didn't sound that condescending."

Tilly held up her forefinger and thumb, only a little space between them. "And btdubs, Mick doesn't have to sneak in and out. I don't care if he spends the night."

With that, she went to bed, where she had to admit to herself that if there had to be a guy around here, Mick wasn't a bad one to have. Quinn should probably keep him.

Quinn should keep *both* of them and at *that* thought, Tilly flopped to her back. "Talk about cheesy," she muttered.

Mick slid out of Quinn's bed. It was crowded with him, Quinn, Coop, and Tink.

Especially since Tink was taking up more room than anyone else, mostly because Coop didn't want to get within hissing range.

Behind him, only Quinn stirred and sat up, looking heart-stoppingly gorgeous in the puddle of moonlight and wearing nothing but a sated glow and some whisker burn at her throat, breasts, and between her thighs. Just the sight stirred him again, but he'd delayed long enough already.

"You're leaving?" she murmured.

He pulled up his jeans and left them unfastened as he searched around for his shirt, finding it on top of her lamp. Shaking his head, he snatched it and pulled it on. Then he met her gaze and her smile faded.

"Yeah," she said. "You're leaving."

That had been the plan. Especially since Quinn had so clearly pulled away and he'd promised himself to respect her barriers.

But that had been before her "I love you," the one she hadn't meant to say but that he couldn't un-hear because it had given him something he hadn't had all that much of in his life—hope.

All he had to do was give her the space and time she needed to catch up to him. He could do that.

He *would* do that.

"I've got a meeting in the morning," he said.

"So you're going to drive home in the middle of the night?"

"I don't mind." He planted a hand on either side of her hips and leaned in to kiss her.

She kissed him back, which was gratifying. As was the way she wrapped her arms around him without hesitation, deepening the kiss. When he reluctantly pulled back, he wasn't the only one breathless. He gently touched his forehead to hers. "Quinn."

She made a soft sound and kissed him some more, until he wanted to strip back down and climb into bed again, but before he could, she gave him a push. "You've gotta go."

What else could he say to that?

It was three in the morning when he finally got home to his high-rise condo in the city. He grabbed a few hours of sleep in the bed that felt too big to be in alone.

His phone woke him at six thirty.

"Your gut's right, as usual," Colin said. "The construction companies contracted to build the two new Wildstone motels and the brand-spanking-new community center that's about to break ground were the only companies contacted. The locals weren't given a chance to bid. I went snooping into the city manager's finances."

"And?"

"Over the past two years, he's paid off his rather large mortgage, put in a pool, bought himself a new car, a motor home, and a motorcycle. All high end. All paid for up front. He also went to Cabo, Maui, and the Bahamas. No credit card debt."

"Kickbacks?"

"Unless he won the lotto."

That Mick's suspicions were true didn't make him feel any better. First of all, Wildstone was still in trouble. It couldn't really sustain two new motels, and it wasn't a good time to build a community center when so many businesses were in trouble. It was an unnecessary expense in uncertain times. "This isn't good."

"Not for the city manager, no," Colin said. "You going to stir up the hornet's nest?"

Mick had already done so, intentionally or not, first by buying up the properties and leasing them back to the current businesses, and then at the city hall meeting when all that had become public knowledge.

"You still going to buy the Wild West B and B you're staying at, the one that's going under?" Colin asked. "I mean, that is the reason you're staying there and not somewhere nicer down the highway, right?"

Mick blew out a breath. The building itself was a historical monument, which meant that hopefully it couldn't be destroyed, but Mick didn't want to take a chance on that if the B & B went under. "Probably," he said.

"I figured." Colin sounded amused. "Sucker."

Mick disconnected and shook his head. Colin didn't know the half of it. Because if Quinn had trouble managing the café or the house and ran into financial problems, he'd do what he could there as well.

The definition of sucker.

Shit. He had it bad. He looked at his phone and realized he had a missed call and a message that he played back.

"Mick Hennessey," came a voice he knew all too well. It was rougher than his son Boomer's, but Tom had the same sarcastic, wry tone. "You've been busy, butting into my business. Too bad you didn't stick around to see it through. You always did run away like a little girl."

Mick hit redial before he thought it through and when Tom answered with a knowing low laugh, Mick knew he'd made a mistake.

He'd shown his hand. After all these years of learning the hard way how to hide his emotions and feelings, one voice mail had turned him back into an idiot teenager who put it all out there for the world to see.

But if Mick had shown his hand—and his weakness—then so had Tom. "Don't mistake my absence for running," he said. "Because I'm not gone."

"You hate this town," Tom said. "Stay out of it or you'll regret it."

"Was that a threat?"

"A promise," Tom said, and disconnected.

Chapter 34

I miss when my mom would come into my room and ask why everything was on the floor and I'd say gravity.

—from "The Mixed-Up Files of Tilly Adams's Journal"

To celebrate Tilly surviving the first day of finals, Quinn bought them pizza for dinner and then . . . gave Tilly her mom's journal.

They were sitting on the couch in the living room and Tilly stared down at the bound book in her hands. "I forgot all about this."

Quinn blinked. "You knew about it?"

"I used to watch Mom write in it all the time. She'd sit at the kitchen table with some hot tea and write down all her secrets." Tilly ran her fingers over the cover, not opening it. "She used to say that when she died, I should sell it to Hollywood and insist on the starring role because I'd win an Oscar." She lifted her gaze to Quinn's and her eyes were damp. "She didn't want me to read it, not until . . ." She shrugged and then shook her head and swiped an arm under her nose. "It's what made me start my own journal."

Quinn's gut squeezed and she scooted closer, wrapping her arms around her sister. "I didn't know you had a journal."

"Yeah." Tilly held herself still, hugging the journal as Quinn hugged her. And then slowly, she let her head drop to Quinn's shoulder.

Just like Tink, and it broke Quinn's heart. "You don't have to read it now," she said quietly. "You can hold on to it until you're ready."

Face still pressed into Quinn's throat, Tilly nodded. And then let go of her two-handed grip on the journal to wrap an arm around Quinn to keep her close.

AN HOUR LATER, Quinn lay in her bed staring at the ceiling. She needed to talk to Tilly about their plans, but things kept derailing that conversation. Tilly wanted to play summer league softball. Greta and Trinee wanted a vacation, and Quinn would need to fill in. They needed more staff and she'd have to do the hiring. And then there was the fact that she hadn't yet sold her car, so none of the house updates had been done.

Lots of loose ends.

"Liar. You're still afraid to admit that you want to stay."

This from Beth, who was sitting on the top of a stack of craft supplies in a bathrobe, eating a bowl of cereal.

Quinn sat up. "I'm not afraid." She was petrified. "Tilly's going to turn eighteen in less than three years. Maybe she'll take off. You ever think of that?"

"And you're worried about where that would leave you?"

"Yes!"

Beth snapped her fingers and her bowl of cereal vanished. "You *know* where it'd leave you."

Yes, here in Wildstone . . .

"You're happy here, Q."

She was. She loved working at the café. Maybe not in the same way that she loved the restaurant, but in a different way. A better way, actually. It wasn't as creative as the restaurant, but there was no tension. Any criticism was given with a dose of laughter. It was . . . freeing.

As was Wildstone in general. "I am happy here," she said softly. Feeling in control and proud of herself, she looked up.

Beth was smiling from ear to ear and . . . fading away.

"No!" Quinn said. "Don't go!"

"You should go to L.A. and break the news to Mom and Dad in person," Beth said, her smile so beautiful. "I'd say do the same to Chef Wade but he already replaced you."

"What?"

"Yeah, he just hasn't found the nerve to break it to you yet." She blew Quinn a kiss. "Love you. Stay happy. It suits you . . ."

"No!" Quinn said, panicking because Beth's voice was somehow different. This was good-bye. For real. Well, as real as a ghost got anyway. She jumped up. "Don't you leave me again!"

But Beth was gone.

Tilly was lying in bed using Snapchat to take a selfie with horns coming out of her head when Quinn knocked and came in.

Quinn looked at the pic with the horns and snorted. "There's a stretch."

"Ha-ha," Tilly said, embarrassed to be caught doing the selfie thing. Not that she was about to admit to that.

Quinn leaned against the dresser, trying to look casual, but the expression on her face was anything but.

"What's wrong?" Tilly asked.

"Do you ever . . ." She grimaced. "See your mom?"

Tilly blinked. "You mean my *dead* mom?"

Quinn shifted uncomfortably. "I'm talking about her . . . spirit. Do you ever see her . . . spirit?"

Tilly took a beat. "Like . . . a ghost?"

"Never mind." Quinn ran a hand over her face.

"Do *you* see my mom?" Tilly asked her carefully, feeling a little bit absurd but oddly hopeful at the same time.

Quinn dropped her hands and sighed. "I see my sister."

Tilly's gut tightened. Beth. Of course. Because Quinn didn't really think of Tilly as her sister. "You see Beth's ghost."

"I said never mind!"

"Dude." Tilly paused. "Maybe you need a vacation."

"I can't afford one," Quinn said and shook her head. "Forget all that. I need to talk to you about something else."

At this, everything inside Tilly went still. *Never let 'em see you sweat* . . . She forced her muscles to relax and met Quinn's gaze. "You do realize nothing good has ever come from that sentence, right?"

"It's nothing bad," Quinn said. "I need to go see my parents. How do you feel about this weekend? We could make a shopping trip out of it, get some new clothes or something."

"I thought you were broke," Tilly said.

Quinn blew out a breath. "Well, there's broke and then there's broke."

Tilly drew in a careful breath. "So . . . you want to go shopping."

"I realize I'm resorting to blatant bribery, but I need to talk to my parents and my boss." She paused. "We're doing okay, the two of us, right?"

Tilly shrugged, not ready, or willing, to comment.

Quinn searched her expression. "I just don't want to jeopardize that by leaving you here to remember how much you loved living at Chuck's."

Tilly let out a low laugh that wasn't really a laugh.

"So . . . you'll come?"

Tilly shook her head. "I don't like L.A."

"You ever been there?"

"No," Tilly admitted.

"You don't have to come, I won't make you. I just have some business to take care of and thought you might enjoy the trip."

Tilly shook her head.

Quinn looked disappointed, but turned to the door. Tilly warred with herself and lost.

"Quinn?"

"Yeah?"

"You're still going?"

"Yes. We'll talk to Chuck tomorrow." Her phone buzzed. "Cliff returning my call," she said and stepped out of the room.

Tilly stared at the door Quinn shut behind her and then leaped out of bed and pressed her ear to the wood.

"Thanks for finishing up the paperwork," she heard Quinn say. "I can't keep Tilly floating adrift like this any longer, a toe in each world. She's got roots here and she's not interested in L.A."

Tilly froze. So with or without her, Quinn was leaving. The betrayal of that cut deep but she'd gotten good at operating from a place of pain. Real good.

Time to make her own plans.

Quinn stared at her phone. She'd changed her mind. She didn't need to go to L.A. This was about Tilly. So even though it was ten o'clock at night, she'd called her parents. She'd called Brock.

None of them had been surprised at her decision to stay.

She'd called Chef Wade, who had reluctantly confirmed that yes, he'd hired someone. It was a temp but she was working out so well he'd like to make it permanent. Quinn told him she didn't blame him one bit, she completely understood, and she was sorry that she hadn't come clean about not wanting to come back sooner. He told her the door was always open for further discussion.

She sat there for a few moments after the call, wondering how, if Beth's ghost was just a figment of her imagination, she'd known Wade had hired someone . . .

But since that hurt her brain, she moved forward and called Skye, who had squealed in excitement.

"You do realize I just told you I'm moving away," Quinn said.

"Yes, but you're following your heart!" Skye sounded like she was grinning. "I'm so proud of you. And so happy. You've got the right temperament to live in that crazy-ass, old wild west ghost town."

Quinn laughed. "Thanks. I think." Smiling, she disconnected and texted Mick with a simple: I'm staying.

When she didn't get an immediate response, she slid into bed, not sure if she was confused or hurt. She was asleep when her phone finally buzzed with an incoming call.

Mick.

"Hey," she said. "Thought maybe I scared you into a coma or something."

"I'm on my way home." His voice was low and gruff, and just the sound of it brought her an aching smile, so it took her a moment to absorb his words.

"I thought you were already in the Bay Area," she said, confused.

"I meant home to Wildstone. To you."

She sat straight up in bed, her heart starting to drum. "What does that mean?"

"I'm not doing this over the phone. I'll be there in a few hours. Try to get some sleep."

Was he kidding? "Mick—"

"I love you, Quinn." And with that shocking statement, he disconnected.

Quinn stared at her phone, emotions she hadn't felt in too long welling up and out of her chest, spilling into every corner of her being.

Hope.

Excitement.

Completely unable to sleep, she got up. Now that she'd made the hard decisions—which hadn't been hard at all—she felt an inner peace fill her. A calm. She was 100 percent certain she was doing the right thing, just as Carolyn had somehow known she would.

She couldn't wait for Mick to get here. Couldn't wait to wake Tilly up in the morning and tell her it was official. In the meantime, she prowled to the kitchen. She and Mick were going to be a team and she was hoping like hell she and Tilly were going to be a team too. Trying to keep as quiet as possible, she went through the cabinets. She needed to cook something. No, this was a celebration, which meant she needed to bake something, even though that was out of her comfort zone. But hell, her entire life was out of her comfort zone, so it felt oddly symbolic.

She found the ingredients she needed for a cake and was in the middle of it when her phone buzzed again. Thinking it was Mick, she pulled it from her pocket with a smile, but it was an unknown number. "Hello?" she asked, wondering who the hell was calling her at midnight.

"Is this Quinn Weller?"

"Yes," she said. "Who's this?"

"California Highway Patrol, ma'am. There's been a car accident with a minor who says she lives with you."

Quinn gasped. "Tilly?"

"Yes, we want to let you know that she's at County Hospital—"

"What? Is she hurt?"

"Minor injuries. We need you to come down here."

"I'm already out the door," Quinn said even though she had no idea how Tilly had gotten in an accident when she'd been supposedly asleep in her room. She ran down the hallway and flung Tilly's door open, flipping on the light.

The room was empty of one sullen teenager.

Oh, God. Still holding the phone to her ear, Quinn ran back into the living room and grabbed her purse, yanking open the door, only half-listening to the CHP officer.

"—was in a Lexus that's registered to you—"

"But that's impossible." Quinn moved to the living room to peer out the window. "My car's right here—" But it wasn't.

Tilly had stolen her car.

Chapter 35

Why is it that it's only after an argument when I think of the awesome things I should have said?

—from "The Mixed-Up Files of Tilly Adams's Journal"

Tilly closed her eyes. "She's going to kill me."

"She's not going to kill you," Dylan said calmly.

He was always calm.

She wished she had half his calm. "Yes, she *is* going to kill me. And if for some reason she doesn't, she's going to run to L.A. even faster now, without looking back."

"You stole her car, Tee. You crashed it into a tree and demolished both. I'm not sure what the hell you were thinking, but you must've known you were pretty much saying fuck you when you took her car without permission, not to mention without a driver's license."

Is that what she'd been doing? Trying to push Quinn away

before Quinn did it first? Yes. Yes, okay, fine, that's *exactly* what she'd been doing, which made her . . . a child.

Her head was killing her from the cut above her eyebrow, but they said she didn't have a concussion, just a broken arm.

The ER nurse had called her lucky. Tilly laughed bleakly at the thought of being lucky. She hadn't been lucky a single day of her godforsaken life.

Except maybe the day Quinn had come into it . . .

The thought made her want to cry. Luckily she never cried. At least not that she'd admit to. "How did you get so smart?" she asked Dylan.

"The smartest girl I know taught me."

She snorted. "Maybe she's not really all that."

"She is."

She blew out a sigh. "I don't know why I did it. I wanted to stop hurting. I wanted to be somewhere I'm wanted—"

"Tee," Dylan whispered, voice pained.

She shook her head, unable to say anything else.

"From what you've told me, you're like her, you know," Dylan said. "Quinn. You're both stubborn. Single-minded." He paused and smiled. "And always sure you're right . . ."

"I don't know why I called you."

". . . beautiful."

She met his warm gaze.

"Courageous," he whispered.

Her throat got tighter.

"Cares about other people like no one else I know," he went on and paused. "I think you got scared because you're afraid to believe in love."

"Well, look who's talking," she managed.

Holding eye contact, he set a hand on either side of her hips and leaned in. "You've been sweet and kind and patient with me, Tilly."

She couldn't tear her eyes from his, so deep and dark and full of the haunting, hollow experiences he'd had in his life, none of which had anything to do with sweet and kind and patient. "It's easy to be those things with you," she said. "I love you, Dylan."

He closed his eyes briefly, as though both pained and moved, and then he looked at her again. "I know you do. And I'm even starting to believe it. I love you too, Tilly."

Completely melted, she lifted her one good arm and set her hand on his biceps. "Dylan—"

"So maybe you can try to be as kind and sweet and patient with Quinn," he said. "Because she's going to barrel in here any second now, frightened, freaked, and half out of her mind."

"How do you know?"

"Because that's how I felt when you called me."

Guilt swamped Tilly. Guilt and remorse, because she hadn't even called Quinn herself, she'd let the cop do it.

They were still staring at each other when Quinn came running into the room looking just like Dylan had said—frightened, freaked, and half out of her mind.

"Oh my God," Quinn said, tears in her voice as she rushed to the bed.

Dylan backed away, making room for her. She cupped Tilly's face, staring at the butterfly bandage over her eye, taking in the cast on her arm. "*Oh my God.*"

"You already said that," Tilly said.

Chuck had come in behind Quinn. Probably he'd given her a ride.

Tilly met Chuck's gaze and he gave her a very small, relieved smile.

Quinn expelled a breath of air like she'd been holding her breath for too long. And then to Tilly's horror, Quinn's eyes filled with tears.

"No," Tilly said. "No, no, no . . . there's no crying allowed in the hospital. It's a rule, I swear it!"

"Are you okay?" Quinn demanded.

"Yeah." She swallowed hard. "I'm sorry about your car."

"Forget the car," Quinn said and hugged her tight.

So tight she couldn't draw in air. "Um, you're squeezing me pretty tight—"

Quinn's arms tightened even more.

"Okay," Tilly squeaked out and patted Quinn awkwardly on the back. "Okay, but I. Can't. Breathe—"

"I was worried sick about you!"

Over Quinn's shoulder, Tilly met Dylan's gaze, the one that said *I told you so.* She tried to sigh but couldn't draw a breath. "No, really, I don't need any air or anything—"

"Do you have any idea what could have happened?" Quinn demanded, voice quivering. "You could've—" When she broke off, clearly unable to speak, the reality of the situation hit Tilly.

Quinn had lost Beth in a car accident. The loss had devastated her, and now Tilly's stupidity and selfishness had brought back all the pain and horror and shock.

She was the biggest jerk on the planet, and knowing it, wrapped her arms around Quinn and returned the hug. "I'm sorry," she whispered. "I'm so sorry for . . ." Well, everything. But before she could say it, a nurse bustled in, doing her nurse thing.

After checking Tilly for what felt like the thousandth time, she said, "I'm getting your release papers ready. We've got some paperwork to go over."

It was an hour and a half before they actually got to leave. Then they spent another half an hour at the pharmacy.

The car ride home was tense.

Quinn had said very little after hugging Tilly tight enough to crack her ribs. She was vibrating with tension and emotions though, and Tilly wished she'd just let them loose but had no idea how to make that happen.

Chuck dropped them off at the house, where they found Mick waiting for them on the porch. Mick hugged both Quinn and Tilly, and they went inside, Mick moving to the kitchen to give them some privacy.

Quinn stood in the living room and tossed her purse to the coffee table before putting her hands on her hips and staring down at her shoes.

Tilly stood there uncertainly. She wanted to sneak away to her bedroom, pull the covers over her head, and wait for her mom to come bring her hot chocolate.

But that wasn't going to happen.

Quinn finally seemed to find her words. "Running away is never the answer, Tilly."

Tilly was smart enough to know that already, but she wasn't smart enough to keep her mouth shut. "You ran away from L.A. and your parents."

Quinn gaped at her like a fish for a moment. "I didn't run away! I ran *to* something. To *someone*, as a matter of fact. A someone who doesn't seem to give a shit."

Tilly's stomach hit her toes. "I—"

"Oh, no. You had your chance to speak and you chose to open

a can of worms, so let's do this," Quinn said. Actually, yelled. She was totally yelling. And also crying, which made Tilly feel like the biggest asshat on the planet.

"Maybe you don't realize it," Tilly said. "But you're talking in all caps."

"Do you think this has been easy for me?" Quinn pressed a hand to her own chest. Or at least that's what Tilly thought she said, but Quinn was an open-mouthed crier and it was getting harder and harder to understand her.

"I know nothing about raising someone! But I'm trying, okay? And I get that I fail a lot, but I'm not going anywhere. You hear me, Tilly? I get that I'm not Carolyn, not even close, but you know what? I'm willing to try for second best because sometimes that's just how life works. But you have to meet me halfway."

Tilly opened her mouth but Quinn jabbed a finger at her and kept talking. "I never got to ask Carolyn questions, and I have questions, Tilly. I mean, did she also have one foot that was half a size bigger than the other? Or get murderous urges during PMS? And how about love, huh? Did she suck at it as badly as I do, because . . ."

The rest of that sentence was lost behind the crying, but it sounded like "and now I can't even afford to fix that damn shower and I really need more hot water!"

Okay, she'd totally sent her sister over the edge. *Completely* over the edge. "I'm sorry," she whispered.

Quinn stopped talking and crying to blow her nose, and then she . . . walked away. She went down the hallway and a minute later her bedroom door slammed shut.

Which was shocking because Quinn never slammed doors. She never lost her shit at all and Tilly was standing there wondering what the hell to do when Mick appeared at her side.

"Come to the kitchen," he said.

"But Quinn—"

"—needs a moment." Without another word he moved back to the kitchen.

With a sigh, Tilly followed him.

Mick pushed a mug across the counter toward her.

Hot chocolate.

She blinked away tears and that's when she saw the ingredients . . . everywhere. Bowls, mixer, eggs, milk . . . Flour was tipped over and spilled out across the counter and floor, like someone had knocked it over in a rush.

"That was Quinn," Mick said quietly. "She dropped everything to get to the hospital the second she got the call."

She lifted her shocked gaze to his. "Why was she baking? She cooks all day. Baking is the last thing she'd want to do."

"She signed your guardianship papers," Mick said. "She wanted to surprise you with a cake."

"But she hates to bake."

He just looked at her.

She closed her eyes. "She said she was going to L.A."

"Yes. To tell her parents she was moving to Wildstone. To stay."

Tilly was stunned.

"And because you're a minor and you don't have a license," Mick went on, speaking kindly but not sugar-coating it, "and because she signed those papers, you're her responsibility. And that includes legally. She could be in trouble for you driving underage and without a license, and be held liable for all damages."

And still, Quinn's first and only concern had been for Tilly. About getting to her. Seeing her with her own eyes. "But it wasn't her fault," Tilly whispered past a throat that felt like she'd swallowed shards of glass. "Isn't there anything that can be done?"

"Yes," Mick said, not pulling punches. "To soften the blow for herself, Quinn could have you charged with stealing her car."

Tilly was pretty sure she was going to pass out. She gripped the counter and stared at the spilled flour.

Mick gave her arm a gentle squeeze. "But we both know that Quinn would never in a million years do anything like that to you. Or at least I'm hoping you know that."

Tilly nodded. Because she did know it.

"Do you know why?" Mick asked.

"Because she loves me," Tilly whispered.

"She does." There was a smile in his voice. "Although once the dust settles, she might be a little pissed about not having a car to sell. She'd planned on using the money from it to update this house and the café."

Oh, God. She covered her face and felt Mick turn her to him and pull her in for a hug. "I'm not trying to hurt you," he said. "But I'm not going to stand around and let you use her for a punching bag when she's trying so hard either."

Tilly nodded and sniffed.

"Did you just wipe your nose on my shirt?"

She choked out a laugh. "No!" When she pulled back, she saw that he was teasing her and realized it had worked. He was a really good guy. Maybe as good as Dylan. "Mick?"

"Yeah?"

"I'm not the only one all screwed up, you know. My sister has trust issues."

He nodded. "I know."

"She'd never put this into words, but she'd been hurt, big time. By her adoptive parents. By my mom. By that Brock guy." She paused. "By me." She shook her head. "I don't think she believes in love."

"I know that too," he said. "And until she came along and changed my mind, I'd have said she wasn't the only one."

She stared at him.

He let her, seemingly unbothered by her scrutiny.

"I broke her heart," she said quietly. "I'm going to fix it and then I'm never going to do it again."

"Good."

"But now I need you to look me in the eyes and give me your word that you're not going to ever do it either," she said.

He held eye contact and nodded with the solemnness the moment called for. "You have my word."

"Okay." She nodded back. "Now there's something I have to do." She went back to her room and pulled out the box she'd been hiding under her bed. She set it in the hallway next to Quinn's shut door. She hesitated, wanting to knock, but she was afraid to make things any worse.

Mostly she just felt like crap. She'd known Quinn wanted to go back to L.A. and she'd assumed the worst. That she'd stay in L.A. and Tilly would have to go back to living with Chuck.

Chuck had been good to her. He'd done the best he could, but his place had never been home.

This was home.

And she'd blown it.

Chapter 36

My mom used to say that the fastest land mammal on earth is the teenager who sees Mom pulling into the driveway and realizes they forgot to do some chores.

—From "The Mixed-Up Files of Tilly Adams's Journal"

Quinn got up the next morning not letting herself think too much or she'd lose it. When Mick had finally joined her in bed last night, they hadn't talked. She hadn't the brain power for it. Instead, he'd done his best to distract her from her stress and anxiety, and he was a most excellent distractor. It had proved all but impossible to think of anything past her desperate need for him when he had her in bed.

Or in the shower.

Or up against a wall.

He wasn't in the bed now, but given that his side of the mattress was still warm and that Coop was still snoozing in the corner, he hadn't gone far. On a run, maybe.

She got up and nearly tripped over Tink.

"Mew," she said in a tone that suggested she was close to starving to death.

Just beyond the cat, just outside Quinn's bedroom door, was a small chest she'd never seen before. She picked it up and moved into the kitchen with Tink on her heels, finding the place clean of her baking mess.

Tilly stood at the stovetop making breakfast. She'd even made coffee, cast on her arm and all. The teen nudged a mug toward her, gave a tentative smile and . . . burst into tears, sobbing out words like "sorry" and "I don't know what I was thinking" and "please don't hate me . . ."

Quinn set the small chest down and moved in close. She took the spatula out of Tilly's hand, turned off the flames, and then pulled her in for a hug. "Of course I don't hate you."

But apparently it was Tilly's turn to lose her collective shit. She was crying so hard she was shaking and still talking nonsense, something about their deal and how she'd messed everything up.

"It's okay," Quinn told her, stroking her back, pressing a kiss to her temple. "You're safe, and the rest will fall into place. It's going to be okay."

Tilly managed to subside into hiccups. "How?" she asked soggily. "How will it fall into place? I've ruined your car and your life. You'll un-sign the papers and go back to L.A."

Quinn pulled back just enough to look into Tilly's face. "Is that what you think? That I'd just walk away from you?" But she could see by Tilly's expression that she truly feared exactly that.

And why wouldn't she? Her dad had walked away. Her mom had left her too, albeit very unwillingly . . . So why shouldn't Quinn? "Tilly," she said quietly but with utter steel, as she meant every single word. "I would never leave you. You're my sister.

You're stuck with me, okay? Through thick and thin. That's what family means."

Tilly stared at her, eyes searching so desperately that Quinn could scarcely breathe. "You really want to stay?"

"Yes."

"With me."

"Yes."

"In Wildstone."

Quinn laughed. "Yes! Especially now that I know you've got cleaning skills." She looked around. "You've been holding out on me."

"You're choosing Wildstone over L.A.," Tilly repeated, refusing to be drawn into a good mood.

Quinn let her smile fade. "I'm choosing *you*."

"But—"

"No buts. It's you and me," Quinn said. "It's also your choice. If you wanted to go to L.A., we'd do that. We'd live in my condo or figure something else out. But if you want to stay here, that's fine too. And actually . . ." She met Tilly's gaze. "So do I."

"For reals?"

"For reals," Quinn said with a smile.

"What if you change your mind?"

"I won't."

"Dad did."

"His loss," Quinn said quietly. "But neither of us is built that way. We don't walk away from those we love. Ever. And I do love you, Tilly."

Tilly eyes spilled over again, but this time Quinn was pretty sure it was relief, not worry or anxiety.

"I have something for you," Tilly whispered.

"A promise to never scare me again?" Quinn asked.

Tilly grimaced. "I can work on that, but no."

"A promise to make me coffee every morning?"

"A box of your baby clothes," Tilly said. "My mom—our mom—made them for you." She gestured to the small chest. "I found it a while ago, which was mean and selfish of me. I'm sorry about that too."

Quinn opened the chest and gasped softly. "These are mine?"

"Handmade," Tilly said. "She was excited about being pregnant with you. Happy. I don't know what happened or why that changed, but she was really young." She met Quinn's gaze. "I mean if it was me, I wouldn't be grown up enough to be able to keep a baby, you know?"

Quinn nodded.

"I thought you'd want to know that she did want you."

Quinn's eyes shimmered brilliantly and she nodded. "Thanks," she whispered. "You're a good sister."

Tilly chewed on her lower lip, her gaze saying she hadn't been a good sister and she knew it. "I wanted to end our trial period a long time ago," she burst out with. "I just didn't know how."

Sometimes it was the big things. Death. Love. Life. But sometimes it was the small things. A hug. A few words. Quinn set aside the chest of clothes and smiled. "Took you long enough."

Tilly let out a low laugh. "We're not going to have to hug again, are we?"

"Yes," Quinn said and hauled her in.

Her face smushed into Quinn's shoulder, she asked, "Are we going to have to hug a lot?"

"Yes. Deal with it," Quinn said and Tilly smiled against her neck and knew everything was going to work out. Messily, no doubt, but they'd be okay.

Far more okay than she could've hoped for.

Mick was knee-deep in negotiations with the owner of the Wild West B & B when he got a call from Tom. Mick stepped outside to take it, knowing it wasn't going to be anything good. Colin had sent him the evidence he'd alluded to in their phone call. A full accounting of expenses Tom had incurred in the past year—which didn't come close to matching up with his salary. The discrepancy was more than a million dollars.

He could give it to the county prosecutor's office and Tom's fate would be in their hands.

"Heard you and your girlfriend had an exciting night," Tom said.

"What do you want, Tom?"

"I want what I've always wanted. You to go the fuck away and stay away. You were a shitty influence on Boomer all those years ago and you still are. He was doing fine until you came back and now he's in rehab for fuck's sake."

It took everything Mick had to not refute that statement but he did because Tom didn't understood Boomer and never would.

Boomer deserved better.

"I know that you think you've got something on me," Tom said. "You're wrong."

"If that was true," Mick said, "you wouldn't be calling."

"Fine. Then let me spell things out for you. If you don't drop this vendetta against me, you're going to be sorry."

"Am I?" Mick asked, squatting to rub Coop's belly.

"You will be when I have Quinn deemed an unfit guardian, and then have Tilly taken away from her and put in foster care."

Mick rose to his feet. "Try proving Quinn unfit. She's an amazing guardian."

"Let me remind you that not once but *twice* now, Tilly's run away. She's driven without a license, crashed a car, and damaged county property—while under Quinn's care. And I'm sure if I think real hard, I can come up with even more charges. I've got a lot of influence and pull in this county and you damn well know it."

"What I know," Mick said evenly, "is that you've been taking kickbacks instead of providing jobs to this town. That's on you and no one else."

"Even if you manage to prove that and take me down, facts are facts. The girl's been acting out while under Quinn's care. On top of everything else, there's also evidence she's been shoplifting."

"Bullshit," Mick said. "Where and when?"

"Let's just say that if there isn't evidence of it yet, there will be," the slimy bastard said. "So stand down, or I take you and yours down with me. Oh, and one more thing. You're going to stand up at the next town meeting and announce that you've reconsidered your position and you're backing me and my projects one hundred percent."

Mick wanted to reach through the phone and punch his smug face. Because now he was faced with either letting his old friends and neighbors down, or watching Quinn be publicly deemed unfit and lose Tilly.

Neither of which he could let happen.

Quinn knew something was wrong when she got a call from Cliff that afternoon. "What's up?" she asked, immediately moving down the hall to peek into Tilly's room.

When she saw the teenager sprawled out on her bed, lost in her own world with headphones on, she took a deep breath.

No one had run away, stolen the car, crashed the car . . .

"I just had an odd phone call," Cliff said. "I was questioned about you and Tilly by someone at the county."

"Questioned?"

"About the legality of your taking guardianship of Tilly," Cliff said. "Something doesn't feel right to me. I'm going to look into it, but I wanted to warn you that I think something's up."

Her stomach tightened. She'd had just about all the drama she could take. "Like what?"

"I don't know. I'll call you back tomorrow, sit tight."

But Quinn didn't do sit tight very well. She waved at Tilly, who sat up and pulled the headphones away from her ears. "What?"

"I need to go talk to Mick," Quinn said.

"Is that what the kids are calling it these days?"

"It's a *real* talk! Jeez. I'll be back in a few," Quinn said and went to the garage. She cranked over Carolyn's old Bronco, drove to the Wild West B & B, and knocked on the door of the room Mick always used when he was in town.

He opened the door wearing a pair of low-slung basketball shorts and a set of headphones around his neck. His laptop was open. Clearly he was working, and just as clearly, he was surprised to see her. "Hey," he said. "I was coming to you in a little bit."

"Beat you to it." She ducked under his arm and let herself in.

"Is this a booty call?" he asked hopefully.

She wished. "No, I have to get back to make Tilly dinner."

"You know, if you wait long enough to make dinner, people will just eat cereal. It's science."

She laughed, but the smile fell quickly from her face. "I just got an odd call from Cliff. Someone's questioning my guardianship."

Mick's eyes darkened with anger, but not, she couldn't help but notice, surprise. She let out a breath and sat on the edge of the bed. "What's going on, Mick?"

He hesitated and then came to sit down next to her. "Tom

Nichols called me," he said and then told her the rest, what Tom had sworn to do if he didn't back down.

"But you're not going to back down, right?" she asked.

Mick looked at her as if she'd lost her mind. "Quinn, there's no way in hell I'm letting you get caught in the crosshairs."

She jumped up, unable to sit. "Are you kidding me? There's no way in hell I'm letting you back down and eat crow before that horrible man! I mean it," she said, choked up as he rose and slid his hands up and down her suddenly chilled arms. "Over my dead body, Mick."

He held fast and gently reeled her in even though her feet had turned to lead. "Quinn, he's going to destroy you, which will destroy me."

"You're not the one who did illegal things!"

"Listen to me." He cupped her face and tilted it up to his. "It's not too late. If you stay away from me, make it clear that I don't mean anything to you, he'll find another angle to try and hurt me."

She stared at him. "You want me to walk away?" Because hell no. "I've already tried that, Mick, and I won't do it again."

"Quinn," he breathed softly, his voice achingly full of emotion. "I don't want whatever happens to be the end of us. I want to keep you if you'll have me. But this is your decision, your last chance to avoid more heartbreak."

Her forehead dropped to his chest as an escape from the intensity of his gaze. She knew he was right. Despite all the wonderful things about the man, he came with flaws. But so did she. If she wasn't already in love with him, she would've fallen in love with him for giving her the time to think it through.

As if she needed any time at all.

She turned her head to rest her cheek against a warm, hard pec, thoughts racing. She couldn't lose Tilly now, she just couldn't. She'd fought tooth and nail for her.

The way Mick fought tooth and nail to help his mom, and anyone else he cared about. The way Skye had driven up to Wildstone for one day just to make sure she was okay. The way Greta and Trinee had each other's backs.

The way her own mom had spent her life just wanting Quinn to be happy, when they both knew that emotion was elusive as hell. A lump formed in her throat. Love wasn't in the words, love was in the deeds, trying to give your daughter everything you'd never had, including buying a restaurant just to give her the job she wanted.

Or in Tilly's case, giving up a chest of things that her mom had made with her own hands in order to give someone else some peace. And in Mick's . . . lending her a Jetpack, saving her from bugs, buying her a damn bed so she wouldn't have to sleep on the couch, among so many other things she couldn't even count them all. She struggled to take it in and came to a conclusion.

Happiness *was* real. It was a state of mind. So was love, and she had more than her fair share of that.

Time to give some back.

She lifted her head. "I want you to fight for Wildstone, and the people in it."

"But—"

She put a finger over his lips. "I can handle the fallout. I won't let anyone take Tilly from me, even if I have to sell my condo or borrow money from my parents to get a good attorney who'll make mincemeat out of the city manager."

"Quinn, this is my fight. I've got this."

Stupid, wonderful man. She looked into his eyes and echoed back his own words from when he'd been angry over Brock's visit.

"You might be having trouble understanding what constitutes a relationship," she said. "But I'm happy to explain it to you. It means I'll be standing at your side, no matter what, no matter who we have to take down."

He tugged her in closer. "Bloodlust. I like it."

"I mean it, Mick. I don't have a lot of people in my life, but the ones I do have, I feel very protective of and would fight to the death for."

"Now you're just *trying* to turn me on."

She gave him a little, teasing smile. "Gonna kick ass and take names."

He slid a hand into her hair and lightly tugged her face up to his. "I love you, Quinn." His voice was gruff and honest. A promise, and more than she'd ever dreamed of.

"I'm not going to let anything happen to you or Tilly," he said. "Do you believe me?"

Did she?

Could she?

The answer was simple. Yes. She believed him and she believed *in* him.

His eyes warmed and his smile was a balm on her aching heart. "I like the way you're looking at me," he said.

"Yeah?"

"Yeah." He shifted closer and ran his hands up her back and then down again to cup her sweet ass in his palms. But just as he leaned over her with fierce intent, there was a knock at the door.

Mick groaned. "Ignore it."

That was a good plan and she pressed her face into his throat and inhaled deep, feeling like she needed the scent of him to survive.

There was a second knock, and with a sigh, Mick went to the door.

Joe, the old-timer who owned the gas station, stood there with a few of his cronies behind him. Lou, Not-Big-Hank, and Big Hank.

"I've got your problem solved," Joe said in a been-smoking-for-five-decades voice.

"What problem?" Mick asked.

"Your city manager problem."

Quinn could only see Mick's back and broad shoulders, but she sensed his surprise.

"How do you know I have a city manager problem?" he asked.

"We've got eyes in our head, don't we?" Lou asked.

Mick just leaned against the doorjamb, arms crossed, deceptively casual. "And?"

"And . . . we planted a spy kit," Joe said. "No, hear us out," he added quickly when Mick shook his head and started to speak. "We bought it on the interweb and bugged Tom's office. We caught him admitting everything to you on the phone earlier."

"You bugged his office," Mick said.

"Yep."

"That's . . ." Mick shook his head. "Disturbing. Not to mention illegal."

"It's okay," Joe said. "Let 'em throw the book at me. What'll I get, five years in the big house?" He glanced behind him at the others, who all nodded like a row of geriatric bobbleheads.

"We figured it all out. I'm the one with the biggest dental problems. But I can't afford a dentist, see? So I'll get free dental." He beamed. "Win-win."

The others nodded in unison again. "And if Joe kicks the bucket before his time's up," Big Hank said, "I'll offer to finish it up for him. My lease is coming up next year and they're going to raise the rent on me anyway."

Mick craned his neck and looked at Quinn, seeming just as amused/horrified/touched as he was. She moved to his side and slipped her hand in his.

"I'm honored," Mick said. "But there's no way I'm letting any of you go to jail for me. And how did you even know what was going on anyway?"

"Shoot, you've been gone from Wildstone too long if you don't know how this works," Joe said with a snort. "Lou's niece's boyfriend's sister works in the city offices. The city manager yelled at her last week for spilling his coffee and made her cry. She's the one that bugged the office using the spy kit. Plus, he slept with the county recorder's wife—her sister. That's what everyone's saying anyway."

"Well, then it must be true," Mick said with a straight face.

Joe nodded. "The bastard is done."

"I appreciate that," Mick said. "But none of you are going to jail for me. We're going to give the justice system a chance to handle this."

"Can we go downtown and beat him up?" Joe asked.

"If we stop for doughnuts first," Lou said. "What," he said defensively at Hank's long look. "I'm hungry."

"Revenge, *then* food," Joe said. "You in, Mick?"

Mick looked at Quinn. "I don't need revenge." He looked at Quinn. "And if you'll all excuse me, I've got something much better to do anyway. I've got a hot date with the woman of my dreams."

And then, to the hoots and hollering of their audience, he hooked an arm low on Quinn's hips, his other hand coming up to slide into her hair to hold her head where he wanted her as he kissed the thoughts right out of her head. When he pulled back, he smiled into her undoubtedly dazed face as someone rode down the hallway on a bike.

Someone with a cast on one arm. "Nice 'talk,'" Tilly said.

"You rode over here with only one good arm?" Quinn asked, horrified. "What's wrong?"

"Nothing. I made dinner, but you left your phone, so I couldn't call you. I thought you didn't need a man."

"She doesn't," Mick said. "Truth is, *I* need *her*. In fact, I need your sister like I've never needed anyone or anything in my whole life. And," he went on, smiling into Quinn's face as he reached out and hooked an arm around Tilly's neck and dragged her into the hug too. "I'm pretty fond of her nosy, know-it-all sister too."

Tilly snorted but she also melted a little, Quinn could tell. She felt her eyes burn even as she laughed and held tight to the two most important people in her life. "I love you both," she said fiercely. "So much."

Tilly sighed with dramatic flair. "You promised no more hugs."

"Didn't promise no more kisses," Quinn said and kissed her face all over while Tilly squirmed and yelled, "*Ew!*" Quinn kissed Mick's face too and that also grossed out Tilly.

"Right in front of me?" she asked.

Quinn smiled up at Mick. "We're a team."

"A team," Mick said. "Tilly?"

"Yeah?"

"You okay with me loving your sister and making her mine, since I'm already hers?"

"Seriously. You two have a problem."

"Yes or no, Tilly," Mick said, eyes locked on Quinn.

Tilly blew out a sigh, but she couldn't quite hide her pleasure at being asked. "Sure," she finally said. "But you should know, she hugs *way* too much."

Mick smiled into Quinn's eyes. "A team," he said, repeating her words. "We're in it together, always."

"Always," she whispered back. She didn't hear Beth's voice in her head, and hadn't since her sister had said good-bye, but she felt a warm peace settle over her as the last piece of her heart clicked back into place.

Epilogue

Six Months Later

Quinn found one of Mick's shirts in her laundry and it made her smile. He hadn't left it for her to do. She'd stolen it.

On the nights he was in San Francisco, Quinn slept in it. It should've felt like a silly, juvenile thing to do, but wearing it gave her comfort.

When she'd washed and folded the laundry, she opened the drawer in her dresser that she'd designated as his. She wasn't even sure how it had happened, but it made her smile as she crouched down and scooted a pair of his basketball shorts aside to make room for the shirt and . . .

Exposed a little black box.

A jewelry box.

She stared at it, whispered, "Oh my God," and then shut the drawer like she'd seen a bomb. A ticking bomb.

"Did you say something?" Tilly asked, passing by on the way

to her bedroom. She had blue streaks in her hair, like the ones Quinn had worn when she'd first gotten to Wildstone—courtesy of Lena, of course.

"Nope," Quinn said, shaking her head. "Didn't say anything. Not one little thing. Nothing. Nada. Zip . . ."

Tilly narrowed her eyes and stepped into the room. "Try it again without looking guilty as hell."

Quinn pointed at the drawer. "I found a box. A little box. A little black box."

Brows up, Tilly came into the room. The past six months had been good for all of them. Tom Nichols was in jail for collusion and an assortment of other charges that would keep him in a cell for five to seven years. Dylan's mom had been able to make charges against his dad stick and he was also currently sitting out the next few years in jail, making license plates for the state of California. This meant that Dylan didn't have to work for the guy digging ditches. He was still working at the café—which was more popular than ever—and talking about trying for a scholarship at a local tech college when he graduated.

Tilly was doing better than Quinn could have asked for. Her grades had held firm, and she had her eye on a liberal arts school in San Francisco. She was quicker to smile and laugh these days, for which Quinn was grateful. She was also driving, legally, and giving Quinn gray hair.

Which Lena helped her hide with highlights—*not* blue.

Tilly moved to Quinn's side and crouched down in front of the drawer. "Show me."

Quinn opened the drawer, where together they stared at the box.

"It could be a bracelet or something," Tilly said.

"You think?"

"No."

Quinn sat on the floor because her knees were weak. "Well, since I'm already sitting . . ." She reached for the box.

"Figured you wouldn't be able to help yourself," Mick said from behind them.

With a gasp, Quinn jerked around and tilted her head back to stare up at him, the damning evidence in her hand.

"Go ahead," he said. "Try it on. You know you want to."

"She really does," Tilly said.

Quinn shot her a look and then turned back to Mick.

He kneeled in front of her, took the box from her hand, and removed the ring.

A beautiful, sparkling diamond ring.

"Wow," Tilly whispered reverently.

Quinn turned her head and looked at her sister.

"Just saying," Tilly said.

Tossing the box to her bed, Mick took Quinn's hand in hers and pulled it to his chest, over his heart. "I fell for you that very first day when you demanded I come into your room at the B and B."

"I didn't do that," Quinn said to Tilly.

"She did," Mick said. "She wanted me to get the bug out of her tub."

Tilly laughed. "That, I believe."

Mick looked at Quinn again. "And then I tasted your crappy pancakes and I fell for you, hook, line, and sinker."

"Those were crepes!"

He smiled. "Loved them. And your smile. And your strength. And your kindness. And—" He looked at Tilly. "Cover your ears for a second." He turned back to Quinn. "Your sweet ass. Love that a lot, actually. Love everything about you, Quinn."

Tilly sighed dramatically. "Oh my God," she said to the room. "They're being gross again."

Quinn wrapped her arms around Mick and pressed close. "Keep going."

He slid his hands into her hair, holding it back from her face. "I'm over commuting back and forth from San Francisco. I'm moving my office to Wildstone to be with you and Tilly. You're my entire world, my heart and soul. I love you. The forever kind of love."

"Do I get to be in the wedding?" Tilly asked.

"If there is one," Mick said, eyes on Quinn. "I can do with or without the ceremony, babe; as long as I have you, I'm good. Your call."

Quinn wasn't prepared for the wave of emotion that swamped her. "First," she managed. "I love you too."

"The forever kind," Tilly added helpfully, nodding at Quinn encouragingly when Quinn once again met her gaze.

Quinn turned and looked up into Mick's steady, dark eyes, feeling the love he had for her enfold her. "The forever kind," she agreed.

"And second?" he asked.

"*Yes.*" She'd never been more sure of anything in her life.

Mick hauled her in tight and kissed her, and from far, far away, Quinn heard Tilly sigh dramatically.

"They're at it again," the teenager told Tink, who'd come in to see what the commotion was about.

"Mew."

"Tell me about it . . ." Tilly scooped up the cat and cuddled her in close. "Seems we're a good fit after all."

A great fit, thought Quinn. A forever fit . . .

About the author

About the book

Read on

Insights,
Interviews
& More . . .

About the author

Meet Jill Shalvis

Emily Rademacher

New York Times bestselling author JILL SHALVIS lives in a small town in the Sierras full of quirky characters. Any resemblance to the quirky characters in her books is, um, mostly coincidental. Look for Jill's bestselling, award-winning books wherever romances are sold, and visit her website for a complete book list and daily blog detailing her city-girl-living-in-the-mountains adventures. ~

Author's Note

I started writing when I had three kids under the age of five and badly needed an escape. I wanted to write something real but not depressing. So I started with romance—hugely cathartic for someone whose daily wish was just to make it to the bathroom alone.

I wrote a lot of books while surrounded by little kids and sticky fingers. I wrote some more while raising—count 'em—four teenagers. Girls. I still shudder at the memories of all that estrogen. But with a little distance, I realize how much fodder that gave me to do something a little different for me. Something where I could still be funny (hopefully), still a little sexy and sassy, still create warm, close relationships . . . but also more. Like the complicated relationship between sisters including the good, the bad, AND the ugly.

For a long time, I've been fascinated by the idea of Quinn's character. How many of us haven't wondered at one time or another what it would be like to find out you're adopted? Would it rip the foundation from beneath your feet? Would it make you wonder how much you knew of yourself wasn't . . . you? Or would it be like finding a whole new beginning?

As I outlined the book, I really believed it was going to be all about Quinn learning about her adoption. But once I started writing, I realized it was so much more than that. It was about a woman devastated by the loss of her sister to the point where she'd stopped feeling. It was about that same woman finding out ▸

Author's Note ***(continued)***

she'd been betrayed by the people who she thought loved her more than anything else. And then she was further staggered to realize that though she'd lost one sister, she'd suddenly found another. And more than that, Quinn wasn't the only one experiencing loss and grief.

Enter Tilly, stage left. Honestly, I didn't see her coming. But from the moment we first see teenage Tilly hiding in the tree, chipped black fingernail polish and untied sneakers—as big a wreck as Quinn—I was in love. Another thing I didn't see coming? Dylan. (Or Mick, but I can admit, I fell a lot in love with Mick so he got a bigger role than planned . . .)

In any case, I hadn't raised four teenage girls without learning about young love. A whole lot, as a matter of fact. Going through it was . . . traumatic, to say the least. But writing about it with 20/20 hindsight? Heaven. I absolutely fell in love with the idea of Tilly and Dylan being in love, so I make no apologies for the extra romance. ☺

Now, normally in my books, the relationships between the men take center stage but *Lost And Found Sisters* was all about the girls. Quinn. Tilly. Carolyn. Beth . . . It was about love and loss and life coming full circle, about what it's like to have something come back and bite you on the patoot and to make it out on the other side all the stronger for it. I think we can all relate to that in different ways.

And no story about the story would be complete without touching on the setting of Wildstone, a character in its own right. So much so that I intend to revisit Wildstone with a whole new story soon. So stay tuned . . . And thanks to all for coming along for the ride!!!

Happy Reading!
Jill Shalvis
www.jillshalvis.com

Reading Group Guide

1. Do you think Quinn really saw her sister's ghost or was it all in her head?
2. If you think she was imagining it, was she was trying to work something out in her head? What might that be?
3. Did Carolyn do the right thing?
4. Did she wait too long to tell Quinn? If yes, do you find her sympathetic? If no, why do you think she took as long as she did to say something?
5. If Quinn hadn't met Mick, do you think she could've been happy with Brock?
6. Was Carolyn a good mother to Tilly? In what ways?
7. How does Tilly's relationship with Dylan compare and contrast with Quinn and Mick's?
8. Were Quinn's adoptive parents right to keep the adoption from her? How do you think you would handle a similar situation?
9. Was Quinn's reaction to it understandable?
10. If Quinn hadn't lost her sister, do you think she would have accepted her role in Tilly's life as quickly?
11. Cliff started out with a minimal role, but by the end, he seemed to be a peacekeeper—why do you think he was so invested in seeing Quinn and Tilly's relationship work out?
12. What do you think of Chuck? Was he someone who could have given Tilly a good life if Quinn had left?
13. Why do you think Quinn is happier cooking at the café than back in L.A.?
14. The rough-start relationship between Quinn and Lena seemed to lead to a real friendship. Do you think Lena can be a real friend?

Read on

Coming Soon . . .

An Excerpt from *Chasing Christmas Eve*

Chasing Christmas Eve, the next heartwarming romance from Jill Shalvis, is on sale September 2017.

Keep reading for an exclusive sneak peek!

Chapter 1

#SonOfABeanBagChair

"Spencer Baldwin?" an unfamiliar female voice asked.

Shit. Anyone who used his full name was most definitely *not* someone he wanted to speak with. After the past few months, he knew better than to answer his phone without looking at the screen but when he was buried in work like he was, he always forgot. With both hands busy directing a drone around the room, he'd answered on voice command without thinking about it.

"Wrong number," he said, his drone hovering with perfect precision—and engineering—above his head. Then, to prevent a repeat, he took one hand off the controls and chucked his phone out the high, narrow window of the basement.

Which felt great.

Directing the drone to continue hovering, he moved to the far wall of the huge basement below the Pacific Pier Building and climbed the three foot ladder that was against the window for just this sort of situation.

Yep. His cell phone had landed directly into the fountain in the center of the courtyard. "Three points," he murmured just as the elevator doors opened and Elle entered.

"Are you kidding me?" she asked in a tone that only she could get away with and not die. "You killed another one? Why don't you just stop answering to the reporters, wouldn't that be easier?"

He turned his attention back to his drone. "Am I paying you to bitch at me?" he asked mildly.

"As a matter of fact, yes," she said. "You're actually paying me a hell of a lot of money to bitch at you. Why don't I just change your phone number again?"

"He can't," Joe said from the other side of the room. He wore only a pair of knit boxers and stood in front of one of the three commercial grade washer and dryers, waiting for his clothes. "Me and the guys like it when he gets all the marriage proposals."

"You mean you like the nudie pics that come *with* the proposals," Elle said and her eyes narrowed in on Joe's body. "What the hell are you doing in your underwear?"

Joe was an IT wizard who worked at Hunt Investigations on the second floor. He was second in charge there, a master finder and fixer of . . . well, just about anything, and fairly badass while he was at it. And although Elle terrified almost everyone on the planet, Joe just grinned at her. "Had a little tussle earlier on the job," he said. "Spence let me in down here to use the machines."

Elle was not impressed. "If by tussle you mean a take-down went bad and you got blood all over yourself again, you best not be using those machines."

"Hey, at least it's not my blood. And I'm fine, thanks for asking."

Elle went hands on hips. She managed this building for the owner, who happened to be Spence and she often mistook the job for world domination, trying to run his personal life as well.

But Spence had nixed his personal life a long time ago. It was the Baldwin curse. He could be successful in his business life or his personal life – pick one – but not both. Since he objected on a very base level to going back to abject poverty, he'd long ago decided business was a safer bet than love.

Although, to be honest, he'd made a few forays into attempting both and had failed spectacularly.

"Hey," Joe said to Elle. "Did you hear that Spence here is ▸

Coming Soon . . . ***(continued)***

probably one of the top ten nominatees for San Francisco's most eligible bachelor?" He snorted as if this was hysterical.

Spence leaned forward and banged his head against the wall a few times.

"Don't bother, your head's harder than the concrete," she told him. "And yes," she told Joe. "I saw the news. Why do you think he just threw his phone out the window?"

"I could just scare everyone off your ass," Joe said to Spence.

He was kidding. Probably. And actually, Spence was more than a little tempted. This mess was all his fault, trusting someone he shouldn't have. As a result, the press had been having a field day with his success in a very large way, threatening his privacy and also his sanity.

Just thinking about the most eligible bachelor thing had him groaning.

"Listen," Elle said more kindly now. "Go take a break, okay? Then you can come back and do what you do best, shut out the world and work."

It was a well known fact that Spence's ability to hyper focus and ignore everything around him was both a strength and a huge flaw. Great asset for an engineer/inventor, not so great for anything else, like, say, relationships. But actually, he was hungry, so a break sounded good. He headed toward the elevator only to be stopped by Elle.

"Uh," she said, gesturing to his clothes. "You might want to . . ."

"What?" he asked, looking down at himself. So he hadn't shaved in a few days, so what? And okay, maybe he lived out of his dryer, grabbing clean but wrinkled clothes from there in the mornings when he got dressed. Whatever. There were worse things. "Joe's in his *underwear*."

"Hey, at least I was wearing some today," Joe said.

Elle took in the guy's nearly naked form, clearly appreciating the view in spite of her being very taken in the relationship department by Joe's boss Archer Hunt. She finally shook it off and turned back to Spence. "You know damn well when you walk across the courtyard talking to yourself, hair standing up thanks to your fingers, just the right amount of stubble in place and those black-rimmed glasses slipping down your annoyingly perfect nose, women come out of the woodworks."

"They do?" Joe asked.

"It's the hot geek look," Elle said.

"Huh." Joe rubbed his jaw, where he too had stubble. "Maybe I should try that sometime."

"No," Elle said. "You can't pull off hot geek. Your looks say sexy badass, not geek, which apparently is like a siren call to crazy women everywhere."

Joe looked pleased. "I'm okay with that."

Elle ignored this and looked at Spence. "After your last romantic fiasco, you vowed to take a break, remember? So all I'm saying is that you might want to change up your look."

"How?"

"I don't know. Slouch. Get a beer gut. Fart. Whatever it is that guys do to organically turn us off."

"Wait," Joe said. "You gave up sex after Clarissa dumped you?" Like, *willingly*?"

"Something you should try sometime," Elle said to him.

"Woman, bite your tongue."

"No, really," she said. "How do you even keep all their names straight?"

"Easy," Joe said with a smile. "If I forget their name, I just take them to Starbucks in the morning."

He was totally pulling Elle's leg. Probably.

Elle rolled her eyes. "Seriously?"

"Hey, you know I run on caffeine, sarcasm, and inappropriate thoughts at all times."

"I didn't give up sex," Spence said. Okay, yes, work had taken over his life. His latest project required his 24/7 attention, that's all. He hadn't had time to connect with anyone, and a quick hookup wasn't really his thing. What was his thing at the moment was creating a system for getting meds to people via drones, in far-reaching areas where they were nearly non-existent. Meds and also medical care through a camera-equipped drones, allowing doctors to remotely diagnose and monitor patients.

He'd had problems. Accommodating for the atmosphere and varying weather patterns, for one. The security, for another, making sure pirates couldn't intercept and steal the meds and equipment was a high stakes priority. But he was getting close, very close. All he ▸

needed was time, uninterrupted time. He moved toward the door. "I'm going after my phone."

"You mean the one you just killed dead?" Elle asked.

"I'll bring it back to life."

"You're a genius, Spence, not a miracle maker."

When he kept going, he heard Elle mutter "great" to Joe. "Now I've issued some sort of challenge to his manhood and he has to prove me wrong."

The truth was, Spence could fix a phone in his damn sleep. What he wished he could do in his sleep was get this project up and running. Maybe a part of his problem was that it happened to be for Clarissa's One-World charity and he'd promised her.

And Spence no longer broke promises.

He took the stairs because he hated the elevator, and when he stepped out into the courtyard, he stilled for a beat. He'd grown up hard and fast and without a home. This building had changed all that for him, and normally the sight of the fountain, the cobblestones, the building itself with its amazing, old corbel brick architecture, all worked together to lighten his day.

But when he hadn't been looking, Christmas had thrown up all over the place. There were garlands of evergreen entwined with twinkling white lights in every doorway and window frame, not to mention all the potted trees that lined the walkways had been done up like Christmas trees.

This being winter in San Francisco, specifically the district of Cow's Hollow, the afternoon foggy air burned his lungs like ice. He grabbed his phone from the coin-filled fountain, dried it off on his pants and shoved it into one of his pockets to restore later.

"Spence!" Willa called out from the pet shop that opened into the courtyard. She ran a pet daycare out of her shop and somehow when Spence needed to think, he often did so while walking her clients for her.

She gestured to the large dog snoozing in the sun spot with two cats, one on either side of him. "Got time to help me out?" she asked.

"Sure." The dog was a regular client named Daisy Duke, who came out of a dead sleep at Spence's voice, leaping over the cats in sheer joy right for him. When she got there, she jumped up and down in place, attempting to lick his face. Spence got her hooked up to her leash and they hit the courtyard, heading towards the wrought iron gates so he could walk her to the park.

But Daisy Duke wasn't a walker. She was a runner. More accurately, she was a hundred-and-twenty-five pound bunny, bounding with enthusiastic energy, tugging at the leash.

"Hold your horses, Daze," he said. "Save it for the park." He muscled her to his side, his mind miles away on his drone problems. Lost in thought, he wasn't exactly on his game when a black cat appeared out of nowhere.

With an excited bark, Daisy Duke broke free to charge after it, heading back toward the fountain and the woman now standing there, suitcase at her side, arm primed to thrown a coin into the water.

The cat managed to dodge the woman, but Daisy Duke wasn't nearly as dexterous. Barreling forward at warp speed, she saw the problem at the last minute, letting out a bark of surprise. She was probably mostly Irish Setter, but he was pretty sure she was also part wookie. She was huge and uncoordinated, and a few crayons short of a full box. She did drop her head and try to stop, but her forward momentum was too much. Her back-end slid out from beneath her and she flipped onto her back, skidding, plowing headlong into the woman, toppling her over.

Right into the water.

Jesus. "Stay," Spence said to Daisy and lurched forward as the woman pushed up to her hands and knees in the water, coughing and sputtering. "*Are you okay*?"

Gesturing that she didn't need his assistance, she swiped a hand down her face. "I should've gone to Toronto," she muttered.

She was maybe late twenties, completely drenched thanks to him, and yet she wasn't yelling. She got serious points for that, he thought. And because she was wearing one of those flowy dresses that gave a man thoughts about what might or might not be under said dress, along with a denim jacket and boots—all of which were now clinging to her and fighting her efforts – he stepped into the fountain to help her.

"The water's . . . warm," she said in surprise. "It's freezing out. How is the water warm?"

He looked down at the water. Green. He could feel coins beneath the soles of his shoes. "That can't be good." ▸

Coming Soon . . . ***(continued)***

She choked and he did a mental grimace. He deserved the tears. Hell, he deserved fury. But when she lifted her face, he realized she was *laughing*?

She'd found humor in this shitty situation.

He felt something shift in his chest at that, a zing of attraction maybe, which he hadn't seen coming. In fact, he actually wasn't seeing too much at all since he was now nearly as wet as she, including his glasses. He took them off to wipe the lenses on his equally wet shirt and eye contact was made.

She had big green eyes. Big, green, smiling eyes. "I'm a mess," she said.

That wasn't what he was thinking. Her clothes were plastered to her body. Her very nice, curvy body. He forced his gaze back to her face as he stepped out of the fountain and turned back for her, offering a hand.

She took it, but still struggled because her dress had shrink-wrapped itself to her legs, making moving all but impossible. They struggled a moment, hands grappling for purchase on each other until finally he just wrapped an arm around her waist and lifted her out, setting her down on the cobblestone ground.

"Wuff!" Daisy had flopped around on her back for a few seconds, trying to right herself. Finally she'd given up and stayed on her back, tail wagging like crazy, her tongue hanging out the side of her mouth.

That is until she eyed something in one of the big potted trees lining the courtyard, now decorated to within an inch of their lives with lights and ornaments.

The black cat.

"Stay," Spence warned the dog and turned back to the woman.

"Thanks," she said, her voice matching her husky laugh. "Appreciate the help . . ." She paused, clearly waiting for him to fill in with his name.

"Spence," he said, purposely skipping his surname. Anonymity was hard to come by lately, but he kept up the effort.

"Well," she said. "Thanks for the help, Spence." And then she . . . turned to walk away.

"Wait—" He'd gotten her drenched and he felt terribly about that. He wanted to make sure she was okay, that he got her dry and warm. "You didn't tell me your name."

She looked back, seeming oddly reluctant. "Colbie," she said. "My name is Colbie."

"Colbie, I can't let you just walk away. You've got to be freezing cold. At the very least I owe you dry clothes and a warm drink."

"No, really. It's okay." She started to wring out her long, dark hair and paused. "You might want to stand back, my hair needs it's own zip code when it's wet."

This made him smile.

"Oh, I'm not kidding," she said.

Out of all the women Spence had known in his life, he couldn't think of a single one who'd be taking this so well, and shit, he realized she was absently rubbing her elbow. Gently, he pushed up the sleeve of her denim jacket and found an abrasion along with an already blooming bruise.

"It's nothing," she said.

Maybe, but her skin was broken and he had no idea what was in that water. "We need to clean that cut and ice your elbow. And of course I'll pay for your clothes to be cleaned or replaced—"

"*Wuff!*"

He shot the impatient Daisy a long look that promised no cookies today just as Elle came out of the elevator, striding toward them with a concerned look on her face. "Hi," she said to Colbie. "I'm Elle Wheaten, the building manager. What happened? Are you okay?"

"She took a header into the water," Spence said. "Daisy's fault."

They all looked at Daisy, who was sitting there smiling wide, not a concern in this world.

"I'm taking Colbie upstairs," he said. "To clean out her cut and get her some dry clothes."

Elle turned to him in shock.

Spence understood the surprise. He usually avoided dealing with people, especially people he didn't know. And then there was the fact that his penthouse apartment was an inner sanctum that he didn't let just anyone into. "The gym," he clarified, which was on the top floor next to his apartment. It had its own entrance, separate from his living quarters and office.

"I'll take her," Elle offered, doing as she always did, which was keeping herself between Spence and the rest of the world.

"Really," Colbie said, her voice firm if not a little shaky. "Not necessary. I'm fine." ▸

Coming Soon . . . ***(continued)***

Spence didn't claim to know all that much about women, but even he knew that 'fine' didn't mean fine. The scale went: great, good, okay, not okay, I hate you, fine. And as a bonus, she was beginning to tremble from the cold as she gripped her suitcase and tried to walk off—not that her dress was having it. Tangled around her legs, it was suctioned to her limbs.

Colbie stopped fighting it, sighed, and tilted her head back. "Really? Are we serious with today?"

Both Spence and Elle glanced up at the sky. Nothing but clouds. He looked over at Elle, who was brows up, giving him a slow shake of her head. And while it was true that Elle was one of his best friends and he trusted her with his life, he didn't agree with her silent opinion to just let the woman go.

He couldn't. There was just something about the very wet, cute-yet-sexy Colbie No-Last-Name that appealed to him in a way that nothing else had in a long time. So when she tripped over her dress yet again and swore with a low, muttered "*son of a beach*!", he grabbed for her, keeping her upright.

"Please," he said as her clothes bean to soak his. "*Please* let me help you."

At his other side, Elle's mouth fell open. She wasn't used to hearing the word 'please' from him. Ignoring her, he kept his gaze on Colbie.

Wary, she rolled her eyes but gave a slight nod. She'd let him help her out, but she wasn't happy about it.

Fair enough. ~

BOOKS BY JILL SHALVIS

LOST AND FOUND SISTERS

A Novel

Available in Paperback, E-Book, and Digital Audio

A bombshell secret and a mysterious inheritance send Quinn Weller reeling…and back to her hometown, where a world of possibilities awaits—once she decides if this new life is the one she was always meant to have.

ACCIDENTALLY ON PURPOSE

A Heartbreaker Bay Novel

Available in Mass Market, E-Book, and Digital Audio

There's no such thing as a little in love . . .
There's no such thing as a little in lust . . .
There is such a thing as . . . Accidentally on Purpose

ONE SNOWY NIGHT

A Heartbreaker Bay Christmas Novella

Available in E-Book and Digital Audio

A long road trip in a massive blizzard might be just what Max and Rory need to face their past… and one steamy, snowy night is all it takes to bring them together at last.

THE TROUBLE WITH MISTLETOE

A Heartbreaker Bay Novel

Available in Mass Market, E-Book, and Digital Audio

If she has her way . . .
He'll get nothing but coal in his stocking.
Unless he tempers "naughty" with a
special kind of nice . . .

SWEET LITTLE LIES

A Heartbreaker Bay Novel

Available in Mass Market, E-Book, and Digital Audio

Choose the one guy you can't have . . .
Fall for him—hard . . .
And then tell him the truth.

Discover great authors, exclusive offers, and more at hc.com.

Available wherever books are sold.